A SUITE TEMPTATION

A Billionaire Romantic Comedy

ROYAL RESORTS
BOOK 2

JESSICA GREGORY

Copyright © 2023 by Jessica Gregory

Cover design by Qamber Designs & Media

Cottman Data Services Pty Ltd

All rights reserved.

No part of this book may be reproduced in any form or by any electronic or mechanical means, including information storage and retrieval systems, without written permission from the author, except for the use of brief quotations in a book review.

The characters and events portrayed in this book are fictitious or are used fictitiously. Any similarity to real persons, living or dead, is purely coincidental and not intended by the author.

All brand names and product names used in this book are trademarks, registered trademarks, or trade names of their respective holders. Cottman Data Services Pty Ltd and Jessica Gregory are not associated with any product or vendor in this book.

PROLOGUE

Somewhere in the wilds of Iowa

Jordan Royal rested his aching head against the bars of the jail cell and sighed. Everything hurt, even his hair. *And I stink.* His gaze took in the state of his bespoke Saville Row suit and hideously expensive Italian leather shoes. It wouldn't take a genius to figure out what was caked all over them.

This week on jail cell Jeopardy. For $200, what is horseshit?

And while he mightn't have actually reached the lowest point in his life, he was certain he could see the bottom from where he currently stood, banged up in a county jail.

What happened last night? And how did I get here?

The loud clang of the main cell door being opened and pushed against the wall had him wincing. It only added to the pain of the bright glare of the overhead lights. The world this morning was far too bright, loud, and putrid. The only comfort to be found was in the cool metal of the bars which covered the front of his old-fashioned cell. The touch of the rolled steel against his face soothed his tortured head.

A gray haired, sheriff's deputy stopped in front of the cell. He took one look at Jordan and slowly shook his head. "You look an awful sight, young man. And you stink. Now you, go on and move back a bit. Give me some room while I open the door. I don't want any trouble."

Jordan did as he was told, his woozy head protesting all the while. He stood hugging himself as the door slowly slid open, flinching when it clanged loudly against the hinges.

He rubbed his hands against his sides, grateful that someone had taken the handcuffs off once he'd been thrown in here. It had been a welcome blessing. Cuffs were his least favorite part about getting arrested. Those things pinched.

"Come on, Mister Royal. Time to go. Paperwork to complete," huffed the deputy.

They were letting him go. *Thank god.* "Did I make bail?"

"No. The charges have been dropped." There was a definite note of disappointment in the lawman's voice.

Thank fuck. Not that I can remember what I did anyway.

He followed the deputy out the door and into the main reception area. Matthew stood in the foyer, flanked by two gentlemen in midnight black suits. They may as well have had a huge sign hanging above their heads which read LAWYER. Not that Jordan was complaining. He was just relieved that they'd succeeded in getting the charges against him withdrawn.

Matthew's gaze ran up and down Jordan's disheveled clothes. "You look like someone dragged you backwards through a swamp." Lifting his head, he sniffed at the air. "And you stink."

Jordan mustered a strangled laugh. He was exhausted and badly hungover. "You should see how it looks and smells from this side. Thanks for coming to get me." He turned to the pair of stony faced legal eagles and sketched a bow. "Thank you, gentlemen. As always, I appreciate your time and efforts."

His brother sighed. "Speaking of time, yours was, as always damn near impeccable. I was about to fly to the sunny beaches of Greece when you called. My vacation plans didn't include a side trip to Iowa. The next time you get thrown in jail, you'll have to make your one phone call to someone else. I'm done with hauling your ass out of the shit, Jordan." Matthew sniffed the air once more. "Urgh, is that what you were rolling around in last night? Shit."

Jordan couldn't honestly answer that question. He had a few hazy memories of what had happened the previous evening. On a whim, he and some friends had flown out to Iowa, to watch a night rodeo, but apart from some vague memories of bulls and horses, he had absolutely no recollection of how the night had ended. Or what had happened to result in him getting arrested. He'd woken up sprawled on the floor of the jail cell a little after five am. Unfortunately, the whole hazy brain, handcuffs, and legal team scenario was a familiar one for Jordan.

This is one thing I have a talent for, the one thing my high achieving brothers and cousins can't lay claim to—black sheep of the family.

After retrieving his cell phone, and some other personal effects from the clerk at the front desk, Jordan was handed several sheets of paperwork, and made to sign them. He gingerly put his sunglasses on his face, then followed Matthew out the front door. The pair of lawyers who kept a guarded distance, trailed in his wake.

Once they were outside in the parking lot, Jordan stopped and quickly checked his wallet. His credit cards, with their unrestrained spending limits, were still there, but all his cash was gone. Jordan had a vague recollection of handing over a fistful of hundred dollar bills to a shady guy behind a cowboy bar. *Guess that answers that question.*

His queasy stomach growled its need for attention.

"Do you have any money on you, bro? I'm not sure if they take credit cards at the local diner. I'm in desperate need of some coffee and food."

Matthew angrily snatched the paperwork out of Jordan's hand and passed it to one of the lawyers. "It goes without saying that none of this should go officially through the Royal Resorts company accounts. Make sure it gets hidden somewhere as research costs. If anyone asks, just tell them I was out here looking at possible resort development sites. Thanks guys, I'm sorry to have called you out so early."

Stifling a grin, Jordan nodded. "Yeah, um, thanks. And sorry."

With their task now complete, the lawyers got into one of two nearby cars and drove away. Jordan watched them go, staring at the road until the car was out of sight.

And cue the disapproving lecture from my brother...

He turned to Matthew. His sibling shared the same shade of dark brown hair and green eyes as Jordan, but that was where their similarities ended. Jordan's hair was normally groomed to within an inch of its life, whereas Matthew wore his long locks past his shoulders.

While Jordan was currently wearing a five o'clock shadow, which he would shave off as soon as he could, Matthew rocked a lumberjack, unkempt bearded vibe. Anyone who happened to wander by wouldn't pick them for brothers. And while they looked more like two characters out of a cheesy '80s road movie, Jordan didn't need a map to tell him that Iowa was a long way from *Walley World*.

But there was no humor on Matthew's face as he reached out and punched Jordan hard on the side of the head. Jordan's teeth rattled. "You fucking idiot. Do you have any idea how close you got to having to front a local judge? And unlike all the other times when either Bryce or I bailed you out from jail, if you had ended up in court, there would've been no hiding a prison sentence from Mom and Dad."

The only good part of having such a terrible hangover was that Jordan barely felt the punch. His ear and cheek were stinging, but the rest of his body hurt so much it made little difference. The threat of Edward and Alice Royal discovering the truth of their middle son's latest transgression pained him more. Jordan was the undisputed black sheep of the family. A constant source of shame.

"I'm sorry, Matthew." His half-baked apology sounded hollow and trite. He'd offered it too many times for either of them to believe it. "Um. Do you have any idea what happened last night? Things are kinda patchy in my brain. I don't remember much of anything between leaving Jackson Hole and then waking up alone in the jail cell."

Yesterday afternoon, Jordan had been attending an economic summit in Jackson Hole, Wyoming. He hadn't actually made it to any of the formal sessions, rather he'd embarked on a bar crawl with a couple of other pampered sons of commerce. Someone had a private jet at their disposal, and the lure of mischief was too great to resist.

Jordan racked his brains. He couldn't even remember who he'd been with last night, or what sort of drugs he had taken. The booze however would have been his usual, vodka shots ... and keep 'em coming. The cold light of day was having its spiteful revenge.

I feel really dizzy. God, I hope it's just from low blood sugar.

Matthew brushed his fingers over his soft, bushy beard. "You had a busy night, Jordan. According to the rap sheet, which was short but quite spicy, you stole a tractor. You then took it on a cross country rampage where you crashed it through several fences, before finally drowning it in a farm dam. The tractor was *DOA*, and they are still fixing the fences."

That explains the strands of strange, damp weed in the pockets of my pants.

"How much?"

If the authorities had dropped the charges against him, it must have been because the farmer didn't want to press the issue. And the only way this whole thing would have been made to go away was because someone had handed over some serious House of Royal cash.

The look on Matthew's face was one of great sibling displeasure. His brother hated waste of any kind.

"Twenty four grand for the tractor. From what I understand, the farmer was more than happy about that as he has a brand new John Deere arriving later today to replace his eighteen year old work horse. Fortunately he only asked for a few hundred bucks for the fence. According to our team of lawyers, the guy seemed pretty pleased about getting a new tractor. Said to tell you thanks, and that if you wanted to wreck any more tractors, he knew some guys who would be more than willing to take your money." Matthew made a great show of loudly clearing his throat. "Sorry, *Dad's* money."

For the sort of immense wealth that the Royal family had at its disposal, the settlement funds were a drop in the ocean. But for Jordan the fallout from his little misadventure could have cost him dearly. It would be bad enough if the local press got a hold of it, but if word got back to New York City, to his father ... another wave of nausea washed over him. This time it was more than just a hangover. It was embarrassment. The knowledge that he was a constant disappointment to the House of Royal.

The sooner he got out of Iowa, the better.

The warmth of the August sun was beating down on his

head. His body was at war with itself. He was either going to pass out or throw up. Or both.

I stink. I'm hungry, and I just want to go home.

"I'm sorry Matt, and I promise you can punish me all you like once I am feeling human again. Just please for the love of all that is holy, tell me you came in one of the company jets."

Not only couldn't he imagine trying to get on board a commercial flight in his current disgusting state, but he had no idea where the nearest town was, let alone a proper airport.

Matthew appearing to finally take pity on him, nodded. "Yes, it's at a local aeroclub. Come on, you can wash up on the plane. I'll see if I can find some clean clothes for you."

Jordan's luggage was still in a hotel suite in Jackson Hole, but he wasn't game to ask Matthew to make such a large detour rather than head straight back to NYC. He would get someone from Royal Resorts to call the hotel later and make the necessary arrangements to retrieve his belongings.

His brother pointed at Jordan's stained jacket. "You might want to take that off and place the... clean-ish inner lining face down on the seat of the hire car. Oh, and take your shoes off. I'm not paying for an extra cleaning fee."

Fearing his brother would make him strip completely, Jordan sheepishly did as he was told. He climbed into the passenger seat of the small rental car, and casually adjusted his sunglasses. "Come on let's get out of here."

Matthew climbed into the driver seat. He glanced at Jordan and shook his head in disgust. He was still shaking his head as he turned the car out of the parking lot and onto the main road.

When Jordan caught sight of the Royal Resorts corporate jet a short time later, he let out a large sigh of relief. The sooner he was on board, and they were in the skies, the better. The plane would have catering of some sort, and he could wash some of the shame of last night off his skin in the private bathroom.

I can't wait to get home to New York and climb into my bed. Sleep.

Filthy shoes in hand, he followed Matthew up the steps of the jet. But the moment he set foot into the main cabin, his blood turned to ice.

Seated in the first of the luxury white leather armchairs was Alice Royal.

His mother rose, gave a nod to Matthew, then turned her steely gaze on Jordan. "Don't bother attempting to blame your brother for me being here. When he tried to change the flight plan for the jet from Greece to Iowa, a call was immediately made to Janice. Fortunately for you, your father's EA decided I might be the lesser of two evils, so I was the one she messaged."

Jordan swallowed down a lump of dread. He had dodged a major bullet. If Edward Royal had been informed of Jordan's arrest, there was every chance he would have let his middle son sit and stew in a prison cell for the next few days. His father was big on giving him ample time to think on his sins.

And I've done a lot of thinking over the years. Not that any of it has done me much good. I'll never live up to family expectations.

"I will make sure to personally thank Janice for her discretion as soon as we get home tonight. And I'll keep a low profile for the next few days." He could only hope that was enough to placate his mother.

Alice's bottom lip quivered, and tears shone in her eyes. "I'm afraid it will be some time before you get an opportunity to talk to Janice in person, darling. The jet is heading back to New York today, but on the way home, we will be making a short stopover in Philadelphia."

"What's in Philadelphia? Are we picking someone up?" asked Jordan warily.

Alice took a hold of his hand and gave it a gentle motherly squeeze. "There is a world-class addiction treatment center in Philadelphia. You can't go on like this Jordan. It's time you got sober and clean."

Rehab. They are sending me to rehab.

CHAPTER ONE

Berlin, Germany
 Four and a half years of tortured sobriety later

The throbbing techno beat of the tightly packed nightclub pulsed uncomfortably through his body. In his former life, as Jordan liked to call his pre-rehab days, he would have soaked up the ear-splitting, pulse-racing music. The party favors and alcohol coursing through his veins would have seen him in the middle of the dance floor, busting out all the slick moves. In his heyday he had been one hell of a dancer. He'd also been a world-class drug addict. Now, clubbing simply annoyed him. Three months of treatment, with the occasional top-up spot of therapy had stuck. He was clean and he was sober.

Jordan wouldn't have normally come to a place like Berghain, the famous Berlin nightclub located in a former Soviet era heating plant, but his German cousin Leon had convinced him to set aside his *dull New York brain* and take in some cutting-edge music. Jordan's personal assistant, the red-headed Sheila, had been banging on all week about visiting

Berghain, so that had also played a part in his decision to come tonight.

Being a local minor Berlin celebrity meant Leon could get through the front door without having to suffer under the withering gaze, and swift 'nein' of the club's bouncers. The bouncers at Berghain were as famous as the club. Only a select few guests were given approval to step inside. Tourists were routinely turned away.

Holding Sheila by the hand, Leon made his way through the crowd, and toward a short set of steps which led up to the next level of the club. Jordan trailed behind them. He barely noticed the scantily clad men and women moving in time with the music. The scent of body sweat, perfume, and alcohol hung thick in the air. He might be a recovering addict, but Jordan's nose could still pick out the notes of various alcoholic drinks. His eyes caught the sleight of hands, which signaled that other small *pop-in-the-mouth* items were being handed around.

This was a dangerous place for him. Temptation was everywhere. He did a quick mental check of his escape plan. If he found his resolve being pushed to the limit, he was to send a message to a private number. A House of Royal security team would be immediately dispatched to discreetly extract him from the club.

"Here we are, this is our table," announced Leon. He ushered a smiling Sheila into the minimalist designed wooden booth and followed closely behind. Jordan stifled a grin as his two companions quickly got cozy with one another. They had first met a year or so ago and seemed to have hit it off. Now whenever Jordan happened to mention to his cousin that he might be coming to Germany, Sheila's name inevitably found its way into the conversation, along with a less than subtle hint that she might also want to make the trip.

Sheila's hopeful pleadings had finally overcome Jordan's

reluctance to visit the nightclub. Considering the amazing work she did in supporting him, having to endure a couple of hours of electro, ghettotech, and psy sounds mixed by a Colombian DJ was the least he could do. Table service meant expensive bottles of booze, with a minimum four-figure dollar spend to secure a table. Since Leon was paying, Jordan didn't mind. Just as long as they offered a decent nonalcoholic range of drinks, he was content.

Sheila was beaming. As was Leon. Jordan couldn't decide which of his two companions looked the most like a kid on Christmas morning, all bubbling with excitement.

Such a cute pair. I wonder if Leon is ever going to make a move. Sheila won't wait forever. Better snap her up and soon, cuz.

And as much as he privately shipped *Lesh* or was that *Shon*, Jordan was more than happy to admit that the romantic affairs of his relatives and company employees were actually none of his bloody business.

He wasn't here in Berlin to play cupid—he was here to check out the city's recently opened Royal Resorts hotel. To see how the furnishings looked, and possibly steal one or two ideas for the new Laguna Beach resort he was going to project manage in California later in the year. The European design team had a great eye for little touches, ones that would be sure to delight guests. And delighted guests were what every hotelier wanted.

His older brother Bryce ran the European arm of Royal Resorts, and from what Jordan had seen of his other completed projects, he had no doubt the Berlin hotel would be exceptional.

How do I compete with that? I don't know if I can.

A server arrived at their table and conducted a quick conversation with Leon in German. He pointed at Jordan. When the woman repeated the words "bitter lemon", Jordan held up four fingers. He'd been clued up on how things worked in the clubs. Nonalcoholic drinks didn't come with the same markup or profit as bottles of booze, but if he ordered four glasses, the bar staff would charge a full bottle of champagne to Leon's minimum spend tab and everyone would be happy.

As soon as his drinks arrived, Jordan was going to settle in for a hopefully not too long a night of soberly appreciating the decadent electronic music and alternative culture. While it was easy to see why all the other clubs envied Berghain, Jordan would have preferred to be somewhere quieter.

That odd thought sent a shudder through him.

I'm thirty two years old and I'm beginning to sound like my father.

Berghain, the giant concrete and steel nightclub was world-famous, but then again so was Chloe Fisher. The double takes and stares she got as she made her way through the cavernous venue spoke volumes as to how instantly recognizable, she was—everyone knew Chloe.

The loud cries of "Chloe?" "Is that?" "Wow, das ist sie!" followed her every step. So did several large well-trained security men who kept the crowd at bay. No one was getting anywhere near the pop princess, not without her say so. Anyone who tried would soon find themselves deposited outside in the cold Berlin night.

Her small select party of guests was ushered to a private area in one of the upper levels of the club. Their austere booth sat at a right angle to the rest of the room, which afforded Chloe a welcome degree of privacy as she dropped wearily onto a spot on the wooden bench out of clear sight of the dancefloor.

I am so tired. Why did I agree to come here?

She knew the answer to that question only too well ... because her entourage had forced her into it. It was alright for them, they hadn't just come off stage after playing a full two and a half hour concert at the Mercedes Benz Arena. While she had sore feet and a blinding headache which the pumping beat of the heavy DJ mixed music at Berghain did nothing to dull, her people were fresh and ready to party.

Thank god, we are headed back to the States at the end of the week. I want to go home. I miss my house.

Chloe and her entourage were flying to Paris late tomorrow. Two days from now she would perform the final show of her whirlwind European tour. At least it wasn't a full tour, just eight of the major capital cities. By Sunday night, she would be home in LA and back in her own bed. *Yay.*

A club server arrived and handed each member of Chloe's party a glass of champagne. The other three members of Chloe's official touring entourage—Marta her number one personal assistant, Gabriela her assistant's assistant, and Stixxluv, Chloe's stylist—all downed their drinks in one go, but Chloe was content to nurse hers.

True to form, her companions immediately began bickering over what hideously expensive bottle of booze they were planning to order next. On a night like tonight, when her people were in a mood to party hard, the bar tab could easily be in excess of twenty grand by the end of the evening.

Her tight knit little group was getting set up for a long night of partying. Life would be easier if Chloe gave a damn about clubbing, but after working her ass off all night, she had zero interest in letting loose. The headache was partly to blame, but truth be told, she was far more interested in the three other guests who were seated in the booth opposite to hers.

The other party consisted of two men and a red-headed woman. They looked so out of place, that Chloe couldn't imagine how they had gotten through the front door. The woman was rocking a pale pink ballerina dress and matching high heeled boots, which had to be the very antithesis of the nightclub's unofficial all-black uniform.

And the two men? They were dressed so achingly conservatively, it actually made her teeth hurt. Both wore black tailored pants and white Oxford dress shirts. Either one of them could have featured in a Hugo Boss fragrance ad.

Yet all three of this odd little group seemed perfectly at home in their little bubble, oblivious as to how much they stood out. From the way they behaved, it was clear they were used to being able to find a table at an exclusive techno club. *Fascinating.* Who were these people?

Over the heaving beat of the music, she caught the occasional word. They were all speaking English. The dark-haired guy sitting next to the girl in pink, was tapping his finger in time to the beat. His body language was both obvious and telling—he was hot for her. The red head, in turn, made no effort to move away when her male companion leaned in close. She crossed her long legs and preened, smoothing the edges of her skirt. Sexual tension vibrated between them.

But it was the third member of this well-dressed ménage à trois who really caught Chloe's eye. His dark brown hair was lazily adorned with a pair of designer sunglasses. He wore his boredom like a shiny badge of honor. His confidence came with a noticeable lack of the cocky edge that was the hallmark of most men she met in LA.

I'll have twenty bucks on that one being an American. Only an American male would wear his sunglasses perched on top of his head at night and not think he looks like an idiot. He probably thinks it's cool.

Unfortunately, her American compatriot had it wrong. Berlin's version of cool was defined by its artists and students, even its nightclub bouncers. Not preppy college boys.

You're trying too hard buddy.

As if the object of her interest could read her mind, he suddenly slipped the sunglasses off his head and placed them on the low table in front of him. Tilting his chin up he raked his fingers through the strands of his short, dark brown hair. The elegant movement had the sleeve of his white shirt pulling taut around his bicep. *Nice.* Mister America, might be over dressed, but he had all the right moves.

Chloe's heart skipped a beat as he turned and gave her a panty dropping smile.

Oh hello.

CHAPTER TWO

Chloe might well be used to the limelight, to having people constantly staring, but the way this guy looked at her, she was certain he could see right into her soul. And as much as she tried to tear her gaze away, it was held fast. His sexy, all-knowing grin informed her that not only did he know who she was, but that he wasn't intimidated by her fame. That he was up to any challenge she might think to throw his way. This guy had *Big Dick Energy* coming out his pores.

Who is this guy?

"Chloe. Chloe." A hand appeared in front of her face. Startled, she turned to see Gabriela waving furiously at her. *Huh?*

"We are ordering two bottles of Cristal Rosé, and Stixxluv wants to get a bottle of Patrón for shots. I know you are watching your waist, but do you want anything?"

Bed. Sleep. And to meet that hot guy who is doing a great job of screwing me with his eyes. Not necessarily in that order.

She was always having to watch what she ate and drank. Her number one personal assistant Marta made it her business to have right of veto of all and anything Chloe put in her mouth. It sounded harsh, but the life of a pop star was so intense that having someone else manage the mental load of her diet just made things easier for her.

"No thank you Gabriela ... actually, change of mind. I will have something. If they have Grey Goose on the menu, let's get a bottle."

The stranger from across the way looked like someone who would drink vodka, not because he loved it, but because it helped to make him appear edgy. In the privacy of his own home, he likely drank and enjoyed an old-fashioned American beer.

While her entourage busied themselves with ordering an insane amount of booze, Chloe, and *Sunglasses Guy* continued their little game of seeing who could blink first. He might have money and an attitude, but she had survived a shitty upbringing, followed by four years of living rough on the streets. He was going to have to try a lot harder to beat her.

I can play this game all night.

When the ballerina girl and the other suited guy both moved and got to their feet, Mister *Too Cool For School* America, had to stand in order to let his companions leave the booth. He broke off eye contact with Chloe. She could have taken that as a minor win, but decided she was having far too much fun to end the contest.

Chloe was waiting for the moment when the dark haired hunk would look her way once more.

Leon and Sheila were holding hands. "I've spotted a good friend of mine down on the dancefloor and I want to introduce Sheila to him. We might be back. Will you be alright on your own, Liebste?"

"Sweetheart?" laughed Jordan. Leon loved to offer him these little German terms of affection. Anything to get his blood up. As his cousin and assistant made their way past him, Jordan gave Leon a friendly slap on the back. "Just go easy on whatever treats your friend downstairs might be selling. Don't forget you promised me a tour of the new hotel before I leave tomorrow."

Jordan picked up his glass and took a long drink. There was every chance that he wouldn't be seeing either of his friends again this evening. He was now on his own.

With the others gone, Jordan turned his attention back to the booth opposite, to where the world-famous pop star, Chloe, sat pretending to sip from a flute of champagne.

She was more than nursing it, the drink had barely shifted from the top of the glass. Being a recovering addict meant Jordan tended to notice those sorts of things.

Chloe stood and waved a hand in his direction, beckoning him to come join her. Jordan didn't need a second invitation. He'd barely taken a step in her direction before two burly gentlemen appeared in front of him. Instinctively, he lowered his gaze, not daring to meet their eyes. *I am not a threat to her.* Only an idiot would give the slightest bit of attitude to a man the size of a mountain, let alone when he had a muscular friend.

"It's alright, Martin. I asked him over." Chloe's hand rested on the arm of one of the men. She was a fully grown woman but in comparison to the size of her security detail she looked like a child. These men were paid to protect her, and Jordan had no doubt that they wouldn't hesitate to sit him on his ass if he made the wrong move.

His billionaire family background had given Jordan a lifetime of experience in dealing with people protection. Of how they worked, and how not to get on the bad side of a large, well trained Navy SEAL. He remained exactly where he was, not daring to twitch a muscle. It was only when Chloe finally came to stand in front of him, offering Jordan her hand, that he deemed it safe to lift his head.

"Hi, I'm Chloe."

He was immediately struck by the warmth and sincerity in her smile. Her deep brown eyes reminded him of liquid chocolate. Her long raven hair was glossy and smooth. *Stunningly beautiful.*

The way she shared her name was as if she genuinely expected that not everyone would know it. It took Jordan a moment to gather his wits.

"I'm Jordan, its lovely to meet you, Chloe." He took her hand, holding and shaking it with the right amount of pressure. His father had taught all his sons how a gentleman should shake a woman's hand. To Jordan's surprise, Chloe's handshake had a degree of firmness to it.

Her smile, however, remained soft and inviting. "I see you've been abandoned by your friends, Jordan. Would you like to come and sit with me?"

Jordan checked over his shoulder. Sheila and Leon were still nowhere to be seen. Since his cousin had paid for full table service, at some point in the night, Leon would return and spend more cash on drinks. But who knew when that might be, or whether his own presence might make things awkward for Sheila and Leon.

Never let it be said that I am a cock blocker.

Then again, he might be making fanciful assumptions about his cousin and assistant. "My executive assistant might be back eventually ..."

"Oh, that's alright. She can join us as well. What about your other friend?"

"Leon? Oh, don't worry about him, he's only my cousin. He lives in Berlin and can take care of himself."

And I was right, he is an American.

Chloe brushed her hand over Jordan's chest. The way the white button down fitted his form so perfectly, it was clear he didn't shop at Gap. And his pants had the unmistakable cut and fine cloth that could only come from a gentleman's tailor. Which meant, Jordan either had money or his family did. "Come and sit with me, Jordan. I am keen to meet someone new."

It was all an act on her part. Her way of protecting herself with strangers. People wanted to meet Chloe the pop star, and in public that's who they met. Few got to know the real Chloe Fisher, and she was determined to keep it that way. Maintaining an invisible wall between her and the rest of the world kept the girl from Nebraska safe.

She motioned for her entourage to move along and make space. When Marta and Gabriela let out a collected huff of disgust at this imposition, Chloe glared at them. Stixxluv eyed Jordan's bespoke suit with bored distaste but shuffled over. For their troubles, Chloe banished them to Jordan's booth. Grumbling about their lot and how unfair the world was, the three of them snatched up the bottles of champagne and tequila and beat a hasty retreat.

Gabriela, bless her, who had a little more manners, brought Jordan's drinks over and placed them with care on the table in front of him and Chloe. She offered a polite. "Enjoy," then scooted back to rejoin her drinking buddies.

With everyone now settled in their new places, Chloe

turned her attention back to Jordan. "So what brings you to Berghain, Jordan? You don't look the type to be getting all hot and sweaty on the dancefloor."

She was interested to see how he would react when she placed a touch of emphasis on the words *hot* and *sweaty*. In the music business, it never paid to be too subtle.

The pair of dark green eyes which met hers had Chloe swallowing deep. There was no mistaking the strong intelligent mind behind them. Chloe both liked and appreciated clever men.

"My cousin Leon's side of the family runs a number of hotels and resorts in Germany and Eastern Europe. I'm here to catch up with him, and also to visit the new hotel they have just opened here in Berlin." He picked up his drink and took a generous sip. "And as for getting hot and sweaty, my days of destroying what's left of my youth on the dancefloor are mercifully well behind me."

Jordan threw back the rest of his drink. Chloe wasn't sure if he was thirsty or nervous.

"What about you, Chloe? I saw on CNN that you were going to be performing a concert in Berlin tonight, is this the sort of place you come to wind down?"

"I came off stage not long ago, but I didn't want to come here, they did." She gestured in the direction of her entourage. "I much prefer to go back to my hotel and watch TV after a concert, but you have to give the touring party their little perks."

There was nothing worse than touring with a group of unhappy assistants. Getting them through the front door of Berghain and straight to a full service booth was one way to keep the peace.

Her show at the Mercedes Benz arena had been an instant sell out. Foster, her longtime manager had pressured her to announce a second show, but Chloe had held firm. This was a limited tour. Starting later in the year, after she had her brand new album released, she would embark on a grueling world tour. There wouldn't be a corner of the planet where she didn't perform.

As soon as I get home I need to get back into the studio and finish laying down more tracks. This album is taking forever to write and record.

Thoughts of her pressing commitments could wait— tonight she wanted to sit and share a drink or two with the hot guy she had just met.

"Was it a good show, I mean the crowd?" he asked.

"Oh yes. The Germans really know how to go off at a concert. Security was getting worried at one point when Chloe's Garden just cut loose."

"Chloe's Garden?"

"That's what my diehard fans call themselves. Though since they are mostly young women, the crowd is usually well behaved— they don't even like to mosh all that much. My fans are into hugs and being nice to one another."

Another artist might be offended at someone not knowing the lexicon of their fanbase, but Chloe didn't mind. If Jordan didn't know about Chloe's Garden, then he wasn't a fanboy. *Thank god.* Over the years, she'd encountered her fair share of fanboys all hoping to use their inner knowledge of Chloe's world as the means to flatter their way into her bed. Many had tried, none had succeeded.

He picked up a fresh glass from his selection of drinks and took a sip. "I can't remember the last time I went to a concert, but I hear yours are amazing. And Chloe's Garden sounds lovely." Her gaze followed his glass as Jordan set it down.

Is he staying off the alcohol so he can do drugs?

It pained her, but she had to ask "Jordan. Are you avoiding alcohol because you intend to do pills?"

His face blanched. A muscle twitched in his suddenly tight jaw. "Absolutely not."

"I ask, because I have a reputation I need to protect. I can't be linked to a user."

With his fingers balling on his thighs, he avoided her gaze. "I'm not a user."

Huh. Then what is his deal?

"So, would you like a glass of champagne or perhaps some vodka? We just opened a couple of new bottles."

He shook his head. "No, thank you. I don't touch the booze." There was a sense of finality in his words. A subtle warning for her not to ask anything else about why he wasn't drinking alcohol.

Since coming to sit with her, Chloe had noted that Jordan was polite but guarded. It could have just been an act, a way of getting her attention. Some guys liked to play the mysterious hunk, but he just appeared a touch uneasy. His all American swagger had somehow disappeared. In its place she got a sense of him actually being genuine. What she was seeing was the real Jordan.

Surprising.

"You don't like this place all that much, do you?" she ventured.

There I said it. He's here under sufferance, just like me.

He gave her a tight smile. "Sorry. I don't mean to be a downer, but if I'm being completely honest, I hate it. I'm not exactly dressed for a nightclub, which is why I'm slugging my drink down. It's unbearably hot in here and the air smells of sweat. The only reason I haven't already abandoned this concrete cavern is you, Chloe." A laugh escaped his lips. "God, that didn't half sound like a well-used pick up line, did it? But I mean it. You are the nicest thing here."

Chloe brushed the tips of her fingers along Jordan's thigh. "It's not my scene either, but I don't see those three leaving anytime soon." She nodded in the direction of her team. None of them acknowledged the move—they were too busy fighting over the drinks menu and deciding what bottle they would order next. *There are going to be some very ugly heads in the morning.*

She moved a little closer to him. "What would you say to us ditching my people. I mean we could go somewhere quiet and have a bite to eat. Just the two of us. I don't know about you but I'm starving."

Am I really doing this? It had been a long time since she'd spent any real time away from Marta and the others. *I just want a few hours with someone else.*

Jordan curled his hand around hers, the pads of his fingers brushing seductively against the skin of her palm. It sent a spark of lust racing straight to her core. Then to her surprise and distress, he set her hand aside and got to his feet. "I apologize if my compliment implied something I didn't intend. It was lovely to meet you, Chloe. I wish you all the success in your future, you are an incredible talent. Enjoy the rest of your evening." Jordan began to move away.

What? He's brushing me off. How did I misjudge this?

Chloe shot to her feet. Her glass of champagne teetered then fell, spilling its contents over the table. While her bodyguards quickly scrambled to clean up the mess, she moved out of the way, taking a hold of Jordan's muscular arm in the process. "What's wrong with me? I thought we were making a connection, but now you are leaving."

And you don't sound the least bit desperate, do you, Chloe?

He glanced at her hand, then lifting his head, fixed her with his emerald eyes. "Is that what you want, Chloe? I'm happy to go and find some food, but I'm not looking to be anything else for you tonight. You are gorgeous, and wow … it's just that I don't do casual these days." The words *I'm not a fuckboy fan were heavily implied.* "You seem a really nice girl, but ..."

Chloe the global pop star disappeared in an instant. In her place stood Chloe the girl from Nebraska who couldn't handle any form of rejection. And especially not from a man who appeared as genuine as Jordan. Her hand tightened on his arm.

She couldn't fault his manners. Someone had raised him right. Jordan was clearly doing his best to give Chloe all due respect and not cause offence.

They'd met mere minutes ago, yet the thought of him simply wishing her well and saying good night had Chloe stumbling to the edge of panic. None of it made sense. *I've just met this guy.* She barely knew him beyond his first name. But the combination of fatigue and deep-seated fear of abandonment was all too powerful.

She released her hold, then proceeded to gently pat his upper arm. "The offer for food is real. I'm sorry if I came across as, sexually aggressive. I guess I'm just conditioned to how things work in my world. Subtle isn't much of a thing."

Jordan nodded. "I can see how that would be, especially in your line of work. Where you just ask for something and it happens. I know what it means to have a life of privilege, but unlike you, there is no magic in me. I'm just a guy from the East Coast. What you see is what you get."

She couldn't remember the last time she'd been around a regular person. The Hollywood set considered themselves to be gods. If you weren't rich and famous, you were a mere mortal. And mortals were only put on this earth to serve the gods.

Chloe leaned in closer to Jordan, so he could hear her lowered voice over the rapid-fire beat of the music. "I would really like to go and find somewhere to eat with you, Jordan.

But we'll need to slip away from my assistants. If they know I'm leaving with you, they will want to tag along."

He placed a hand over hers and gave a gentle squeeze. "Trust me, when it comes to the ancient art of making a sly exit, I am a grand master. Though your body guards might have something to say about it being just the two of us. And so they should, since you don't really know me."

Even if she and Jordan had known one another, Chloe wouldn't risk leaving the club alone with him. Not tonight. Her concert might be over, but plenty of her fans would still be out and about in the city. The chances of them getting caught up in a selfie-hungry mob were too great.

"Let me have a quick word with Martin and come up with a plan." Her head of security could be trusted to run interference with her people if needed, delay them while he helped Chloe and Jordan make their escape.

Chloe's body thrummed with sexual need. For a man's touch. It was a shame that Jordan wasn't looking for a casual hook up. The ache between her legs spoke of an unsated hunger.

Just remember he is only agreeing to food. You need to keep a lid on your lust.

Jordan was right in stating his position. Tonight was simply a chance meeting of strangers, an opportunity for them to go and share a meal. She might be a world renowned superstar with money and fame, but even Chloe understood the word 'no'.

CHAPTER THREE

Sharing small talk over plates of tapas and salad with a musical megastar hadn't been in Jordan's plans for the evening. And yet here he was. He and Chloe were tucked away in a far corner of Matanga, a restaurant, a few minutes' walk from the nightclub.

Martin, her senior bodyguard had taken up a position at a table close to theirs which made it virtually impossible for anyone other than the waitstaff to approach them. Jordan could well understand the need to protect Chloe.

He'd been counting on the fact that this was Berlin where people tended to value their privacy, and in doing so, had assumed the other diners wouldn't disturb her. But not long after they'd arrived, Jordan had come to see the folly of his ways. The restaurant was a favorite haunt of the city's tourists.

Idiot. You could have picked a dozen other places, but you had to come here.

Worried, Jordan had spoken to Martin, who'd reassured him that at the first sign of trouble, he was to get the hell out of the way while Chloe was quickly hustled out the back of the café and into a waiting car. Jordan was in no doubt that if push came to shove, he was on his own.

Chloe sat toying idly with her salad. The tomatoes, avocado, and green leaves were pretty, but he could almost hear them pleading to be dressed in the homemade vinaigrette which she'd asked to be held back.

"This tortilla is really good, would you like to try a bite?" he offered, pushing the plate toward her. Chloe briefly licked her lips, then shook her head. He pushed the plate a little closer. It was like trying to tempt a wild bird. She shook her head a second time. There was a real battle going on here. Temptation vs. resolve.

Hang on. You don't like it when people do that to you. When they shove a beer under your nose. Don't be that guy.

She had respected his stated boundaries earlier, he should give her the same courtesy. Jordan pulled the plate back. As he did, Chloe let out a sigh of relief. She'd obviously wanted to taste the egg and potato omelet but wouldn't allow herself. Wouldn't permit it. His brows furrowed as Chloe dragged the salad bowl closer and she stabbed her fork into a leaf.

Jordan's phone pinged. He glanced at it. The nightclub privacy sticker was still stuck over the camera. It had occurred to him that if the clubs in NYC had been doing that during his wild hellcat days, it would have saved him a gut load of pain, not to mention lawyers, and bail money.

Grainy pictures of Jordan in *various* stages of undress with *various* young women in *various* nightclubs still lurked in the recesses of the internet. House of Royal money, vast that it was, could only buy so much anonymity.

He peeled the sticker off and turned the phone over. The screen shone with an angry message.

> The skanky folks who've stolen our booth r royally pissed at you. Did u really kidnap a pop star?!!

Trust Sheila to put it so eloquently. Jordan could understand where Chloe's people were coming from. They didn't appreciate being ditched by their boss.

Well, tough. She's with me. And we aren't doing anything wrong.

> No I didn't, her bodyguards are with us. We went to get food. Ignore the others.

> Ok. But still giving them 😒 Be a good boy. C U tomorrow.

> R U still with Leon?

😶

"Who is that?"

There was a distinct sense of worry, almost suspicion in Chloe's voice. Jordan dropped his phone into his coat pocket. "My assistant, Sheila. The woman I was with at the club. She wanted to know if I had left. Apparently, your people are not happy that you slipped out with me."

Chloe nodded. "Oh. Ok."

"Why? Am I not supposed to use my phone when I'm with you?"

A patch of red flushed Chloe's cheeks. "Of course you can. It's just that I get a little edgy when people I'm out in public with start suddenly texting. In my experience the paparazzi are not normally far behind."

Ouch. Jordan scrubbed a hand over his cheeks. *Do I have douchebag written all over my face?*

"A guy would have to have a serious death wish to want to

lure you and your hefty bodyguards out of a Berlin nightclub just to get a photo for a pap," Jordan huffed. He was annoyed at the insinuation. Retrieving his phone, he unlocked it, then pushed it screen facing upward toward Chloe. "That's the exchange Sheila and I just had. Other than that I haven't touched my phone since we left the club. Feel free to check. I've nothing to hide."

She had the good grace to look away from the phone before whispering. "Sorry. I'm sorry."

But Jordan was the one feeling sorry. Sorry for Chloe. He pitied her. Was there no one in her life whom she could trust without first having them sign an NDA?

This woman lives at a whole other level of fame. Where everything she says or does is closely scrutinized. Including apparently her food. That's not success, that's a prison sentence.

"Chloe, I have no interest in crashing your life. Or ruining your evening. If any of this is a problem, I'll get the check, and we can say goodnight. I promise, you won't be seeing any quotes from me on the gossip sites or in the *Daily Mail*. I wouldn't do that to you."

Chloe had barely touched any of the delicious food he had ordered, and now she was worried about him tipping off the paparazzi so he could sell her image. But he was the last person who would go talking to the press.

You have no idea how much I don't ever want to see my face in the newspapers again.

"I'm sorry, Jordan. I'm sorry, forget what I said. Please, can we just eat?" she pleaded.

Chloe was sensibly wrapped up in a large black overcoat, beret, and scarf. March in Berlin was bitterly cold. The snow still thick on the ground. The coat was miles too big for her, but Jordan could see how it would come in handy for hiding from the public. Between her rust brown beret and the coat lapels, only her face showed. He caught a glimpse of the stray lock of her black hair which had escaped, and his fingers itched to tuck it back behind her ear.

Don't touch her. She is like a cat on a hot tin roof.

Her warm disguise was necessary, but it was also a shame. He'd liked what he'd seen in the nightclub. The tight silver tank top and jeans. The sky high heels of her boots. And those sexy silver hoop earrings. He'd always had a thing about girls and hoop earrings.

And here he was, giving her his best rich boy attitude. Chloe was clearly not used to dealing with people who didn't come into her life without their own set of agendas. She didn't know him, or his background. His family's billions shouldn't even come into this—he should just get over his ego and let her enjoy this moment of freedom.

A change in topic might help. Give her something else to talk about other than the worry of stalker fans.

"Are you headed back to the States after tonight, or do you have more shows in Europe? I honestly only found out about tonight's concert by sheer chance when I turned on the TV in my hotel suite."

Chloe handed Jordan's phone back to him. "Yes well, you don't fit the usual profile for Chloe's Garden. I think it's close to ninety-five percent female Gen Z and Gen Alpha." As he reached out to take it, their fingers brushed over one another. In a moment that could only be described as pure serendipity, they both let out a small gasp at the heated touch.

A thrill of lust went straight to Jordan's cock. His head shot up and he met Chloe's stunned gaze.

She felt it too. I would have to be the world's biggest idiot right now. I've just told this girl I wasn't interested in a fling and yet when we touch—lighting bolts.

Her heart had definitely skipped a beat—maybe two at his touch. It was a brief half second, but it had her mind suddenly filled with images of the two of them walking hand in hand along an empty beach. Across the water, the setting sun lit the sky with gold. As Jordan stopped and pulled her into his embrace for a long toe-curling kiss, one of Chloe's own power ballads kicked in as the soundtrack.

Sorry, Celine Dion, you got Titanic, this is my moment.

A loud crash from the café's kitchen broke the spell. Chloe's senses went on high alert. She looked to Jordan who was gazing back over her shoulder in the direction of the disturbance.

"It's alright, someone just dropped a stack of plates."

"Oh." She wasn't normally like this around men. Her *I'm the world's biggest pop star* protective armor usually stayed firmly in place. But not tonight. With Jordan, things were different. She was unsettled. The answer was all too obvious.

I want him to like me.

"Chloe?" What had he said before that? Oh, yes, he'd asked about her travel plans. A nice safe question. She could do safe.

"No, I won't be back in the US for a few more days. Tomorrow we are heading to Paris for the final concert of my mini European tour. The day after, I'm meant to be flying home to LA. And then I have an album to finish and promote. And then my manager wants me to announce a global tour."

She waved her hand idly about. The *yada yada* was heavily implied.

"I couldn't begin to imagine how hard you must work to

hold it all together, to make it look so seamless. I trust you have an amazing group of people around you."

Chloe nodded but deep down she knew the next few months were going to be utterly exhausting. She wasn't looking forward to the moment when her manager Foster spoke the dreaded words, 'we need to confirm dates for the world tour.' It all sounded wonderful and glamorous, but tours mostly consisted of hotels, sound checks, mindless press interviews, and very little real interaction with her fans. But with the advent of streaming services, touring was the way artists made most of their money these days.

She paused and mustered a smile. *Where are my manners?* This conversation shouldn't be all about her. "So, where do you live, Jordan? I know you mentioned being from the East Coast when we were at the club."

His answering grin warmed her heart. "New York City born and bred, but I do travel around a bit on company business and to catch up with family. I'm actually going to head out to the West Coast in a couple of weeks for a long work assignment. I'll be based at Laguna Beach until the end of the year."

Jordan was coming to California. Chloe sent a prayer to heaven. *There is something about this man that has me intrigued. Please don't let him be a handsome-as-sin stalker.*

If they were going to possibly meet up again, she would need to get Martin to do some serious background checks on Jordan just to be safe.

In her coat, Chloe's cell beeped. She dug her hand into her pocket and after a moment or two of frantic searching, managed to locate her phone, and set it on the table.

> Bad. Bad. Chloe. You r buying us 3 bottles of Dom for taking off with that guy.

Reprimand and demand all in one. She shouldn't be the

least bit surprised that Marta was planning to hit the expensive stuff tonight. Every time they went clubbing her number one personal assistant always wanted to drink the *top, top-shelf* booze. Nothing else was good enough for Marta, especially when her boss was paying.

Jordan tapped a finger next to Chloe's phone. "Tell her she can have one. And if she wants any more, she can damn well pay for it herself."

Chloe had a sudden flash of how well that would go down with her team. Tears and tantrums. She never said *no* to them. She was so scared that they might decide to leave her, that she didn't dare. "It's ok, they're just having fun. And I did leave without telling them."

> Sorry, I'm selfish. Yes get 3. Enjoy. C U on the jet.

Jordan picked up his knife and fork and after putting a piece of the omelet into his mouth, set his cutlery down. As he sat chewing his food, his finger tapped a frenetic beat on the table right next to Chloe's phone.

Chloe's cell pinged again. Jordan's hand shifted toward it, and for a second, she feared he was going to snatch it away from her. The message was another one from Marta. It was rare for her to only send one.

> Stay off the carbs. You have to look fab for France.

It was quickly followed by another.

> I love you.

Chloe picked up the phone and quickly typed her reply.

> I love you too.

Setting the phone down, she lifted her head. Her gaze settled once more on Jordan. He was staring at the screen of her cell, reading it, taking in that last exchange. His brows were knitted together in undisguised displeasure.

"You think I'm a pushover, don't you?"

"It's actually none of my business," he said, though his tight tone betrayed that he wished it was. "If you want to pay for bottles of Dom Pérignon then that is entirely up to you. But if you ever want to talk about setting and enforcing boundaries with your people, feel free to give me a call."

Wow. Mister Judgey McJudgeface.

It was rare for anyone outside of her small circle of staff and management to speak to her in such a way. Chloe was taken aback. "You are an arrogant son of a bitch, aren't you?"

Her hand shot immediately to her mouth. She'd actually said what she was thinking. Her frazzled brain hadn't seen the big red stop sign in time, and she had crashed straight through it.

Chloe couldn't blame Jordan if he got up and left without paying the bill. In her world, guys didn't like being called out on their self-importance. Especially not by women.

But instead, he burst out laughing. Jordan's whole body shook. Chloe sat in stunned silence while her date helped himself to a long, rolling guffaw. She couldn't quite decide whether it was at her expense or not. But it was still interesting to watch.

"Oh that is priceless. I can't remember the last time I was put so firmly in my place. I deserved that," said Jordan, wiping away a tear.

He grinned at her, his eyes still sparkling with mirth. "I've been behaving like a big-headed ass, one who has absolutely no right to be telling you what to do. You can blame my cousin Leon for my rude behavior. I've spent the past day engaged in a battle of egos with him and I forgot to dial things back with you."

His laughter and apology had taken the heat out of the moment, but Chloe knew that Jordan believed what he'd said. She had no doubt about that. He disapproved of the way she let her people treat her.

He's probably right. Of course he is, but I need them.

It was a pretty screwed up arrangement in anyone's language for a major recording star to pay people to push her around. Oddly enough, Jordan was the first person to have actually called her out on it. And even he had backed off when she got defensive.

Jordan drained the rest of his cup of coffee. When he pushed his plate away, Chloe wondered what was about to come next. Most likely, he was going to call for the check, offer his polite farewells, and wish her all the very best with her future career. Like others before him, Jordan would take his leave of her, and not look back. Her team might not be the best people in the world, but at least they stayed.

Please don't go. I just want a little of your time.

"Do you know Berlin well, Jordan? I hear it looks amazing at night. I'd love to go for a drive and see the Reichstag Building and the Brandenburg Gate when they are all lit up."

Chloe hated the desperation in her voice, it left her wondering if she would ever stop reaching out to people this way. Like a puppy at a refuge center trying to find its forever home.

Jordan's gaze shifted to her security detail. "Could we check with them first? I don't want the Berlin Police having to deal with the mountain of paperwork that will drop on them if my lifeless body washes up on the banks of the River Spree tomorrow morning."

Chloe snorted. He had a sense of humor. "The members

of my protection team are good men, and they are also very discrete. I promise, no one will ever find your body."

A grinning Jordan rose from the table. "Let me go and settle our bill, back in a minute." He headed to the front counter of the café, while Chloe squared things with her bodyguards. She had just finished buttoning up her coat when Jordan reappeared at her side. "What hotel are you staying at?"

"The Berlin Hyatt." She was a global pop star, which meant that her management wouldn't have Chloe stay anywhere other than at a five-star major branded hotel. She liked the hotel. Her private suite was gorgeous, and the hotel service was impeccable.

Maybe she was playing it safe. In an historic city like Berlin there would be far more interesting and edgier hotels for her to stay in if she chose. But safety was something Chloe needed, something she craved.

As they headed toward the door, Chloe wrapped her scarf around her neck and adjusted the collar of her coat. She kept her gaze fixed firmly ahead, not looking at any of the other diners. Chloe loved her fans, but tonight, she wanted something else.

The limousine was waiting for them out on the street. Chloe's bodyguards climbed into the front, while Chloe and Jordan slipped into the spacious, and private, rear passenger section.

Jordan took the seat next to Chloe. As the car pulled away from the curb he leaned in close. "I think we might have gotten off on the wrong foot. At the club and in the café, I made some pretty big and to be honest arrogant assumptions about you. That wasn't fair."

Chloe's heart did a little dance of joy. *He's actually a nice guy.* Jordan had more insight of his behavior than most guys she knew. LA was full of people who lived and died by the *never explain never apologize* rule of law.

"I think we are both guilty of a bit of pre-judging. I certainly took points off your score for wearing your sunglasses on your head in a nightclub."

He winced. "I'd forgotten they were there. Thank you for not calling the fashion police and having me placed in handcuffs."

He has a self-depreciating sense of humor. I like it.

His fingers brushed over her hand and Chloe shivered. The musical soundtrack of their romance started up once more inside her head. She liked Jordan's touch even more than his smile, especially when it lingered.

"I'm also seriously regretting giving you the "you're a nice girl but ...' line."

Chloe laughed. He really was a nice guy. It had been such a long time since a man had been this close to her without it being in a professional capacity. Her stylist and bodyguards were the only other males permitted to lay their hands on her. And only when it was absolutely necessary. Even Foster rarely touched her, but then again, her manager hadn't ever been one for displays of affection.

"In fact, I'm regretting it so much, that I'm now formally retracting that statement so I can do this." Jordan took her hand and raised it seductively to his lips, he then proceeded to kiss each one of Chloe's finger tips in turn. One by one. Slowly. *Kiss. Kiss.*

Chloe swallowed deep. He had to know what this was doing to her pulse. And to her panties.

"Hi, my name is Jordan Royal. It's a pleasure to meet you, Chloe." His voice was so rich and smoothly silk it had her legs parting in anticipation.

Jordan Royal. He hadn't given her his full name until just

now. *What a unique surname.* It had a certain weight about it. And it suited him.

Chloe shifted closer, one hand working the buttons of her coat free, while the other slipped her scarf from her neck. She wanted more than sweet enticing words. "Touch me. Please, Jordan."

A gruff breath of barely restrained hunger escaped Jordan's lips. It went straight to her core. He gently tugged the beret from her head, then casually tossed it across the limo onto the opposite seat. As her long black tresses cascaded down, settling around her shoulders, he murmured, "You are so beautiful."

Chloe hesitated. She hated herself for feeling so needy, for wanting Jordan's hands all over her. He moved forward, dropping a kiss on her forehead. "So damn beautiful." His fingers speared into her hair, lighting up the nerve endings. *Perfection.* This was exactly how she loved being held by a man when he was about to kiss her.

The all-consuming, bone deep desire for him to kiss her threatened to scramble Chloe's brain. He *was* going to kiss her, wasn't he? She was getting dangerously close to the point of begging.

Please. I need so very badly to be kissed. It has to be you.

Chloe gripped the front of Jordan's coat, holding him to her. Their gazes met. "I would like very much to kiss you, Chloe," he whispered. The heated promise in his voice went straight to her already aroused sex. This was happening. And if her bodyguards tried to intervene, she would fight them both off with her bare hands.

Oh yes. Please. Please. Kiss me stupid. And don't stop.

"Jordan," she murmured, offering him her mouth.

When his lips touched hers, it was with such heartbreaking tenderness it brought her to the verge of tears. His kiss was soft. Slow. Dare she say, loving? Jordan had it all wrong—he was the one who was beautiful.

In the dimly lit rear of the limo Jordan revealed himself to be a man far removed from his public persona. He might give off the vibe of being all sharp edges and a man of business, but it was clear Jordan had a gentler side, one he wasn't afraid to share with a woman. His embrace was warm, affectionate. Chloe's heart stirred to life.

Yes. Yes. Where has this man been all my life?

His tongue swept into her mouth, and Chloe groaned. She gripped even tighter to the folds of Jordan's gorgeously soft wool coat. It was so divinely supple, that she had to force herself not to think about his clothes and concentrate on the kiss. Talk about a scattered mind.

She wished his clothes would magically disappear. *I need him naked.* Sex in the back of the limo was rocketing up the charts of her to do list like a bullet. If he offered to play, she would say yes. The mere thought of his hands on her bare ass sent her pulse racing.

Jordan deepened the kiss, working his mouth and hers together in an embrace that showcased his mastery of the act. If this was how he kissed, Chloe couldn't begin to imagine what he could do to her when she was naked and in his arms. What his skillful tongue could do to her clit. Her fevered imagination stripped her own clothes away, leaving them pressed together skin to skin.

Why did I have to wear jeans tonight, a skirt would have made it so much easier.

While she wrangled with her poor choice of wardrobe, the gentle whir of the divider screen being raised reached Chloe's ears. Thank god for Martin and his innate sense of decency.

The driver would be politely cautioned about any sort of attempt to sell the story to the press. Her security team could be very persuasive. What ever happened tonight, they would stay silent. Chloe was confident that none of what transpired in the car would be getting back to her entourage.

She waited with bated breath for Jordan to make the next move. To slide down the zipper of her jeans and see just how far she was prepared to let him take things. To slip his hand inside and test the edges of her G-string. To discover how horny and wet he'd already made her.

I don't want him to stop. I want his hands and lips all over me. Fuck. These. Jeans.

Chloe's unsated hunger to be groped and pawed was fast reaching fever pitch. She wanted to feel alive. Wanted to give herself to this man. To know pleasure.

There was nothing stopping him. They were two consenting adults. And for the sort of money that the limousine company charged, she was certain they would find a fresh box of condoms in one of the small storage cupboards.

Please. Forget who I am. I'm just a girl wanting a guy to make love to her.

A sharp pain speared into her heart as Jordan's hands slowly released their grip, and he drew back from the kiss. Chloe knew that pain. It was the all too familiar ache of rejection. She was a world-famous pop star, but she still wasn't good enough for the people she wanted to want her.

I will never be enough for anyone.

Jordan glanced at the divider screen, then back to her. "Sorry, I got a little bit carried away. We were meant to be taking a tour of the city and seeing the sights of Berlin at night."

Chloe reluctantly let go of his coat, her fingers drifted down his lapels then away. He didn't want to take this any further, and he was well within his rights to say no. Just because she was famous didn't mean she could make demands of him.

No means no.

She shifted further along the bench seat, making it clear she was giving him space. "Yes, we were going to see the city. And then drop you off at your hotel." Chloe hurriedly scooped up her beret and scarf and put them back on. She buttoned up her coat, mentally sliding her emotional armor on.

She'd learned the hard way that if people wanted to be in her life, they made it their business to be there. And when they didn't, they tended to make it pretty damn clear. Some of her earliest memories were of doors being closed as people walked away.

With her clothes back in place, Chloe settled into polite mode, displaying the pattern of behavior that she reserved for interviews and red carpets. "So Jordan, where are you staying?" Her bland, unthreatening tone carried the right amount of 'just friends' interest. When her emotions protested at this sudden change of heart, she sucked in a deep breath and forced them down.

"I'm staying at one of our family apartments, it's only a short walk from your hotel. So once we arrive at the Grand Hyatt, I can make my own way from there. You don't need to worry about dropping me off anywhere."

Jordan had made his position clear. They were going to go for a drive and do a little night sightseeing. Nothing else. But Chloe was intrigued. Who was this guy? There was just something about him. Something she couldn't let go.

His family must have money if they can afford to have an apartment in Berlin. His clothes are tailored, and that coat felt super luxurious.

Chloe touched the button on the divider screen, making herself comfortable as the private space opened up once more. She and Martin exchanged a brief nod of understanding. His boss would be going back to her hotel suite alone.

"Could you please ask the driver to take us past the Brandenburg Gate?" asked Jordan. "I think Chloe would really enjoy seeing it."

She offered him her best smile. The one she used for people who tried to let her down gently. A silent reward which was meant to convey *'thank you for thinking of me'* without her having to actually say it.

"Yes, let's go and look at the lights."

It was time for Chloe to once again tuck her heart's disappointment back into its glittering box. She was one of the world's biggest pop stars, but Jordan had just relegated her to the friend zone.

CHAPTER FOUR

Jordan's head was a mess about the pop princess. He'd been thoroughly invested in kissing Chloe, of engaging in some serious heavy petting as they drove around Berlin. His plan was to see if she responded favorably to his advances. And if she did, to ask if she wanted to spend the night with him. He wanted nothing more than to give Chloe hours of intoxicating sexual pleasure. The mere thought of having the dark haired temptress writhing beneath him, groaning his name as she came, had his cock hard and demanding in his suit pants. She wanted him, and he wanted her.

But right in the middle of it all, his father's voice had exploded into Jordan's lust-filled mind, obliterating every other thought and emotion in its wake. Talk about terrible timing. Edward Royal was banging on about responsibilities and how much was riding on the company's new Californian resort.

"I am depending on you, Jordan. There is a billion-dollar development at stake. I had to convince the board you are up to the task. But I believe in you, son. Jordan? Jordan? Why the devil are you kissing that girl? Do you even care about the opportunity I've given you? You

don't have what it takes to balance a relationship and work, we both know that ..."

He'd done his best to push his father's thoughts out of his head, but he'd failed. The words kept eating away at Jordan. *Billion dollar. Depending on you.* His father just wouldn't shut the fuck up.

His semi-hard erection had wilted and disappeared. If he couldn't get his father out of his head, he wasn't going to be able to perform in the bedroom. It was with a sense of deep reluctance that Jordan released Chloe from his embrace. A man only got one chance with a woman like Chloe. Leaving the superstar unsatisfied in bed would be a sure-fire way to guarantee she wouldn't want to see him again.

Nope, not happening. With his old man's words still ringing loudly in his brain, Jordan wasn't prepared to take that risk. He had an impeccable track record of being able to deliver exactly what a woman wanted in the bedroom, and he was determined to keep it that way.

If I can't bring her to orgasm, she'll think I'm a dud. Oh god. What if she writes a song about me?

Cold dread slid down his spine at the hellish thought of having to hear about his bedroom failures every time he tapped into Spotify. Sleeping with famous people really should come with a warning.

He'd made the right decision by bringing their passionate kiss to an end. But while his manhood might be in a weakened state, his ego was more than ready to take up arms and resume the battle.

He was Jordan Royal, the king of comebacks. The lord of second chances. He was the bloody poster boy for *where there is life, there is hope*. Just because he and Chloe didn't end up between the sheets tonight, didn't mean it wouldn't ever happen.

I just need to find a way to stay in touch with her. And get Dad out of my head.

What had she said about the rest of her tour? *Ah, yes.* With his charm dial set to high, he turned from gazing out the window and smiled back at Chloe. "Where are you staying in Paris? If we exchange numbers, maybe we could catch up. Spend some real time together."

Chloe's merry little band of assistants were mercifully still out on the town when she finally made it back to her suite at the Grand Hyatt a little after four am. Marta's text asking about the extra bottles of Dom Pérignon had been several hours ago. Knowing Marta, Gabriela, and Stixxluv the table tab would be well past that by now.

And if publicity whore Stixxluv stuck true to form he would have gotten bored and dragged the other two out of Berghain and gone in search of somewhere new to party. Somewhere that allowed him to take Insta worthy pics to share with his two-million devoted followers. He might be working with Chloe at present, but Stixxluv had his own loyal fanbase, his own groupies. The demand for him to supply them with new fashion and style material was never ending.

Chloe resisted the temptation to check her stylist's social media. She'd be hearing every sordid detail of the night's high and low points on the flight to Paris later that day.

As long as they don't get arrested or end up in the hospital, I don't care what they do.

She wanted what was left of tonight to ponder why a guy like Jordan would turn down the opportunity to get hot and heavy with a world-famous pop star. She'd thought she'd made it pretty clear that she was a sure thing.

As they drove around Berlin, her come-hither glances had been a bust. He seemed determined to play gentleman tour guide. As soon as the limousine pulled up in the private parking garage below her hotel, Jordan had wished her a polite good night, kissed her on the cheek, then headed for the exit.

Her only consolation was his second request for them to meet up again in Paris the day after next. They'd exchanged phone numbers. That at least had left her with some hope.

Chloe was prepared to wait. Just as long as Jordan's reluctance to seduce her tonight had everything to do with his manners and nothing to do with him having a girlfriend or—god forbid—a wife waiting for him back in the States. While they'd sat and ate at the well-lit café, she'd checked Jordan's left hand for the telltale signs of a wedding ring. But she knew far too many serial cheaters and it was rare for one of them to make such a rookie mistake.

Fame was a peculiar beast. There were some women who would have no issue with their boyfriend or even husband sleeping with a pop star, just as long as he came home and told them every single, sleazy detail. The trash magazines would be more than willing to pay good money for pictures of a teary-eyed woman whose man had been tempted into cheating on her by a sultry songstress.

LA, and especially Hollywood, seemed to have a different set of morals and codes of behavior than the rest of the world. Money and power was all that truly mattered. Decency tended to get shoved aside by inflated egos.

Jordan had her intrigued. The guy was devilishly handsome, that much was obvious. He was also extremely self-assured, which only made his behavior tonight that more unfathomable. She was Chloe, famous, talented, and beautiful, but when he'd found himself in a position that would have seen close to ninety-nine percent of the straight male population not hesitate to fuck her in the back of the limo, Jordan had let her go.

Her security people would do a full background check on Jordan before she met up with him in Paris, but for now, Chloe was determined to find out as much as she could herself. To rule out any obvious reasons as to why she shouldn't ever see him again.

I need to know everything I can about him.

Retrieving her laptop from the suite's extra-large safe, Chloe typed "Jordan Royal" into Google. A ton of pages about the Jordanian royal family, an airline, and basketball sneakers immediately appeared. After scrolling unsuccessfully through several pages of information, none of it about her quarry, she narrowed her search.

"Jordan Royal. Royal Family". Nope, more things about the Jordanian royal family. It was only when she finally typed in "Jordan Royal, New York, rich" that she finally had success.

Chloe leaned forward over the keyboard, staring hard at a grainy picture. It wasn't the best paparazzi effort she had ever seen, but it was clearly Jordan. He was standing next to another man, whose name was listed as Edward Royal. The image might be a hastily snapped piece of photographic crap, but the familial similarities were still clear. The older man had to be Jordan's father.

"Royal Resorts Announces Billion Dollar Resort, Laguna Beach, California."

The article was from one of the financial newspapers. It talked about the international brand conglomerate House of Royal. Among a glittering array of luxury brands, many of which Chloe recognized, they also owned Royal Resorts. Jordan was part of the mega billionaire Royal family. The

American side of the global powerhouse was apparently based in New York City.

Well that explains the bespoke suit, fancy coat, and superior attitude. He comes from old, serious money.

The limousine, bodyguards, and bottles of high-priced liquor wouldn't have impressed Jordan in the slightest. "He probably eats caviar for breakfast, served to him on a silver platter," she whispered.

Some more quick finger work saw Chloe clicking into her subscription for *New York Magazine*, where she did a deep dive into the society pages. As a pop star it was part of her job to know what was being said about her, and by whom. While she left the trashy gossip magazines and sites to her assistant's assistant Gabriela, Chloe liked to keep tabs on the main US based press and influential magazines herself.

It quickly became apparent that Jordan Royal maintained a low social profile. Apart from the occasional gala charity dinner or official hotel opening he was conspicuously absent from the society pages. Intrigued, she dug a little deeper, her search going back a few more years. It took time, but she eventually struck gold.

A small paragraph with an accompanying photo of Jordan lazing against a wall, while dressed in a formal evening suit, bow tie hanging loosely around his neck, and sunglasses hiding his eyes, caught her attention. It was only a couple of lines, but it told a very different story to the one she imagined he'd been trying to sell her tonight.

"Troubled, billionaire bad boy Jordan Royal reported to have checked out of rehab. No comment from the Royal family as he returns to New York City to pick up the pieces of his life."

That was over four years ago. And if his behavior this evening was anything to go by, Jordan was still living clean and sober. She hadn't seen him touch any booze, and he'd been adamant about not using drugs when she'd asked. This was all good news.

So why did warning bells still ring so loudly in her mind?

Because every guy you've ever dated turned out to be a user trying to further his own career. Or had his own agenda.

He might well be reformed, but since she had little experience with real relationships, getting mixed up with a former addict probably wasn't the right place to start finally looking for love. A guy like Jordan Royal could well turn out to be a cautionary tale.

After twirling her hair round her fingers until they lost sense of feeling, Chloe gave up and tied it into a messy bun.

The newspapers and magazines showed a carefully curated image of Jordan, but Chloe was interested to see if perhaps he let his guard down just a little on social media. She picked up her phone.

Another half hour of searching and scrolling revealed no Facebook account, no Instagram. She assumed a guy like Jordan wouldn't be the type to watch dancing goats on TikTok, but she still checked. Nope, nothing. If Jordan was on any social media platform it wasn't under his own name. He was keeping his secrets to himself.

The familiar warning signs of what having the wrong kind of people in her life could cost her, were right there in front of her. Red flags were posted every half mile. She should know better. She *did* know better. But the painful ache of loneliness was strong.

None of her heart or head's sensible pleas could stop her from sending Jordan a message.

> Still want 2 meet me in Paris. I can put your name on the door for a backstage pass. Concert on Thursday. The Arena. La Défense.

It was now nearing six am. She really ought to try and get some sleep. Her people would soon be wandering back to the hotel, and if they got even a sniff of her still being awake, they would come knocking.

If she didn't have the show in Paris the day after tomorrow, she would have changed their checkout and flight times. But soundchecks and concert rehearsals didn't wait. Nor did the fans who would be waiting patiently for the *Chloe Jet* to land at Paris Le Bourget airport.

And we don't back out of commitments. The fans want this show. So do I.

Her cell buzzed.

> I need to see you. Unfinished business. No backstage pass.

He didn't want to come to her show. Didn't want to see her perform. That stung more than it should. Maybe he was just keeping true to his need for a low profile. Heart racing, Chloe sent another message.

> Paris. Late Thursday night. Le Meurice. Presidential Suite. I will leave your name at reception.

She'd barely had time to send it, before a reply pinged back.

> Private liaison. Come to me, Chloe.

> 21 Rue Benjamin Franklin.

He wanted her to come to him. Chloe went straight back onto Google and checked out the address. It appeared to be an elegant block of private apartments situated a short distance from the Eiffel Tower.

Dare she risk it? Going to see a man who was basically a

stranger. And what might happen once she arrived at the place where he was staying? Her fingers curled into tight balls of nervous energy. She could just visualize the headlines.

"Pop Princess Goes Missing. Fans Hold Candlelit Vigil".

"Don't be ridiculous," she sighed. "He's from one of the richest families in the US, not that money matters, but if he decides to kidnap me, it won't take much for The Feds to find out who and where he is. And Martin will know."

Jordan was playing hard to get. She really ought to tell him to go away. That she was Chloe and men didn't tell her what to do. They were the ones who begged for her attention, not the other way round.

And yet, you know damn well you are going to do what he says.

Memories of their all too brief a kiss dropped tantalizingly into her mind. That moment when Jordan had made her toes curl up in her high heel boots. His luscious scent had held her spellbound. She would have given anything for him to have slipped her jeans off and taken her there and then in the back of the limo.

Chloe brushed a hand over her silk pajama top. Her nipples were hard and sensitive. The pulse throbbing between her legs begged for intimate attention. Lust clouded her mind.

"Come to me," she whispered. The lure of his words held her fast.

Her fingers tapped out a longer, more strategic reply to Jordan's message.

> Have checked U out online. No socials? Security team compiling dossier on Mister Jordan Royal. C U in Paris. C 🤍 🤍 🤍

She'd added the heart emojis and sent the message before she realized what she'd done. What would he think of them? She didn't want to consider. Hopefully Jordan would barely notice, or just think she was being cute. So much for sultry siren.

Chloe set her phone on the desk. The thought of seeing Jordan again had her body making its demands known. It wanted release, and now.

After turning off all the lights in her suite, Chloe carried her laptop over to the bed. She propped it up with some pillows, then clicked open the website where she'd found the article and photo of Jordan. She enlarged the image with a quick tap and focus.

Her gaze remained on the photo of him standing in his beautifully tailor-made suit, bow tie teasingly askew, smiling at the camera. His whole seductive bad boy pose held the promise of everything, but mostly mischief.

Chloe spread her legs and settled back on the bed. Her hand slipped beneath the waistband of her PJs. A finger teased the entrance to her sex, and she let out a gasp.

Oh god, I am soaking wet.

She slid one, then two fingers deep into her heat, arching her back as she played with the sensitive bud of her clit. "Oh yes," she murmured. Her other hand went to her left nipple, squeezing it hard. Punishing herself for pleasure. Self-love was the greatest release.

Imagining that it was Jordan who was touching her body, Chloe moaned as his fingers pleasured her long and slow. His smiling mouth sucked hard on her tits, driving her wild.

She crushed her nipple between her fingers, as the pace of her strokes grew more frenzied. Chloe crashed through into a blazing climax, crying out, "Jordan" as she came.

It took her a few minutes to regain her composure. Lying slumped on the soft hotel sheets, Chloe opened her eyes, and stared at the ceiling. It had been a long time since she had brought herself to orgasm so fast. Her clit pulsed.

Jordan Royal had done that to her, and he hadn't even

been in the same room. She could barely begin to imagine what being naked with him in Paris would be like. How having his hands on her body would feel. *Heaven.*

Come to me. She hoped she had read that message right. That what he really meant was *come for me.* If things went according to plan, Chloe had every intention of doing just that for Jordan, and more than once.

CHAPTER FIVE

Sheila stepped out of Jordan's bathroom and announced, "All clear. I'll upload the screen shot and details to human resources. They will send your certificate through later today. In my considered opinion, this morning's sample looks like a young Riesling, which means you should watch your water intake."

"Um. Yeah. Thanks, Sheila."

Jordan was heading to Paris today. His executive assistant was on her way to Scotland to visit family. A little while earlier, Sheila had sprung a random drug test on him. He'd been waiting for it to happen. The standing request from the House of Royal HR people was for him to undergo a monthly drug test. As part of her job as his personal assistant, Sheila got saddled with the not-so-glamorous task of testing Jordan's urine.

Sheila classifying the color of his pee against the shades of a wine chart was a sick private joke between the two of them. She'd stood steadfastly at Jordan's side through many of his bleakest moments. His sponsor might be able to talk to him over the phone, but it was Sheila who was downstairs at three am with a packed suitcase in the trunk of a town car, ready to spirit her boss back to a secret stay in rehab when things got serious. If there was one person who knew Jordan almost as well as himself, it was Sheila.

She worked hard for her money. Jordan was glad to be able to send her home first class to Edinburgh to spend time with her extended family.

This morning, he held back a secret smile. Sheila thought she was going to Scotland just to see her grandparents. What she didn't know was that he had also arranged for her parents and siblings to fly first class from New York for a Kirk family reunion. He would love to be a fly on the wall when Sheila set foot in her grandparents' house.

But Jordan would be in Paris. And hopefully seeing Chloe once more. He couldn't stop thinking about her. Other people didn't normally occupy long periods of time in Jordan's brain, but for now he was more than content for Chloe to live rent free in his head.

"Well, have a great trip back to Scotland. Give your grannie my love. I'll see you in New York in a few weeks. Then it's off to LA. I'm looking forward to some of that California sun."

Sheila suffered his kiss on her cheek. "It's alright for you, you're going to be based in LA. I'm the one who is going to be flying back and forth between the two places, while also juggling my studies. I have a feeling these next few months are going to be interesting to say the least. Oh, and when you see that shit of a cousin of yours this morning, could you let Leon know that what he thinks is funny, actually isn't."

She didn't add to that last remark, and Jordan knew well enough to leave it alone. Sheila was the kind of woman who would be more than happy to vent, but horrified if her boss actually went to war on her behalf. The embarrassment would kill her. And then she would come after him.

I'm going to miss you when I'm in California.

"I'll let Leon know he is a dick, but it won't be news to him. Have a safe flight. Call me in a few days when you're bored and need to bitch about the weather in Scotland."

Sheila huffed. She tapped Jordan a little too firmly on the arm, then added a second huff for effect. "Are you going to bloody well tell me what happened with the pop star last night or not? You left early. And when I got back to our table, her strange little clique had not only taken over both booths and were partying hard, but they were making it plain that they were seriously pissed about the guy who had stolen their Chloe away. Very possessive bunch. I will never understand you Americans and your need to cling to famous people."

"It's only some of us. And don't tell me you wouldn't drop your panties in a heartbeat if Gerard Butler winked at you."

Sheila laughed. She had a thing for the Scottish actor.

"Nothing happened with the pop star, as you call her. Chloe and I went and got a bite to eat. Then we went for a drive around Berlin, and I showed her the sights. Her bodyguards were with us the whole time."

He didn't elaborate further, as far as he was concerned, he didn't have to. What had happened in the back of the limousine was no one else's business. Jordan understood the need for privacy. Chloe had the right for hers to be protected.

Sheila gave him one final, and mercifully more gentle pat on the arm. "Let me know if you need anything. And say hello to your family in Paris for me."

"Will do." He didn't have the heart to tell her that his plans for the French capital had changed. If he got time, he would call in and see his uncle and aunt at their chateau outside of Paris, but the truth was, he was more concerned with getting to the Royal family apartment in the 16th arrondissement and making sure that everything was perfect ahead of Chloe's arrival.

As soon as Sheila had gone, Jordan picked up his phone and clicked on his messages. He went straight to the last one he'd received from Chloe, the one which had ended with all those love heart emojis.

It doesn't mean anything. She probably adds them to the end of all her messages. I shouldn't read anything into them.

His silly, hopeful heart oddly did.

CHAPTER SIX

Paris La Défense Arena
Thursday night

Hoping to fit in with the concert crowd, Jordan had dressed as low-key as possible. He was wearing jeans, a dark green cashmere sweater and the only pair of Doc Marten boots he owned. But as a thirty-two-year-old male he still stood out in the sea of young women. Chloe had been spot on about the composition of her fanbase. At his estimation, Chloe's Garden was at least ninety-eight percent female, with a smattering of boyfriends, and the odd male Chloe fan.

He hadn't originally planned to attend her show, but he couldn't resist the temptation of seeing Chloe perform live on stage. Jordan had called the head concierge at one of the Royal Resort hotels in Paris and asked if they happened to know of any spare tickets that might be available. A VIP pass to a private box had been delivered to the Royal family apartment in less than an hour.

Standing with a bottle of Evian water in his hand, Jordan

took in the vibe of the crowd. Being mostly young women, it had a definite friendly, safe feel to it. Squeals and excited words of delight drifted in through the open window of the private box. Fortunately he could speak fluent French, so he understood what was being said. Most of the conversations consisted of general chit chat about clothes and how much the fans were looking forward to seeing their favorite pop star. There was also a good deal of discussion about the merits of choosing comfortable shoes over fashionable ones.

He chuckled at that, recalling a female friend's horror story of wearing white sandals to the Glastonbury music festival in England, only to discover upon arrival that it was actually held in a mud-soaked field. While her toes sank into the ooze, everyone else had happily got about in sensible rain boots.

I wonder if Chloe would ever play Glastonbury.

When the support act came on, Chloe's fans were enthusiastic in their welcome. The artist was a local up and coming French singer and had her own fans. Jordan bopped along with the music, nodding his head.

She's good. Probably not megastar material, but she'll have a solid career.

He was alone in the private box, content with his own company. Chloe's generous invite for him to have a special pass for the show hadn't sat right with Jordan. After their time together in Berlin, he wanted her all to himself. If he'd gone back stage tonight, he would have been just another body in her already crowded entourage. Jordan Royal wasn't one for being part of the party crowd. He'd done that and had the emotional scars to prove it.

Beyond the stage and the bright lights, he ached to discover who the real Chloe was—she was the woman he wanted to get to know, not the pop star. And as far as he could see, the only way he was going to do that was for them to be alone. But he was still intrigued enough by Chloe the artist to want to see her in concert. Tonight was too good an opportunity to pass up.

The support act came and went, followed by a half hour of people moving around the arena, eating, and drinking.

As the time for Chloe to come on stage drew closer, Jordan sensed a certain change in the air. People put their bags under their seats. Empty food containers headed for the trash cans. Phones were gripped tightly in hands.

There was a growing mood of anticipation, waiting for the lighting strike.

When the recording of one of Chloe's biggest hits boomed over the arena sound system, forty-thousand fans roared as one. They applauded and stamped their feet. A million selfies launched onto the web.

Chloe's Garden was getting ready to party. When their leader arrived on stage, the roof of the giant arena would be blown off. He'd never seen anything like it before, the tension as thousands of Chloe's fans collectively held their breath.

A hush rippled through the mass gathering as the lights went out. Jordan set down his drink. The entire arena fell into dark silence.

This is incredible. I had no idea. All this is for her.

A small drum beat broke through the quiet. *Boom. Boom. Boom.*

A chorus of beats came back from the crowd.

The drum answered.

The crowd replied. Slowly, the beats and the feedback built. From somewhere in the darkness a violin joined in, the soaring strings breaking through the drum. Cameras flashed.

Jordan snatched up his bottle of water and took a deep drink. His heart was pounding in his chest. He didn't fully understand what was happening, but he was caught up in the raw power and emotion of the crowd. With every note, Chloe's Garden was rising.

A small red light lit the stage, and he peered hard at it. Then another light appeared. And another. All the while, the music kept on building.

He glanced down. His hands were shaking. And just when Jordan started to wonder whether he could take much more of this suspense, the stage suddenly erupted into bright light. Music filled the arena, and the monster of a crowd roared as one.

"*Chloe! Le Jardin de Chloé est arrivé! Chloe! Chloe!*"

Chloe's Garden had arrived.

And so had she.

Jordan's gaze settled on the small figure of a woman who stood centerstage. From here at the side of the arena, he could just make out her dark hair, and the glittering silver two piece costume she wore. Four giant jumbotron screens which sat either side, and on top of the stage now came to life. Chloe's image filled every one of them.

Everywhere Jordan looked, he saw Chloe. The music and the crowd all fell away. His world became her.

The only thing for him was Chloe.

CHAPTER SEVEN

The French certainly knew how to enjoy themselves at a show. When it came to enthusiastic audiences, Paris could certainly give Berlin a run for its money. The crowd in Chloe's Garden had been pumped to the max before she had even set foot on stage. Her support act, a talented French pop starlet, had received a rapturous welcome. Watching from the side of the stage, Chloe had beamed with happiness. It was nights like this that she lived for, when the fans and the music were in perfect sync.

And now the concert was over. The crowd was streaming out of the arena and since it was a midweek night, she expected most would be making their way straight home. She couldn't blame them. Two and a half hours of concert had left her exhausted, and her fans had been singing and dancing along with her from the very first note.

Her entourage had hit it hard in Berlin and were still in recovery mode. Marta and Gabriela had barely made it through the first half of tonight's show before calling it quits and going back to the hotel. Stixxluv was his usual super professional self and had remained. His role as Chloe's stylist meant he had to make sure she looked mind-blowingly fantastic on stage. And tonight she had.

The costume, hair, and makeup had played a significant part in how amazing she felt tonight, but there was something extra. A bubble of excitement which bounced around in her belly. A secret. After the concert she was going to steal away and meet with Jordan Royal.

She was eager to see if he would take things further than he had in Berlin, and also worried. What if he didn't want them to be anything more than friends?

Ok. Ok. You can do friends. Friends is good.

It wasn't. There was something about Jordan that kept him constantly at the forefront of her thoughts.

"Are you coming back to the hotel?" asked Stixxluv.

"Um. Yes. Yes. I am."

Chloe was slowly coming back down from the adrenaline high of the concert. Of accepting the adoration of forty-thousand fans. She'd showered, and all traces of her heavy waterproof stage makeup were gone, replaced by a light powder and barely there classic eye. Her hair was brushed and blown out. Her makeup and hair stylists knew how to have her shine on stage, but only Chloe handled her day-to-day makeup.

Her glittering costumes were being carefully handled by the tour team and packed away, ready for the trip home to the US.

She was dressed in a short black dress, a demure contrast to the deep pink matching bra and panty set she wore underneath. Her soft leather knee-high boots had been a gift from a new LA based designer, keen to have his hand-crafted footwear worn by the one and only Chloe. The gold hoop earrings were her lucky earrings. They had been the first thing she'd bought for herself when her debut album hit the top of the charts.

Hopefully they will bring me luck tonight.

"I'm coming back to the hotel, but I'll be holing up in my suite tonight. I have a one am Zoom meeting with a potential new business contact in the states." She pointed at her dress. "Hence the subdued choice of wardrobe."

It was a flat out lie, and if her stylist actually cared for anything other than the clothes and how working with Chloe progressed his own career, he would have asked why the meeting couldn't have waited until they returned to the USA in a matter of days. Him not giving a shit about anything that didn't personally involve him or money, played into her hands. Stixxluv could suit himself. Chloe had other things on her mind.

She couldn't stop thinking about Jordan. In the shower this morning, she had closed her eyes and imagined it was his hands roaming all over her body. Stroking, touching, and bringing her to climax once more.

God, I hope he doesn't want to waste too much time in getting to know me first. I'm not sure if I'm capable of more than a couple of minutes of idle small talk.

She'd already read the file her security team had put together on Jordan Royal. Her cheeky message to Jordan that they were compiling a dossier on him, might have sounded like a joke, but it wasn't.

His past had sent up some red flags. Drugs. Rehab. Party pictures which featured fully naked women. Fortunately, his transgressions seemed to be in the dim and distant past. If they hadn't, she wouldn't be taking a chance with him.

Jordan had come to the glaringly obvious conclusion that hanging around outside at night in the middle of March wasn't such a smart idea. According to his phone's weather app, it was minus three degrees Celsius. He did the rough calculations to convert it back to Fahrenheit. Twenty-six degrees might be a bigger number, but it was still freezing. The wind chill factor had to be pulling it down another notch or three.

His jeans were a merino wool and denim blend. Comfortable and warm. His all-weather Ugg boots were lined with wool, and his deep green peacoat was the finest money could buy. But his face and hands were icy cold. He'd accidently left his scarf and gloves upstairs in the apartment. With his coat collar turned up and both hands stuffed deep into his pockets, he was giving off sleezy drug dealer vibes rather than Parisian suave.

It was a little after eleven. He'd checked his phone a few minutes ago. Since leaving the concert he had been on edge.

Give her time to shower, change, and find her way here.

His phone was set to buzz just in case she messaged him.

Maybe I should message her. No. That would make me look desperate.

He would do anything not to appear like an overeager fanboy; to have her see him as a real man, one who was interested in her as a woman. His years of being a billionaire playboy were well behind him and he wanted something more meaningful in his life. Why he felt like that could be found with someone like Chloe he hadn't the foggiest of ideas. But he knew, deep down, he wanted more than a one night hook up with her.

Jesus, Jordan. You're not a player high on power anymore. You shouldn't even be thinking of words like hook up when it comes to her. She's a woman, not a conquest.

Yesterday, on the one hour and forty-five-minute flight from Berlin to Paris, he'd done some homework and checked out more of Chloe's background. He knew a bit about her music, and that she was famous, but until now, that had been the extent of his knowledge.

She'd said she was having her people create a file on him, so tit-for-tat, he'd done the same. He now knew she was almost twenty-nine years old. Originally from a small town somewhere in Nebraska. She'd moved out to LA eight or nine years ago and been discovered by her manager after she'd posted a song on YouTube. That track, "No One Is My Hero", had eventually become the first in a string of massive hits.

There wasn't much else to be found online about Chloe before she'd become a star. Various articles and gossip pieces made mention of her having been raised by a paternal aunt and uncle. But the rest of her past seemed to have been buried deep. He had an inkling that someone had gone in and made a point of erasing Chloe's original pre-fame life. In its place sat a carefully curated *lite* backstory.

Don't we all wish we could go back and clean out our life's browser history? Delete. Delete.

When his cell buzzed, Jordan quickly pulled it out of his coat pocket. Hope flared in his heart as he took in the message.

> Are we still on? Food?

He recalled how Chloe had been around the tapas in Berlin the other night. While she had been stabbing at her salad, her gaze had been locked on his food. The pressure for her to maintain her figure had to be immense. And while it wasn't his place to try and make her change any of that, earlier in the day before heading out to the concert, he'd paid a visit to the grocery store conveniently located next door to the apartment complex. There, he had stocked up on, well ... everything. One hundred and thirty euros of food would hopefully cover whatever Chloe might be in the mood to eat.

> Yes. And yes. I got some cheese.

By some, he meant, Brie, Camembert, Raclette, Emmental, Comte, and a seriously stinky blue. He'd even snuck in a fresh pâté. And if Chloe didn't eat any of it, come tomorrow morning, the apartment's manager was in for a lovely treat.

> Sounds fab. C U soon. 🤍 🤍 🤍

> C U soon. 🤍 🤍 🤍

When did I become such a sucker for little emojis? I wish I knew the one for eager to see you.

His excitement grew at the thought of Chloe being here. She wanted to see him. He did a little jig on the spot.

Ok get it out of your system, but when she gets here be cool. Ice cool.

A well-dressed Parisienne passing by gave him a disapproving glare. He could just imagine what they were thinking. *Imbécile.* But Jordan didn't care. He had a warm apartment, with views of the Eiffel Tower. A kitchen full of wonderful food.

And a beautiful woman to woo.

His cold hands trembled at the thought of how she had affected him at the concert. How his blood had pumped hard through his veins. What he felt for her, what he craved was more than the music, more than her songs.

For the first time in a long time, Jordan was suddenly caught up in his own self-doubt. Would he be enough for her once they were both back in the US?

CHAPTER EIGHT

The sleek, silver town car came to a halt out the front of Twenty-one Rue Benjamin Franklin just before midnight. Chloe's bodyguard opened the passenger door and Chloe stepped out. She wore a black silk scarf over her head to hide her face from any prying eyes. She loved her fans, but she'd given enough of herself to them already tonight.

From the doorway of the apartment complex, a figure moved toward the car. Martin immediately placed himself between Chloe and the approaching stranger.

The stranger, who wasn't a stranger, held out a welcoming hand. "Hi, Martin. I'm Jordan, we met in Germany." He then turned his attention to Chloe. "Hi, gorgeous, would you like to accompany me inside?"

Chloe bit down on her bottom lip. Anticipation coursed through her body. She followed Jordan into the building with her bodyguard walking close behind, constantly on alert.

As soon as the front door closed behind them, Chloe threw off the scarf. "Phew. It was hard to breathe underneath all that." She patted at her hair, hoping to settle it down.

So much for the smooth moves, Chloe.

Jordan's brows knitted together in confusion, and Chloe couldn't help but laugh. "I was going for the mysterious unknown lady in the back of the car guise. Now I probably just look a mess."

Out of the corner of her eye, she caught a glimpse of a smirking Martin gently shaking his head. She was grateful that her head of security would be taking many of her foolish secrets with him to the grave.

Chloe's heart gave a squeeze as Jordan stepped forward and bent to place a tender kiss on her cheek. At that gesture, her hopes for the evening rose. "You look beautiful, Chloe. Perfect. And I'm thrilled that you came."

Her already flushed cheeks now burned hot. Chloe didn't quite know where to look. She barely knew Jordan, yet he made her feel all the feels. A breathy, "Hi," was the best she could manage in reply.

"Bienvenue à Paris, Chloe. You certainly rocked the Arena tonight. Chloe's Garden was amazing to watch."

He came to my concert?

She wanted to ask if he had indeed seen her show, but first she wanted the two of them to be alone.

It was silly, she was a fully grown woman, but asking her bodyguard to leave still felt weird. Martin had always been a bit of a surrogate father figure to Chloe. He'd treated her far better than her real father ever had. "I'll be staying with Jordan for a little while."

His gaze settled on her well stuffed tote bag, and he gave a nod of understanding. The bag contained more than what she would need if she planned to only stay a few hours. Martin was nothing like her deadbeat dad—he cared about her welfare. Her bodyguard met her gaze. "Call me if you need anything, Chloe. The hotel is only three minutes away." He gave Jordan a quick look, heavy with warning, and headed for the door.

Chloe softly laughed. "I'm surprised Martin didn't give you his iron handshake while looking you dead in the eye and calling you 'son'."

"I wouldn't have been the least bit surprised if he had," added Jordan.

"Sorry, he is protective of me."

"And so he should be. It's his job to look out for you. I get the distinct impression he really cares about your well-being, and having someone like that protecting your life is worth its weight in gold."

Martin had been thorough with his background check of Jordan, but it was only after he'd reached out to some other navy SEALs currently employed by the House of Royal that he'd finally given Chloe his reluctant approval to her plan to stay at the apartment, while he went back to the hotel.

She took Jordan's offered hand, and he led her over to a winding set of stairs. At the bottom he took her tote bag, saying, "I'm afraid this is Paris, and few apartments have elevators, so we will have to climb all the way up to the fifth floor. We can stop for a breather every now and then if you need."

Chloe gave him a look of mock outrage, as she plucked her tote back out of his hands. "I've just got off stage following nearly three hours of dancing and singing. If you think I can't manage a few flights of stairs in one go, you are sadly mistaken, Mister Royal. Now kindly step aside."

She'd seen a similar scene in an old 1950s movie starring Audrey Hepburn and took great delight in grandly instructing Jordan to move out of the way.

He was laughing at her teasing for the first few floors, but by the time they finally got to the top, Jordan was huffing and puffing. Chloe in turn, had barely raised a sweat. Her pulse quickly returned to its resting rate. She turned and smiled sweetly at him.

"I dare you to try and tell me you have an old college football injury. Bad knees perhaps?"

He winced. "Harsh. I'm out of shape because I've been avoiding the cardio classes at the gym. I never made it to college. Barely got through high school, kept getting kicked out of places."

And here I was assuming that all billionaires went to Harvard. He really was a bad boy in his younger days.

She wasn't going to mention that she hadn't finished school. It was impossible to afford books when you were struggling to find enough money to eat.

From his coat pocket Jordan produced an elegant key and, stepping up to a nearby door, slipped it easily into the lock. Chloe's excitement grew as she heard the bolt draw back. An old apartment in Paris and a fancy key, it was all so European and romantic. Just like in the movie.

But instead of Audrey Hepburn in A Roman Holiday, I am Chloe in Paris.

She finally snapped out of her day dream when instead of opening the door to the apartment Jordan turned and quickly punched a code into a nearby ultra-modern security pad. They definitely hadn't had one of those in the movie. "The touchpad ruins the old apartment in Paris look, don't you think?" she offered.

"Yes, but modern security systems are essential these days, especially in this part of Paris. The sixteenth arrondissement is notorious for break-ins." he replied, pushing the door open.

He ushered her through the doorway and into the apartment. Chloe waited patiently while Jordan locked the door behind them. "LA isn't great for burglaries either. I'm fortunate that I live in a gated street and have twenty-four-hour security on site. There is a certain notoriety to be had from robbing the homes of stars."

Wannabe Bling Ringers can't touch my house.

Jordan pointed to a small red button on the wall. "I expect you've got one or two of these panic buttons at home." *Yep, thank god.* "This one is linked to the House of Royal security team. Most of those people are ex-military and some even former special forces. I would put good money on them beating Martin to this place if either of us hit that button."

It took a great deal of effort for Chloe to pay real attention to the security briefing. She'd been on tenterhooks all day, eager to see Jordan again. In the aftermath of tonight's performance, she was still coming down from the high. Her thoughts were scattered. But one thing was certain. All she wanted was to be with Jordan. To spend the night together as normal people. Or at least as normal as a famous person and a billionaire could be with one another.

You don't want to be normal. You want it all. And to be loved.

A glance at her clothes, boots, and the two thousand dollar Gucci tote in her hand had Chloe silently chiding herself. How many women would kill to have the life she had. The success. The fans. The money. Millions of women was the obvious answer.

"Chloe?"

She lifted her head to find a concerned Jordan studying her. "Sorry. I'm still recovering from the concert. It takes a bit to get the body to process all the adrenaline. For my brain to slow."

There was a lot to concentrate on when she was on stage. Choreography. Her position on stage. Her back up dancers. Costume changes. Even the lyrics to her own songs. And heaven forbid if she ever got the name of the city she was playing in wrong.

He bent and gave her a kiss full of promise. "Come on, let's go and find you a drink and some food. You must be starving."

She followed him down a narrow hallway. On either side

of the cream painted walls hung black and white framed photos. Dozens of them. In each and every one of them were of groups of people smiling and laughing. Family.

"Who are all these people?" asked Chloe.

Jordan waved his hands left and right. "I'm assuming you now know a bit about my background. These people are various members of the Royal family. Brits, Americans, French ... you name it. My German cousin, Leon, who you saw the other night at the club is somewhere in one or two of these photos."

At the end of the hall, he stopped in front of the very last picture. "That's my mom, dad, my older brother Bryce, and my *pain in the ass* younger brother Matthew. Oh, and me of course." He laughed. "The New York branch of the family."

Chloe studied the photo. It seemed to have been taken on an idyllic island somewhere. There were palm trees and clear skies. In the background, on a crystal blue sea, sat a luxury yacht. Everyone was smiling. Everyone looked happy. Chloe didn't care about the yacht or the stunning location. All she saw was a family, people who loved one another. People who cared. Something she had never experienced.

She'd noted Jordan's casual remark about his brother Matthew. "Why is Matthew a pain?"

Jordan shrugged. "We've spent most of our lives as rivals, but I'm pleased that over the past couple of years we have been working on our relationship. Tried to be more grown up about things. Then again, I would be lying if I said I wouldn't take the chance to get one over on Matthew if it presented itself. And he would likely do the same to me."

"But you love him?"

"Yes of course I do, and if anyone ever tried to hurt him, I would be the first to go into battle for my brother."

A real family. Wow.

At the end of the hall, the apartment opened onto an

expansive living space. Chloe slowed her steps. To her right was a long kitchen bench, made from what appeared to be solid marble. On the top of it stood two ornate porcelain vases filled with beautiful white and red roses.

Oh, My favorite. They are stunning.

An antique dining table came next. Its wooden surface bore a graceful patina of age. Chloe could just imagine all those various members of the Royal family gathered together around the table at some point or other. A family sharing and creating precious moments. Her heart ached with longing.

Her gaze now settled on a large glass platter which sat at the nearest end of the table. On top of it was with a gorgeous array of cheeses, fresh fruits, and— "Oh my god, is that French pâté? Yum." Chloe took two hurried steps toward the cornucopia of delights, then stopped. "I really shouldn't but— you went to all this trouble. Maybe just tonight."

Jordan came to stand alongside her. "One night enjoying the delights of Paris won't ruin you. I promise."

Chloe's stomach rumbled as she picked up a piece of thick sourdough bread, she couldn't wait to slather it with a liberal helping of the rich pâté. She reached for one of the short flat bladed knives.

But her hand fell away as another marvel caught her eye. The view out through the floor to ceiling glass doors of the rooftop apartment. The bright golden lights of Paris's famous Eiffel Tower filled her vision. "Wow," she whispered.

"The French call her *La dame de fer*, the Iron Lady. She is gorgeous. But then again so are you."

Chloe turned from the stunning view of the Parisian icon and gave him a shy smile. "Did you rehearse that line?"

He had the good grace to sheepishly nod. "Was it too much?"

"A little, but this is Paris, and you do have pâté. And when you look at me that way, with your wicked, promising smile, I could probably forgive you a thousand corny pick up lines."

Jordan slipped his arm around her waist. "I'm glad you came."

Kiss me like you did in the limo in Berlin. Then tell me you want me to stay tonight.

CHAPTER NINE

She was here and she'd dismissed her security detail. The size of her overstuffed tote bag confirmed Jordan's hopes; Chloe intended to stay the night. He hadn't needed to use his terrible pick up line on her, but it had broken the ice.

Just calm your nerves and be yourself. She came here because you asked her.

Jordan pointed to the table. "Let me get you some pâté and a drink. You must be starving after the show. I know I would be if I'd put that much energy in over three hours. I don't think you stopped moving for more than a minute at any one time. Your stamina is incredible."

She playfully narrowed her eyes at him. "So you did come to my concert?"

"Yes, I did. I couldn't stop thinking about you, and decided I had to see the show."

"I'm glad you came, but how come I didn't see you back stage? No one mentioned your name."

Jordan shook his head. "I didn't come back stage. I was alone in one of the private boxes. I wanted my first Chloe concert to be special. It might sound ultra-cheesy but when you were up on stage, I pretended that it was just me who you were singing for, no one else."

Tears glistened in her eyes. "Not cheesy at all. Just lovely. And how was your first Chloe concert, Jordan? Did I reach out and touch you?"

"You did. I could barely breathe when you sang that really soft, slow song. The one about being left behind. I'm sorry I don't know the name of it, but I can honestly say I am now a lifetime member of Chloe's Garden. I just need to get around to buying the T-shirt."

Chloe moved a step closer and took his hand in hers. "I think the song you might be referring to is *Ice Flowers*. It won Song of the Year at the Grammys. It's the origin song for Chloe's Garden. The super fans have the garden symbol inked into their skin." She turned her left arm over and on the underside of her wrist was the CG logo with its floral twist wrapped around the initials for Chloe's Garden.

Jordan's heart squeezed in his chest. This woman was more than just a singer. She was a wonder. Someone who had the ability to reach out to people and touch their lives. His emotions swelled and he was momentarily lost for words.

He bent and placed a soft kiss on her wrist, right over the fine ink. "Come and eat."

He was the sexiest, most alluring man she had ever encountered, which was saying something. Chloe was constantly surrounded by beautiful, enticing people. Los Angeles was called the City of Angels for good reason. Every handsome man on the planet seemed to congregate there. But here in this Paris apartment, none of the bright lights of

Hollywood could hold a flame to Jordan Royal and his tender kisses. Or to his charm.

He'd come to her concert. Listened to her music, and somehow through the darkness and the thousands of her fans, she had touched him. As the flames of hope burned bright, Chloe did her best to silence her inner voice. She'd heard all the warnings of what might come from being with a man like Jordan. The risk of him leaving her broken hearted, and alone.

But if I don't risk my heart, I will never know.

She had heard and understood her inner counsel. But her choice was already made. None of this made sense, but then again, her aching need for love never had.

I want to be with him tonight. For him to know that I am more than just my music.

At the table, Jordan carefully covered a piece of crusty bread with pâté and handed it to her. As she took it, Chloe wondered if there might come a time when he would feel comfortable enough to hand feed her such delicate delights. She'd always found something sensual about having a lover offer her food. To open her lips and take from a man was an intimacy that went well beyond the boundaries of friendship.

I want him to be more than just a friend. Tonight I want us to become one.

"Would you like a chilled glass of Pinot Gris to go with your food?"

"Yes, please." Chloe was thinking of what else she would like to taste this evening. Top of the dining list was Jordan. The memory of their first kiss and how it had set her blood on fire still lingered in her mind.

Wicked. Wicked girl.

He poured a glass of wine and after handing it to her, set the bottle down. One glass. Jordan didn't touch the wine. She was tempted to ask why, then remembered the picture she'd seen online and the short piece about him having gone to rehab.

Jordan met her gaze. "I've been clean and sober for over four years, but I'm what's known in rehab circles as an HRRC. High Risk Relapse Candidate. Occasionally, I take myself off to a treatment center for a bit of a mental top up, just to make sure I stay on track."

She admired his honesty. And his resolve. He owned his issues and had enough self-knowledge to know when he was on the verge of failing. "I did see a snippet on the web about you coming out of rehab," she confessed.

The glass in her hand felt heavy. *I don't want to drink in front of him.* She went to set the drink down, but Jordan shook his head. "It's alright. I'm fine around people who are drinking. I don't miss the booze all that much, well most of the time. Alcohol wasn't my biggest downfall. Drugs were."

He was giving her an opening. Inviting her to ask the obvious question. Trusting her with his pain.

"What sort of drugs did you take?"

"Mostly the good old white powder, but just before I really went off the rails, I discovered they sold some other really nasty stuff in the dark corners of nightclubs. I went into a bit of a spiral in my mid-twenties which only ended when I got banged up in a jail cell in Iowa. After Matthew got the charges dropped, my mother had me involuntarily committed to a facility in Pennsylvania." Jordan scrubbed his hand over his face. "I made my mom cry, and I swore I would never do that again."

The wine and rich pâté had lost their taste. She wasn't used to this sort of honest conversation. To such open candor. In her world, people lied as easily as they drew breath.

She took one final sip of the wine and put the glass on the table. "Thank you." It wasn't just her gratitude for the food, but also for having shared such a private part of his life. Of having opened himself to her. Chloe valued honesty.

Moving away from the table, she reached for Jordan, but as she did the terrace outside was suddenly plunged into darkness. "Oh," she gasped. The lights on the Eiffel Tower had all gone out. "What happened?"

"Relax, its nothing to worry about. At 11:45 every night they turn the lights off. Just a minute." He crossed the floor and pressed one of the switches on a nearby bank of buttons. Fairy lights flickered to life on the terrace, bathing the apartment in a soft silver glow. "I could put some more of the main lights on if you wish."

"No, this is lovely. I like it just as it is. Thank you, Jordan." The terrace lights along with the mood candles which Jordan now lit, gave the private space a sense of warmth. She liked the effect.

I hope he gets the not so subtle message that I want the lights low for other reasons.

She might be one of the world's biggest musical artists, but she was still a young woman. On stage she could shine in the bright lights, but when it came to being with this man, she could admit to being more than a little nervous.

Chloe didn't have an extensive list of ex-lovers. She'd had a number of short-lived and very public relationships, several of which had been carefully curated by her management team. Men chosen to serve either one of Chloe's current album narratives or to help with their own record sales. The tabloids had tracked the highs and lows of her love life, the joys and supposed heartbreaks. But the truth was Chloe's love life was mostly based on business.

This hot fling with Jordan could be different. *I hope so.* He wasn't from the world of entertainment. He wasn't someone who would seek to use a romantic connection with Chloe as a means to furthering his career. The Royal family already had immense wealth and power—Jordan didn't need that from her.

The need tonight was very much on her part.

"As long as you are comfortable with the lights being low, Chloe, so am I. Whatever it is that you want, you only have to ask. I am yours."

He moved closer and she stepped into his arms. Jordan brushed a kiss on her forehead and whispered, "We can stay here and talk, or we could move into the bedroom. Whatever happens tonight is entirely up to you. I would love for us to continue what we began in Berlin, but again, it's your call."

Berlin. They hadn't got all that far, and it had preyed on her mind. If Jordan had been unsure about them hooking up in the back of the limo, then why hadn't he simply asked her to invite him to her hotel suite? He'd said goodnight and then left.

"Can I ask why things didn't happen in Germany? I mean I thought they would, and then ..."

Jordan nodded. "Rehab made me clean up a lot of things in my life. It taught me a good deal about respect. I didn't want us to fool around in the car, and while hotel rooms are nice enough, I've used far too many for casual sex and I don't do that anymore. That's why I wanted you to come here tonight. This apartment only ever has family members stay in it."

She hadn't expected that kind of reasoning from him. "But your family owns hotels and resorts."

"Yes, we do. Several hundred of them. Does that make me a bit of a hypocrite? Probably. But the truth is, I like myself better when I stick to this code of behavior."

Had self-loathing been a factor in his drug use and eventual arrest? The fact that Jordan had highlighted how living a better life made him feel good about himself, set Chloe wondering if that had been the case. And good for him.

Jordan had reached a level of maturity that many others, could only ever dream of attaining.

Chloe drew in a ragged breath. She had come here tonight with one thing in mind. To have Jordan make love to her. Every minute she spent with him had her questioning that intent. He was open and honest with her, inviting her into his private world, while her first thoughts had been all about sex.

He gave her a feeling of expectation, of maybe there being something between them that went beyond tomorrow. Chloe caught her thoughts.

Don't be silly, don't start building little dreams.

There was every chance that after tonight they may never see one another again. Jordan might be dressing this evening's encounter in words of honor, but they were adults, and she wasn't nearly naive enough to think that Jordan had invited her here for a lesson in chivalry.

Keep it simple. Keep it about sex and let tomorrow take care of itself.

"You seem like a really nice guy, Jordan. And this apartment is beautiful. So yes, I would like for us to spend the night together."

He bent and softly kissed her cheek, then whispered in her ear, "The bedroom it is."

CHAPTER TEN

The master bedroom was as beautifully decorated as the main living area. A large curved, wooden sleigh bed sat in the center of the room. The duvet cover was a cream, blue, and gold leaf pattern. A dark blue woolen blanket had been artfully draped over the end of the mattress. Chloe had stayed in some of the most luxurious hotels in the world, but they had always felt like hotels. This room had the same warmth and soul as the rest of the apartment. It spoke of it being a home.

As Jordan pressed his body against hers, Chloe didn't bother to take in the rest of the room. She offered him her lips and he claimed them with unrestrained hunger. His hand slipped down her back and settled on the curve of her hip. He pulled her gently toward him, and she reveled in the sensation of his firm erection as it pressed into her stomach. An ache settled between her legs. She wanted Jordan. And he wanted her.

They remained this way, holding one another and kissing deeply for a gloriously long time. When they finally broke the kiss, Jordan let Chloe take a small step backward. His gaze lowered and settled on the swell of her breasts, sending a ripple of lust rushing through her body. He liked what he saw. She hoped he wanted it all.

"I've been thinking about you nonstop since Berlin. And what you would look like stripped and standing naked before me. Watching you up on stage tonight, I have to confess a great deal of my time was spent staring at your gorgeous breasts. Whoever designs your costumes certainly knows how to make them cling perfectly in all the right places."

No doubt there would have been others in the crowd tonight thinking the exact same thing, and then imagining what it would be like to have Chloe naked as their hands roamed over her body. But only one person, one man, was going to get that opportunity tonight.

"Touch me."

Jordan's fingers brushed over Chloe's nipples, making them pebble. She loved this tender foreplay, but she wanted his mouth on them, licking and sucking hard. But asking for what she wanted had always been a challenge.

He gave one of her nipples a firmer tweak and on a pleading sob she closed her eyes. He had to know what this was doing to her. "Tell me, Chloe, how would you like this to proceed? A gentleman always lets the lady set the rules. Let me be that gentleman for you tonight."

His warm invitation had Chloe swallowing deep. She kept her eyes closed. If she didn't look at him, she might just be able to find the right words to speak her desire.

"Hmmm?"

"I want you to strip me naked. I want you to lay me on the bed, and I ..." Her breath caught and she paused.

He brushed a kiss against her mouth, then parted her lips with his tongue. Jordan's kiss dared her to speak her truth. "Go on, Chloe, you can say what you need. Tell me what you want me to do to you. Your desires are my command."

He made her want to feel brave. To step into the limelight and show him the real Chloe. Could she dare to reveal that much to him, to this stranger?

Her breath was ragged as she finally answered. "I want you fuck me slowly, and deep. I want it gentle, and so beautiful that I weep as I come."

There. She had said it. Her deepest desire. To have tears in her eyes as she crested the wave of pleasure and crashed down the other side.

He let out a groan at her words. "Oh, Chloe, I promise to fuck you so tenderly, so sweetly, that the angels in heaven will shed tears when you climax."

Jordan's lips came down on hers once more, capturing her mouth in a deep, lingering kiss that held all the promise of a magical night. Their tongues brushed together, sending a shiver down her spine. He was a master of the embrace, teasing, nipping, and making her desperate for his mouth to be all over her body. She clung to him. She wanted tonight. This moment was for them. To give in to her desire.

Her lust took firm control. "No more talking, Jordan. Just imagine we are back in the nightclub in Berlin. I know about the sex rooms where people let others watch as they indulge. Could we pretend that we have a crowd watching us?" She would never do it in real life but fantasizing about it had always turned her on.

A large, warm hand brushed over her cheek. "I like that you trust me to keep you safe. In this place, we can do whatever we want. It's just you and me. And when you want your imaginary onlookers to disappear, just wish them away." He bent and whispered in her ear. "I do have one particular fantasy I would love to indulge with you, if you are willing."

Chloe forced down her fear. There were some things she was prepared to do, but she had her limits. On the rare occasions that she'd slept with a guy, she'd made her position clear.

No matter how insistent a man might be there were some sexual acts she'd never let them pressure her into doing them. She could only hope Jordan's wishes were on this side of that line. Her imagination was there to fill in the gaps of what her body wasn't comfortable doing.

He kissed her slowly once more. She remained fully dressed as his hands roamed over her body, touching her curves. Chloe would have given anything for Jordan to take the lead and tug on the zipper of her dress.

Had he noticed her apprehension? Some men cared to read women, perhaps Jordan was one of them. Fearing a repeat of Berlin when Jordan had pulled away, she summoned her courage. "What would you like to indulge in, Mister Royal?"

His gaze lowered. "I love a pair of killer heels, and those boots are as hot as. I want you naked except for them. And then I want you seated before me with my cock in your mouth. And when I think you have been a good girl, and only then will I spread you out on the bed and give you exactly what you want. A slow, deep, tear-filled orgasm. How does that sound, Ms. Fisher?"

How did it sound? Like all her porny dreams had come true at once. Chloe let out a whoosh of air. She was relieved that while his request was wickedly delicious, it was well within her plain vanilla kink boundaries. She'd never been with anyone long enough to learn trust and explore new horizons.

I can do that. No problem.

The thought of laying on the bed, legs spread wide, while Jordan buried himself to the hilt was hot enough to set her pulse racing. But his idea of her servicing him while dressed in her knee high boots was sizzling hot. Any second now she might spontaneously combust.

She turned in his arms and touched a finger to the top of

her dress's zipper. "Would you like to unwrap me? See what's underneath. And then you can decide if you really do want me fully naked or if I should leave the rest of my things on while you fuck my mouth."

His wicked chuckle had her sex throbbing. "I can't wait to see what you have on under that sedate black dress. I have a feeling it's going to be the best."

The cool night air touched her skin as he lowered her zipper. The dress fell to the floor and when she stepped out of it, Jordan picked the dress up and tossed it aside. She turned to face him, and he let out a hushed. "Oh, that's ... that's ... oh, Chloe."

He slowly shook his head, she sensed he was torn about what to do next. "You've given me the devil's choice. That pink is so... *wow*, but then again." His gaze roamed hungrily over her body. He licked his lips and Chloe mirrored the action.

"I'm going to have to go with the barely there pink G-string and bra staying on." He paused for a moment, then met her gaze. "You are absolutely gorgeous, and I can't wait to feast on every inch of your body. But now is the time for us to have an adult moment before we proceed. I get tested regularly, for many things, including all the nasties. If you want, I can go and get my laptop and log on to a secure site. Then you can see all my latest medical results, including my drug tests. I'm negative for everything."

Whoa. Full disclosure. A real man.

It was refreshing to meet someone who understood how a real man should behave. And how attractive a woman would find a man who openly owned his personal history.

If he's offering to do that for me, then I suppose its quid pro quo.

"I also get tested. My tour promoter has it standard in all contracts. They can't get insurance without me undergoing a full medical and having all my results come back negative. I'm happy to share my results too."

"Of course." Jordan motioned to the bedside table where a small blue ceramic dish sat. It contained several packets of condoms. Chloe had also brought some with her, just in case. Since she knew where hers had been, they would be the ones she and Jordan would be using.

A high-backed chair in the corner of the bedroom caught her eye. She moved toward it, but Jordan beat her to it, saying, "Let me get this for you, it's an antique and a lot heavier than it looks."

He carried the chair into the middle of the room and set it down. Chloe stifled a nervous grin, but a chuckle still escaped. "This looks like one of those racy scenes in an art house film. A girl and a guy in a swanky apartment in Paris, where they embark on a steamy torrid affair. The soundtrack is all edgy and moody, but usually once the hot scene is done and dusted the movie turns dark."

Jordan moved closer, his hand coming to rest about Chloe's waist. "My French cousins have made me sit through enough of those existential crisis movies over the years. Give me a good old fashioned boy meets girl, happily ever after rom-com any time over an art house flick."

An image of her and Jordan curled up on a couch watching a Netflix movie while sharing a bowl of popcorn slipped into her mind.

Stop playing happy families. You know that doesn't exist for you.

She had to get out of her own mind. Her secret longings were threatening to derail the proceedings. "Just give me a minute."

Hurrying from the room, Chloe retrieved her leather tote from the living space. She carried it back in one hand, while in the other she held the strip of condoms she'd stuffed into the side pocket. "If you don't mind, I will insist that we use these. It's not that I don't trust you, but I know where these have been. No offence intended."

"None taken. It pays to be careful."

They stood staring at one another for a long minute, while Chloe racked her brains trying to figure out the best way to get this all back on track. She'd taken them off on a side road and now feared the mood had shifted.

Her relief was palpable when Jordan gently took the condoms out of her hand and lay them on the bed. "Come here, you." She did as she was told, accepting his soft kiss, then leaning in as the embrace deepened and he speared his tongue into her mouth.

He seemed to know exactly the right thing to do with her, how to handle her dotted thoughts and bring them back to where they should be—with him, with them. In this moment.

The kiss was the tonic she needed. A calming balm. A place where she could find herself.

"Are you back with me?" he asked.

"Yes. Sorry, just …"

"Don't worry, I will take good care of you. But first things first, I would like your lips on me."

Chloe toyed with Jordan's dark green cashmere sweater. "Still rocking the preppy boy look. It's hot and this color matches your eyes."

Jordan traced a blazing trail of kisses up her neck and whispered in her ear, "This preppy boy got kicked out of all the good schools." He took a step back, throwing off the sweater, and the T-shirt underneath. His fingers rested on the button of his jeans. "I might be a reformed bad boy, but for you, I can be as dirty as you want."

Jordan Royal was just what Chloe wanted. He didn't tell her how to behave. How she should feel. Her pleasure was all hers to claim.

Settling on the edge of the chair, Chloe spread her legs.

The sharp heels of her boots claiming purchase in the highly polished parquetry. Jordan kicked off his boots and slipped out of his jeans. He had just reached for the waistband on his briefs, when she gave him a disapproving "tut-tut," for his troubles. Her curled finger beckoned him over. "Don't spoil the surprise for me."

A grinning Jordan took a step toward her, and Chloe's pulse kicked up another notch. With his every step, her hunger grew. When he finally stood in front of her, Jordan brushed his hand over Chloe's hair. "I'm all yours, do with me as you wish."

The tip of her finger traced along the edge of his waistband. Chloe smiled as the bulge in the front of Jordan's briefs grew larger, straining against the seam. Lust coursed through her body. The time for playful sex talk was over.

Gripping the side of his briefs, she tugged them down. Jordan's erection sprang free and slapped against his stomach. The pleasing sound had a pulse throbbing in her sex. His cock was everything she'd hoped it would be, big and thick. She couldn't wait to taste him. She licked her lips.

Now this is what I have been hungry for all evening.

He shuddered as she bent her head and ran her tongue along the length of him. When she reached the head of his cock, she placed a gentle kiss on the tip before opening her lips and taking several inches of it into her mouth. She breathed in and took him deeper. He settled his hand on the top of her hair. It rested there for a moment, but when she drew back, sucking hard, his grip firmed. "Fuck," he growled.

It was all the encouragement she needed. Chloe set to her task with relish, licking and teasing him. Her hand wrapped around the base of his shaft, and she began to stroke up and down. In the quiet of the room, the only sound was Jordan's labored breaths as she pleasured him with her hands and mouth.

She loved doing this to him, giving Jordan exactly what he desired. She'd always found oral sex to be a more intimate act than intercourse. There was a degree of trust involved, which made the connection stronger. The fact that she was still in her pink bra and panty set and high heeled black boots only served to heighten the experience. Giving him pleasure had her nipples hard and her sex begging for his wicked attention.

She worked him hard, right to the point where she sensed he was getting close to the end, then she backed off. There was a moment when she released him entirely from her ministrations, but when Jordan took a half step back, she commanded him to return, saying, "I'm the one who will tell you when you're done."

He returned, and as she took the head of his cock into her mouth once more and drew back hard, he murmured. "I have a feeling you are going to make me beg before tonight is over."

Damn right she was.

CHAPTER ELEVEN

If he hadn't been a fan of hers before tonight, he was now. Jordan stood naked, his hand fisting her hair while she worked his cock in and out of her mouth. He'd heard the urban legends about singers having great tongue and breathing control, he now knew them to be true. This woman, seated in front of him, wearing an outfit worthy of a wet dream, was slowly tearing all his walls down. Her deep-throat skills were the sort he hadn't thought possible.

He was getting close to a mind blowing climax, his brain completely sex addled. She'd brought him to this same point four times already and each time she had left him teetering on the edge until his blood and mind had cleared. But fifth time might not be the charm. He was only a mere mortal.

"I don't think I can hold out if we keep going. And I really want to be ... fuck." Struggling for control, Jordan gritted his teeth. "Chloe, please."

Achievement level unlocked. She had reduced him to a state of begging. His cock came free of her lips with a pop, and Jordan winced. He dared not touch himself, fearing that even the slightest brush of his hand could tip him over.

Chloe, the dark haired temptress, sat back in the chair and offered him a self-satisfied grin. "I'll give you a minute to regain your sanity before we see how close I can get you next time."

Jordan shook his head. He was done. "No. I'm right on the edge, and I want to be inside you when I fall."

The tremble in Jordan's voice told Chloe all she needed to know. He was barely holding on. It would have been so easy to simply take his cock back into her mouth and put him out of his misery, but she was feeling greedy tonight. Lust ruled her head.

Rising from the chair, she unclipped the lacy pink bra and slipped it off. She gave a little wiggle of her hips before hooking her fingers into either side of the dainty pink G-string. Jordan fixed her with a desperate gaze and pleaded, "Show a little mercy."

Still toying with her G-string, she turned and bent over, pointing her ass at him. Her sexy little move was instantly rewarded. Jordan gave a low growl of manly hunger. But Chloe was having far too much fun to yield to his appeals.

Large, warm hands took hold, seizing her by the waist. "Smart girl. Now I want you to hold onto the chair," he commanded. His words were firm, but his touch was surprisingly gentle as he thumbed her G-string down her legs. By some miracle they didn't catch on the top of Chloe's boots. The scrap of satin joined the rest of their scattered clothes on the floor.

Hot, searing kisses traced their way down her spine, and Chloe shivered. Jordan cupped her ass, then slipped a finger deep into her wet heat. He stroked her. Her already hardened nipples turned to pebbles. They could have cut glass. He continued to stroke her sex. "So beautiful, and such a good girl." With his arm wrapped about her waist he held her to him, teasing her clit as he thrust a second finger into her. "Two can play at this game. I want you as hot and needy as you have made me."

She sobbed at his deep penetrating touch. "Jordan."

When he finally, mercifully released her, Jordan dropped to his knees, and turned her to face him. He unzipped Chloe's long boots and took them off. She waited, expecting him to get to his feet, but instead, he slid his hands up the inside of both her thighs. When he reached the apex, to the tiny thatch of hair at the opening to her sex, he leaned forward and kissed her.

Chloe held a hand to her mouth. No man had ever done that to her before, and it was beyond perfect. "Jordan," she whispered. She didn't know what else to say. His name seemed enough.

His thumbs parted her soft folds. Her head fell back as Jordan licked deep into her pussy. His tongue laved over her sensitive flesh in a carnal dance of pleasure.

Oh god. Oh ...

The tables were now fully turned. She was the one spearing her fingers into his short brown hair, while he tortured her clit. The vanquished becoming the victor.

"Jordan, please."

"Is that begging I hear?"

His face was still buried between her legs, his laughter only stopping when he plunged his tongue deep into her sex once more. This man was amazing. Incredible. Skilled. Where had Jordan Royal been all her life?

"Yes. Yes. I am begging. Please, I need to be fucked."

With the world's sexiest grin on his face, Jordan slowly

rose to his feet. He held out his hand, and weak-kneed she took it. "Come to bed, Chloe. I want to give you want you need. I am going to make love to you so slow and deep. And with tears if you wish."

He led her over to the bed and lay her down. Chloe barely had time for her head to hit the pillow, before he rose over her, condom in hand. She took the packet, ripped it open with her teeth, and with all due reverence for his hard but very sensitive erection, rolled it on. She opened her legs, their eyes locking on one another as Jordan parted the folds of her sex and slowly pressed his cock in.

"Oh god," she sighed.

"Now I am going to fuck you slow and deep, Chloe, and I will only let you come when I see tears shining in your eyes."

CHAPTER TWELVE

Chloe woke the following morning wrapped up in the warmth of Jordan's arms. The curtains of the bedroom were open, and the sun's rays were peeking through the iron lattice framework of the Eiffel Tower. What more could a girl want than to be in Paris with her secret lover?

"What time is it?" she muttered.

"Just after eight."

She rolled over and was greeted by a smiling Jordan. The sight of the man, with his mussed up bed hair, who had shown her such an amazing night of sexual pleasure had her heart dancing with joy.

She'd lost count of the number of times he had brought her to a tear-filled climax. Jordan had taken such wonderful care of her, acknowledging her need to achieve her release this way without any form of judgment. She'd never been able to trust a guy like this before, fearing they wouldn't understand.

And yet he had.

"Good morning, my goddess of music, are you hungry?"

Chloe had barely eaten a bite of the delicious food Jordan

had laid out for them last night. "I'm starving. I've normally had my protein booster and vitamins by this hour of the morning. Marta makes sure of it."

Jordan snorted in obvious disgust of Chloe's usual morning fare. "Well I don't have any boosters or personal assistants at hand, what I do *have* are fresh croissants from the bakery next door. I kinda forgot you might not want to eat those. I can get rid of them if you like. I also have the best, hot Parisian coffee waiting in the kitchen for your delectable lips. Would you be allowed that?"

He'd gone to all the trouble of getting freshly baked croissants and coffee, it would be churlish for her to refuse his hospitality. "They sound delicious. Thank you, Jordan. Let's eat, I'm hungry."

He threw back the duvet and leapt out of bed. "Come on, let's have coffee and croissants on the terrace while we stare in wonder at the Eiffel Tower."

Her back and hips protested, but Chloe did as he asked. She caught the thick, fluffy gown he casually tossed her way. When she left the bedroom a few minutes later it was with a grin on her face.

She padded into the kitchen and took a seat at the island bar. Happy morning vibes bubbled through her. The scent of freshly ground coffee beans and the heady aroma of warm butter, and freshly baked pastries filled her senses. The delicious man pouring her a hot brew had her mouth salivating.

I wish we could go back to bed. Spend the rest of the day hiding away from the world.

He pushed a croissant ladened plate toward her, then took the seat next to Chloe. "The bakery next door opens at five am and I called them and asked the delivery boy to bring us up these buttery goodies."

Jordan sipped his coffee. Black, and strong by the look of it. The nearby sugar bowl looked untouched. Her strict touring diet meant she wasn't allowed sugar or dairy, but as she reached for the small unopened carton of milk on the countertop, Chloe decided this morning she was going to break all those rules.

While she filled her cup, Jordan brushed a hand over her cheek. His touch was soft and caring. "So how much longer are you in Paris, Chloe?" he asked.

"We are due to leave for home late tonight, but that can always change. My assistants want to go shopping on the Champs-Élysées, but I think I might just go back to my hotel and get some more sleep. For some strange reason I find myself utterly exhausted this morning. Besides, I can't really go out in public like they do. I tend to do my shopping after hours or online."

She'd love to be able to go wandering through the stores, aimlessly window shopping for bits and pieces. The glamourous Parisian mega store Galeries Lafayette had a private service for celebrities and on her next world tour Chloe intended to have a night arranged for herself and her entourage to go shopping. Without the crowds.

Jordan broke off a piece of his croissant and held it up near to her face. Chloe opened her lips. Her heart gave a little flip as he fed it to her. And it was so delicious. Butter and carbs. Yum.

If only every morning could be like this, my life would be complete.

The gods clearly had ears. The second that thought popped into her mind, her phone buzzed. With a resigned sigh, she slipped off the chair and hurried back to the bedroom to retrieve it. The message from Marta was brief, but it spoke volumes.

> Where the hell R U?

> With a friend. I'm fine.

Three dots appeared on the screen. Then they disappeared. Wandering back into the kitchen, Chloe set the phone down on the countertop, giving Jordan a tight smile as she did. She almost jumped out of her skin when the phone rang.

Steadying her nerves, Chloe hit the receive button. "Hi, Marta. How are you?"

"What friend? You disappear without telling any of us. You lied to Stixxluv about a business meeting, and no one knows where you are. What's going on?"

She turned from Jordan and moved toward the terrace doors. Her hand settled on the handle, but it was locked. *Damn.* There went any hope of her discretely slipping out of earshot. He might not be able to hear exactly what was being said, but Marta was loud enough that her angry shouts would have echoed their way across the River Seine.

"Martin knows where I am," Chloe calmly replied.

"Huh, Martin. He doesn't count. He's just your hired muscle. We are the people who really care about you. Aren't we?"

"Yes, you are."

"The only ones who love you. Aren't we?"

Chloe lowered her head. She knew this scene and its script all too well. "Yes, you are."

Even from where he sat a good ten feet or so away, Jordan could still make out most of the conversation. What he couldn't get his mind around was why one of her employees was yelling at her. Chloe paid these people's salary—where she went after hours and with whom was none of their goddam business.

You don't know Chloe or her people. Marta might well be family.

But being family didn't give someone a free pass to treat others poorly. The way Marta spoke to Chloe set Jordan's teeth on edge.

"Yes, I won't be long. No I haven't eaten anything bad. I will see you soon."

Marta ranted on, ending her piece with a half yelled, "I love you."

"I love you too." Chloe ended the call on a sigh, her shoulders slumped. She'd kept her back to him the entire phone call, but Jordan sensed what was about to come next. He braced himself. She turned to look at him, and there was no mistaking the expression of resignation on her face. Their brief time together was at an end.

"I have to go, Jordan. I'm really sorry. If I don't, I won't hear the end of it."

Of course she was leaving. Her people had found out she wasn't in her hotel suite and called her to heel. And like a well-trained pet, she was going to do as she was told. He wasn't the least bit surprised, just disappointed. Chloe wasn't his, she belonged with her people.

I just wish you didn't come at their beck and call.

Heartsore that their morning was being cut short by one of Chloe's minions, Jordan climbed down from the stool and went to her. If she had to go, he wanted to claim one last moment with her before she left. He wrapped his arms around her.

"It's alright. I understand you have commitments, and I wouldn't want to get you into trouble."

Even if Marta does sound like she needs taking down a peg or two.

Chloe rose up on her toes and offered him her mouth. Jordan accepted her kiss, doing his best to keep his hunger for her at bay. Her fingers settled on the front of his dressing gown, and she teased the fabric nervously. "Will I see you again? I mean, if you wanted to ... um ..."

His heart leapt at the thought of Chloe wanting to see him again. He'd forced himself to hold no expectations about either last night or this morning. Chloe might just view her time with him as the final part of her European tour, a nice way to end things. He hadn't dared to allow himself to hope that when they were both back in the US, they might see one another again.

Do I want to see her again, is she kidding?

He bent and their foreheads touched. "I would love to see you again, Chloe. I'm heading back to New York the day after tomorrow, but I will be coming out to the West Coast at the end of this month. If you have time in your schedule, then yes, it would be fantastic to catch up. Last night was amazing, and ..." He let out a nervous laugh. "Yes."

The Laguna Beach resort was still many months away from its official opening, but the Royal Resorts board, and especially his father, were keen to have an executive presence on site to ensure that things went smoothly. A lot was riding on the billion-dollar Platinum Collection resort. Now was probably not the best time for him to be making any sort of relationship commitments, but that didn't mean he and Chloe couldn't catch up when they had the chance.

I really like this woman. But she's not just any woman. She's Chloe.

He met her warm brown eyes, taking in the gentle soul which he now knew lived within. *God you are beautiful, I'm so lucky to have been able to have last night.*

Jordan wanted more. He just wasn't certain how to have more while keeping it a secret from his family. They wouldn't understand. Would make him choose between having a real relationship and managing his career.

I can't tell them. Not yet.

"Could we maybe make a tentative date to catch up in a couple of weeks? I've got to go back into the studio in LA to finish up a couple of the tracks on my new album, but we could still chat in between. If you like," she offered.

The uncertainty in her voice, the utter lack of ego called to Jordan's protective side. A side that until now he didn't know existed. The image of a knight in shining armor upon a white steed suddenly popped into his head. He would go into battle for this woman.

"Chats and messages sound good. I'm a legend at GIFs, but don't be surprised if I stuff up on the emojis. I've been known to send a poop one when I actually meant to hit the smiley face. Fat fingers."

Chloe laughed. "Yeah, I have that problem. I'm always having to send follow up texts to explain myself."

It went without saying that whatever passed between them was private, but if she insisted, Jordan was more than happy to sign a non-disclosure agreement. Whatever it took to make Chloe feel comfortable sharing her thoughts with him. If only she could stay here with him this morning.

"I really wish you didn't have to leave so soon." He buried his nose in her hair, breathing in her scent. Chloe's perfume was the first thing Jordan had noted this morning when he woke. The soft, floral fragrance was on his pillow. He would be taking the pillow case with him when he left later today.

"If we hurried and finished our breakfast, we could steal a few minutes and take a shower together. From what I understand the hand held shower head was given a five star rating from Cosmopolitan magazine. Something about the various pulse settings. I've no idea what that means, but I'm more than happy to help you uncover its secrets."

She grinned up at him. Jordan took that as an unspoken yes. He tugged on the ties of her robe freeing them from their loose knot. Slipping his hand inside the lapels, he brushed a thumb over Chloe's peaked nipple, giving it a firm squeeze. His hand drifted down over her stomach, then went lower. He pushed one, then two fingers into her wet heat, stroking deep. Chloe clung to him as his thumb circled her clit. Her whimpers of unsated need gave Jordan all the instruction he required for her pleasure.

"Shower or bed?" he murmured. He would be happy with either option, but Chloe's sexual release was foremost in his mind.

"Bed, then shower. I can't get enough of you, Jordan."

It was the perfect answer.

Her entourage could damn well wait. Chloe came first.

CHAPTER THIRTEEN

It was late afternoon when Jordan arrived in London. The Eurostar train from Gare de Nord in Paris had taken three hours, during which time, he had caught up on some much needed sleep. The night and morning spent with Chloe had been wonderful, but utterly exhausting. He already missed her smile. A prior obligation to make a quick trip out of Paris to catch up with some French family members was the only reason he hadn't already sent Chloe a dozen texts. He'd had to settle for just one.

> Thinking of you. C U in LA. Safe journey home. 🩶🩶🩶

He didn't get one back.

From St Pancreas station, Jordan took a cab to the Kensington townhouse where his brother Bryce currently lived. Bryce was well into his four-year tenure as head of European operations, but everyone expected that the eldest of the American Royals would eventually come home.

At Christmas while they were all gathered at the family's private island in the Caribbean, Jordan had inadvertently overheard his brother and father talking. The discussion had been centered around the timing of Bryce's return to the USA. It was clear that Edward Royal expected his first born son to take over as CEO for North America in the future, but Jordan had noted a definite hint of push back from Bryce.

Maybe there is still a chance that someone else in the family could get the gig.

That would have been interesting. But it was also impossible. Matthew had never shown any sort of intention of putting his hand up for the top job, while the thought of occupying the fancy corner office at the company's US headquarters in Manhattan had always filled Jordan with a sense of cold dread. *Bryce is the best man for the job.*

After paying the cabbie and including a handsome tip, Jordan gathered his bags and headed for Bryce's front door. He rang the bell.

Two seconds later, Bryce opened the blue glossy door. Jordan and his luggage were quickly hustled inside. No sooner had he set his suitcase and bag down, than a cup of coffee was thrust into his hands.

"Tell me what you think. It's a secret blend from Jamaica. I found a guy in a street just over from Shakespeare's Globe theatre who brings it in from his family's plantation every month. I'm thinking of securing a regular delivery and offering it to our VIP suite guests."

Jordan had to laugh. His brother was an absolute caffeine fiend. From the second he woke to the time he closed his eyes, Bryce Royal was on the hunt for coffee. The color of his blood wasn't red, it was thick and black, just like his beloved brew.

"I'm glad to hear you've found a new caffeine dealer." Jordan took a sip of the hot joe and raised his eyebrows. *Damn that's fine.* The coffee was excellent—he could almost say it held its own against the famous Jamaican Blue, and that was saying something.

It was only when he'd finished his obligatory first cup of coffee, that he was finally permitted a brotherly hug. Bryce's attempt at a rib crush was quickly defeated by Jordan's five am weight lifting class arms. He grinned when his older brother finally cried, "Uncle." Jordan gave mercy and released him.

"You've gotten strong. I need to get back in the gym and on the weights so I can give you a proper thrashing," said Bryce, struggling for air.

Clenching his fists, Jordan bent and gave his best bodybuilder pose. He would have done the whole arms above his head routine, but the seams of his Italian suit might not forgive him. "I've got strength but no stamina. I was huffing all the way up the stairs of the Paris apartment yesterday, it was embarrassing."

He wasn't going to make mention of the world-famous singer who had left him in her wake as he struggled up the five flights of stairs.

"It's good to see you, Bryce. You need to get home more often." London might only be an eight hour flight from New York in the company jet, but everyone was super busy. At any one time, the three Royal siblings could be on three separate continents, thousands of miles apart.

At least the bonds of a shared upbringing still held.

"How's Matthew? Any more movement on the Colorado project?" asked Bryce. He was busy cutting up some fresh bread and adding it to a charcuterie platter which already contained cheese, sliced meats, and fresh fruit. Bryce was nothing if not the master of Omotenashi, the Japanese hospitality mindset where one looked after guests well beyond expectations.

Jordan rolled up a piece of thinly slice prosciutto and

stuffed it into his mouth, humming with delight as the Italian cured meat set the pleasure response in his brain to *yum* level. While he chewed, he considered Bryce's question about their brother.

Poor Matthew. He'd come across an old, abandoned ski resort in the Colorado mountains and been possessed by a burning desire to buy the site, raze the existing buildings, and create a brand new ultra-modern resort from scratch. Matthew Royal was the king of big dreams. Being the most creative of the three siblings, he had gone on to study architecture at Cornell University.

"Last time I spoke to our little brother, he was trying the divide and conquer route with the current owners of the place. They, of course, saw right through his ruse, and decided to punish him by adding a couple more devious clauses to the deed of sale. Negotiating has never been Matt's strong point."

Bryce winced. "Yeah, I would offer to assist, but like the ski resort, I'm snowed under. Pun intended. I have a horrible feeling we are going to find Matthew has been eaten by a bear in the woods of Colorado long before he can get a signature on that contract. But if he can find a way to get the deal done, it could be an absolute gold mine."

There might be a degree of sibling mirth in the conversation, but the Aspen project was a major piece of work for the American side of the House of Royal. If they could find a way to deliver a world-class resort in the town that was famous for celebrities and rich people, it would be a huge coup for Royal Resorts. It would also go a long way to sealing the USA as the big growth market for the House of Royal. As well as shutting up a few of the condescending European cousins at the same time.

"Dad wants us to stay out of it, says it's Matthew's project and he has to learn to deal with recalcitrant vendors. But as

Mom would say, enough about business. Where have you been this week, Jordan?"

He shrugged off his coat and jacket, making himself comfortable on one of Bryce's overstuffed dark gray couches. His brother set the platter of food on the low coffee table in front of Jordan and motioned for him to eat.

"I went to Berlin to catch up with Leon and check out your new hotel. It looks great, you really know how to deliver the best product. I thought it made sense to see how Leon was handling an opening. Pick up some tips for Laguna Beach. Then, last night I was at the apartment in Paris. I caught the Eurostar this morning."

A bemused Bryce shook his head. "You had the corporate jet at your disposal, but you still chose to take the train. Are you ever going to grow out of your little obsession with all things relating to rail?"

Nope. That was never happening. From the time he could walk, Jordan had had a thing about locomotives. He liked planes, but he *loved* trains. The thundering beat of a train as it approached the station always sent shivers down his spine. And the things that happened to his cock when a steam whistle blew, well that was something he had never dared share with another person. Bryce had his coffee obsession, Jordan had his trains.

As far as Jordan was aware, he was the only member of his family who owned a New York City transit system Metro-Card. He doubted that either of their parents had ever set foot on the subway.

"I like taking the train, especially in Europe. Besides, once I'm out in California for the Laguna Beach project, I doubt I will get much time to travel. It was nice to look out the window and see the passing countryside, and just before we got to the channel tunnel, I took a nap."

Bryce dropped into the seat next to his, slapping Jordan

on the thigh as he did. "I saw some Laguna Beach photos the other day. Construction looks pretty much done. The golf course is coming along beautifully, the design team have done a fantastic job. I bet you're itching to get out to the site."

"Absolutely. I paid a quick visit to the resort a month or so back and the fairway greens are certainly looking green. I can't wait until the first paying guests tee off."

He was saying all the right things, but this morning Jordan's heart and mind were elsewhere. Until only a few days ago, California had long meant the big ocean-side resort, but now it represented something else. LA was where Chloe lived. He couldn't stop thinking of her.

She'd given him her home address in Beverly Hills, and he'd promised to keep it private. Her home was in a gated community, and protected on the ground by security, but Chloe certainly didn't need people finding out where she lived and attempting to illegally fly drones over her house. She'd told him she was always worried about the super fans who went to extraordinary lengths just to get her picture. Her home was her one true place of refuge from the world.

The Royal family knew as much about the need for protection as anyone else. Wealth seemed to always attract the wrong kind of people. People who wanted money. People who wanted power and influence. In Chloe's case, Jordan suspected the members of her entourage were those sorts of people.

"So when are you moving out to Laguna Beach?" asked Bryce.

"Soon. I hadn't planned to relocate until late next month, but you know New York at this time of the year. Cold and miserable. So I'm thinking of packing my things and heading out to California not long after I get home."

Jordan hadn't planned to rush out to the West Coast. The resort wasn't due to start receiving guests until sometime in

September. But if there was a chance that he and Chloe might be able to carve out some alone time for themselves before then, he wanted to be in LA. He'd messaged her earlier to let her know he'd changed his mind and would be in LA the following week.

He was keen to see Chloe and discover what might truly lay between them. To find out if perhaps Paris hadn't been just a one night stand. But in the meantime, he was going to keep his connection with the pop princess a closely guarded secret. The last thing he needed was for anyone in Royal Resorts to find out and start questioning his motives for being in LA.

CHAPTER FOURTEEN

Chloe's home Beverly Hills
One week later

"Now we're in preliminary discussions with several tour promoters, but I'm looking to lock in some concert venues for late August, early September. Your mini European tour went well, but we need you back out on the road as soon as this album is completed."

I've just got home.

"I've been thinking about taking some time off toward the end of the summer, rather than going on the road again. I know you want me touring, but I'm tired. I need a break. And this new album isn't even finished. I'm not a machine, Foster. I can't keep working at this pace."

They were standing outside on the patio of her Beverly Hills home, next to the swimming pool. Foster had a thing for conducting business with Chloe out of earshot of her people. Just the two of them. Like it had always been.

Foster waved his golden ring-laden hand in her direction.

The light from the morning sun caught the expensive jewels and the colorful reflections danced across the water's surface of the swimming pool. He clearly wasn't listening, or if he was, he didn't care. This past year had seen him push her harder than ever to produce new music and be constantly in front of her adoring public.

"You know you need to be front and center with your fans. If you aren't they will forget you. The next younger, prettier star is always waiting in the wings. Ready to take your place."

How many times had she heard that thinly veiled threat? If she didn't continue to feed the fame monster, it would soon turn its attention to someone else. Stars came and went. Fame lived and died. The not so subtle dig about age and beauty always struck home. Foster loved to play on Chloe's insecurities.

Something has changed. He is agitated. But why?

She knew better than to come straight out and ask him what was going on. Foster was the one who had given Chloe her big break. It was rare for her to challenge him on any of his decisions. She owed him her entire career, and he never let her forget it.

Chloe glanced furtively at her watch. Jordan had said he was coming to see her this morning. She didn't want Foster knowing about him. Her manager would no doubt tell her that she didn't have time for romance. Or a private life.

She took a deep breath, summoned her courage, and for the first time that she could actually remember, met his gaze. Eight—almost nine—years of back-to-back success had to have earned her the right to some personal space. God knows she had worked hard enough for it.

"Let's not book anything until this album is done. I don't know if I will be able to manage a full tour."

He narrowed his dark eyes at her, anger creased the

corners of his mouth. Foster wasn't a man used to being told "no". Especially not by Chloe.

"I think you might want to check your contract, young lady. While I'm your manager, you have obligations to meet."

Foster could make life difficult for her, but unlike every other time she had thought to challenge his authority, today Chloe wasn't in the mood for simply taking things lying down. Something within her had changed. "I know I have certain things which I am contractually obliged to do, but I am not a robot. I am a person, and I'm telling you I need a break. I need time for me."

It took all her mental strength to hold back her heart's pleas. To make him finally look past Chloe the superstar and see the young woman. But Foster wasn't that kind of man, she doubted he'd ever been that way. He was all business. All money. She was merely the means to an end. And when he tired of her, when he'd wrung out every last cent of her talent, he would find a replacement.

"We will discuss this further when you are in a more rational state of mind," Foster huffed. Without so much as a goodbye, he turned on his heel and headed back into the house. Chloe followed in his wake. Her manager kept walking. Right out the front door, which he closed behind him with an unnecessary degree of force and headed straight to his car. The roar of his Bugatti Chiron sportscar filled her ears as it tore down the driveway.

By the time Chloe made it outside, the dust and stones kicked up by Foster's high performance racing car were still settling back down onto the drive. She stood hands on hips and glared at the road.

Maybe I should be looking for another manager, not just signing another contract extension.

That would teach him. After a minute she turned, intending to head back inside when another car came into view. It was a small white SUV, and it was driven through the gate at a far more sedate speed.

Thoughts of her high pressure manager and his fiery temper instantly fled as she caught sight of the person behind the wheel. It was Jordan.

Her pulse quickened. When he gave her a friendly wave, it was all she could do not to burst into tears. She hadn't been entirely certain he would come, but he was here.

And unlike arrogant Foster who parked anywhere he damned well pleased, Jordan pulled up in one of the car spaces which were clearly marked for visitors. It reminded her once more that Jordan had manners.

Chloe did a quick check of her clothes. She was wearing a pink and orange striped sweater with faded jeans. Very, at-home-casual. Her original intention had been to head upstairs and change into something more stylish before Jordan's arrival, but the unexpected visit from Foster had put paid to her plans. He was always doing that, pulling the rug out from under her whenever she thought she had a solid footing.

Forget about Foster. Jordan is here. That's all that matters.

With a welcoming smile on her face, she went to greet her special guest.

From the seat next to him, Jordan retrieved his jacket and the box of Grand Cru Chocolates by Pierre Marcolini which he had purchased earlier that morning. The House of Royal had its own private chocolate brand, but he'd thought that might come across as him being a little cheap. He wanted to impress Chloe, not have her thinking he was tightfisted with money.

He glanced at the chocolates. Were they a misstep?

Shit. Maybe I should have gone with a piece of jewelry. Does she wear silver or gold? And what exactly do I buy a woman who has all the money she could ever want?

A tap at his driver's side window startled Jordan's doubt away. A grinning Chloe waved at him through the glass.

It had only been a week or so since he'd last seen her, but seeing Chloe sent joy immediately flooding through his heart. He had never been effected in such a way by a woman before. Never felt the need to wrap someone up in his arms and hold her, like he did with Chloe.

It had to be the jetlag. *Yes, I'm just jetlagged.* He ignored the obvious facts that he'd been back in the US for some time, and the private jet flight out to LA yesterday morning hadn't exactly taxed him.

Chloe stepped back as he carefully opened the car door and climbed out. They stood looking at one another for a moment. He sensed she was as awkwardly shy about this reunion as he was, and also just as uncertain. There was something refreshing about it. Dare he say sweet.

He offered her the box of chocolates. "These are for you."

A beaming Chloe took the gift, clutching it tightly in both hands. Jordan was suddenly reminded of having seen her on TV after winning a major music award. She held onto the box of chocolates like they were as precious as that shiny golden miniature gramophone.

"Chocolates. Ooh, lovely. Thank you." Chloe glanced furtively over her shoulder in the direction of a nearby doorway. "I'm not actually allowed these, but if we're quick, we might be able to eat one or two before they are confiscated."

What the actual fuck? She wasn't allowed chocolates? And who had the right to take gifts away from her?

Let it go. It's not your place to question her life. You barely know the woman.

Perplexed Jordan followed Chloe around to the other side of the hire car, frowning as she dropped down to the stone paving, and hurriedly opened the box. She wasn't joking about no one finding out she'd eaten the chocolates. What happened to enjoying the little treats in life?

He took a spot next to her. The driveway was immaculate, there wasn't a stray leaf to be seen.

I expect they have rules against such untidiness in this part of LA.

Somewhere in the gated community body corporate regulations there would be a clause about nature's litter.

Chloe offered him the box. "Here." Jordan noted that she had selected one of the heart shaped chocolates. He took one of them as well. They'd been sending one another heart emojis in their messages, so it seemed apt.

With the forbidden sweet goodies stuffed into their mouths, Chloe and Jordan sat grinning at one another. When he reached out his hand, she took it, shuffling a little closer to him. "I'm so glad you're here Jordan, I can't wait to show you around my home. This is my most favorite place in the entire world."

You are such a sweetheart.

He hadn't felt anything like this since the time, when aged fifteen, he'd fallen for one of the household staff at his parents' estate. He'd spent months mooning around after her, only ceasing with his foolish devotion when the young woman up and announced she was getting married. And she was pregnant. And she and her fiancé were moving to Texas. His summer crush had well and truly crushed his heart.

But this was different. He wasn't a hormone fueled youth, he was a man.

"Chloe!" A voice rang out from within the house. When Jordan looked to Chloe, she shook her head. It was clear that she didn't wish to be found. Or at the very least not yet.

"Who is that?" he whispered.

"Marta. My number one personal assistant. If she knew I was out here with you gorging on sweets, she'd go ballistic," Chloe whispered back.

I wouldn't call eating one or two handcrafted chocolates gorging, but this is Hollywood.

The *tak tak* of a pair of high heels clicking over the smooth surface of the driveway reached his ears. Was Marta actually hunting for Chloe?

He remembered who Marta was— she was the woman who had demanded the top shelf booze in Berlin. She was also the person who had called Chloe at the apartment in Paris and shouted down the phone at her boss. His skin crawled at the memory of hearing Chloe's almost Pavlovian response of "I love you too" when Marta had offered her those empty words of so-called affection.

The clicking came to a stop on the other side of Jordan's car. It was replaced by a *tsk* and a heavy sigh. "Who has dared to park a hire car in the driveway? Seriously. I bet it was one of the cleaners. Who do these people think they are working for? It's just not good enough. Chloe has standards to keep."

Marta and her angry shoes disappeared back into the house. Her exasperated screeches soon echoed off the stone walls of the mock Spanish dwelling. It was clear, that at Chloe's house, she was the one in charge. That didn't sit at all well with Jordan.

Chloe offered him the box of chocolates once more. "A last one, then we had better head inside. If Marta doesn't find someone to blame for your car, she will march back out here and turn over every last stone until she finds the guilty person."

Jordan selected two more of the contraband treats and stuffed them into his mouth. If he was going to die today, it would be with Belgian chocolate on his lips.

CHAPTER FIFTEEN

As soon as she and Jordan made it into the house, Chloe's attention was grabbed by what was happening outside on the patio. Through the open glass double doors she could see Marta along with the rest of the household staff all gathered by the pool. Her stomach dropped.

Marta stood ramrod straight with her hands clasped firmly behind her back. She was going from person to person. Her hard words drifted into the house. She was conducting an interrogation as to who had parked the offending motor vehicle out front. It looked like a scene out of a war movie, any minute now someone would confess their crime, and Gabriela would be given the job of dragging them away to be shot.

Not this morning. Not in front of Jordan. Please. This is so embarrassing.

"Ah, there you are, where have you been?" snapped Marta, as Chloe led Jordan out onto the patio. Her assistant's disapproving gaze immediately switched from Chloe to him. She could almost hear the last piece of the puzzle as it snapped into place. Marta immediately hurried over to where Jordan stood. "Is that your hire car in the drive?"

Oh, no.

Jordan gave the dark haired Marta a slow withering looking up and down. He sniffed his obvious disapproval of her. "Yes, it is. Why? Do you have a problem with your *employer* having visitors to her home, or is your issue with the brand of vehicle? I'm sorry to say they were fresh out of Mercedes when I arrived at the airport, and the Kia seemed a perfectly acceptable alternative. I didn't realize that there was a dress code for motor vehicles. I will remember that for *next* time."

Marta's face registered the obvious challenge in Jordan's words. Her hazel eyes widened, and her red painted lips became a thin, hard line of disapproval. She might think she was in charge of things here, but Chloe's guest was making it clear he was not going to be bullied.

Chloe really ought to say something, but from the way that Jordan and Marta looked one another in the eye, it might be better if she simply held her tongue. These two seemed more than capable of taking care of themselves.

An interesting silence now descended. Interesting to Chloe, because Marta's authority was being questioned by a stranger in front of the rest of the household team. Knowing Marta, she would be running several scenarios simultaneously in her head in an effort to come up with the most effective way to keep her iron grip on power. She would also be thinking of how she could put Jordan firmly in his place. Marta excelled at this sort of conflict.

"I'm happy to move the car if it's a problem," offered Jordan.

I really should do something. I should, but ...

Chloe was utterly riveted by this encounter. Spellbound. Two strong minded people, seeking to gain an edge.

A smile lit Marta's face. Her expression was victorious. No one ever won against her. And she was going to make certain that Jordan knew his place.

"Would you mind moving it to the visitor car space farthest from the front door? Ms. Fisher doesn't like the driveway to be crowded."

Invoking Chloe's name so formally was Marta's sly way of letting Jordan know that if he refused her request, it would be due to his lack of manners. And by not moving the car, the only person he would be offending was the lady of the house. Chloe.

Ms. Fisher, my ass. That's not what you called me when you found me eating a tiny handful of French fries after the concert in Berlin.

Her assistant excelled in name calling and put downs. All in the supposed noble cause of making sure that Chloe fitted her costumes and looked fabulous. If Foster and Marta weren't as thick as thieves, Chloe would have rid herself of the woman long ago.

Then again if I changed managers ...

With the fragile peace hanging by a thin thread, Chloe turned to Jordan. This moment was all about everyone saving face. If Marta was forced to back down, the rest of the staff would be made to pay. Jordan sadly was the only one without a lot to lose.

"Are you ok to move your car, please, Jordan?" she asked. The plea in her voice made her sound weak.

You are weak. Face it, you will never get rid of Marta.

So much for trying to impress her lover. She really ought to pull Marta into line, but the earlier argument with Foster had sapped Chloe of her strength.

Jordan tightened his grip on her hand. "It would be my pleasure, Chloe. How about you come and show me where I'm allowed to park. It is your home, so you should be the one who decides."

As he led her inside the house, Chloe dared not look back. She was sure Marta's gaze was burning a large hole in the back of Jordan's head. Her number one assistant wasn't one for being crossed. Those foolish enough to challenge her tended to find themselves pushed out of Chloe's Garden very quickly. Chloe had lost count of the number of minor assistants who had tendered their resignation at short notice, usually via text and often overnight.

But it was apparent that Jordan wasn't some mere minion who Marta could intimidate. He walked at a leisurely pace. His casual posture bordered on indifference. There was no anger in his stride or his demeanor. When they reached the door, he stopped. A frisson of heat slid down Chloe's spine as he turned and calmly asked, "Did you want to go for a coffee? I know a place nearby."

There was a simmering heat in his words.

God, I hope he doesn't just want to meet for a coffee.

Her waking moments might well be full of pop star demands, but when she was alone, all Chloe could think about was that night in Paris. Of being with Jordan.

Her purse and cell were on a side table next to the front door. She scooped them up and gave him a hopeful smile, before asking, "Where are you staying?"

"The Royal Resorts Beverly Hills, it's only ten minutes from here." She followed Jordan's gaze as it shifted from her to the patio, where Marta was still giving the other staff hell. No doubt her assistant was making sure that none of the people who Marta designated as being merely *the help* got any sort of idea into their heads of challenging her authority.

Jordan was right, this was her home. These people worked for her, and Chloe knew better than to tell them she was going somewhere with Jordan. Marta and Gabriela would argue against it. And if Chloe persisted, they might cave, but at the same time demand she have a small entourage with her when she left the house. Then the bodyguards would be made to follow. Every time she went out, her people made it a performance piece. It was exhausting.

But if they don't know I've slipped out ...

Mind made up, Chloe opened the front door, quickly closing it as soon as Jordan had followed her outside. "I've just had a coffee, but from what I learned about you in Paris, Jordan Royal, I'm sure you can find something else just as amazing to offer me."

His deep, rough chuckle went straight to her sex. "Your wish is my command, Ms. Fisher."

Jordan pulled the box of chocolates from under his jacket and handed them back to Chloe. "Chocolates for the road. Let's both try a fruity ganache before we leave, then one of the smooth caramels for the trip down Benedict Canyon Drive."

He was being cheeky, but also lovely. Charming. Jordan displayed a degree of grace and good humor that Chloe had rarely seen outside of the big gala events when the press and a thousand cameras were tracking every move of the major stars of the entertainment world. Her own people could learn a thing or two from the way he had behaved in the face of such outright rudeness.

Guilt sat heavy in her heart. She didn't want him leaving here and being reluctant to ever visit at her home again. "I'm sorry about Marta. She is in one of her moods today."

He gave her a look which all but said he expected Marta was permanently in a foul mood. He wouldn't be wrong on that count. Her number one personal assistant had been pushing boundaries for some time now. And Chloe hadn't been pushing back. She was paying people to treat her poorly and tell her what to do.

"I will talk to her. She has no right to speak to my friends like that."

Jordan didn't respond to her apology, he simply jangled his car keys, and smiled. "Forget about Marta—I already have. Come on, let's you and I go have some fun."

They climbed into the hire car. It was only when Jordan reached the end of the drive and they were about to pass under the ornamental archway, that he spoke again. "Something tells me Marta's mood is not going to improve while we're gone." He pointed to the rear vision mirror. Chloe shifted in her seat and glanced back at the house. In the middle of the forecourt, hands on hips stood Marta. She was looking at the car and shaking her head. Talk about a censuring look.

"I don't think your evil henchwoman assistant likes me all that much. Fifty bucks says that when you get home tomorrow morning, she takes you aside and tells you that someone like me shouldn't be in your life. I'm a bad influence," offered Jordan.

Chloe pressed her teeth into her bottom lip. Here she was, riding in a car with a reformed billionaire bad boy. Stuffing forbidden chocolates into her face. And she was running off to spend the night with him in his hotel suite. Her bad influence bingo card was close to full.

Jordan could keep his fifty bucks. Chloe didn't care what Marta had to say on the subject of Jordan Royal. Or where or what she was doing. Her phone buzzed and a message popped up.

> Call me. Dress fitting for the album launch is at 3

Seriously, the album isn't even finished. I want this man in my life. I need to have fun.

> Sorry out of cell range. Get Gabs to cancel fitting. C U tomorrow.

Jordan gave her a sly, sideways look. "You didn't just blow off your personal assistant did you, Ms. Fisher?"

"And my security team." Chloe laughed.

Damn right she had. Chloe felt a sense of having snatched just a tiny bit of her own life back. It wasn't much, but it was a start.

CHAPTER SIXTEEN

The well-dressed concierge didn't so much as bat an eyelid as Chloe and Jordan stepped out of the elevator which had brought them up from the parking garage. Instead, he walked calmly across the hotel lobby and stood in front of Chloe, effectively blocking her from anyone's prying gaze. He looked directly at Jordan. "Good afternoon, Mister Royal, is there anything you require for this afternoon?"

Chloe was impressed. It was a neat trick. With Jordan's strong, protective arm wrapped about her shoulder, holding her to him, she was well concealed.

I forget he knows the tricks of staying out of public view.

"Privacy would be nice. Could you ask that the head of guest services be the only one who comes to my suite? An order for food will be sent down shortly."

The broad shouldered concierge nodded his understanding. "Of course. I will let her know. No one else will be permitted near your suite, Mister Royal."

With an ease that spoke of a lifetime of habit, Jordan produced a keycard out of his jeans pocket and tapped it gently on the wall next to a nearby elevator. A soft ting quickly followed. As the doors opened, Jordan gave a nod to the concierge, who in turn finally looked at Chloe and bowed his head. "Please enjoy your stay."

The concierge held the doors open as Chloe and Jordan stepped into the elevator. Her last view of him was of his back as he stood guard. No one else was getting in the car with them.

"Wow, the staff members of your hotel really do know the meaning of the word discretion. I've been to plenty of hotels where the folk who work the front desk have been yelling my name the second, I set foot in the lobby. They are also the ones who tend to pick up the phone and call the local paparazzi as soon as I am out of earshot."

Jordan spun Chloe into his embrace. His touch sent tingles through her body. They became sparks as he bent and placed a warm, tender kiss on her lips. "You will always be safe at one of our hotels. And especially when you are with me. I will never let anyone hurt you. Trust me."

She blinked back tears. How long had she yearned to hear those words from a man, to know she could trust him? Too long.

All my life.

"Oh shoot," exclaimed Jordan.

"What?"

"I left the chocolates in the car, did you want me to go back and get them?"

The chocolates were lovely, but they were fine where they were. She had other things on her mind. The moment they had stepped out of the hire car, Jordan had put a protective arm around her, and he hadn't let go. The way he made her feel was sweeter than anything she could have eaten.

She planted a tempting kiss on his lips. "I can think of another delectable thing I would like to feast on. Something that will make us both forget about the chocolates."

He kissed her again. "And I'm meant to be the bad influence."

Chloe's lady bits started a now familiar happy dance. They liked what came with being alone with Jordan.

When the elevator stopped at the top floor, the doors opened onto a small entrance area a few feet wide. On the other side of the narrow foyer was a pale cream door.

Chloe grinned as Jordan tugged her to the door. He tapped his card against the keypad and pushed the door open with his foot all in one graceful, *sexy as hell* move.

Today was the first time they'd met in person since Paris. In the days following their encounter in the French capital, Jordan and Chloe had texted, sent DMs, Zoomed, and even emailed one another. But nothing could compare to the heady tactile joy of being able to touch. Skin on skin.

"Would you like a drink? I have various bottles of water, and the coffee machine is one of those super expensive ones that do everything apart from call your name to collect your order. I think there is some decaf somewhere, or peppermint tea."

Chloe shook her head. She knew exactly what she wanted. "I want you. Every inch. Naked. And now. Please."

"Such lovely manners." Jordan took Chloe's phone and purse from out of her hands. His warm fingers settled at her waist. He lifted her sweater and camisole up and over her head. She loved that he wasn't messing around.

He hooked a finger into the front of her bra and pulled her hard against him. She enjoyed his rough playfulness. As she stood, face pressed into his chest, Jordan's other hand worked the clasps of her bra free. The man had skills.

One. Two. He brushed the thin straps off her shoulders. Then with a masterful flick of the wrist, he tore the bra from her body and tossed it onto the floor.

I really should give him a round of applause.

Jordan sank straight to his knees, cupping a naked breast in either hand as he went down. His teeth nipped at her left nipple sending a shiver of pleasurable pain racing down her spine. "Jordan. Oh god."

He set to work sucking and teasing her nipple. Every time he drew back hard, her core clenched. Her sex throbbed with desperate aching need.

Eager to assist, she flipped open the top button of her jeans. But with a large male body blocking her way, Chloe only managed to get the zipper part way down. An accommodating Jordan did the rest. He released her breast from its delicious torture just long enough to pull her jeans to the floor. Chloe kicked them off, along with her slide-on sandals.

Thank god for the warm weather of California. It meant a girl could undress with speed and ease.

"Hmm. A dark blue G-string with diamantes. Very pretty. Such a shame it has to come off, maybe I should get you to leave it here when you go." Jordan slipped the scrap of Italian lace down her legs and tossed it carelessly aside.

Dark green eyes glittered up at her. She could have sworn the word *devil* danced in them. Her own eyes closed as a thick tongue speared into her heated flesh. Strong hands gripped her ass cheeks as Jordan delved deep over and over again. Every time he reached the top of her sex his tongue did a little flutter over her clit. Chloe sobbed. Her flushed bud was so sensitive it had her switching back and forth between pain and the edge of an all body orgasm.

But she didn't want to come. Not yet.

This was beyond heaven. Paris had been merely an entrée as to what this man could do. His fingers spread her soft folds open, and he buried his face between her legs. Chloe cried out. Desperate for what, she didn't quite know.

At the very edge of a shattering climax, he pulled her back. Drawing her away from her orgasm. *What a glorious tease.* Jordan rested on his haunches and slowly nodded to himself. "Now I think it's time you took in the view."

Huh?

He got to his feet and towed Chloe toward a bright red ottoman chair which sat in the middle of the living area. "I would like very much for you to get on your hands and knees and face the window, please, Ms. Fisher."

As soon as she climbed onto the ottoman, Chloe understood the quip about enjoying the view. The skyline of downtown Los Angeles lay before her in the distance.

Jordan ran the palm of his hand over her bare ass. The move was full of promise. "Now spread your legs, wide."

Chloe deliberately shifted her knees only a little apart. She was teasing him, hoping he would pick up on her signal.

The sharp sting of his hand on her ass took her breath away. He'd got the message. "Spread your legs, Chloe."

This was hot as … if he hadn't already brought her to the brink, his commanding well-spoken voice and firm hand would have done it for her.

She moved her legs apart another inch and got a second slap on her backside for her troubles. Chloe hadn't ever been one for this sort of sex play, but after Paris she felt safe with Jordan. Sensed he wouldn't push her to do anything she didn't want to do. She was naked and on her knees in front of him, vulnerable. But he would protect her.

"Would you like my cock to pound into your sweet pussy and bring you to a teary orgasm? Is that what you want. I will do whatever you ask."

She dragged in a shallow, ragged breath. If he had any idea as to how close she was, he wouldn't be saying those things. The slightest touch and she was going to come. "Yes, I want you. I need you."

The hiss of a zipper being lowered, followed by the

crinkle of a condom wrapper was music to her ears. "Are you alright if we use my condoms?"

Chloe nodded. She hadn't thought to bring her own, they weren't something she normally carried in her purse. She welcomed the exquisite pressure as Jordan slowly pushed the head of his cock inside her. She moaned. "Oh, Jordan. Please."

"Take a deep breath sweetheart and cool your blood. We should take our time, so if you think you are close, drop your head. I'll pull out until you have regained control. How does that sound?"

"It sounds like heaven."

The *slap, slap* of flesh against flesh now filled the silence of the room. The heady scent of sex hung in the air. Chloe focused her gaze on the city as she took every inch of Jordan's cock. Again and again. Three times she dropped her head, and three times he withdrew from her body. Each break took a few more minutes than the last for her to wrestle her lust into submission. But when he thrust in deep for what felt like the millionth time, Chloe fractured into a thousand shards of light.

She gripped tightly onto the fabric of the ottoman as Jordan let loose his restraint. His hips pumped his hard erection into her. Over and over again. His arm wrapped around her waist, and he slowed. His thrusts became long and languid. She was utterly destroyed, but with every stroke he put her back together again.

Jordan came on a whispered, "Chloe."

The city outside the window was lost in the sheen of her tears.

CHAPTER SEVENTEEN

Chloe's bedroom,
 A week of sexual delights later.

Chloe shifted in the bed and Jordan let her out of his embrace. Moving onto her stomach, she rose up on her elbows. At the same time, he piled another pillow behind his head and adopted his listening pose. She clearly had things she wanted to say. He'd quickly discovered that when Chloe was in one of her chatty moods, she could talk for hours. Jordan loved these late night conversations.

After a week in LA, much of it spent in bed, he and Chloe had settled into a comfortable easy existence. In the morning Jordan would leave the house and head down to Laguna Beach and the resort, while Chloe continued to work on her album.

In the late afternoon, they would meet up once more. Enjoy an hour or so of hot sweaty sex, before showering and eating dinner. Jordan didn't feel right eating heavy meals in the evening while Chloe was forced to drink protein shakes, so he usually ate a full late lunch and then stuck to fruit at night.

He was supporting Chloe, but he secretly relished watching Marta get all bent out of shape over his impeccable behavior. For every opportunity that might present itself where she could find fault with him, Jordan was always one step ahead. He'd love to have just five minutes alone with Marta. She was a serious piece of work.

"Are you nervous about heading up the resort launch?"

It was wonderful that Chloe was interested in the project. That she asked questions beyond the obvious ones such as opening dates and when people could start booking rooms. Was he nervous? "Yeah, I guess I am. This is a big project, and I would hate to stuff it up. Dad and Bryce both went all in with the board to get their approval for my appointment. When we are closer to opening, I would love to take you down to the site and give you a private tour."

"I'd like that. The pictures you've shown me look fantastic, but nothing would beat actually seeing the place."

The loud roar of a car's engine split the night. Chloe swore. "He has got to be kidding."

"What?"

She climbed off the bed and went to the window. "Yep, it's Foster. Eleven o'clock at night and he just rocks up without so much as a phone call."

They both turned their heads in response to a loud knock pounding on the bedroom door, followed by the sound of an all too familiar—and all too unwelcome—voice bellowing from out in the hall. "Foster is here, Chloe. You had better get dressed."

When did Marta arrive back at the house? I thought she'd left hours ago. And how did she know Foster was coming? There's something not right about all this.

To his disappointment, Chloe didn't question any of it,

instead she went straight to her dressing room. When she returned a few minutes later, she was fully clothed. Their gazes met for an instant and she gave him a small shake of the head. The message was clear. *Just don't say anything.*

This was her life, her career. Much as he wanted to step in and play the role of being her champion, he had no right to interfere.

While Chloe headed downstairs, Jordan hit the shower.

"Hi, Foster. It's a bit late for a house call, don't you think? You do have a phone, you could have called and checked to see if I was available."

Jordan's personality was beginning to rub off on her. Before him, Chloe would never have spoken to her manager like that. Instead she would have been scurrying to the kitchen to make him a coffee.

"I spoke to the team at the recording studio today and your producer tells me the album is still not going well. Has the Chloe talent well finally run dry?"

He was sticking the knife into the soft flesh of her pride and twisting it hard. Foster knew exactly how to hurt her.

"Five tracks are completed, I'm just not sure if the last couple are right. I'm working on them."

"Well maybe if you closed your legs and stopped wasting time with your toy boy, you might come up with a new song. Something that will sell this album. Because right now, none of your fans will buy it because it's a damn embarrassing mess."

Chloe blinked back hot tears. She hated it when Foster

was in one of these moods, the ones where he stood and tore her down. Made her feel small, worthless.

"Jordan isn't a toy boy."

"Really? Well I would beg to differ. I think he's a waste of fucking space."

"You don't know Jordan, or what he means to me."

Foster moved forward, coming to stand closer to Chloe. He towered over her. This was yet another of his many ploys he used to intimidate, to make her bend to his will.

"You are right—I don't know him. All I do know is that the record company is getting fed up, and so am I." He let out a tired sigh. "Chloe, Chloe, Chloe. When will you learn that the only people who know what is good for you are the people who are already in your life?"

She was shrinking. Her childhood trauma was rising to the surface, whispering all its horrible words. Telling her she was no good. That no one would ever want her. That she was unlovable.

"I'll get the album finished, I promise."

Foster reached into his jacket pocket and pulled out a piece of paper. He handed it to her. "That's the day and time the *Chloe Jet* leaves LA at the end of next week. As I told you, I am the only one who knows what's best. I've spoken to the record company, and they have agreed for you to go and work with Kevin Smith in London."

Kevin Smith. *The Kevin Smith?* Chloe had waited her entire career to work with the famous producer.

She was cornered. If she said no because she wanted to stay in LA, the record company might reconsider the whole album, possibly even cancel it. If they did that, the one person who would wear the blame in its full entirety would be her.

But if I go, that means leaving Jordan.

"Can I leave the week after that?" She wasn't above haggling. A week here or there wouldn't make a difference.

"No. Kevin's time is tightly booked. Look, I know you think that guy upstairs is some kind of wonderful, but he's not. He's just another man who wants to get into your panties, and when it's all over, he'll sell his story to the press. Maybe even get himself a nice little reality series out of it on one of the cheaper streaming services."

"Jordan wouldn't do that."

"Are you sure? Are you willing to bet this album, and your entire career on a guy you've only just met? Users like him won't stick around once all the money is gone. He'll bleed you dry and before you know it, you'll have to sell this house to pay off your debts." He waved his arms around and Chloe was powerless to stop her gaze from following.

Foster's words hit home. Right to the deepest depths of her insecurities. This house meant everything to Chloe. It was the only home she'd ever known. If her career faltered, the record company would come looking for its money. Lawsuits and cash-sucking lawyers would soon follow.

Was she prepared to risk everything for a few more days with Jordan?

"Well? Are you getting on the plane that day, or staying in bed with your deadbeat boyfriend?"

She gave a little shrug. Unsure of what to say or do. Either way she would pay a price.

In the final act of his soul crushing play, Foster lay a hand on Chloe's shoulder. "It comes down to who you feel you can trust. It's either me or him. I'm here for you, Chloe."

Jordan stood at the top of the stairs. Chloe was being made to choose between him and her career. Between him and Foster. He could try and offer her all the guarantees in the world, but there were none. Foster, the cunning prick, was playing on Chloe's weaknesses. She loved this house. And the thing that made her life complete was her music. Her fans. Without Chloe's Garden, Jordan feared what would happen to her.

Chloe let out a resigned sigh. "Yes. You are right, the risk is too great. I'll talk to Jordan. Let him know I have to go to London."

Game over.

Foster had pressured Chloe into caving to his demands. And if that wasn't bad enough, she'd agreed with her manager about him. *I'm too great a risk.*

How many times had he heard that remark being said about him? That people liked him, but their trust only went so far. He'd messed up in the past and paid a heavy price for it. Hearing Chloe say that about him stung his pride.

Does she see me as just a temporary thing? And when this album is done and she goes on the road to promote it, will I be left behind?

He hadn't ever been in a long-term relationship. Still couldn't recognize the signs as to whether this thing with Chloe had enough substance to survive or whether it would wither and die. He wanted it to grow.

And what if this album does fail and she views me as being tied to its demise? Like a bad talisman. A link she needs to break. Something to be rid of.

The Royal Resorts board had wanted to be rid of him too, once. His shameful past of partying, drug addiction, and arrests hadn't exactly put him in league with his high-achieving family members. Which—if he was brutally honest with himself—was why he'd fallen into that bad boy spiral in the first place. He'd embraced his own failure without the embarrassment of trying to succeed first.

But he was trying now. Trying to rise up to impossibly high family expectations. To finally show that he had moved on from his past. That he wasn't that guy any more.

But listening to Chloe and Foster as they stood downstairs and argued, his failures all came rushing back to him. With his confidence shattered, Jordan turned away.

As he did, he caught sight of Marta. Chloe's personal assistant was standing at the other end of the hall. She had to have heard the whole thing. Marta gave him a sly, knowing grin then headed back into another room. The click of the door closing echoed loudly in Jordan's heart.

CHAPTER EIGHTEEN

Laguna Beach, California
Four long weeks without Chloe

"Ok, bye. Talk to you tomorrow." Jordan reluctantly ended the call with Chloe. He stuffed his phone into his pants pocket and stared out at the dark waters of the Pacific Ocean. *I need to tell her I love her.* He wanted to say it, but not over the phone. If he was ever going to attempt to have that sort of conversation with Chloe, then it had to be in person, not when there was five and a half thousand miles between them. And especially not when he wasn't 110 percent, *you can bet your life on it*, certain that his growing feelings were reciprocated.

It was late at night in California, but just after dawn in London. Why Chloe had to go all the way to England to finish up the final touches of her new album completely escaped him. "Anyone would think the US doesn't have recording studios," muttered Jordan.

Of course, when she had explained that the producer, she'd waited years to work with was based in the UK capital,

Jordan had been forced to concede the point. One of the first things he'd learned while dating a world-famous person was the need for compromises. And since their romance was still a closely guarded secret, Jordan found himself having to pivot more often than he was used to doing. More often than he liked.

He'd come to a decision. As soon as the Laguna Beach resort was up and running, full of happy, well satisfied guests he would ask Chloe to rethink their relationship. He planned to take her somewhere private where they could talk long and honestly about things. They had to come up with a plan for moving forward as a couple. Being with one another but at the same time hiding in the shadows, wasn't how he wanted things to continue. He wanted them to eventually step hand and hand into the light.

But not yet.

With a thousand balls all hanging in the air at the one time, the last thing he was going to do was to call his parents and inform them that he was in love with a pop star. Alice might see Chloe as being a positive thing in her son's life, but he worried that Edward would consider her an unwelcome and poorly timed distraction.

It was mid-May, and things between him and Chloe had been quietly simmering for the past two months. But for much of that time, she'd either been away in London, or on the publicity trail in the US. Her management never seemed to schedule any real time off for her.

I worry about her. About what this life does to her. These people who surround her don't really care about Chloe, they just see dollar signs. They make me sick.

"I miss my Chloe," he whispered to the waves. It had been four weeks since he had last held her, since they had made love. He'd never thought he would ever need the tender touch of a woman so much as he did each night as he lay alone in his bed. Chloe had stirred a hunger in him, that even regular hand jobs both morning and night couldn't come close to sating. He craved her touch. Her kisses. And her smile.

If he didn't have a billion-dollar resort launch on his plate, he would have got on a plane and gone to her.

He turned his gaze from the water to the bright lights of the main building of the Royal Resorts Platinum Collection, Laguna Beach. It was situated on the top of a long rise. Tradespeople were working late finalizing the laying of carpet and polishing the terrazzo in the resort's elegant lobby. If things went according to plan, the resort would be welcoming its first guests sometime in early September.

But that timetable wasn't the one Jordan was watching closely. It should have been, but his mind was constantly distracted by the thoughts of where Chloe was, and when he would see her again. She wasn't due back in the States until June. Another two long, lonely weeks without her. He raked his fingers through his short, spiky hair, wishing they were her hands not his own. This waiting was killing him.

I have time. We don't open for another three months. I could do a quick trip across the Atlantic to London. See Chloe and be back here before anyone even suspected I was gone.

A plan was quickly forming in his mind. If he got Sheila—who was currently working out of the Royal Resorts office in New York City—to run interference with his father, no one would be the wiser. All she would have to do would be to maintain the illusion that Jordan was still in California.

He hesitated for a moment. It would be well after midnight in New York. Calling Sheila at this hour would be selfish. Jordan retrieved his cell and tapped away a message to his assistant.

> Can we talk in the morning? I'm thinking of going to see Chloe in London for a couple of days. Thoughts?

> Hmm. Every 2nd word out of Edward's mouth is Laguna Beach

Sheila had to be up late working on her studies.

> But if he didn't know?

> Risky. But if only 2-3 days I could cover 4 U

It was unfair of him to put Sheila in such a tricky spot. She'd covered for him enough times over the years but asking her to lie to his father was a stretch.

But I want to see Chloe.

If anything happened, he would make sure to protect Sheila. He would take the blame, telling his father she hadn't known he'd gone to London.

> 3 days max

> You can't take RR jet. Need to fly commercial

Damn. He hadn't thought about that, but Sheila was right. He couldn't risk his father discovering that he'd taken one of the company jets. *Then again ...*

> I'll message you back in the morning. Thxs Sheila, you are a star

He might not be able to take one of the Royal Resorts jets, but he knew someone else who owned a plane. Jordan hit dial. When a half awake female voice answered, he smiled. "Me again. What would you say to having the *Chloe Jet* sent back to California to pick up a lonely billionaire and bring him over to London for a few days?"

The excited squeal from the other end of the line gave him just the answer he was hoping for. "I would say that's a brilliant idea. I'll get my team to sort it out this morning. Oh my god, I miss you so much. I can't wait to see you in the flesh. When can you leave?"

"I can be ready late tomorrow afternoon, just get Marta to liaise with Sheila and sort out the arrangements."

Jordan was still grinning like the Cheshire cat by the time he got back to his hotel suite in Beverly Hills. He was going to England, and soon Chloe would be in his arms once more.

"Are you sure that is the smartest thing to be doing right now? Think of the album. Foster won't be happy. You have to concentrate on your music." Marta threw up her hands in disgust. She was nothing if not predictable. Of course she was against the idea of sending the jet back to California to pick up Jordan.

"And anyway why can't he fly his own plane here? I thought he was a billionaire, or something like that." She nodded at Gabriela, her assistant's assistant, who in turn nodded her own fierce agreement. The tight blonde curls on her head bounced up and down. Hell would freeze over before sycophantic Gabriela ever dared go against Marta's opinion.

Chloe took her time and considered her response. She was well aware that there was little love lost between Marta and Jordan. And things with the album hadn't been going all that well. She was a good six weeks behind on delivering it to her record company. Foster was constantly on the phone berating her about the need to finish *the damn thing and get on tour*.

Everyone was pushing her. Expectations were set high. If she produced a less than stellar album, one which wasn't full of instant hits, she would be crucified in public. Her fans might eventually forgive her, but the press certainly wouldn't. The music industry seemed to revel in watching female artists fail. And pop princesses especially, were considered fair game. Too many people would take great delight in watching Chloe's Garden wither and die.

Right now, with all the world bearing down on her, the one person Chloe needed was Jordan. Even if he could only manage to come to London for a few days, it would be wonderful.

Chloe held out her hand to Marta. "Give me your cell." As soon as it was slapped into her palm, she opened it and tapped on the name *Chloe's Jet* which was on the contacts list. The number began to ring, and she handed the phone back to Marta. She had the number of the flight company on her own phone, but arranging the jet was Marta's job.

I pay her to do this.

"I want Mister Jordan Royal to be VIP boarded at Van Nuys airport and flown to London City Airport tomorrow night Los Angeles time. When you have the arrangements and details sorted, please send them to Jordan's assistant, Sheila. Oh, and send them to me as well."

Chloe headed back toward the recording studio booth. She had pickups to finish on one of the songs. Reaching the door, she turned and gave Marta a blank look. She was determined that her personal assistant wasn't going to get any sort of rise out of her. "Jordan is coming to England on my private jet because I asked him to—that is all either of you need to know. Sometimes I think you forget who works for who."

Her heart was still racing as she took her place in front of the microphone a few minutes later. She'd known she should stand up to her people, but until Jordan had come into her life, she had never dared to do it. The mean girls had run roughshod over her all these years.

No more. I am going to start taking control of my destiny. I will make Jordan proud. Actually scratch that, I will make me proud.

CHAPTER NINETEEN

The glamorous Chloe Jet
  Van Nuys Airport, Los Angeles

Jordan took a seat onboard the famous white and red livered *Chloe Jet*. From what he understood, the plane wasn't just a plane, it was a shining beacon of hope for Chloe's fans. For all those who believed in the power of dreams. Of finding success.

It was a little difficult for him to understand how others could view a private jet this way. Having grown up flying in them from a young age, Jordan saw them as little more than flying cars. It only took a phone call or a quick message to an assistant and one of the Royal Resorts jets would be at his disposal.

But this was Chloe's jet. The interior had been custom fitted with red and white striped seats. The carpet was a plush fire-engine red. Silver fittings and a giant TV screen definitely set it apart from the usual corporate planes he flew in. Alice Royal had always had the final say in the fit out of the family homes and private jets, and she wasn't one for shows of glitz and glamor. Then again, Alice wasn't a pop star.

He'd just got a few things out of his travel bag for the flight, ready to settle in and catch up on some reading, when a loud and all too familiar obnoxious voice filled the cabin.

"I shouldn't have to wait until after we take off to get hot food. You know who I am. I demand full service. Don't make me have my executive assistant call your boss. Because if that happens you will be looking for a new job."

Oh, no ...

Jordan lifted his gaze and took in the sight of Chloe's manager Foster as he stood towering over the flight attendant. The poor woman who had greeted Jordan with such a lovely welcoming smile and perfect service was literally quaking in her shoes.

"I'm sorry, sir, but we weren't informed of your arrival until just now. The schedule only had Mister Royal flying with us to London this evening. I will make the best accommodations that I can, but you must understand that I cannot have the food prepared and do the safety check all at the same time. If you would like to take a seat, I'll bring you a beverage and some food as soon as possible."

"Well you don't seem to understand how important this trip to London is, and Ms. Fisher will certainly hear about your attitude once I land."

Foster shoved his alligator skin briefcase into the poor woman's hands then headed further into the cabin. He stopped at Jordan's seat and huffed. "And someone is sitting in my seat."

Sorry, Papa Bear, but Goldilocks ain't moving.

There were plenty of other perfectly good seats on the plane, including a separate bedroom at the back which Jordan had already snagged, but that was beside the point. He didn't flinch when Foster bent and growled at him. "This is all your fault. If her pussy wasn't doing the thinking for her, this album would have been finished weeks ago."

Jordan lifted his face and gave Foster a sweet smile. "I think you meant my magic cock is what's making her question things. Perhaps that's why Chloe is struggling with the album, she's actually reaching for some happiness."

He hated that Foster was once more trying to lay the blame for the album's issues at his feet. Unfortunately Chloe's asshole manager wasn't entirely wrong. Yes, he was wrong about the relationship, but not about the music. The album wasn't going as well as it should.

The tracks Jordan had already heard were great, but even he'd been forced to quietly agree with those in the know, Chloe's album was missing a killer track. It was customary for an artist to have at least one song on an album which defined it. Whatever that meant. Jordan liked his music, but he wasn't so heavily into it that he felt any particular song could stir his emotions so much that he would class it as being exceptional.

"I'm glad you think this is all a bit of a fucking joke, just remember that when Chloe is the one picking up the tab for the extra production costs and release delays."

Chloe's album recording and the impending Laguna Beach resort launch couldn't have come at a worse time. They were both trying to focus on major projects while at the same time keep the flames of their romance still burning bright. So many famous relationships had failed due to competing career demands, but Jordan was determined that his and Chloe's love would not end up on that long and sad list.

Hiding their love from the world was hard, but he couldn't imagine how difficult it would be if they decided to go public. *Not yet. Not until I'm sure about what is important in her life. If she really wants me.*

Foster righted himself, then moved further down the

cabin, where he then picked up where he had left off on his previous demands for food.

Great. I have a whole transatlantic flight of joy ahead of me.

He could give Foster use of the bedroom as a peace offering but decided against it. The man was a rude pig and deserved nothing.

The crew was continuing to make final flight preparations when Jordan's phone pinged. He glanced at the screen, quietly praying it wasn't his father.

> Heads up!!! Edward is looking for you. I have fobbed him off as best I can.

A heavy cloak of guilt settled on Jordan's shoulders as he stared down at the bright screen of his phone. He'd dreaded this. It was early evening in LA, which made it around eight pm in New York. Sheila wouldn't be sending him a message like this unless it was urgent.

His assistant's text held all the warnings of impending trouble. She was always short and to the point with her words, but Jordan could read the worry in her brief message. If his father got wind that he was in London, not California …

He picked up the phone and called Sheila. She answered immediately. "Please tell me you are still in LA."

"I'm at the airport, on the *Chloe Jet*. We are due to take off in the next half hour. Did Dad say what he wanted me for?"

"You need to get off the jet. I overheard Edward's EA talking just now. Your father left for California midafternoon. He's only an hour or so out of LA. From what Janice said, Edward is going to head down to Laguna Beach as soon as he lands."

Fuck. Fuck. Fuck.

If his father arrived in LA and discovered Jordan had gone to England, there would be all hell to pay. Bryce would be tasked with the job of hunting him down in London and on behalf of their father would be compelled to hand Jordan his ass.

He'd told Chloe enough of his past mistakes for her to have a good understanding of why this new resort was so important. Of the heavy expectations placed upon him by his family and the board of Royal Resorts.

Jordan rose from his seat, with his free hand he began stuffing his things back into his travel bag. He'd made a foolish mistake. He should never have got on this jet. "Ok. I am getting off now."

I'm sorry Chloe.

He caught a movement out of the corner of his eye and turned his head. A slyly smiling Foster stood in the aisle. He had to have heard the conversation. The second Jordan lifted his bag from his seat, Foster pushed his way forward and dropped into the chair. He motioned toward the jet's main door.

"Don't let it hit you in the ass on your way out."

Jordan gritted his teeth and headed for the exit. Foster might well be making demands about the flight's catering, but all he could taste was the bitterness of defeat.

This will break her heart.

Crossing the tarmac, he tapped out a brief message to Chloe on his cell phone.

> Sorry. I'll call when I can.

CHAPTER TWENTY

Chloe had wished for the chance to work with Kevin Smith for as long as she could remember. The Jamaican producer had a reputation for bringing out the best in an artist. For finding the emotional seconds in a song that even the original songwriter didn't know existed. He was experienced and supremely talented. Fortunately for Chloe, he also had the patience of a saint.

Long past the time when her regular producer would have called the track finished, Kevin had Chloe back in front of the microphone trying new approaches to her work. Every hour she spent under his musical direction she felt herself grow as a singer.

But growth and creativity were not what mattered to her manager Foster, or apparently the record company. The time Chloe was spending in the studio was costing money. And when Kevin Smith was in the chair, that meant big money.

It was well past midnight. Through the glass window of the live studio Chloe could see into both the control room and adjoining lounge. In the control room, the dreadlocked Kevin sat at the desk busily working, while in the lounge next door, Marta lay on one of the couches with her face turned to the wall. Gabriela, had been handed the job of going out to the airport and greeting Jordan when the *Chloe Jet* arrived in London.

Chloe was so over this song. She hadn't wanted to put it on the album, but the record company had vetoed her original choice, and insisted she cut this track. It wasn't a bad song, just not one of her best. Besides there were only so many ways she could work her vocal talents into the music.

The song wasn't coming together—her heart just wasn't in it. *I knew it wouldn't work, but they wouldn't listen.* And if the expression on Kevin Smith's face was anything to go by, they were still a long way from making magic.

She stepped up to the microphone, ready for yet another take but Kevin's attention had turned elsewhere. The door of the control room was open, and a grim-faced Foster stood on the threshold.

What? That's all I need. More pressure.

Marta appeared at Foster's shoulder. She brushed her fingers through her hair, before making a great show of welcoming him. They hugged one another. It was sickening. Especially since Foster being here could only mean one thing. Marta had got in touch and let him know that Jordan was coming to London. Her assistant hadn't taken kindly to being told what to do and decided that some petty payback was in order.

Chloe puffed out her cheeks. She was tired. Tired of the album. Tired of the bullshit. Her only joy was the prospect of getting out of here and going to find her man. Sharing a night of passionate love making with Jordan was exactly what she needed. What she craved.

A horrible thought slipped into her mind. If Foster had just arrived, it surely meant he had come with Jordan on the *Chloe Jet*. And if he was here then where was Jordan?

Chloe turned toward Kevin, sending him a pleading look. He nodded his understanding and held up his hand. Over her earpiece came the words she was hoping to hear. "Chloe, baby gal, let's call it a *nite*. I'm *tiad* and you need to rest your voice."

Kevin moved away from the mixing desk and after hurriedly ushering Marta and Foster out of the room began to pack up his things. Typical of them they had rudely barged in and taken over the man's creative workspace. Kevin Smith was a musical genius, but the members of her management and entourage had treated him as nothing more than a well-paid hack. Chloe slipped her headphones off and headed for the exit.

When she reached the lounge, she gave Foster a curt, "Hi." Her gaze searched the rest of the room, hoping that perhaps Jordan had politely lingered outside the studio, waiting for her to come out.

"If you are looking for your toy boy, Chloe, he didn't make the flight. Apparently, his daddy snapped his fingers and Jordan went running. Said he had more important things to do than go all the way to London for some stray pussy."

Marta snorted at the spiteful remark. "Of course he did. He doesn't see Chloe as someone important. Not like we do." She handed Chloe her phone. "Silly me, I forgot to mention, he left you a message hours ago. It was so pathetic that it slipped my mind."

The little spark of joy in Chloe's heart flickered and went out. Jordan wasn't coming.

When she got back to the hotel, she called Jordan. Her call went straight to voicemail. He'd put his family ahead of her. Of course he had. They were family.

And I am not.

CHAPTER TWENTY-ONE

According to the flight tracker app, Chloe's plane was only an hour out of LA, so he should have been able to reach her. Seated at his temporary desk in the management suite of the Laguna Beach resort, Jordan had been trying to call Chloe for the better part of an hour. His calls kept going to voicemail. After six endless weeks separated from her, patience was not Jordan's strong suit.

I just want to tell you how proud I am. Five All American Music Awards nominations is amazing.

The award nominations had been announced earlier that day and it seemed the rest of the world was calling Chloe. He would have to wait until her plane landed to share this fabulous day with her. Hopefully her new album would be received as well as the one she'd released the previous year. *Five nominations, wow. She deserves to win them all.*

The September opening day for the Laguna Beach resort was approaching much faster than he wished. Jordan was feeling the pressure. It might only be a soft opening, but resort reviewers and the press would still be sniffing about, looking for signs of success, and failure.

It seemed that every decision which had to be made somehow found its way across his desk. With Sheila flying back and forth from New York, he was finding it hard to manage the day-to-day process. How the hell Bryce handled the whole of Europe, and the UK was beyond him. Jordan was fast gaining an appreciation of his brother's executive skills.

He'd resisted the temptation to call Bryce and ask for his advice, worried that the minute he did, his brother would wonder if he was up to the challenge. And despite all of this going against his better judgement, he couldn't overcome his desperation to succeed on his own terms. To finally shake off his old reputation.

I wonder what Dad would say to me hiring an assistant manager. Someone to handle the annoying things, like staff rosters and guest supply orders.

But if he hesitated when it came to talking to Bryce, he was even more reluctant to confide in his father. Knowing Edward, he would start asking uncomfortable questions. Jordan's history of messing things up still hung over him even after all this time. He wondered if he would ever be able to shake his past off, if he would ever come up to the exacting standards demanded by Royal Resorts.

I have to stop comparing myself to everyone else in the family and make some decisions. I shouldn't ask, I should just do.

He penned a note to himself in his planner. *Hire assistant mgr. urgently.* If there was one thing, he did have in common with Bryce's management technique it was his love of a good, old fashioned paper journal.

Sitting back in his chair, Jordan turned to gaze out the window. His office overlooked the seventh hole of the resort's golf course—in the distance was the blue of the Pacific Ocean. He'd much rather be out there on the greens than in here, wading through a never ending stream of emails. His daily email count was well over two hundred. Every morning Jordan woke to at least one hundred more of them, all marked urgent, all vying for his attention.

His previous work with Royal Resorts had never had him down this much in the weeds. The amount of detail that went into launching a resort bordered on insane. He had department heads under him, and a functioning management team, but apart from Sheila, so many of his staff were barely past the stage of being raw recruits. He hadn't expected to encounter the labor shortages which existed in LA. Inexperienced resort staff meant Jordan was left managing many problems himself.

"This is not what I thought this gig was going to be," he muttered.

In one smooth move he turned back to his laptop and closed the lid. Rising from his chair, Jordan grabbed his jacket and cell. The emails, phone calls, and people who regularly cluttered the doorway of his office were all going to have to take a backseat today. He had other priorities.

Today Chloe was coming home.

He fired off a message to Sheila.

> If anyone is looking for me, I'm out of the office for the rest of the day. Going to look at bed linen.

His assistant's reply had him smiling.

> Send Chloe my love

Chloe's joy at being home was short lived. As soon as the limousine turned into her driveway, she spotted Foster's black and orange insanely priced sportscar parked close to her front door. In typical Foster fashion he had blocked the entrance, forcing her driver to park further away and Chloe to step around the vehicle in order to get into her own home.

She'd had a couple of peaceful weeks in London without him. His stay in the English capital had been mercifully short. It was clear that once he'd delivered his message about finishing the album, he felt he didn't need to stay. The fact that Jordan hadn't made the trip likely also had a major bearing in Foster's travel plans, but Chloe dared not bring that topic up.

She braced herself. If Foster was here, it was because he wanted to talk. And as things currently stood between them, talking usually meant him berating her until she caved.

I'm so over all this drama. As soon as this album launch is done and dusted, I'm going to start looking for a new lawyer. And then a new manager.

"Now, we need to talk gift bags for the album launch. And also special bonus presents."

Chloe shook her head at Marta's left-of-field suggestion. They had just arrived back in the States after a long flight from England. Gifts for the launch party were not something she really should have to get involved in. And as for the special bonuses, Marta had already decided that she and Gabriela should be gifted new cars.

At the front door of the house, Chloe stopped and faced her personal assistant. She sighed. As she saw it, there were two ways she could answer Marta. One was to tell her to go home, and they would talk about things later. Or two, pander to her demands. A rational person would have seen that this was not the time to be asking about presents, but Marta's self-interest had always ruled.

"Why don't you go home and unpack, and then when you are done go and visit a dealership to choose which make and model you want. Gabriela might want to come with you. Then we can discuss gift bags. How does that sound?"

If I am serious about looking for new management, I can't have these two women hanging around my home all the damn time.

Marta's gaze flittered briefly to Foster's sportscar, and Chloe could almost hear her debating as to whether she should head inside and fawn all over him or go and select her new car.

"Ok, I'll go. See you a bit later."

"Take the rest of the day off, you deserve it. Besides I've got some other things to do once I've seen Foster."

Her personal assistant moved closer and took a hold of Chloe's hand. "You're seeing him again, aren't you?"

Chloe nodded. She hated the way that Marta took pains never to speak Jordan's name. "I haven't seen Jordan in a month and a half. He's coming here in a little while, so it would be nice for the two of us to have some privacy."

"Alright, but I want to say something, and for you to take it with all the love that I have for you. You might be the world's biggest pop star, but you will never be good enough for him. All the expensive gifts and phone calls in the world won't make up for the fact that he put his billionaire papa ahead of you, Chloe. Tell me, does his daddy even know you exist?"

That remark hit home. As far as she knew, Edward Royal had absolutely no idea about her and Jordan's romance. Marta's hold tightened and a knot of tension grew in Chloe's stomach as she replied. "Jordan and I have agreed to keep our relationship private for the time being."

She didn't believe that lie, and from the look on her assistant's face, neither did Marta. Out of the corner of her eye, Chloe caught sight of Foster as he stepped out from the house. The knot in her stomach twisted and burned. Her manager and assistant were going to tag team one another.

"Marta is right. The Royal family is part of New York City high society. You might be world-famous, Chloe, but they will always view you as a white-trash brat from Nebraska. You'll never be good enough for them. Face it, they are not your people." He pointed to Marta and then himself. "We are your people."

She's been crying. The telltale tracks of tears were still fresh on Chloe's cheeks when Jordan arrived at her home early that evening. Despite his best endeavors, his plans to leave the Laguna Beach resort and head up to Beverly Hills had been hampered by design staff and contractors intercepting him on his way from the office to his car. The official handover from the resort builders to Royal Resorts was scheduled for next week, and it seemed that a million minor things still had to be ticked off before then.

The completion handover was a major milestone for the project, and one which couldn't be missed. If the certificates were not exchanged on that day, the party at fault would be facing penalties. He had to make sure that Royal Resorts fulfilled its side of the contract.

But all of it meant nothing compared to the joy of finally seeing Chloe and holding her in his arms again. A joy that disappeared the second Jordan set foot inside her house.

Someone had hurt her. She managed a whispered, "Jordan," before stepping into his embrace. Jordan wrapped his arms around her and let the silence of the house envelop them. He knew enough about this girl to know that she would want physical comfort first. When she was ready to talk, she would.

With his chin resting on the top of her head, Jordan closed his eyes. He'd missed her, but he hadn't realized just how much until this moment.

Jordan brushed his hand over Chloe's hair, then gently tipping her head back, captured her mouth in a long lingering kiss. Every fiber of his being rejoiced in the taste of her lips. Of her scent.

I've missed you. But something is wrong.

"Have you been crying? Why?"

Chloe shook her head. "No. Yes. Oh, it's all so horrible. The album is finished, but it's not the best work I've ever done. I don't know how the fans are going to receive it. No one loves it, and ..." She sighed. "I'm just so damn tired."

He sensed there was more. He knew deep down there had to be something gnawing at her soul. "What else? What have Marta and the others been saying?"

"Nothing."

They might not have seen one another in person for some time, but Jordan had learned enough of Chloe's tells via Zoom and messenger video calls to sense that she was worried about more than just the album. "Please, sweetheart, tell me what has you in tears?"

"My people keep saying that you are ashamed of me, and that's the real reason why we haven't gone public with our relationship."

Bloody Marta, Gabriela, and Foster. They had been working on Chloe's insecurities making her feel that she was less.

I want the world to know about us, but I just don't think I have the capacity to handle all the attention from the press right now, not with the resort launch getting so close. But how do I tell her that without her thinking I'm rejecting her?

Jordan brushed a kiss over her lips, fighting the growing hunger for her body. This conversation was important, even more important than getting naked and heavy with one another. "I want us to go public."

Chloe's eyes lit with happiness. "That's great! We can do it on the red carpet at the All American Music Awards on the fourth of July. That would be the perfect time for us to make our relationship official. Oh, Jordan, thank you."

Damn. That's not what I was going to say.

Jordan steeled his nerves. He could just imagine his father's reaction when he discovered that instead of his son focusing all his attention on the launch of the billion-dollar resort, he'd been busy seducing a pop star. It might not be the truth, but it would surely be how Edward Royal saw things.

"Um, look." *Shit. Double shit.* "Maybe lets hold off on the red carpet appearance. Let's not rush things. We haven't seen one another in weeks, so maybe now is the time to slow it all down. Then when we feel we are ready, we can talk about our future."

He hated himself for being the one to wipe the joy from her face.

"You don't want to tell the world about us?"

This was not the homecoming she'd been hoping for—Jordan was unsure of them. Instead of being happy about her suggestion for them to debut their relationship at the awards show, he'd put the brakes firmly on. *Talk about our future.* She hated how that sounded.

Had their time apart changed the way he felt about her? She'd worked her guts out in London, put long hours in at the studio, in order to get the album finished and be able to come home to him. And now this, the all too horribly familiar feeling of someone preparing to take themselves out of her life.

He's pulling away. Oh god, were Marta and Foster right all along?

"It's not that I don't want to tell everyone about us. It's just that I have so much on my plate at present. The resort is ... well, it's a much bigger job than I ever thought it would be, I barely have a moment to myself. From the time I wake to the time I go to sleep I'm ticking things off lists. People are constantly in my face wanting decisions. I just don't think I can take on the extra wrinkle of us going public. Or of having to defend our relationship to my family."

Wrinkle? Is that how he sees us? As a problem, something to solve or smooth out.

"Ok, so if you can't come to the awards, will you come to the album launch?"

He'd said for them to slow things down. She wasn't stupid, every woman knew that was man code for 'let's take a break.' And what the hell did *defend their relationship* mean?

"I'm in an impossible situation here, Chloe. I want to come to the launch—you have no idea how badly I want to be there to support you and acknowledge the incredible work you've put into this album— but it would have to be in the capacity of a guest. And if work commitments stop me from making it on the night, I hope you'll find a way to understand. I'm not doing this to hurt you."

A guest. Not a friend. Not a lover. Nothing official.

Chloe wiped away a tear. This was not how she had imagined their reunion would play out. Foster and Marta had done their usual number on her pride earlier today, and she'd been hoping, praying, that Jordan would bring her back. And yet here he was, stonewalling her. Confirming what her people had told her. That the Royal family would never see her as good enough.

"Are we breaking up?" She had to know. Was this the end? If it was, she hadn't seen it coming.

CHAPTER TWENTY-TWO

She didn't have time to protest before his arm came round her waist, and he pulled her hard against him. "Goddamn it, we are not breaking up, Chloe."

His lips came crashing down on hers in a fiery demanding kiss. Chloe clung to Jordan as he deepened the embrace, his tongue stroking masterfully over hers. In between breaths, he murmured, "You are mine. No one else. I won't let them tear us apart."

"Jordan," she sobbed. He wasn't leaving, he was here.

Please don't ever leave me. Please.

They'd have to talk things over, but right now, being with him was all that mattered. Touching. Skin on skin. She would remind Jordan just how good they were together.

Chloe's loose leisure pants were no match for Jordan's skillful fingers. He slid them down her hips, and then went for her underwear. As soon as she was naked below the waist, he lifted her onto the table and lay her down, spreading her legs open. Her heart was racing as she stared up at the ceiling, her sex throbbing with anticipation of what was to come next. God, she had missed this man.

There was a scraping sound as a chair was pulled into place, and Jordan sat down.

"I haven't had a bite since lunch, are you going to let me taste you Chloe? Actually scrub that, forget I asked. I'm a greedy boy so I'm just going to go ahead and eat you out."

Oh god. Yes. Yes.

His hot breath blew on her clit, sending shivers down her spine. When the tip of his tongue flicked over her pleasure bud, Chloe's back arched off the table. He rose from the chair, burying his face into her sex. She cried out. "Jordan!" It was too much. All too much. And then not enough.

The heady torture he inflicted on her with his tongue and mouth was exquisite. He fed on her like a man who'd been starved for days. For months. She grasped his hair in her hands and held on tight. He gave no mercy, not a moment to catch her breath. Up the mountain they raced, and right to the edge of climax. She was a sobbing, needy mess.

Only then did he spare her, drawing back to gaze down on her. A wicked, wolfish smile set on his glistening lips. "Oral or cock?"

Her scattered mind struggled for words. But she knew what she wanted. What she craved. "Cock. All of it, deep and hard. No mercy."

Chloe barely had time to draw breath as Jordan rolled a condom on, then grabbing her by the hips pulled her to the edge of the table. Lifting her legs, he placed them either side of his head, then pushed his cock slowly into her. *Oh yes.* This was so much better than trying to talk. Their bodies knew how to communicate.

"I've missed this pussy. My pussy," he growled.

He went gentle and slow at first, giving her the chance to become accustomed to the depth and position of his erection. But the second she whispered, "Now. Please, Jordan," he released his restraint and gave her everything.

As Jordan flicked his thumb over her clit, Chloe raced straight back up the mountain and over the edge. She fell into a deep chasm of pulsing orgasmic pleasure.

His hands gripped her flesh hard as he pounded her sex. *Slap. Slap. Slap.* She loved being ravished by this man. Taken. Branded. He finished in a flurry of hard, deep strokes then stilled. "Chloe I …" Jordan's words trailed off.

She lay utterly spent on the table, but as her mind cleared her thoughts focused on what he'd said, or rather what he hadn't said. Had he almost said the L word? Jordan was reluctant for them to go public, but he might well be ready to say he loved her.

Don't risk it. You've just had a fight.

What would she do if he did say he loved her, and could she find the courage to finally speak those words to someone else and actually mean it? For her the word love had never meant what it did for most people. To her it had always been a form of manipulation.

He slowly withdrew from her body, then helped Chloe to sit upright. While she dressed, Jordan disappeared into one of the nearby bathrooms to deal with the condom. When he returned, she steadied her nerves, ready to stop him from declaring his affections.

"I think you're right. Let's take things slowly. Now isn't the time to be making rash decisions or offering up grand statements to each other."

If he wasn't ready to go public with their relationship, she didn't want to hear those three little words. Words that would change everything. It all made perfect logical sense, but her heart still cried out. *Tell him you love him. Don't give him the chance to ever leave you.*

His brows furrowed. She'd caught him off guard. "I'm sorry if any of what I said hurt you, I just think slow and steady is the best thing. We both have a lot on and forcing things might end up becoming a mistake."

She shoved down her feelings of disappointment. In her mind's eye she'd built this reunion up to be something much bigger. She'd expected a sweeping soundtrack and a room full of flowers, not an argument and hasty sex on the kitchen table.

Silly Chloe, when will you learn that life isn't one of your love songs.

The urgent buzzing of a cell phone cut the air. Her sense of inadequacy only heightened when Jordan answered the call. "Jordan Royal." He listened while whoever was on the other end of the line spoke. "Now? It's late." More listening. "Ok, yes, I'm on my way." He hung up the call, and Chloe braced herself.

"That was the head contractor at the resort. He needs to go over the final work at the beachside café tonight so it can be signed off for completion."

He'd fucked her, and now he was leaving. She could handle almost anything, but not abandonment. This was not how their story was meant to be playing out. Jordan should be staying. Sleeping in her bed and making slow wonderful love to her in the morning. Not slinking off into the night while her body was still thrumming from his touch.

If he doesn't want to be here, then I can't make him stay.

Her heart and mind were still in a whirl, as Chloe moved to the front door. She opened it then stood back, resisting the temptation to usher him out.

"Call me when you have a spare minute."

She accepted his brief farewell kiss, then closed the door. As the sound of his car's engine slowly faded into the night, Chloe let the tears fall.

What the hell just happened?

He'd said she was his, but had her own lack of response to him saying those words make Jordan want to leave? And was that phone call just the thing he needed in order to escape, to avoid talking about them. She wanted nothing more than to hear him say he loved her but saying it back was easier said than done.

"I don't know how to tell him I love him."

And what if her inability to say those words ended up costing her the one man she wanted in her life.

CHAPTER TWENTY-THREE

Chloe's House
 Three weeks later
 The make-or-break album launch

Jordan was convinced that the sheer number of people crowded into the house would make anyone with an ounce of social anxiety immediately book an Uber the second they arrived. The crush of bodies was terrible.

He could only count one or two people he'd set eyes on before, and even then, he didn't know their names. The only people he was on any sort of standing with were Chloe and her inner circle. And from the look of it, they were all upstairs getting their pop princess ready for the album drop.

I think that's what they call it when you launch an album.

He was still a long way from getting his head around the lexicon of the music business. To Jordan's way of thinking it was less of a business and more of a circus. Clowns to the left of him, jokers to the right. He didn't give a damn about any of these people.

I only care about Chloe. I'm losing her, and I don't know what to do.

They had somehow managed to make it through the past few weeks without having had any real sort of conversation. Sex had become the way for them to communicate, but even then, the simple act of lovemaking had begun to lose it connection.

He and Chloe were constantly juggling competing calendars. His rare moments of spare time never seemed to match up with hers. He would arrive at her house just as she was leaving for a photoshoot. Foster and the rest of Chloe's people hadn't done anything to make their lives easier. All they seemed to care about was the album.

She is just a commodity to them. A product. None of these people here care about Chloe or what this is doing to her.

The album's release was late, and the record company had pressed for Chloe to release it on a short pre-order window. If her album dropped just before the All American Music Awards on July fourth, then while the fans were out celebrating her old music, they would be primed to go and buy her new stuff. Jordan couldn't fault that logic.

When a smiling waiter graciously offered him a glass of champagne, Jordan waved the guy away with a polite, "Thanks, but no." How anyone with an addiction could manage to stay clean in this world of constant temptation was beyond him. He hadn't had a drink in almost five years, but even he was feeling the thirst tonight. The small clusters of people huddling in private corners bent over what surely had to be lines of cocaine didn't help with his mental fatigue.

His phone buzzed in his jacket. Jordan pulled it out. *Please don't let it be another crisis at the resort.* His heart sank as he checked the screen. The name Chelsea FC shone bright. Edward Royal followed Chelsea Football club in the English Premier League.

Scratch that, I think a crisis might be better. Terrible timing, Dad.

He was in a crowded room, with dozens of important music industry people, all talking at the top of their voices, all vying for mastery of the scene. Jordan headed for the door to the patio, hitting receive as soon as he stepped outside. "Hi, Dad. Give me a second to find a quiet space."

"Where are you for heaven's sake? It sounds terribly busy," asked Edward Royal, in his crisp British accent.

"Um ... just out and about in LA. You know how loud this city can be what with all the tourists." It was a strange thing to say but it was the first thing which popped into his head. Anything to set his father's mind at ease.

"Yes, I saw several coach loads of tourists on Sunset Boulevard earlier this afternoon. I think they were doing one of those homes of the stars tours, or whatever they call them."

Jordan's body tensed. His father was in LA. Again. Edward rarely travelled out to the West Coast, much preferring New York City, but he had made several trips to town of late. And if he was in town, then it meant he was on business and would want to visit the new resort. His being here, spoke of his father not fully trusting Jordan.

No it doesn't, he means he's a CEO making sure of a billion-dollar investment. You have to stop being so damn paranoid.

"So you are here? In LA tonight?"

A gruff laugh rolled down the phone line. "Well yes, I don't recall Sunset Boulevard being located in any other city of the United States. I was hoping that you and I could take a trip down to Laguna Beach and have a look at how things are progressing. I meant to come down earlier today, but I got stuck in meetings. And I can't delay our flight back to New York tomorrow morning as your mother has a gala dinner I'm expected to attend."

Our flight? Oh no. I'm meant to be going back to NYC with Dad. How the hell did I let that slip through?

He'd been writing the wrong date on documents all week. Still dating things as last week. Sheila had pulled him up on it twice already. Three was not the charm.

Jordan rubbed at his temple. *Damn.* He couldn't say no to the CEO of Royal Resorts. And he couldn't be in two places at the one time. Which meant, something had to give.

He lifted his gaze to the upper floor of the house, and the large window of Chloe's bedroom. Shadows moved among the bright lights. She would be surrounded by make-up people, her stylist, her management, and her two evil henchwomen. He wouldn't have a hope of getting two minutes alone with Chloe to explain why he was not going to be downstairs when she finally made her grand entrance.

The sickening mix of disappointed realization made his body feel heavy. There was no way out of his pressing work commitments. *I am going to miss the album launch.*

"That is alright isn't it, Jordan? I don't wish to be an inconvenience, I just want to take a look at our new resort. It would be nice for my son to show me how things are progressing. I trust that's not asking too much?"

His father was handing Jordan a large slice of paternal expectation. It came with lashings of hot, richly flavored guilt.

Jordan tore his longing gaze from Chloe's window and focused on the fairy lights which hung in the trees on the other side of the swimming pool. "Of course it's not too much, Dad. I was thinking of how you might be pressed for time when I was packing my suitcase earlier this evening. You know how time often loses meaning when you travel."

Oh great, now I'm quoting my secret girlfriend's song lyrics to my father.

"Yes, well that's why I have Janice, she makes sure I am where I need to be and on time."

His own assistant, Sheila was doing her best, but even she couldn't work miracles. Not when her boss wasn't fully paying attention.

It was well after nine, but Los Angeles traffic snarls were terrible even at this hour. It could easily take him over an hour and a half on the San Diego Freeway to get down to Laguna Beach.

"I'm a little way out of the city at the moment, so did you want to meet me at the resort?" offered Jordan. He would have to dash back to his hotel and quickly pack, then head down to the resort to meet with his father.

He'd lied in order to cover his mistake. An old, bad habit Jordan had tried his best to break. The pressure of the resort and his relationship issues with Chloe were beginning to take their toll. He was reverting to his default behavior of ass covering. His therapist would say he was actively avoiding issues, and in grave danger of following a well-worn path to disaster.

Jordan swallowed a lump of anxiety. It refused to stay down, instead coming back up as burning bile in his throat.

Just go pack. See Dad. Take steps you can manage.

"Excellent. I shall see you at the resort shortly, bye." And on that cheery note, Edward was gone. At least he'd made one person happy.

Jordan stood staring at his phone, torn as to what he should do. If he tried to go upstairs, there was every chance that the hyena pack would bar him from trying to enter Chloe's bedroom. The irony of him having woken in that same room earlier this morning wasn't lost on him.

And if I wait until she comes down, she is going to be more concerned with the album launch than talking to me.

This was Chloe's big night. Her time to shine. He had no

place in playing the pouting boyfriend or demanding to see her. Few people here even knew he existed. If he tried to get near Chloe, his actions might well cause a scene.

Marta and her cohort would make sure of it.

He was paying the price for refusing to let anyone know that he and Chloe were a couple. He'd put the resort ahead of her because he didn't want to fail his father, and in doing so, he was going to fail her.

His nerves were rapidly fraying, Chloe didn't need him adding his own problems to her night. That was selfish. But something had to give.

If a miracle happened and their relationship survived the next few months, as soon as he could get away from his obligations at the resort, he planned to whisk Chloe away for a vacation at the Royal family's private island in the Caribbean. And when he did, he would be making doubly certain that none of her people would be tagging along. The time would be spent alone with the woman he loved.

I will make all of this up to you, sweetheart. I promise.

With his father's urgent demand to see him, Jordan was torn. Chloe would be expecting to see his smiling face in the crowd tonight. To know that he fully supported her.

Edward wanted to talk about the billion-dollar resort down the coast. A resort that if successfully launched, might well have Jordan moving into prime position for a role on the Royal Resorts board. Only a short time ago, he thought that was what he wanted. Now, he wasn't so sure. Not if it meant having to be apart from Chloe for long periods.

If this is the life, then maybe it's not the sort of career or success I want.

Time was ticking away. If he was going to make it through the LA night traffic he would have to leave soon. Staying here, waiting for Chloe to make her grand entrance was no longer an option.

Jordan dialed Chloe's number and wasn't surprised when Marta picked up the call. "She's busy, it will have to wait. Go have a drink."

"Hi, Marta. I'm afraid it can't. I need to let Chloe know I won't be able to stay for the album launch."

He could just imagine the mileage Marta would get out of that juicy piece of information. His suspicions were confirmed when a flustered Chloe suddenly came on the line. "What do you mean you can't stay? Please, Jordan. This is important, I want you here. I need you."

Jordan braced himself. "Dad is here in LA, and he wants me to meet him down at Laguna Beach. And I have to go back to New York with him first thing tomorrow." He took in a long slow breath, steadying himself for the next piece of news he was going to have to deliver. The thought of the New York trip had brought to mind another of his forgotten commitments. "I'm so sorry, Chloe, but I won't be back in time for the All American Music Awards. If there was any other way, you know I would do it. Please, I'm doing my best."

Am I? It doesn't feel like it. Especially not when it comes to her.

She put him on hold, leaving Jordan to wait for a good long minute. When Chloe came back on the line, there was a cold, hard edge to her voice. "So, you blew me off over London. You are not staying for the album launch; and now you suddenly drop the news that you're flying home with daddy in the morning. And you don't give a damn about the awards show. I would love to have met your father tonight, but it's now pretty clear to me why you wouldn't think to invite him to my album launch. Or to my home. I'm good enough to fuck, but not good enough for the Royal family. Just go, Jordan. Worry about the people who are important in your life."

The line went dead.

He was certain that right this minute Marta and her friends would all be gathered around Chloe, giving her poison laced words of comfort. Telling Chloe how she was better off without him. How little he cared about her. How guys like Jordan were a dime a dozen.

Her new album was due to drop in less than an hour. He'd already done enough damage, he didn't want to add to her pain. Him going upstairs right now would only end in tears. The press would love to flood the internet with pictures of a broken-hearted pop princess crying during the launch of her new music.

Jordan headed back inside the house, making his way through the crowd toward the front door.

Near the exit, a large gifting table had been set up. Jordan glanced at the expensive gold, red, and white tote bags, all with the logo for Chloe's new album beautifully imprinted on them. Earlier in the day, a small army of assistants had taken over one of the downstairs rooms. The rustle of tissue paper and people checking off guest names had beat a steady cadence all afternoon. There had to be close to two hundred of the bags, all lined up in neat rows. At the end of one row were some specially marked VIP bags.

Jordan nodded to the two publicity assistants dressed in matching white strappy gowns standing behind the table. One girl had a giant clipboard in her left hand, and a red sparkly feather topped pen in the other. Seeing Jordan, one of the girls picked up a VIP gift bag. She took one step toward him then stopped. Her hand went to her earpiece. Someone from upstairs was giving her instructions. She offered him an apologetic smile, then retreated back to the safety of the table, and set his giftbag on the floor.

Chloe had every right to be angry with him. He didn't give a damn about the gift bag, he just couldn't bear the thought of being cut out of her life.

I swear I will make it up to you. You are important in my life.

On the driveway, Jordan pulled his cell out of his jacket. He started to tap out a message to Chloe. He sighed at his attempt at a feeble apology. The word *sorry* seemed so empty. It mocked him. *Is that all you can say to her, sorry?*

He didn't deserve Chloe, he probably never had.

Jordan Royal had wealth, good looks, and every advantage in the world, but he was just a guy who had no idea how to hold onto the woman he loved.

CHAPTER TWENTY-FOUR

"Now, I want to talk about the upcoming awards show. We really need to make a huge impact at the All American Music Awards to help push your new album," announced Foster.

Chloe was hung over, and only half listening to her manager—who was seated across the kitchen table from her. Still struggling with her sleep-deprived mind and aching heart, she squinted at him.

Really, can't I just draw a breath?

The album launch had gone off as they usually do, with everyone telling her it was her best one ever. That she would clean up at all the music award shows next year and how eager they were for her to make an announcement about a world tour. But for the first time in her star-studded career, Chloe didn't really care.

Jordan left last night. He's going back to New York this morning. I'm not important in his life. He doesn't love me.

She'd searched the crowd for him, in the vain hope he'd changed his mind and stayed, but Jordan had gone.

Her management team, ably assisted by Marta, Gabriela, and Stixxluv, had choreographed the whole evening down to the very last minute. Apart from the scant five minutes when she had given a live interview on her Instagram feed, Foster in his role of *manager to the star* had held onto her arm the whole time. It was suffocating, but as with all things relating to her career —apparently necessary.

By the time, Chloe had finally kicked off her Jimmy Choos, and got a glass of champagne in her hand, it was well past four in the morning. Eventually the crowd of well-wishers and industry folk filed out the front door, gorgeous and expensive giftbags in hand.

Among the few remaining gift bags was the one she had personally created for Jordan. The one with a classic Breitling watch inside. The bag Marta had made certain Jordan didn't receive as he left the house.

Morning had dawned on the Chloe website and the streaming platforms showing the results of last night's hard work. The new album merchandise was flying out the door, and she was the topic of every major fashion and music influencer on social media.

That was all good news, but her mind was filled with the worry of what had happened between her and Jordan. She could almost find it within herself to forgive him from having blown off her album launch to attend an important late night meeting. And while his unexpected trip back to New York and its calendar clash with the upcoming All American Music Awards had really hurt her feelings, she knew all about juggling commitments.

But her ability to understand and accept his behavior ended when it came to the thorny subject of Jordan's father. She would love to meet one of the members of Jordan's immediate family.

He wouldn't bring his dad to my home last night. Is Jordan ashamed of me?

Chloe knew how it felt to think she was not good enough. Rejection was an all too familiar emotion.

"My new signing, Sibling Rivalry, is the hottest band in the country at the moment. So, I'm thinking it might be a good idea to have your fans believe there is something between you and the lead singer Zapp. I can just imagine the two of you setting all of LA ablaze if you appear as a couple on the red carpet at the awards show on July fourth."

Chloe stirred from her sad, private musings. "What do you mean, something between us? I have a boyfriend."

Or at least she hoped so, after last night she wasn't so sure. She didn't know what to do about Jordan. She'd been strategically linked with other famous men in the past, but this thing with Zapp would be something else. When she'd pretended to date those other guys, she hadn't had a real boyfriend. Refusing to acknowledge Jordan's place in her life would be lying.

Isn't that what you have been doing for months? For years. How is this any different?

And would Jordan even care? The way things had gone last night, she was wondering just where his head and heart were at when it came to them.

"Um. Can I think on that for a moment, Foster? Maybe get back to you in a couple of hours. I need some sleep."

Foster rose from the table with an indignant huff and gathered up his things. "Alright, but don't take too long. I need to get this romance set up with the publicity people so they can start sending some rumors out to the press."

As soon as Foster had gone, Chloe headed upstairs. Alone in her bedroom, she locked the door. She called Jordan's number, but to her heart's sad disappointment, it was Sheila who answered.

"Hi, Chloe. I've just downloaded your new album. It's fantastic. Congratulations."

She'd gotten to know Sheila over the past few months, and they had become friends of sorts, but as much as she liked Jordan's assistant, she wasn't who Chloe was seeking.

"Oh, thanks, Sheila. Um ... I was wondering if I could talk to Jordan?"

"Jordan's in an executive meeting at the moment, and from the look of it, his diary is full for the rest of the day. Back-to-back appointments, I'm afraid. I can leave him a message and ask him to call you when he gets a spare minute."

A message. She was reduced to leaving messages. "Ok, could you please check and see when he is due back in LA. I really want him to come to the All American Music Awards on the fourth of July."

She wasn't giving up without a fight. They had to talk face to face. Jordan needed to understand her insecurities, and why she'd been so angry last night. If she could talk to him, then maybe he would at least agree to come to the awards. He didn't have to do the red carpet, but knowing he was in the crowd would mean the world to her.

"Of course, let me check his diary. Just a moment."

Chloe waited. This was the sensible thing to do. Sit down and discuss their relationship before things got completely out of hand. But her mind had other ideas, her childhood trauma seeped in and began to whisper.

You know this is how it always ends. With people not wanting to listen to you. With people walking out the door. Jordan won't come to the awards. Don't fool yourself that he actually cares.

Sheila finally came back on the line. "Hi, Chloe, sorry to keep you waiting. I've checked Jordan's diary, and from what I see he is not scheduled to be back in LA for another couple of weeks. Did he say anything different to that when you last spoke? He's busy and I know he can lose track of appointments, but I would be surprised if he hadn't at least mentioned the Royal family barbecue on the fourth of July. It's a big annual thing at his parents private estate in New York."

"Um, yes, I must have forgotten. Thanks, Sheila." She hung up the call. Jordan hadn't made any sort of mention about his family gathering.

I won't beg for his love. If I'm not a priority, then he should have the guts to tell me.

Chloe called her manager. "Hi, Foster. I've had a think about the Zapp idea. And, as usual, you're right about how this will help with the new album. I think we should go ahead and set up the fake romance."

It was her last roll of the dice. Throw another man in Jordan's face and see how he reacted. If things went how she hoped they would, he'd excuse himself from his family's party, get on a plane and come to her. If he didn't, she would accept that he didn't love her. That they were finished. After that she would do as she had always done.

Move on with her life.

CHAPTER TWENTY-FIVE

The Royal family estate
Fourth of July barbecue

The heady scent of the annual Royal family barbecue filled the air. From where he stood on the large stone patio, sipping an ice-cold homemade lemonade, Jordan had the perfect vantage point to observe the enormous hot plate containing enough meat and vegetables to feed a small army. He chuckled under his breath. "Who is going to eat all that food?" Between him, his parents, and younger brother they would be lucky if they made a small hole in the mountain of barbequed delights.

"It's lovely to have most of the family together for the fourth of July. I'm just disappointed that Bryce couldn't make the trip," remarked Alice Royal, coming to stand alongside Jordan. With the opening of a new resort in Edinburgh a matter of days away, the eldest Royal son had not been able to spare the time to come home.

The annual family get-together at his parent's home just

outside of New York City was an important event. Alice had gone to great lengths to have the house decorated in patriotic red, white, and blue. Even English-born Edward was decked out in an apron festooned with sparkly hamburgers and hot dogs. It was the one day of the year when he allowed himself to become an honorary American.

His father's halfhearted efforts at the barbecue were fortunately being closely overseen by the family chef, who pointedly refused to take the day off just in case something went wrong. Edward had a solid track record of burning the meat.

This should be a fun day, but I wish Chloe was here. Today would have been the perfect day to introduce her to my family.

He'd been an unmitigated ass to Chloe. Missing her album launch as well as the All American Music Awards had put him in the running for his own award. *Shittiest Boyfriend of the Year.* If such an award did indeed exist, he'd be a shoo-in for the prize.

She wasn't returning his calls. His emails went unanswered. There was anger in her silence. He'd sent flowers, but according to Sheila their delivery hadn't been accepted.

Their relationship was teetering on the verge of collapse, and while both were struggling with other pressing commitments, he was the one who had to shoulder a great deal of the blame for their current situation.

Once I get back to LA, we need to talk. I have to let Chloe know how I feel about her. We have to find a way to make this work.

He wasn't used to having this sort of relationship with a woman. By now he would have normally ended things, said goodbye, and walked away with no regrets. But what he had with Chloe was different. There was a connection he hadn't ever felt before, one he was desperate to keep. The problem was, he didn't have a clue as to how he could go about it.

"Earth to Jordan. Earth to Jordan. Are you receiving?"

Matthew's voice stirred Jordan from his private mental battle. He glared at his brother. "Very funny, Matty boy. Some of us have a lot of things on our plate at the moment. Not everyone has the time to go wandering the Colorado wilderness and staring up at the trees. Or was that hugging them?"

He got a clip over the ear for his troubles. On any other day if Matthew had done this to him, Jordan would have retaliated. But not today. His mind was too full of indecision for him to summon up the energy.

Over at the barbecue, Edward was protesting his meat-handling skills with the chef. Alice gave a *tsk* and hurried over to her husband.

That's one relationship that has stood the test of time.

While his parents had always made their marriage and family a priority, Jordan was frustrated with himself over not being able to do the same for Chloe.

Matthew gave him a gentle nudge. "I will have you know that my trips out to Colorado have not been all fun and games. The owners of the old Green Tree resort are still holding out for a ridiculous amount of money. And the planning laws in the city are designed to drive everyone mad. Your resort is almost finished, mine hasn't even started."

Be careful what you wish for, bro.

Jordan shook his head. In his current tired and distressed state, he couldn't muster an ounce of sympathy for Matthew. "Yeah, well when you wake to several hundred emails every day, then come and talk to me. Until then, you can keep playing at pretend. Trust me, it's better than the real deal."

"What's got you in such a down and miserable mood? I thought you'd be happy to be back home," asked Matthew.

He hadn't told anyone in his family about Chloe, but now seemed the right moment to share with his brother. "Can I trust you to keep a secret?"

"Hmm."

"You know the pop star Chloe? Well, I've been in a relationship with her for the past three or so months. No one else knows, so please don't tell a soul. Things aren't going great at the moment, and all the stuff with the resort launch is not making it any easier for us."

Matthew let out a low whistle. "Shit, Jordan. How on earth did you land a girl like Chloe?"

Their mother moved away from her husband and began to slowly make her way back toward where Jordan and Matthew stood. Any moment now she would be within earshot.

"I met her in Berlin. I think I'm in love, but juggling the new resort along with dad's sky high expectations is doing my head in. I just wish Chloe could be here with me today."

Matthew leaned in closer. "Priorities suck at the best of times. I hope you are doing everything you can to keep her. It would be brilliant if come this time next year she is able to be here with us."

"I'm trying. And yes, it would be wonderful for her to share this day."

As their mother drew closer, Jordan quickly changed the subject. "The staffing rosters are a struggle, finding good people is impossible."

"Yeah, I hear LA is a tough market," replied Matthew, loud enough for Alice to hear. She gave a tut of parental displeasure as she came to stand between her youngest two sons. "What have I said about not discussing business at family gatherings? It's hard enough to get us in the one place, at the one time, we shouldn't be wasting such an opportunity on talking about work."

"Sorry, Mom," offered the brothers. Matthew who was standing on the other side of Jordan and out of his mother's clear line of sight, gave him a wink. Jordan's secret would be safe.

"How long are you back in New York, Jordan? I've barely

seen you all year. It's bad enough that we haven't seen Bryce since Christmas." It was the first question Alice usually asked of any of her sons the moment they set foot in the front door when they returned home.

"What about me? I'm home all the time." Matthew huffed. Moving from his spot beside Alice, Jordan came to stand next to his brother. He slung an arm around Matthew, then dropped a wet, sloppy kiss on his cheek. "Yes, but you don't really count."

He turned back to their mother. "I'm booked in for a retreat this week, just a few days. A quick top up of the mental health. After that I'm back to California. Things are really ramping up at Laguna Beach, so I don't expect I'll be back on the East Coast before we do the soft opening in September."

A moment of silence followed, and he suspected that both his mother and brother were thinking the same thing. *Jordan is taking time to make sure he stays clean and healthy.*

Matthew patted him on the arm, and after slipping out of Jordan's hold, he headed over to where his father and the chef were busy turning the meat. Jordan was grateful for his brother allowing him a private moment with their mother.

Alice accepted Jordan's non-sloppy kiss on the cheek. "I know Matthew loves to tease you. In fact you both enjoy giving one another torment, but he does worry about you, darling. We all do. So tell me are you well? Are you happy?"

Alice, god bless her, kept to a regular schedule of checking up on Jordan's sobriety. He expected she was privy to his drug tests, but he was grateful that she didn't ever bring them up. Instead, his mother stuck to offering him words of support every six months or so. The Fourth of July and Christmas Eve had become by default those exact dates. No doubt she was also well aware of the company sanctioned *health retreats* Jordan attended at least once a year. Health retreat looked better in the board minutes rather than drug treatment facility.

"I'm okay, Mom. Busy, but I'm taking care of myself."

Alice nodded her silent acceptance of his words. Like all good mothers she worried about her children, but she didn't push things. Jordan was grateful for her support. Even now all these years later, he still carried the heavy burden of the memory of his mother signing the papers to admit him to the rehab facility. And as the nurse led him away, watching her collapse sobbing into Matthew's arms. It had been the lowest point of Jordan's life, one he was determined never to repeat.

The folly of not telling the rest of his family about Chloe now laid itself bare. If he'd been man enough to raise the subject months ago, he would be in a position to confide his relationship issues with his mother. As it was, his earlier choices now compelled him to hide the truth. More lies.

When will I learn that keeping things from the people, I love always costs me, and them, so dearly?

Alice would love Chloe, he was sure of it. His mom would see the amazing, sweet woman behind the bright pop star image, and welcome her into the family.

I want to tell her about Chloe, but then she would have to tell dad. I can't do it, not yet. A couple more months, then the time will be right.

In the meantime, he'd take Matthew's advice about doing his all to keep Chloe in his life. Tomorrow, he'd ask Sheila to reschedule the health retreat booking—a few weeks wouldn't hurt. It was more important for him to get back to California. Back to Chloe.

And save our relationship.

CHAPTER TWENTY-SIX

He wouldn't eat again for another week. The burgers and barbequed vegetables had been excellent. By the time he left his parent's home in the early evening, Jordan was certain he had eaten close to his own body weight.

His father had politely begged him to stay, but Jordan was determined to get home and watch the Fourth of July, All American Music Awards as they were streamed live from LA. As soon as they were over, he'd try and call Chloe.

Back at his elegant apartment in New York City, Jordan changed into a pair of sweatpants, grateful for their relaxed waistband. Clicking on the TV he tuned in to the station which was scheduled to be broadcasting the show. Shifting some clean laundry from his favorite spot on the couch, he settled in to watch. Jordan caught sight of his red and white *The World is My Lover* Chloe tour T-shirt which was on the top of the pile of clothes. Grinning as he recalled the night a well-sated, Chloe had given it to him, he snatched the shirt up and put it on.

Now I do look like a true Chloe fanboy. A member of Chloe's Garden.

But unlike all the other fans, she was the only one who screamed his name. Who sobbed *Jordan* as he brought her to climax.

I should have made her my priority. I should be with her tonight. I'm going to book the jet and get back to LA first thing in the morning. I am going to make everything right with her. I love this woman.

The big gold All American Music Awards symbol filled the screen. It was accompanied by the grand introductory music, and the voice of some well-known TV host.

The screen cut to an image of the bright lights of downtown California and the red carpet. Famous people and celebrities were all gathered in front of the cameras. All smiling, waving, and being utterly fabulous. Jordan didn't honestly give two shits about any of them—he wanted to see Chloe.

He'd been an utter dick. Too worried about the optics of all this and how other people would view it. About what his father might say. He'd let Chloe's possessive little entourage get under his skin. He was less of a man for it all.

Matthew had been right, priorities did suck. But only when you didn't understand which ones of them were truly important. What really mattered. Chloe mattered.

This amazing woman, who lights up my life. I've let her down. I've hurt her.

None of what anyone else might think of the two of them as a couple counted. No one else but him and Chloe. He loved her. He should have said something by now, but he'd allowed his constant self-doubt to hold him back.

The night she came back from London. I nearly said it then. Why didn't I?

The second he got back to LA, he would tell her how he felt. He would wait patiently for Chloe to rip him a new one, and then when she was done, tell him what she wanted. If it was him, then he was ready and willing to hand her his heart.

To take that risk. If she asked for them to go public, he would do it. All the lies and hiding would be behind them.

We can do this Chloe, you, and me.

"And now the moment you have all been waiting for, the arrival of pop princess, Chloe. Her latest album is racing up the charts. And ... rumor has it she has fallen in love with a sexy new man."

Jordan beamed at hearing those words. Was she sending him a signal through her publicity people? Letting him know that despite the missteps of the past few weeks, she forgave him. She loved him.

He clasped his hands together and sighed. "Oh, thank god. Chloe, I love you too."

His heart leapt as a vision of loveliness filled the screen. Chloe. His woman. She was dressed in a long rich red gown, with a stunning train. The bodice was almost nonexistent. The silken fabric showed a great deal of her breasts, and barely covered her nipples.

Jordan licked his lips. Stixxluv must have employed a great deal of Hollywood tape in order to keep Chloe's gown modest enough to pass the TV censors. Jordan might not particularly like her stylist, but the man knew how to dress the brightest musical star on the planet.

She looks so hot. I wish I was there with her.

His fingers itched to touch her naked skin, to shimmy that gown up her thighs and feast on her sex.

"Here is the man who is reported to have captured the queen of pop's heart. Zapp!"

Jordan's heart stopped beating in his chest. *What The Fuck?*

A tall, heavily tattooed male slipped his arm about Chloe's waist. But instead of her giving him a dirty look or taking a step back, she leaned in. She offered him her cheek, giving him a saucy grin as he placed a soft, teasing kiss on the side of her face.

Jordan shot off the couch. He shook his fists at the TV and bellowed, "Who the fuck is Zapp? And what the fuck is he doing with his hands on my fucking woman!"

The walls of the luxury apartment were sound proofed, and even if they hadn't been, Jordan wouldn't have cared. He was all for marching down to the center of Times Square and screaming out his rage.

"Zapp—lead singer of the heavy metal band, Sibling Rivalry, who have recently signed with Chloe's management—makes a wicked addition to her already star-spangled look. And you can see how the loved up couple have worked to coordinate their outfits. Zapp is wearing red leather boots, and a ruby earring. And that gown that Chloe is rocking, whoa! They are so unbelievably sizzling hot together. Someone get me a fan!"

The insanely irritating voice of the entertainment reporter kept droning on, but Jordan was no longer listening. His ears were full of the rush of his heated blood. Jealousy coursed through his veins, turning everything to fiery, volcanic lava. He stared at the television screen, his brain still struggling to register the truth of what his eyes were taking in.

She'd kicked him to the curb and moved on with another guy. He was in the past.

"No. No. That's impossible. She wouldn't do that to me. This is just punishment. Payback for me acting like a selfish prick."

God, he hoped that's what this was—Chloe seeking to cause him pain, for the hurt he had inflicted when he'd missed her album launch. And for every other time he'd let her down.

A commercial came on, and Chloe and her new man were

gone. Jordan scrambled for his phone, punching the button to call. She wouldn't answer, but he could leave a message. Heck, he'd leave a hundred if that's what it took to get Chloe to call him back.

On the fourth ring, Marta picked up the call. "Hello." Her voice was sickly sweet.

She wasn't going to grace him with saying his name, even though it would be right in front of her as she hit receive. *Petty bitch.* If there was one member of Chloe's crowd Jordan could own up to hating, it was Marta.

He sucked in a deep breath. "Hi, Marta. It's Jordan. I was wondering what time Chloe will be finished with the awards. I would like to speak to her when she is available."

I sound like I am trying to book an appointment with my doctor.

Silence sat on the other end of the line. He wasn't the least surprised. He could just picture Marta quietly composing a cutting remark or two. She seemed to have a particular skill for them.

"Jordan. Oh, yes. Thank you for calling. I'm sorry but I don't know when Chloe will be available—if ever—to speak to you. She has a new man in her life, and he is filling up her every waking moment. If you get my meaning."

Smarmy bitch, yeah, I get your meaning.

Hot tears stung his eyes. He was paying the price of having played cool with Chloe's heart. She had taken his insecurity, his lukewarm reluctance as an outright rejection. And now she was throwing it all back in his face.

He gripped the phone hard in his hand. "Could you please let her know that I called, and I will be waiting here for her to call me back."

"She said you might call, and I was asked to give you this exact message. 'I'm with Zapp now, don't bother calling again'."

The beep of the ended call echoed in Jordan's ears.

CHAPTER TWENTY-SEVEN

Jordan's brain was about ready to explode. He sat through the rest of the awards show, crying and pleading at the TV whenever Chloe got up on stage to accept an award. She'd been nominated for five of them and had won three.

Fate being a perversive creature of torture had made sure that the two other awards had gone to her new boyfriend's band. For three and a half agonizing hours Jordan sat, slumped on the floor of his living room, surrounded by an ever growing pile of scattered, soggy tissues, watching as the woman he loved thanked everyone for their amazing support. Everyone but him.

When an emotional Zapp personally thanked Chloe for her love and guidance, Jordan was all but ready to test the so-called unbreakable floor to ceiling windows of his apartment. The only thing which stopped him from launching the round silver paperweight which sat on the nearby side table, was the fact that Bryce had given it to him.

After all that shouting at the TV, his throat was rough and raw. His mouth dry. Jordan needed a drink. For the first time in a long time, he wanted a *real* drink. Anything to numb the pain.

He was in dangerous territory. Words of self-hate rose whispering in his ear. Telling him that just one drink would make him feel ok. He just needed one. And then he should call up an old dealer friend and see what else was on the menu.

No. Remember how far you have come. And the pain your fall would cause.

Jordan got to his feet, then slowly, methodically he cleaned up the mess. He yanked the Chloe tour T-shirt over his head and dangled it precariously over the top of the garbage disposal unit. "Fuck," he muttered, tossing the shirt onto the kitchen countertop. She might have torn his heart out, but he still couldn't throw it away.

The problem of having no alcohol in the apartment would be easy to overcome. It wouldn't take much for him to walk out of here, go downstairs and find a seat at a bar. It was the fourth of July, the city would be pumping. No one would notice one more casually dressed guy intent on getting seriously hammered.

His hands were trembling as he picked up his phone. More tears threatened when Sheila answered. "Hey, happy fourth of July from the Scottish contingent." In the background he could hear the thumping beat of a live band, and the roar of a hundred people all talking at once. The irony that Sheila was in a bar wasn't lost on him.

Words failed Jordan for a few seconds. The shame of finding himself in the place he was certain he'd left behind him for good, tore at his soul. The cold truth offered up a harsh lesson. Yet again he'd failed to acknowledge his weaknesses, to respect them. To learn.

He'd stopped going to meetings. Let one too many things

slide. Ignored the signs of impending doom. And the beast which lurked in the shadows had been waiting.

"I'm really sorry to call you on your day off. I just don't think this can wait. Could you change my booking for the health retreat. I need to go to the other place tonight." He wiped away a tear.

I am such an idiot.

The sound of the music and the crowd were gone in a matter of seconds. In their place Jordan caught the hum of street traffic. Sheila had immediately left the party. She was coming to his aid.

"Where are you? And have you taken anything?" Her questions were standard protocol. Blunt, but they would immediately inform both Sheila and the rehab people as to the severity of the situation with which they were dealing. Crisis management was her strong suit.

"At home. And no I haven't touched a drop or taken any drugs, but the cravings are building. The therapy at the normal place isn't going to cut it. If you can come, I'll get a travel bag packed. I'll really sorry Sheila, but I'm desperate."

"No need to apologize, I'm just glad you called. I'll have a town car waiting to meet you out the front of your building in half an hour. Do you want me to come with you?"

He nodded, grateful for her support. "Yeah. Please. I don't want to do the car trip on my own. I think I might need you to talk me down before we get out of the city. And Sheila, please don't tell anyone. I swear I am clean, I just need help."

"I'm on my way."

An hour and a half later, Jordan checked himself into a private drug therapy clinic in New Jersey.

CHAPTER TWENTY-EIGHT

He hadn't called. After the awards show and a long evening of interviews and photo opportunities, Chloe retrieved her phone from Marta's care and checked her recent messages and calls. There were dozens from friends and well-wishers in the music industry, but nothing from Jordan. Her silent treatment of Jordan, and then the grand Zapp reveal should have ensured an angry jealous response.

Not even a text. Am I that disposable?

He either hadn't watched the awards show—or if he had —Jordan hadn't cared enough about her to call. News of her and Zapp was all over the internet, Jordan couldn't possibly have missed it.

In the back of the limousine on the ride home after the whirlwind of after parties, Marta and Gabriela offered their heartfelt condolences. "I'm sorry, but we did tell you he was no good. Those sorts of guys, the ones who come from money, they don't treat women well."

"You will be better off without him."

"He was only holding you back."

"We are the only people who really love you."

Their words were cold comfort to a shattered heart.

She'd agreed to the Zapp experiment but not for Foster's reasons, that it would be good for album sales. Chloe had wanted to see what Jordan would do. Would her being seen in public on the arm of another man stir his jealousy? Make him finally take a stand for their love?

All she wanted was for Jordan to go into full cave-man mode, get on a plane, and come claim her. Take her to bed and fuck her brains out. To agree to make their relationship public, and finally admit that he loved her. Was that asking too much?

But silence had been his answer. She had so many unspoken words of rage rolling around in her mind. *Jordan doesn't care. He is ashamed of me. I'm not good enough.*

As the car pulled up out the front of her house, Chloe climbed out. Her assistants were still prattling on, offering their sympathies, but her thoughts were elsewhere. Her sleeping muse had woken. The lyrics of a song were forming in her mind. She didn't want to hear anything more from Marta or Gabriela, their words were just noise.

"Thanks for your support tonight, I appreciate it. I'm going to go to bed. I'm exhausted. I won't need anything else tonight, so the two of you can both go home."

Gabriela shifted on the seat and leaned out the car door. "Are you sure? My girlfriend is out of town this weekend, so it's not a problem if you need someone to sleep over."

"Thanks Gab, but I'm fine. Tonight was great. Three awards. And this dress made it to the top of all the best dressed lists. That's another win for Stixxluv and his talent. I'll see you girls tomorrow."

In the privacy of her bedroom, Chloe quickly changed out of her daring outfit, and gently peeled the Hollywood tape from her breasts. After scraping all the heavy makeup from her face and brushing out her hair, she hit the shower.

Standing under the hot water, her creative mind shifted into full flow.

At three am, she called and left a message on Kevin Smith's voice mail. "Hi, Kevin. It's Chloe. Do you remember how we said we were missing a killer track for the album? Well I think I might have found it a few weeks too late, but we could still release it as a single."

He called her straight back. "If you can describe the song for me in a couple of words, I might be able to fit you in, baby gal."

Chloe sucked in a deep breath. "How does a breakup, revenge song sound?"

"Get on a plane."

CHAPTER TWENTY-NINE

Laguna Beach aka Jordan's version of hell
  Mid-August.
  Five long weeks post break up

"And now for the song of the summer, the song which is on such high rotation at our radio station that we have stopped scheduling any other songs. Only kidding, folks. We thought the pop queen might have slipped with her latest album, but it turns out she was messing with us. And Zapp, wherever you are, bro, you picked the wrong woman to cross. So, here it is, Chloe's, 'Bitter Babe.'"

The opening strains of what was now a very familiar tune filled the cab of Jordan's SUV. He'd only been back at Laguna Beach for two weeks, exposed once again to the outside world, and he'd heard this song more times than his broken heart could count.

Berlin was cold, but you heated my blood

I thought I knew what pain was
But you took it to a new level
Am I bitter, babe
What do you think?

On the hour—every fucking hour—he was treated to the joy of what the press were calling Chloe's rogue revenge song. Rogue because it hadn't been on the album. Revenge, because Zippo or whatever his damn name was, had apparently been a douche and broken her heart. The fact that Chloe's rebound romance had been short-lived—barely three weeks—didn't make it any easier on Jordan. While he'd been stuck in rehab, she'd been busy with a freaking rock star. A douche who was now her ex.

The song was pure torture. He knew damn well that Chloe wasn't singing about the lead singer of Sibling Rivalry when she said he'd lied to her and stolen her happiness.

She was singing about him.

He flicked the dial in the SUV's entertainment system to another radio station. "Bitter Babe" was just ending on that one. "Who knows? I might make it all the way back to the resort without having to hear it in full again."

Then again, he might just start listening to the *This Date in Weather Podcast*. Hearing the guy list all the insurance losses was far more soothing than having to endure Chloe tearing literal strips off him over the airwaves.

The August weather in Laguna Beach was mild, but for Jordan he was living in the center of a burning hell. His former secret ex had written a mega hit in which she'd told the entire world what a piece of work he was, and he couldn't get away from it. All day every day, it found its way into his life. Whenever the song came on the radio in the office at the resort the staff turned it up. Jordan spent so much time gritting his teeth, that his jaw ached.

If the song had been the only issue in his life, he might have been able to handle it, but the resort launch was fast looking like it was going to be a billion-dollar failure. During his three week stay at the clinic in New Jersey, all the balls he'd been so desperately juggling had hit the ground. In his absence, Sheila had done all she could, but with his stay at the clinic a closely guarded secret, she'd had her work cut out for her.

I've been so focused on getting control of myself, that I've lost control of things here.

Once he arrived back at the resort, he parked his SUV and headed for the main office. He barely had time to throw his jacket over a chair and sit behind his desk before his new assistant manager Austin Brown appeared in the doorway and handed Jordan this afternoon's shitlist.

"The budget is over on food and linen. Oh, and the new wine delivery has been delayed by two days."

On and on it went. A never ending list of things that needed his attention. Jordan dragged his fingers through his unkempt hair and sighed. "Do you have any good news for me?"

Rehab had helped sort him out, but he was having to use every trick at his disposal to keep his mind focused on the job at hand.

The eager Austin brightened up. "I do actually. I'm thinking we could make some savings on the linen order. We won't be full when we open, and if we can get through the first couple of months without all those sheets and towels, we can use the money from guest receipts to fund the final part of the order."

Once they were open and the resort was running properly the respective team managers would shoulder the bulk of the workload. His job would shift to more of a hands-off management role. At the first chance he got he would be asking the board to find a replacement for him.

I don't want to manage a resort ever again. Not after this.

And while his assistant manager was full of good ideas, Jordan was quickly learning that when it came to resort launches, Austin was as green as him. They'd both read the books. Attended the lectures. Even watched while others did it. But it was a bit like having sex for the first time, until your dick was in the heat of a woman's body, and you had to move, you weren't quite sure if you had the hang of it.

This was not how he'd envisaged popping his resort cherry. There was no pleasure to be found.

"Ok, let's halve the linen order and see how we go. If guests start complaining, we might have to order the rest. What's next?"

Austin tapped away on his iPad. "Opening week. The Head of Special Events wants to meet up with you and discuss a few ideas he has for our first couple of weeks."

Jordan's interest picked up. Bryce had always said that he made it his job to dazzle the first guests whenever he opened a new hotel. If those guests went home happy, they would tell their friends. Word of mouth was a powerful tool in the hotel industry.

"I'll go and see him now. If he has some really great ideas, you might need to find some more dollars somewhere else in the budget, so keep looking. Thanks, Austin."

The Royal Resorts board had already approved two increases to the operational budget, Jordan didn't want to have to go cap-in-hand to his father and ask for more. He'd managed to keep his stay at the clinic quiet, working from his room between therapy sessions, but he still wanted to avoid talking face to face with Edward until after the resort was open.

Jordan left his office and went in search of the Head of Special Events, eventually locating Claude in the resort's main ballroom. No sooner had he and Claude locked eyes on one another, than a song suddenly blasted out of the music system.

Jordan watched with dismay as the man launched into a full dance number. His moves perfectly in time with Chloe's revenge song, "Bitter Babe".

For fuck's sake.

He couldn't stand it. Jordan waved his arms about. "Stop! For the love of god, stop!"

Claude stopped dancing and the music mercifully cut out. The brief silence was heavenly. Jordan braced himself as the man made his way over. "Sorry, I always get a bit carried away. You can take the boy out of the dance troop, but you can never take the dance from him."

"You're quite the light foot," replied Jordan. "Austin tells me you have some ideas for opening week."

Claude clapped his hands together. "I do. That song. The one by Chloe, got me thinking. She lives in LA, and I happen to know her manager, Foster."

Oh, no. Please no. "Do you?"

"Yes, and I was thinking we could approach him to organize for her to do a mini concert here during the week we open. She could perform 'Bitter Babe'. Imagine the crowds."

"I don't think we have that sort of budget available."

Claude waved Jordan's concerns away. "I know this is your first resort, but I would expect with your background you'd understand that hotel launches are all about creating buzz. I know Chloe would cost a penny or three but think of the publicity. We could sell tickets and have her perform on a special stage on the golf green. Imagine a gorgeous sunset in the background. People would love it. And that song is amazing."

"Yeah, well I hate it. It's a spiteful slap down of some poor schmuck who got on the wrong side of a famous woman. And the idea of having a pop star open a high-end resort is ridiculous. No. Think of something else."

He turned and stormed out of the ballroom.

With opening day for the resort looming, Jordan was now living on site. He'd moved into one of the guest suites. His days started early, and his nights went late. But no matter how hard he tried, he couldn't get his brain to focus on the simplest of tasks. His therapist had suggested he was overstressed and the excess of cortisol pumping through his body was doing him real harm.

But he was committed to the launch date. No matter what transpired, they had to open on time. If they didn't Edward and the board would be asking some serious questions. Jordan had resorted to avoiding his father's calls as much as possible, only replying via email.

His nerves and sanity were hanging by a thread.

In his room, he clicked on the TV, in search of something mindless to watch. A late night chat show was on. The host happily babbling away to the studio audience. Jordan turned the volume up.

"And now the special guest we've all been waiting for, the world's biggest pop star, Chloe!"

Jordan threw the TV remote on the bed in resigned disgust. The universe had won. No matter how hard he tried, he couldn't avoid her. "Just bring it on. I'm fucking done."

The woman he had loved, still loved, bounded onto the studio set in a lime green and black jumpsuit. On anyone else it would probably look like trash, but on Chloe it was fabulous. He watched in muted pain as she kissed the show's host then after taking a seat on the guest couch turned to happily wave at the audience. And then for those watching at home.

He couldn't tear his gaze away. That smile. Those compelling brown eyes.

"So, Chloe, what a massive hit 'Bitter Babe' has become. I hear it everywhere. Even with your stellar career, you must be surprised by how much that song has resonated with the public. Tell me, where did this song come from? I know people are talking about you and Zapp, but is he really 'Bitter Babe'?"

She gave the host a shy smile. "'Bitter Babe' isn't about a person. It's more a feeling. It's a song from the heart. It's for all those people who thought they had found the one. That the person they were with believed in them. Had their back. But sadly, when things got tough, they walked away."

"Or as you say in the song, they go running back to their daddy like a little boy."

"Exactly."

The audience gave a collective 'Boo'.

Jordan picked up the Chloe tour T-shirt and hugged it to his face. He'd kept it, refusing to wash it in case the last of her scent disappeared.

"And I hear your fans are taking selfies outside of a famous nightclub in Berlin. They're not even bothering to try and get in."

Chloe gently laughed. "Yes, hashtag Berlin Bitter Babe."

"We'd love for you to sing the song for us tonight. What do we think folks?"

The primed Chloe's Garden loaded audience screamed and applauded. A chant of "Chloe, Chloe," started up. Jordan felt sick in the pit of his stomach. It was bad enough having to hear the song about their failed romance on the radio, but having to watch Chloe sing it was the worst.

But he was nothing if not a glutton for punishment. Dropping onto the bed, Jordan sat cradling the T-shirt while the woman he loved sang her song.

> *All that's left are memories of what we had.*
> *Regrets of what could have been.*
> *Only little boys go running back to daddy.*
> *Are you bitter babe?*

She'd dumped him for a three week fling with some hack singer of a band that in time no one would remember. Her people had wanted him gone, and she'd listened to them. Chosen her gilded cage over being free. Over him.

Bitter, Babe? You bet the fuck I am. Bitter and burned.

He tossed the shirt onto the floor. At some point he'd pick it up and hold it to himself once more. Chloe was a habit he couldn't shake. And for this, there was no rehab.

She'd just finished the song when Jordan's phone rang. He glanced over at it and caught the name *Austin Brown* on the screen. His assistant manager wasn't the sort of guy to call him late at night unless it was urgent. Jordan picked up the phone.

"Hi, Austin. What's happening?"

"Claude just quit."

Shit.

"He was pretty angry when you said that trying to book Chloe for the opening was ridiculous. But that's not the end of our problems. We have a bigger one—the head of catering followed Claude out the door."

They could muddle through for a time without a head of special events, but without a head of catering, they were dead in the water. "What? Why did he quit?"

Jordan couldn't recall having offended the guy but pissing people off seemed to be his current specialty.

"He's Claude's husband. Said you shouldn't be in charge of a hot dog stand, let alone a major resort."

Oh no. If word got back to New York that he'd managed to lose two senior members of the resort team mere weeks from opening, his father would be on a plane to LA. For a millisecond, Jordan toyed with the idea that having Edward onsite might not be such a bad thing. But then the words of Chloe's song came back to haunt him.

Only little boys go running back to daddy.

She'd certainly sucker punched him with that line. Telling him exactly what she thought about him having put the resort and his need to please his father ahead of their relationship.

I can't call dad. He'll come, take one look at me, and know I'm a mess. Know I've lied to him.

Edward wouldn't let him manage anything ever again. And while he was fast coming to the realization that he didn't think he even *wanted* to manage anything ever again, he knew he had to fix this mess himself.

"Thanks, Austin. Let me make some calls. I'll talk to you in the morning. In the meantime, could you go back through the budget and see where we can find some more money to spend on the opening. I'm thinking gift bags for the first guests. Bottles of wine. Spa vouchers. That sort of thing."

"Will do. Talk to you tomorrow."

Jordan's gaze flitted back to the TV. On the late night show Chloe was taking a bow and waving to her fans. His heart stirred in his chest. Aching, longing for her.

The hypocrisy of employing the use of special gift bags

for the opening of the resort when he'd looked down his nose at them at Chloe's album launch wasn't lost on Jordan.

He'd lost the woman he loved, and now he was walking eyes wide open into a billion-dollar disaster.

Jordan glanced at his phone, then dialed the number of the very last person he wanted to call to ask for help. To his relief Matthew picked up on the second ring.

"Speak of the devil, I was just about to call and see how you were. Did you catch Chloe on TV just now?"

Old memories came flooding back. All the times he'd messed up and all the times he'd called his arch nemesis to come bail him out. His life was fast unravelling, and he was backsliding into bad habits.

I can't put Matthew in a situation where he has to lie to dad, or worse, feel compelled to go tell him the truth.

"Yeah, I did, but can't I just want to say hi to my kid brother and see how things are going with him?"

A gruff snort drifted down the line. "I'm calling bullshit on that Jordan. I know you must still be struggling after the breakup with Chloe. I'm guessing from your silence over the past weeks that you didn't go to the health retreat after the fourth of July, but rather went to the other place. So please, just tell me what you need?"

There had been times over the years when the two of them were more frenemies than friends, but Matthew had always come through for him, no matter what. Jordan took a deep breath, knowing that if he didn't ask for something, Matthew would worry.

"Do you know of any Catering Managers who might be looking for a job, mine just quit?"

His new resort might be about to fall flat on its face, but he couldn't let the guests go hungry.

"Let me make some calls." There was a moment of silence on the other end of the line and Jordan braced himself for what might come next. Matthew had always been one for calling in favors as soon as they were granted.

"I'm doing a short trip out to LA mid-week and when I leave on Friday, I want you to come back to New York with me. I'm worried about you, Jordan, and I think a relaxing weekend away from the resort would do you a power of good."

Jordan glanced at the TV, relieved to see that the segment with Chloe was over. She was gone.

Matthew was asking him to come home for two days. It was a tempting offer.

It would be good to get out of the place even for a couple of days. And if he can find me a new catering manager then that will take my biggest worry off my mind.

"Ok. Friday, then back here Monday."

He would go home to New York for two days. What could possibly go wrong between now and Monday?

CHAPTER THIRTY

Los Angeles
December, five months since she and Jordan imploded
Not that Chloe was counting

"You look divine in that silk top, but I wonder if they have it in another color. I don't think pale pink is you, you look like death warmed up in it." Chloe rolled her eyes at Marta's cutting remark. But her assistant was right, the dusty pink did wash her out.

"Could you ask the sales assistant if they have it in a green or a blue?"

Taking the top with her, Marta hurried off to find the assistant. Chloe continued perusing the racks of clothes. She wasn't really in the mood for shopping. It was a week and a half out from Christmas and the holiday season always made her sad. While everyone else would be heading home to see family and share the wonders of a Christmas vacation, she would be spending the holidays at home alone.

Her version of home alone was unfortunately nothing like

the movies. She wasn't running around the house celebrating the fact that she had made her family disappear. No. They'd done that themselves, abandoned her without any regret.

She was shopping with Marta, and Gabriela for clothes in a high-end boutique in Robertson Boulevard, West Hollywood. It was late in the afternoon, the perfect time for a famous person in LA to go out. The paparazzi and the out of town tourists who were always on the hunt for pics of celebrities were usually done for the day.

Martin lingered outside on the pavement. The store had a strict, no security personnel rule. Apparently having large, armed bodyguards roaming the place tended to kill the fun shopping vibe.

The front door of the store opened, and she caught a glimpse of a well-dressed middle aged woman. She carried herself with a regal Hollywood air. Several designer label shopping bags hung from her arm. More than likely she was the wife of some producer or studio executive.

Chloe moved further down the line of garments, stopping to pull out a cream and silver striped blazer, which featured feathers on the lapel. It was a bit too busy for her taste.

I'm not sure about this, I don't think it sticks the landing.

When she found something that didn't quite work, Chloe liked to quote Stixxluv's favorite line. It was cutting but bitingly accurate. The jacket was trying to be too many things, when it would have been fine without the feathers. Even the mix of silver and beige-tinted cream was a no.

The other customer moved closer, and Chloe's senses immediately went on high alert. Any second now, she would be asked for either her autograph, a selfie, or in all probability, both. But an artist had to keep their fans happy.

"Excuse me."

Chloe took a deep breath and offered the woman a smile. "Hi."

The woman then proceeded to rummage in one of her shopping bags. "Are you Chloe Fisher? I'm such a big fan. I was wondering if you wouldn't mind ..."

It was the holiday season, of course she didn't mind. She'd had a successful album, and a massive summer hit. Foster was going to announce Chloe's world tour early in the new year. Part of her job was to make the people who bought her music and her concert tickets happy. "Sure, do you have a pen and paper that I can sign?" Chloe held out her hand. But instead of receiving a random piece of paper and a pen, she was handed a large buff colored envelope, along with the words. "Ms. Fisher, you have been served. Have a nice day."

She was left staring dumfounded at the paper in her hand as the woman headed straight toward the door.

Being a famous person, lawsuits came as part of the territory, but she hadn't ever been personally served before. Those things normally went through her management. Foster was paid to deal with such things. The public act of having been handed a law suit felt like a violation of her personal privacy. Unease slid down her spine.

Where is Marta? Gabriela? I want to go home. Now.

After folding the envelope in half and stuffing it into her bag, Chloe frantically went in search of her number one and number two personal assistants. Having an emotional breakdown in the middle of a fashion store was the last thing she needed, because if she did, then someone somewhere would surely have pictures of a weeping Chloe posted online within hours.

She kept her nerves under control all the way home. Fortunately, Marta and Gabriela were too busy with some juicy piece of LA gossip to pay her any real attention. Neither had witnessed what had happened in the boutique, and Chloe kept her own counsel about the envelope. Something wasn't right, and until she could get to the bottom of it, she didn't want to share it with anyone.

Back at her house in Beverly Hills, she hid the bag containing the envelope in her wardrobe and feigned taking a nap, waiting until Marta and Gabriela had both left for the day. This was her home, and she loved it more than anywhere else in the world, but she'd never truly felt a real sense of privacy here. Too many people were always coming and going. Too many eyes and ears, all watching her every move. She'd come to the recent realization that this wasn't her home—it was her prison.

She retrieved the envelope and called the number at the top of the cover letter. After giving the reference number and a few other details to identify herself, the call was forwarded on to an agent.

"Hello, are you are calling on behalf of Ms. Chloe Fisher?"

"Yes." She tucked her hair nervously behind her ear. The man on the other end couldn't see her, but Chloe was self-conscious. She rarely spoke to anyone outside of her tight social circle or the press. This was the real world.

"This debt has been outstanding for some time. From my records, it appears that we have tried to contact you on a number of occasions. Oddly this debt is in your name, not your company. But as I am handling those collections as well, and since you are a director, I can also discuss those matters."

There is more than one bad debt?

The agent was thorough with his explanation, and he was kind. By the time she finished the phone call an hour later, Chloe had a clearer idea of where her finances stood.

The house was eerily quiet as she logged on to her laptop and clicked the website where he'd instructed her to download her credit score. The list of debts owed by her company CGN Entertainment was long. Late payments. Partial payments. Summons after summons had been served. Even a notice of demand from the finance company who owned the *Chloe Jet*.

Every single one of them had gone to Foster's office. All except this one. Somehow this small demand for a three-hundred- and seventy-eight-dollar catering bill had slipped through.

"I don't understand. How can this be? I'm a huge success, but I have no money."

She was alone, and for the first time in a long time, she was truly afraid. There was no one to reach out to—no one she could trust.

"Okay. Okay. Let's not panic. You are Chloe, your fans love you. And you owe it to them to dig yourself out of this mess. Come on, think."

Confronting Foster was the obvious solution, and he would no doubt give her his usual condescending lecture, telling her to let him worry about the business side of things and for her to concentrate on making hits. But all of this, all this demand for money was headed toward her whether directly or through her company. When the buck stopped it was going to be at Chloe's front door.

Foster had to have known about the debt collectors. And he had deliberately left her in the dark.

"When you are ready to talk boundaries, let me know."

Jordan's words from that night in Berlin spoke loudly in her mind. He might have shown himself to be an ass, but he'd been right about her letting people run roughshod over her. Foster. Marta. Even Gabriela. They had all taken her for granted.

Chloe's life stood at a crossroads. She could continue down this same path, accepting the inevitability of her life, or she could take another road. Be on her own once more.

I can do this. I survived all those years with no one to help me.

Things were different from the way they'd been back then—she might currently have money issues, but she also had means and resources at her disposal.

"I have to get out of here."

She quickly stuffed a few things into a travel bag, taking care to leave behind such personal items as her toiletries, the absence of which would signal her unexplained disappearance to anyone who came looking. The minute Marta or Gabriela suspected something was up, they would be on the hunt.

A check of her bank account showed a depressing balance. A trail of cash withdrawals revealed the truth that her assistants had used her money as their own private kitty. Chloe chided herself for having let others handle her accounts. For giving them free access to her life.

But today that all came to an end.

CHAPTER THIRTY-ONE

Avoiding her bodyguards, Chloe snuck out of her house and drove herself to a nearby stationery store. Using her own personal credit card, she purchased a journal and some gel pens. Putting things down on paper meant she wouldn't leave an electronic trail. The sales assistant in the store was lovely and attentive.

"I adore your music. 'Bitter Babe' was such an amazing song. I've just played it over and over again all summer."

"I'm not her ..." The words died on Chloe's lips as she handed over her credit card which bore her name. "Sorry, just an auto response. Would you like my autograph?"

She wasn't going to offer to do a selfie. If the girl loaded it up to the social media platforms tonight and tagged her, Marta and Gabriela might see it. They would wonder why Chloe was out by herself purchasing stationery.

I need to update lots of passwords tonight. The sooner she closed off access to her life, the quicker she could make changes. Take her future into her own hands.

With her floral journal and gel pens in hand, Chloe got back into her car. She didn't want to go home. And she feared that all the people she did know in Hollywood were somehow connected to her management team.

This is where a girl could really do with having a good friend. Like they do in the movies. Someone whose shoulder I could cry on, and who has a comfy couch and some white wine to share.

But her life had never quite been a rom-com.

She hopped online and changed the password of her credit card. It was rare for her to use it, but she wasn't taking any chances. Her level of mistrust was now high.

The elderly night porter at the two star hotel in Koreatown didn't bat an eyelid when Chloe handed him her credit card. And when she gave him a different (false) name for the registration, he merely shrugged his shoulders. His job specification didn't include interrogating the guests. She'd paid for three nights and that was all that mattered.

He glanced over Chloe's shoulder at her silver Mercedes EQS. "That's a nice car you have out there, Miss. You might want to park it out of sight around back. This is a decent enough neighborhood, but you know ... temptation."

"Thanks, I will."

Chloe's room was all a two-star hotel was meant to be: a tiny bathroom, a lumpy bed, and a mini fridge that no one with any sense of hygiene would think to food put in. The dank scent brought memories of her old life flooding back. As panic rose within her chest, Chloe forced herself to suck in some deep breaths.

I am not going to lose my shit.

From her travel bag, she retrieved her laptop and got to work. At least the Wi-Fi was decent. With her journal beside her, she worked up a list of all the accounts and things that Foster and her people had access to, then methodically worked through it changing passwords and removing user rights.

Around two am her phone started pinging. Martin's name

was the first one on the ever growing list of messages and missed calls. Chloe turned her phone to silent and kept working.

At three am, she took a shower.

At four am, she ordered uber eats from the nearby all night Korean BBQ.

At five am, she managed to scrub the kimchi stains out of her top. Eating and working was a delicate business when you only had a tiny side table to work on.

At six am, she took another shower.

At seven am, she finally returned Foster's fourth missed phone call.

"Hi. Were you trying to get in touch?"

"Where are you?"

"Out with friends. Why?" Chloe curled her toes up as she forced out the lie. She'd never been good with trying to tell Foster falsehoods. He was a master of the game.

"What friends? Oh, never mind. Somethings wrong with your bank account. Marta says she thinks it and your credit cards might possibly have been hacked. But when she tried to get into your email to check any notifications from the bank, she'd been locked out."

Damn right she has been locked out.

His remarks raised a raft of new questions in Chloe's mind. Why would Marta be trying to access the credit card in the middle of the night? And why was she telling Foster about that? *Of course.* Marta hadn't been able to get hold of her, and so had tried to access the spend details on Chloe's credit card to find out where she had gone.

"Everything is fine. I just decided to change some passwords. I'd forgotten some of them. I'll sort it out later in the morning." She made a point of not apologizing for ignoring his calls or inconveniencing her personal assistant.

Foster huffed his frustration. "All right, but make sure you give the new ones to Marta and Gabriela as soon as you get home. And fix up their access to your emails. And for fuck's sake, call Marta." He hung up.

Understanding finally dawned. Foster and Marta were working together. Foster was keeping tabs on her through her personal assistant. He was controlling her life. Her money. And the people she paid to work for her were his accomplices. "You silly little girl. You fool."

No wonder they'd been so keen to get Jordan Royal out of her life. He'd posed a threat to their money train. Their issues with him had never been about her focusing on her work and getting the album finished. They wanted him out of the way because he asked too many questions. And if he'd stuck around long enough, she might have started questioning the status quo.

Chloe was nauseous, sick to her stomach. It was like waking up and suddenly discovering that she didn't live in the world she thought she did. That her entire existence for the past nine years had been a dream.

"Yeah, well I'm fully awake now."

Later that morning, after having searched, 'entertainment industry lawyers Los Angeles', Chloe drove herself to a house in the Hollywood Hills. By the time she left late that night, she had a new powerhouse industry lawyer.

In the middle of the afternoon on the second day of Chloe's bid for freedom, her lawyer Sandra did a very unlawyerly thing and gave her pop star client a big hug. "I'm not going to sugarcoat this for you, Chloe. The next few months are going to be horribly tough."

On day three as Chloe was checking out of her hotel, her new legal team went to Foster's offices in Century City and served him with a formal notice of contract severance, along with the promise of future legal action. He was not to make any attempt to directly contact his former client.

By the time she got home, her entire entourage, all except for Martin, had been fired. Her head of security would be working out a period of notice while he oversaw the changing of locks and keypads. Chloe felt particularly bad about that, but Sandra had counselled her to make a clean break. To her relief, Martin had graciously agreed with Sandra's advice. A new high security front gate was also on his to do list.

The guards who manned the security box at the entrance to the gated community were given a new list of people authorized to visit Chloe's home. Foster, Marta, and Gabriela were not on that list.

Chloe's final act of the long, emotionally exhausting day was to make a personal phone call to her stylist. "I'm so sorry about all this, I had no idea things had gotten this bad. I'm beyond embarrassed. You've basically been working for free since the European tour."

Stixxluv sighed down the phone. "Yeah. Look I suspected something was up, especially during the album launch. I'm sorry I should have said something at the time, and I didn't. Marta and Foster were acting weird. They were doing everything to keep people away, including that guy, Jordan, who you were seeing. I think they felt threatened by him."

When news of her financial problems eventually leaked, and they would, she could just picture how Jordan would view it. His concerns about her people had been vindicated. He was fully entitled to think. *I told you they were not good for you.*

"Once I get things sorted and have a clearer picture of my finances, I'll make sure to pay your invoices."

"What will you do now?"

The past few days had been a whirlwind of meetings with lawyers and accountants. Chloe needed time to process it all. "With Christmas coming up soon, I think I'm just going to take a break. I'm exhausted."

"Good idea. Look, do me a favor will you, let's agree that

you and I parted professionally a little while ago. You know how important optics are in this business. I don't want to get caught up in the shitstorm when all of this goes public."

Trust Stixxluv to be thinking of how this would impact his image. And after all his support, it was the least she could do. "Let me talk to the lawyers. I expect they will ask me to wait until I get a new manager to issue any formal statement. But yes, let's agree on that, and when the time comes, we can send some messages of support to each other on social media."

"Thanks, Chloe. Take care."

Ending the call, Chloe set her phone on the kitchen table. The house was the quietest she'd ever known it to be. She'd given both her housekeeper and cleaner three months paid notice, along with a generous Christmas bonus. December was not the best time to fire staff, and she felt a heavy degree of guilt over having to part with them at such short notice. But Sandra was right, she didn't know who to trust.

Wandering out to the pool deck, glass of wine in hand, she considered the events of the past few days and pondered her future. With Foster, Marta, and Gabriela all gone, there was no one left to tell her what to do. No one to check on what she ate. No one dictating her life.

She'd wrestled control from out of the hands of people who spent years effectively gaslighting her. All decisions were now hers.

It was both liberating and scary as ...

"Come on, Chloe. You can do this, for yourself and the fans. We are Chloe's Garden—and we will survive."

CHAPTER THIRTY-TWO

Downtown LA
 An accountant's office
 The last place anyone wants to be on Christmas Eve

This was not how Chloe thought she would ever be spending her Christmas Eve. Instead of embarking on her annual last-minute flit through the stores on Rodeo Drive buying expensive gifts for friends and her team, she was sitting next to Sandra, in the board room of an accountant's office as they went through a hefty stack of paperwork. Every single piece of paper on the table in front of her told the same dreadful story.

Chloe Fisher, the biggest pop star in the world, was broke. Or as darn well as near to it as she could get without actually declaring bankruptcy. The papers she'd been served in the boutique were from a catering company who'd supplied some gluten free cupcakes for the album launch. It hadn't occurred to her until now, that she had always been the one on the hook for such events. Her record label rarely picked up the tab.

After a team of forensic accountants had been through her company finances, Chloe understood the awful truth of her glittering life. Her long-term management team had screwed her over. For every dollar she made, they took a sizeable chunk. What was left after Foster got his money, wasn't all that much.

He'd given Chloe her big break and promised to look after her. Treat her like she was a part of his close-knit family. The sort of family she'd never had. But what Foster had really done was milk her for all she was worth.

"We have been through as much of Ms. Fisher's finances as her previous management team's lawyers have allowed. The rest we have tried to put together from tax filings and corporate returns. I'm afraid that the situation is dire to say the least, but not irretrievable," announced the accountant.

To his credit, he delivered the news in a calm manner. There was no judgement in his tone. Chloe got a sense that that her accountant would do whatever he could to help her. But it did little to ease her rising panic.

It was hard to breathe. The notion that she could be on the verge of losing everything had a knot growing tight in her chest. She wasn't Chloe the superstar, she was Chloe the little girl lost. The one that no one wanted. Her fingers gripped the laminated edge of the table.

Oh god, I am going to cry in front of these people.

Her lawyer thankfully nodded her understanding of the situation. "Ms. Fisher has terminated the contract with her previous management team, but it's going to take some time for her to get clear of them. We are investigating the possibility of suing, but again it could be years before she sees any of her money."

"As I said, things are not irretrievable, but some serious

financial decisions are going to have to be made if we are to avert declaring bankruptcy," replied the accountant.

Bankruptcy. The word had bile rising in her throat. She couldn't bear the thought of such public humiliation.

There has to be a way out of this, I can't lose it all.

Chloe placed a hand over her face. She didn't give a damn what it did to her carefully applied makeup. She'd already made some major changes in her life, but apparently things were still spiraling out of control.

I've had both the number one album and single in the charts for the past four months, yet I'm sitting here.

"We've put together a proposal, which should see Ms. Fisher able to meet her commitments for the first quarter of next year."

Pulling herself together, Chloe lowered her hand. The accountant slid a document across the table. He tapped a finger on the top of the paper. "Have you settled on a new agent or manager?"

Chloe and her legal team had met in secret with a number of top entertainment industry people. They were looking at the sort of agents and managers who not only represented the biggest and best artists in the business, but who had solid reputations for protecting their client's wealth. Lesson learned—Chloe's new agent/manager would not be handling her personal or company finances.

"Yes, I signed with Nancy L Rusen this afternoon," replied Chloe, forcing herself into the discussion. She'd let other people make decisions for her in the past, and as much as her nerves were on edge, she had to have her voice clearly heard.

The accountant offered her an encouraging smile. "That is good news. Ms. Rusen has a great standing in this town, if anyone can get your career and earnings back on solid track, Chloe, it is Nancy. But for the next little while you are going to have to rein in your spending."

Moving the slim document closer to herself, Chloe turned over the cover page and began to read. When she left the accountant's office an hour later, it was with a hard, but achievable plan for survival. If she was to have any chance of keeping her home, and not suffering the public humiliation of declaring bankruptcy, she had to cut spending. Designer clothes. Lavish parties. Even her beloved *Chloe Jet*.

It all had to go.

Nancy had promised she would work on securing a new contract with the record company and better royalties. She would also make sure Chloe got a bigger cut of the ticket sales from her future tours. But for the time being the world's biggest pop star would have to live within a strict monthly budget.

I still can't believe I used to let Marta spend fifty grand a month on flowers.

Along with a lot of other things, having fresh blooms every day was an indulgence Chloe could easily live without.

CHAPTER THIRTY-THREE

Royal Resorts
 Laguna Beach, LA
 It's New Year's Eve, I have to get home.

Closing up his suitcase, Jordan rang for his driver. New Year's Eve was one of the worst days of the year for travelling. Thank god, his father had relented and agreed to send the Royal Resorts private jet from New York to collect him.

The last time he'd been sent back out to LA in mid-November, Jordan had been in disgrace and Edward had forced him to fly commercial. Jordan couldn't blame his father for his anger. He had been in charge of the billion-dollar Laguna Beach resort launch, and in the words of one scathing press article: *Jordan Royal has failed to deliver.*

Six weeks of working nonstop in order to get the new Laguna Beach Platinum Collection Resort back on track had taken a heavy toll. He was both mentally and physically exhausted. But he could also admit to being proud of himself.

What was left of his career at Royal Resorts was still in

tatters, but he could now hand the resort over to its incoming manager with a sense of confidence. The issues with food, staff, and guest amenities had all been handled. It had taken an army of people both here and in New York, but the job was finally done.

This year had seen the best and the worst of his life. He was ready to put it all behind him.

Climbing into the back of the town car for the short drive from the resort to John Wayne private airport, Jordan pulled his phone out of his jacket pocket. Being New Year's Eve, there were plenty of messages wishing him all the best for the New Year. He opened the one from his now former assistant Sheila and let out a laugh.

> Farewell to the year where you almost shat the bed. But seriously you survived and that's what counts. I'm proud of you. C U soon.

Almost? No, he could own up to the fact that he'd ruined his relationship with Chloe and managed to stuff up the launch of a billion-dollar resort. Sheila was being kind. In any one's language he had well and truly shit the bed.

> Happy New Year, Sheila. Thank you for saving my sanity over the past six months. I hope Bryce realizes how amazing you are. I'm relying on you to give him hell

He smiled wistfully at the screen. If he had done one thing right this year, it was to encourage Sheila to talk to Bryce and ask the newly appointed CEO of Royal Resorts USA, for a job. Working for his brother, Sheila would have a much better career path than the one she'd had under him.

Another message popped up.

> Wishing you all the happiness and success in the New Year Chloe. 🩶🩶🩶

He gasped. "Oh, sweetheart."

He read the message a second time and shook his head. The message had to be Chloe's version of a New Year's Eve, Hallmark card. It was probably a group message and she'd added him purely by mistake.

I'm surprised she kept my number.

He wasn't going to add to their shared embarrassment by replying. Chloe probably didn't even realize what she had done. He put his cell away.

I should just try to forget her. She forgot about me.

It had been nearly six months since their passionate affair had flamed out. Six months of him trying to dig his way out of the black hole their break up had thrown him into. So only a fool would go online looking to see what the girl who had written a 'fuck you, buddy' smash hit might be up to on New Year's Eve.

Cursing himself for being that fool, Jordan retrieved his phone once more. He tapped on Chloe's certified Instagram profile. In a moment of weakness, he'd broken his self-imposed social-media ban and joined Instagram. Figuring since Chloe had one-hundred and ninety-million followers, and her account followed no one, there was a good chance she wouldn't ever find out that he had checked up on her latest posts.

Her last post had been put up earlier today. It was a black and white one of the Eiffel Tower. And while it looked similar to a million other pictures he'd seen of the Parisian landmark over the years, Jordan immediately recognized where the picture had been taken. The balcony of his family's Paris apartment was unmistakable.

His heart squeezed in his chest as he read the words of

the accompanying caption, "Wishing we were still here, and it was all so new again. #bitterbabe #brokenheart".

There were over three hundred thousand comments under the post. He didn't check how many likes or loves it had. It didn't matter.

Jordan screwed his eyes shut. Any minute now he was going to start blubbering in the back of the car. Why did she have to post that?

I knew I shouldn't have checked. I should have stayed away.

But the damage was done. He may as well keep going. Scrolling through her socials, it soon became apparent that all of her posts after her and Jordan's breakup had become more stylized, less spontaneous than in the past. A sense of joy and warmth was lacking.

Then things had changed once more in the week running up to Christmas. Instead of holiday wishes and vacation plans, Chloe had taken to offering up odd snippets of advice and thoughts on painful lessons she had learned.

Only one post actually showed Chloe, and that had been just her hands. She was journaling. Writing.

Something was off with the world's biggest pop star. She was hiding from her fans. But why?

When will I stop torturing myself over this woman?

His new year resolution should be to block Chloe's number and delete her old messages. #NewYearNewMe.

CHAPTER THIRTY-FOUR

Chloe spent New Year's Eve alone at home. She couldn't face anyone. The official termination notices and non-disclosure agreements had gone out to her staff late the previous day, along with their final payments. When other people talked about a new year, a new me, this was not what she'd had in mind.

The abusive texts arrived not long after, the first was predictably from her former number one personal assistant.

> I loved you. After all I have done for you, this is how you treat me?

Gabriela had dutifully signed her paperwork and sent it straight back. Knowing her, she had probably done that so that Marta couldn't talk her out of it. At least one of her former team members was behaving like an adult.

Stixxluv, who happened to be at an exclusive retreat in Mexico, sent a more strategic reply.

> Thank you for paying my outstanding invoices. In light of our previous conversation I would like it made known that you and I ended our creative partnership not long after the All American Music Awards in July. I don't mean to be hard about this, but I have a business to run and a baby on the way.

If clients saw a gap between his leaving and her change of management, it would look better for him. And for his career. *I owe him that much.*

> Congrats on the baby, wonderful news. Agreed that we make that the official line.

She sent the reply, then turned off her cell.

Chloe rang the new year in while lounging on the couch in her sweat pants and watching the fireworks on TV. A bottle of champagne and some soft, French cheeses were her only indulgence. It made sense to hunker down at home, and ready herself for the inevitable public fall-out which severing ties with Foster and Marta would surely bring. Her former manager and assistant were not the kind of people to go quietly. They would try to extract as much money out of her and cause as much damage to Chloe's reputation as they could. Spite was a strong motivator.

When Nancy arrived at Chloe's house a few weeks later, her new manager came bearing two large hot takeout coffees and a hard set of battle plans. They set up Nancy's laptop on the kitchen table and got to work.

"Now, the first good thing which has happened this morning, is that your new bank account has gone live. I've checked with the accountant, and he has confirmed that no money will be going into any of your old bank accounts. Speaking of money, have you got around to cutting up the rest of your credit cards?"

Chloe shook her head. She'd actually got the scissors and the cards out late last night but couldn't summon the strength to go through with it.

"I wasn't sure which ones I was meant to destroy," she lied, setting them out in front of her on the table. How was she going to survive without them?

Nancy lay her hand over Chloe's. "This is the dark hour before the dawn. Just remember that. Now you don't need to cut them all up, just these." She stacked six of the eight cards into a pile, then shifted the remaining two back toward Chloe.

There was a platinum Amex, but it was not one of the *by invitation only* Centurion cards which all the major celebrities had. The other card was a basic ATM and debit card. Chloe brushed her fingers over them. How naïve had she been before all this, and how long had she stood unwittingly on the precipice of disaster, one debt collector notice away from defaulting on her life.

Nancy waited patiently while Chloe retrieved the scissors and proceeded to cut up the remaining credit cards, nodding her approval when the last of them was added to the small pile of tiny plastic slivers. A lack of money meant a lack of spending choices.

It's all up from here. God, please let it be.

"Now, Sandra's team and your accountant have done a great job in helping to stem the outflow of money. There will of course be some lawsuits and ugly rumors, but that can't be helped. What can be helped however is finding ways to get money coming in. Money that your previous manager won't be able to make a claim on. That is what I have been focusing my energies on."

There was a hopefulness in Nancy's voice. Chloe clung to

that like it was a life raft. She would do whatever it took to get her finances back on an even keel. To have control of her future.

"Whatever it takes, just tell me. If I have to do a pay for view TV special, or a Netflix series just in order to keep my home, I'm up for it."

She didn't want to give up her house. To leave her forever home. It was the only one she had ever known. Her sanity, her soul, were tied to this place.

"The whispers are already starting in Tinseltown. Some of your former employees haven't stuck to their employment NDAs. Marta for one seems determined to cause trouble. News of your money problems is not going to stay secret for too long. We need to get ahead of it. Which is where this new Las Vegas deal comes in."

Chloe's brows furrowed as Nancy produced a manila folder from out of her oversized leather tote and set it on the table. As soon as she opened it, Nancy commenced the hard sell.

"Now, you can either do the Las Vegas deal, or look to take your new album on a world tour. I've spoken to some people, and the earliest you could be out on the road would be mid-year. That's of course if you can get a full live show up and running by then, and we can secure a tour agent who can get us into the big arenas. And we are able to sell tickets in time." Nancy waved her hand in a rolling motion.

And. And. And. Not a hope in hell.

Chloe's faint hopes of a world tour saving her finances crashed around her. Booking major venues was something that artists did a long way ahead, often a year in advance. The sorts of stadiums which she normally filled would already be committed and unavailable.

"Ok, tell me about the Vegas deal."

Nancy chugged down her coffee, then got to her feet. She

paced back and forth across the kitchen. "Las Vegas was once the place where careers went to die, but not anymore." She stopped and pointed a finger at Chloe. "Did you know that the singer Adele is rumored to have made two million dollars a show?" She lowered her hand and pointed at the proposal document.

"To be honest, I'm surprised your old management hadn't already gone down that road with you. Well ... before 'Bitter Babe', anyway."

They had. Chloe had said no. She didn't want to perform at a casino in Nevada. To her way of thinking she was much bigger than that, and she didn't need the money.

Oh how the mighty have fallen.

"Foster put the idea of a Vegas residency to me a couple of years ago, but I said no."

Her stubborn ego was finally paying dividends. If she'd said yes at the time, god knows how much money she would have lost on the deal. And it wouldn't be an option for her to consider now.

"But you are no longer in a position to be able to say no to a solid opportunity. And this contract is more than that—it's your way back. I can't stress how much this deal will mean to your long-term career and finances. It will allow you to clear up your debts and keep most of the things you value."

Most of my things?

Chloe swallowed deep. "What will still have to go?"

Nancy returned to the table, she dropped into her chair and sighed. "The *Chloe Jet* has to go. It's gorgeous, and I think it's fabulous branding, but you can't afford to have a sixty million dollar jet continuing to lose value while it sits idle on the tarmac. And it sends a poor message to the creditors who are still waiting for payment."

The custom painted and fitted out *Chloe Jet* had been the ultimate passion project. Chloe's big public statement to everyone who had ever doubted her. Who had ever abandoned her. It was the loudest way she could say *I don't need you,* to the people who had failed her. Letting it go would be hard.

She met her manager's gaze. "When will the jet have to go? It would be nice to be able to take it for one final flight. To say goodbye."

Nancy's eyes softened with pity. "Unfortunately, the finance company repossessed the plane just before Christmas. Apparently, the repo notices had gone to your old management, and they hadn't bothered to do anything with them."

Foster. He really had done a number on her.

"That's unfair. No one told me." It hurt not to be able to give her plane a proper send off. She gave a resigned sigh. There was no point fighting to keep the jet. And as Nancy had stated, people who had trusted in Chloe's good name were still owed money.

Come on, Chloe, you're a big girl. Remember we don't cry over these things.

It had been many years since she'd been forced to rely on those words. The strong inner mantra which had helped her to survive the constant revolving door of family services and disinterested parents now gave her comfort.

She picked up the Las Vegas proposal. "I'm ready to hear the rest of it."

"Good, now the company we are dealing with is called Royal Resorts. They have just done a one hundred million dollar refurb of their Las Vegas casino and resort complex. I'm thrilled that you are willing to sign up for the residency. It was a hard battle to beat off the two other major recording artists, who were also vying for this gig. Everyone wants to do a Vegas residency. I think the success of 'Bitter Babe' sealed the deal for them."

Irony of all ironies.

Chloe flicked through the pages, grateful that Nancy had taken the time to highlight the important things. A couple of months of rehearsals, followed by six months of shows in Vegas. *Doable.* They were open as to how many nights a week Chloe played. *Good.* The amount of money per show involved had her smiling. If she could successfully pull it off, her finances would be set.

Maybe even look to do a world tour next year. Then all this would be behind me.

"Take some time to read through the proposal carefully and come back to me with any queries. There were a couple of details I had to concede on."

Chloe's ears pricked up. She was determined to pay full attention to any and all contracts that she put her name to going forward.

"Like what?"

"The Royal Resorts people want to appoint their own manager to help handle the weekly shows in Las Vegas. Of course my LA based team will be involved in overseeing things, but since their manager will be working more along the lines of being your personal assistant, I figured you wouldn't have a problem with that minor detail. And it will also give you some breathing space to consider what people you will need working for you in the future. I'm assuming you will eventually replace some of your former employees."

Chloe hadn't put much thought into the people she might bring on board to replace Marta, Gabriela, or even Stixxluv. If she was honest about it, she'd been enjoying the peace and quiet without people constantly in her ear.

She didn't miss having a chorus of voices all telling her what to wear, what to eat, and whose company she should keep. The silence had become rather liberating. She could also admit to it being more than a little scary.

"Do they have anyone particular in mind to work for me?

I mean that could be a deal breaker if the two of us don't get along."

Nancy frowned, then hurriedly flicked through some of the other papers in her folder. She pulled out a printed email. *Gen X, old school. She prints out emails.* "Ah yes, actually this is really positive news. They are clearly taking this contract seriously. They've offered to have one of the members of the family who own Royal Resorts act as your manager."

Cold dread slid down Chloe's back. Royal Resorts were owned by Jordan's family. She couldn't imagine having to work with someone who knew her ex, while at the same time having to keep their failed romance a closely guarded secret. One wrong word and things could get messy, fast.

"They have suggested Jordan Royal."

Chloe's breath caught. *Damn. Damn. Of course its him. How stupid was I to think that the universe was done with slapping me around.*

"From the look of it, he works in the resort business here in the USA." Nancy lifted her gaze and smiled at Chloe. "The House of Royal actually owns a ton of businesses around the world. If this Vegas thing works out well, who knows, we might be able to secure some other deals with them. Clothing, perfume, beauty, you know all those things could help to extend your brand. And make you some serious money. Your debts could be cleared in no time. We can't expect that Foster will be looking to settle any pending legal cases in the next few years."

Her former manager would do his utmost to drag it all out. To make Chloe suffer as much public humiliation as possible.

But she wasn't all that bothered about Foster. Her lawyers and accountants would deal with him. Chloe's brain had fixated on the name *Jordan Royal.* It was scrambling to figure out how she could get out of having to do the Vegas gig while still managing to save her beloved home.

What must Jordan be making of all this? And why had he agreed to work with her, when he'd been the one who'd walked out and ended their relationship? He hadn't even bothered to respond to her New Year's Eve message.

I still don't know why I sent him that text. He probably hates me by now.

Likely Jordan had a new woman in his life, and he had moved on.

And as for the extended brand pieces, she could just imagine what Edward Royal would say to having a pop star cheapen the Royal brand. She might well be the biggest artist in the US, but to an old money stuck up billionaire, she would still be nothing more than a girl from Nebraska. Fame and wealth didn't change who she was or where she'd come from. His people didn't mix with folks like her.

Which is why Jordan didn't want to bring his daddy here for my album launch. He was ashamed of me.

Las Vegas, of course, would be the exception. Rules didn't apply in sin city, money spoke loudest. The executives from Royal Resorts would be in town for the concert announcement and more than likely her opening night. Other than that, they would treat her like she was just another employee.

Focus, Chloe. This is important. Don't worry about rich people and their egos.

"Did they say why they had chosen this Jordan guy? I mean, he's a guy. Doesn't that seem a little odd to you?"

Nancy quickly turned the pages of the contract to the section where the amount of money Chloe would earn per concert was clearly set out. She waved the paper under Chloe's nose saying. "I would suggest you worry about this dollar figure and let the Royal Resorts people deal with the rest. It's not as if you and this Jordan Royal person will be living in one another's pockets. You will have your own private suite in the hotel, and he will simply be helping to make sure you've got everything you need."

She was in a bind, and Nancy was offering her a multimillion dollar way out. "I'm sorry. I have a terrible habit of being my own worst enemy at times. Did you want me to sign the contract now?"

Her manager gave her a soft smile and handed Chloe the contract. "No, Chloe. What I want you to do is read this from front to back at least a half dozen times. We are going to train you to have a laser focus on everything you put your name to from now on." Chloe noted the hint of patronizing in Nancy's tone. "And I'm not joking when I say there will be a pop quiz on the contents of the contract before you get anywhere near a pen."

Okay. Chloe wisely held her tongue. This woman had been brought in to save her career. To do all the things her former management team hadn't done. Making Chloe take the time to be across the details of contracts was an important part of her new manager's job.

"Thank you, Nancy. It's good to have you on my side of the contract negotiations."

"That's what you pay me the big chunk of commission for, Chloe. Now, if we are in agreement with this deal, I'll get in touch with the Royal Resorts people to arrange the details of the contract signing. In the meantime, if you have any questions drop me an email."

After her manager finally left, Chloe sat down and read the contract. She made some notes. The Vegas deal looked fantastic on paper, and she could understand why several other stars had been keen to secure the residency. It all made perfect business sense. The only thing she couldn't get her head around was why Jordan had been appointed her special manager.

A message buzzed on her cell. It was from Nancy.

> RR all good to go ahead with contract. Agreed to have JR fly out here next week to sign at your house. Talk soon. N

Chloe's heart was thumping hard in her chest. Jordan was coming to her house to sign the contract.

He's coming here.

She hadn't ever thought to see him again, let alone have to work with him. And now their first face to face contact in the long months since he had walked out on her was going to be here with her manager and lawyer present.

But why was he handling her Vegas gig? Did he possibly think she was going to cause some sort of trouble for his daddy's company, was that it? He wanted to baby sit his ex to make sure she complied with the terms of the contract. To make sure she stayed silent about their relationship. Seriously, had he never trusted her.

You did write a withering breakup revenge song about him.
Okay, so there is that.

But if Jordan was going to play games, she would play along. And if he was counting on her to be the first one to blink, Chloe was going to show her "Bitter Babe" ex just how long a girl who'd survived living on the streets of Nebraska could hold out. This was her home, and she would do anything to keep it.

CHAPTER THIRTY-FIVE

Los Angeles
January, but it feels more like groundhog day.

Clusterfuck. *noun.* vulgar slang. A disastrously mishandled situation or undertaking. Jordan was certain that if you looked that word up in a dictionary, it would include the additional line, *see also Jordan Royal*.

At least his brother hadn't fired him. Bryce would have been well within his rights as the new CEO of Royal Resorts USA to have terminated Jordan's employment following the disaster at Laguna Beach. The board had made it clear Jordan wouldn't be given another chance at managing a resort— thank god for that— but at least they had offered him the opportunity to make some amends. To partially redeem himself.

One final chance. If he stuffed up again, he was out. His father and older brother had gone in to bat for him for the Laguna Beach resort, and their trust had been burned.

Jordan's SUV slowed outside the gate to the private estate

in Beverly Hills. The two burly security guards were the same ones as before. He lowered his driver's side window and showed them his New York driver's license. "Hi, I have an appointment at number twenty five. My name is Jordan Royal, hopefully I am on your list."

He had learned a lot of hard lessons over the past year and one of them was not to assume people would remember his name. When things had gotten really bad during the resort launch, he'd tried to call in some favors. It had been humiliating for him to discover that many of those markers were not owed to him, but rather his father. Humility had been a bitter pill to swallow.

The contents of the security guard's silver clipboard were promptly checked, and Jordan was waved through. As the gate closed behind him, he let out the breath he'd been holding. He was nervous. His usual cocksure self was nowhere to be seen. He'd been well aware that it had been missing for some time, but today its absence was more keenly felt. The Jordan Royal who'd thought he'd conquered his past and his fears was nowhere to be found.

I just hope Chloe and I can find a way to work together. To put our past behind us.

If he'd had any say in this, he would have suggested they chose someone else for the job of managing Chloe for her Vegas residency, but with some members of the company board making it clear they wanted him gone from Royal Resorts, he had been left with little option than to agree. He might not ever want to manage another resort, but until he could decide on what he did want to do with his life, he'd do what the company required of him.

Dread filled him. He'd wiped his sweaty hands on the leg of his pants several times on the drive over here from his hotel. He was certain Chloe, and her people were going to treat him like yesterday's news.

Marta and her accomplices are going to do everything to make my life hell.

But after the mess he'd made of the new resort, he owed it to his family to suffer whatever fate could throw his way.

The SUV moved around the long winding bend, and as he caught his first glimpse of Chloe's house, memories of the two of them came flooding back. Of the nights they had shared together. He smiled as he remembered the gentle, almost shy way she used to take him by the hand, and quietly lead him up to her bedroom.

And the lust filled vixen she transformed into as soon as they got between the sheets.

"Wrong time to be thinking of Chloe like that. Get your head in the game. This is your final chance."

He turned the car into her driveway, waiting while a large security gate slowly opened.

That's new. I wonder why she's had that installed.

After passing through the gate, and making his way down the drive, Jordan parked his SUV in the visitor spot furthest from the front door. There were several other flashy cars parked close by, none of which Jordan recognized. Had Chloe gone ahead and bought the new cars she had promised to her team? *Generous bonuses.*

Turning off the ignition, Jordan sat for a moment and gathered his thoughts. He could do this, he had to, there was no other choice. If he failed to get her signature today, he might as well not bother returning to New York. The top of a mountain somewhere in the Himalayas would be a better option than going home empty handed to face his family.

"Ok. Let's do this, time to suck up whatever is left of your pride and get Chloe's name on that contract."

The front door was open when he reached the main entrance to the house. That was odd. Chloe's people were usually insane about making sure all the doors and windows were closed. And where was Martin and the other security team members?

Knocking on the doorjamb, he poked his head inside. "Hello."

There was the sound of approaching feet. A silver haired woman in a dark gray designer pants suit soon appeared. She took one look at Jordan and a broad smile immediately lit up her face. She held out her hand to him. "Hi, you must be Jordan Royal. Nancy L Rusen, I'm Chloe's manager. Please come in we've been expecting you." She beckoned for him to follow.

She's got a new manager. I thought she and Foster were fused at the hip.

He stepped into the all too familiar kitchen area. Chloe's favorite space. The place where she'd said she always felt the most comfortable. Around the table were seated several people in suits. One by one they rose, each offering Jordan a firm handshake. There was a new lawyer. A new accountant. A whole set of new faces. But no Chloe.

"Ms. Fisher will be downstairs shortly. We thought it would be good for you to meet the rest of her management team before she joins us."

He desperately wanted to ask what had happened to the old crew, but that would mean revealing his prior connection to Chloe. She may well have brought her new team into her confidence, but he wasn't going to risk putting a foot wrong so early in the meeting. Especially not before he had got her signature on the contract. Jordan was convinced that the three finalized and agreed upon versions of the deal, which he had brought with him, were burning a hole in the bottom of his leather document holder.

Jordan took a seat at the table, relieved when Nancy filled him in on who was who in the zoo. "You will have to excuse us if we appear a little awkward around the table. Ms. Fisher has recently had a change of management and staff and we are all still getting used to working with one another."

It was an opening, and one Jordan was sorely tempted to utilize, but now was not the time for asking about Chloe's people. Not until he knew exactly who had gone and who was still around. He would have to wait.

"Yes, well it's my first time handling a deal like this, but I have gone through the contract numerous times, and hopefully I can reassure your client that everything and anything she needs from Royal Resorts and myself, will be provided."

Nancy nodded. "Good." His words of reassurance were exactly what he hoped she wanted to hear. "Speaking of my client, here she is."

Jordan steeled his nerves. This first meeting was always going to be the hardest. If he could get through it without tripping over his tongue, he would be mightily relieved.

Get the contract signed. Then you can go back to the hotel and call the office.

His father's words of instruction rang loudly in his mind. "Stay in town, get to know Chloe. It would be good for the company." There would be no getting on board the company jet and heading back to NYC. Jordan was once again stuck in LA.

Taking a deep breath, he rose from his chair and turned to face his ex.

CHAPTER THIRTY-SIX

"Chloe, this is Mister Jordan Royal from Royal Resorts. He is here to sign the contract with you, and also to have a bit of a meet and greet," announced Nancy.

Painting a smile on her lips, Chloe gave a regal nod to Jordan's outstretched hand. "How do you do, Mister Royal." Their gazes met for a brief instant, after which Chloe shifted her attention and focused on the end of his chin. Avoiding his deep green sexy eyes was a must. They reminded her all too much of their shared past. Of long nights filled with passion.

He dropped his hand. "Please, call me Jordan. Since you and I are going to be working closely together over the next little while, Chloe, may I suggest we dispense with the formalities. I would also like to offer you my full assurances that whatever you need or want, you only have to ask. I am at your command."

Smooth. Charming. Egotistical asshole.

At least no one else seated at the table knew of her and Jordan's romantic past. Of the wicked things he had done to her in this very house. Her gaze lingered on the table.

He'd made love to her on that table, brought her to

completion right at the spot where one of the lawyers now sat. Chloe's mind quickly, furiously scrubbed away at the memory of Jordan seated in a chair eating her out as she lay spread out before him like a damn feast. Of her fingers grasping for purchase on the cold, hard surface.

When she involuntarily licked her lips, Chloe could have sworn Jordan swayed a little on the spot. Her eyes flickered to his, catching the unmistakable look of pain which burned within them.

Good. I hope this is as awkward for you as it is for me.

If this gig wasn't the lifeline to her keeping this house, she would have pulled Jordan up on the use of her first name. In showbiz it was customary to address the artist in a more formal manner. Egos and all that bullshit. Chloe hadn't ever felt the need to enforce it, but her entourage had. She'd lost count of the number of people Marta had mercilessly ripped into when they had make the simple mistake of not addressing Chloe as Ms. Fisher.

You might hate him, but he and his family's resort is the only way back.

"It's a pleasure to meet you, Jordan. I expect I will have one or two things which will require your attention once I arrive in Las Vegas."

The thought of him being at her beck and call suddenly held a great deal of appeal. She could exact some moments of sweet, petty revenge against Jordan. While nothing she did would be able to pay him back for walking away, she could still make his life more than a little uncomfortable. The prospect of many months of torturing Jordan Royal, and showing him what he was missing, had a wicked smile sitting on her lips.

Hey buddy, I am going to give you hell.

He tore his gaze away and directed his attention toward

the table. "Would you like to take a seat and we can go over the contract? Did you have any final questions?"

Chloe settled into a chair across the table from where Jordan resumed his seat. She didn't want to be anywhere near him if she could help it. Sitting on the other side of the table next to Nancy gave her a sense of power. Jordan was the interloper in her home, and she was going to make sure he not only sensed that he wasn't welcome, but that he damn well knew it.

The Chloe Fisher who Jordan had known was no longer. In her place was a woman who knew every clause of the Vegas contract and had even memorized the payment schedule at the back. These days, she checked her bank account and credit card balances every morning, without fail. Even the regular emails from her accountant noting which bills were to be paid and when, were given due attention. Chloe knew the value of this deal right down to the very last cent. And she was going to make sure she collected everything which was due to her.

She was still deeply embarrassed that she'd been forced to reset all her personal bank account passwords. Marta and Gabriela had been handling Chloe's money on a day-to-day basis. And from what she had discovered, it was clear her two former assistants had treated her money as their own.

"I have read the contract thoroughly, so I don't have any final questions regarding the terms. But once I sign here today, I will be expecting to see the first payment in my company account by close of business tomorrow. Rest assured, Jordan, I will be making certain that Royal Resorts sticks to both the spirit and the letter of the contract."

Under the table, Chloe curled her toes up in her Nike sneakers. She had practiced that last line in the mirror a little while earlier and was proud that she had managed to say it in a calm, even voice.

A rosy blush appeared on his cheeks. He hadn't been expecting her to be so forthright. So blunt.

Nancy, god bless her, took up the chorus. "Yes, we want to make things very clear. Your father negotiated this deal, but we expect you to fulfil it. That includes personally guaranteeing that my client gets everything she needs. And that starts from today, until Chloe's very last performance at Royal Resorts Las Vegas."

There was a familiar clench in the lower of Chloe's belly. There had once been a time where Jordan had given her everything she needed. Almost. *He never said the L word.*

And despite where their connection now stood, the past couldn't be undone. They were still linked.

Some nights she rolled over in bed and could have sworn the scent of his cologne still lingered on her sheets. Or was it her skin?

"Very good. I understand. Are we all ready to get started on signing the various sections and copies of the contract?" replied Jordan. His voice was steady, but he wouldn't meet Chloe's eye.

You should be afraid, I'm not going to make your life the least bit easy while we are in Vegas. There is going to be some serious payback, buddy.

"Yes, I am, thank you. After that we can look to discuss the launch announcement in Las Vegas. I know Nancy and Edward agreed it would be next week, but I've decided it should be pushed back. I trust that won't be a problem, Jordan."

The pop diva routine wasn't normally her vibe, but for Jordan, for the man who had broken her heart, Chloe was willing to make an exception. By the time she stood on the stage at the Royal Resorts Platinum Collection Resort in Las Vegas, Mister Jordan Royal would know exactly who was in charge.

CHAPTER THIRTY-SEVEN

The writing was on the wall. Chloe was going to make his life utter misery. His worst fears were about to come true. He had walked out on her, and she was determined to make him pay.

They may have been seated mere feet away from one another, but their relationship was a million miles from what it had once been. Jordan had to stop reminding himself that this was the same woman who he'd spent night after night making love to in this very house.

He had to forget that she had once been his.

That's a lie and you know it. She could have been mine, but I threw our chance at happiness away. I will always regret not introducing her to my family. I should have made her a priority in my life.

His mind continued to drift. This house was a constant source of triggered memories. Even when he tore his gaze away from the papers in front of him, all he could see was the garden. The lounger where he'd laid her down and sunk his cock deep into her body. Of Chloe's soft cries of 'Jordan' as she'd reached climax.

And their silly, foolish giggles when the noise had

disturbed the neighbor's dog and they'd had to make a naked dash back inside the house.

The disastrous launch of the Laguna Beach resort was going to be a picnic compared to the next eight months of his life.

And yet he was secretly proud of her.

She was giving him the exact amount of punishment he deserved. He'd not stopped to fight for their love. He'd let her down by not staying for the album launch. Had refused to come to the awards ceremony. Kept their relationship a secret from the entire world including his family. All because he was too afraid to be a man and own her love.

Any wonder she moved on with Zippo. Or whatever his name was.

The thought of the guy who had replaced him had Jordan letting out a slow, nervous breath. The new boyfriend hadn't lasted but what if Chloe had some other douche now in her life? If she brought a boyfriend to Vegas, he didn't know what he would do.

Okay. Okay. Get your head out of your ass and be a grown up. Talk to her.

"So, for the Vegas shows, will you be travelling back and forth at the end of each weekend, Chloe? I mean I'm assuming you will coming home here between shows."

He could only pray that was her plan. If she did leave the Vegas resort after her Sunday night show each week, then he would at least get a few days' respite. He could use the time to get out of Vegas and go into the desert. To walk, think, and hopefully find a way to maintain his mental health.

With his career at Royal Resorts all but over, he had to find a new path in life. His spare time in Las Vegas would be spent in making plans for his future.

Jordan placed the copies of the contract on the table, and Chloe's lawyer, Sandra, retrieved them. She flicked through each document checking they were all in order, before leaving them open at the signature page which had been marked for Chloe to sign.

"I haven't yet decided what I am going to do in the days between my performances, but I do expect that you will have a suite available for my personal use over the entire duration of my residency. I may have weeks when I decide to stay in Las Vegas."

Fabulous. I'm really looking forward to those weeks. Not.

Chloe picked up a pen and signed the contracts. She handed them to her lawyer, who added her signature. Jordan waited for his turn, then added his. He put two copies of the executed contracts carefully back into his document case and handed the last one back to Sandra.

Chloe flipped her pen onto the table. "As I don't plan to be hauling costumes and clothes back and forth between here and Vegas. I'll need the exclusive use of the suite for the entire duration of my contract. Only the approved members of my entourage will have access."

It was not a request—it was a flat out demand. Someone had been teaching Chloe how to stand up for herself. *Bravo.* He sorely wanted to give her a round of applause.

"I have already booked out the very best of our sky villa suites for you, Chloe. It will be ready and waiting for you when you arrive."

Jordan continued forcing himself to use Chloe's name, determined that he wasn't going to start addressing her as Ms. Fisher. Not while there was a tiny little bit of his pride still breathing.

Chloe turned to her manager. "What do you think, Nancy? I will need to arrive in Vegas early, but I would prefer to travel incognito. We want the buzz to explode when I get up on stage next to the new Royal Resorts CEO, Bryce Royal and he announces my shows."

Ouch. Jordan didn't even rate a mention, but his brother did. She really knew how to stick it to him.

"I could arrange to send one of our company jets. It would be our pleasure to fly you from LA to Vegas," offered Jordan. The Royal Resorts executive team had made it plain that the Chloe shows were going to bring in big money for the refurbished Las Vegas Platinum Collection hotel, so sending a jet from New York shouldn't present too much of a problem. "I can meet you at the airport and accompany you into Las Vegas. That's of course if you don't mind sharing the ride with me."

He made a point of looking Chloe dead in the eye as he spoke the last few words. He dared her to challenge him. She might be thinking to exact her revenge on him, but it wasn't going to be all one way.

I dare you. I double dare you to tell your manager about us.

"Hmm," said Chloe adopting a thoughtful air. She twirled a stray lock of her gorgeous black hair around her finger. "I've never been able to make the drive from LA to Vegas, so now might be the perfect time. Who knows if I will ever get this opportunity again."

She met his gaze and sweetly smiled. "Do you have a car that we can use? I'm thinking the two of us in a cozy get-to-know-you-better, private little road trip could be fun."

Oh damn. He was going to have to drive her all the way to Las Vegas. Five hours minimum, and if the LA traffic sucked it could be much longer. Add a few stops along the way for bathrooms et cetera. and Jordan was staring down the barrel of a good seven or eight hours alone with Chloe. And if this new Chloe was anything to go by, she was going to make him suffer for every single minute of it.

Score check. Chloe 1, Jordan 0.

CHAPTER THIRTY-EIGHT

She hadn't planned to drop the road trip on Jordan. In fact the notion of driving from LA to Las Vegas hadn't even crossed her mind. But watching him squirm as she laid out her plans for them to share a road trip was pure gold. This was a moment of priceless revenge for every woman who had been done wrong by a man. Her next album would feature a track dedicated to the look of abject horror which now sat on her ex's face.

The world enjoyed "Bitter Babe", wait until I slip out the next song.

Chloe moved in for the kill. "I want to leave on Friday. That will give me some time to get settled into my hotel suite while I decide on the exact date when I'm going to ask Royal Resorts to make the big announcement. I trust that is convenient with you, Jordan?"

She'd been a world-famous pop star for eight years, but it was only now that Chloe was finally beginning to understand the truth of what it meant to be a superstar. Without her old management team to tell her what to do, her requests had become demands. They were politely made, but with the full expectation of them being met as soon as possible.

I'm looking forward to having you as my personal bitch, Jordan.

"Nancy, if you fly over on the night before the press conference, we could go somewhere nice and have dinner. I'm sure Jordan knows an excellent Thai restaurant which he can arrange to book out entirely just for us. At Royal Resorts expense."

She held back her smile this time, afraid that she might actually burst into a solid, knee-slapping laugh. Watching the self-important, self-designated lady killer squirm in his seat was worth all the music awards Chloe had ever won. She should get up and give a thank you speech to herself for having come up with such a cunning plan on the fly.

Jordan cleared his throat. "Nothing is too much to organize for our Las Vegas star. I will make sure everything is perfect for your arrival." He gathered up his things and rose from his chair. After shaking hands with the various other people at the table and finally Nancy, he turned to Chloe. "Would you be happy if I arrive here at say eleven o'clock on Friday morning? If we leave around that time, it will help us to avoid some of the peak hour traffic."

Chloe rose and offered Jordan her hand, confident that she had won any and all battles of the day. But the moment their fingers touched, a jolt raced up her arm. She went to pull away, but he firmed his grasp. "I look forward to working with you, Chloe. And I'm excited about our impending Las Vegas road trip. As you say, it could be fun. I shall see you on Friday."

As the lawyers and accountants followed Jordan out the front door, Nancy stayed behind. She placed a gentle hand on Chloe's shoulder. "I would watch out for that one, I have a feeling he has a smooth tongue. He could talk you into all sorts of trouble if you're not too careful."

Chloe slowly nodded. Nancy as always, had the right of it. Jordan did have a smooth tongue. He'd already talked her into enough trouble in the past.

Her biggest concern now, however, was trying to find a way to resist her lustful memories. Of holding at bay the thoughts of what that smooth tongue had done to her naked body on many occasions. Her sex clenched as she glanced at the top of the table and recalled the heady nights when Jordan and his clever mouth had tortured her clit. Even now the echo of her screaming his name and begging for release still filled her mind.

And I insisted on a freakin road trip with him.

When would she learn? Traveling all the way to Vegas with her ex had to be the stupidest idea in the entire history of stupid ideas.

Well done, Chloe.

CHAPTER THIRTY-NINE

Jordan brought the green Land Rover Defender up to a smooth stop at the security gate. He'd brought the vehicle for his stay at Laguna Beach, figuring he would use it on short getaways to tour California and down into Mexico. With his head a mess and his management of the resort a drawn out disaster, he hadn't got any further than a quick trip down to San Diego to see a baseball game.

The security guards ticked his name off of their list and ushered him through. The car was a sweet ride, the music system top of the range. A Beyoncé track was pumping loudly through the speakers as he turned into Chloe's drive. He waited while the security gates swung slowly open. At the end of the driveway Jordan drew up outside the front door. He was done with using the visitor carpark.

Leaving the motor still running, Jordan opened the door of the SUV. The neighbors wouldn't appreciate the loud music, but then again, he was past the point of caring.

Enjoy the tunes, Chloe.

If he had been in less of a fighting mood, he would have done the polite thing and parked the SUV elsewhere. But not today. Not this morning. Jordan was fired up and ready to rumble. He wasn't going to take any shit.

In the days since he'd last been here for the contract signing, he'd thought long and hard as to how he was going to approach the time he spent working with Chloe. If her behavior toward him at the meeting had been any sort of indication, she had decided to play the diva card.

I bet Marta and her sidekick, Gabriela put Chloe up to it.

He'd found it strange when none of Chloe's usual cohort had made an appearance the other day. But knowing them, they were probably hiding, watching, and listening out of sight. Making plans.

Nope. They were not going to get the better of him. He might have messed up the Laguna Beach gig, but he was still Jordan Royal, part of a global family of billionaires. He'd never been a part of Chloe's entourage, and there was a limit as to how much he was prepared to grovel.

He had a contract with Chloe's signature on it. He'd checked every single clause, and nowhere did it say he had to act as Chloe's personal servant. It was also silent on the subject of what kind of music he could play in his car. She could make all the demands she wished, but he was going to stick to the letter of the contract. Or at least until they got to Vegas.

Standing in the driveway, music pumping, he waited for one of Chloe's people to rush out and demand he turn the volume down. Or move his vehicle. Or both. This morning, he wasn't going to do any of those things.

If I'm gonna do the time, first let me do the crime.

This stupid road trip of hers had played right into Jordan's hands. From LA to Vegas, Ms. Chloe Fisher was going to be subjected to some deep probing questions. Top of the list was the one about Zippo, and how quickly she had moved on. In the confides of the SUV, she would have nowhere to hide.

"Baby, it's time to tell the truth."

Oh great, I've been here 2.3 minutes and I'm already quoting lyrics from her last album. And that stupid song, "Bitter Babe".

When it became clear that no one was going to race out of the house to scold him, Jordan turned the car off and climbed out. He'd made his point.

Where are her security people? She can't be living here alone, can she?

The front door of the house opened, but instead of Marta or one of her brethren it was Chloe who came bounding out. She was dressed in jeans, a white T-shirt, and wore a pair of battered dark blue chucks. The rucksack which she carried over her shoulder made her look more like a girl heading out for a camping weekend with her boyfriend than the world's biggest pop star.

Don't think of her like that, she is the enemy.

She took one look at Jordan's SUV and casually tossed the bag to him, calling out, "Here, bell boy, earn your keep."

The rucksack landed against his chest with force. "Jeez, what have you got in here, bricks?"

Chloe shrugged. "Just a few things. And you're late. Don't make me have to call my manager and tell her that you are not meeting expectations."

Jordan sniffed at the air, turning his nose up in mock disgust. "Is that what happened to Zippo? He wasn't up to your high standards?"

She shook her head. "His name is Zapp. I don't know what your problem is, at least Zapp came for my album launch. And he supported me at the All American Music Awards. In my book that makes him a bigger man than a guy who just ghosts a girl."

Ouch, that one landed square in the middle of his face. He was batting one to two on this, and Chloe was swinging hard.

This new version of her was someone he hadn't met before. She was sharper around the edges than the girl he had first met in Berlin. He was struggling to find the Chloe who had spent that magical night in his arms in Paris. The woman he had fallen in love with, then lost.

There was a spark missing. This Chloe was a battle hardened, super defensive, take no prisoners, all-terrain version of her former self. And by defensive, he meant she was always ready to attack.

He'd also come armed for battle, but it was now apparent that if one of them didn't change their tactics, they were going to be constantly at one another's throats. Resigned to his fate, Jordan decided he was going to have to take care in which battles he picked with Chloe.

Placing the rucksack carefully into the back of the SUV along with the rest of his belongings, Jordan reached into the front and pulled out a take-out coffee cup. He handed it to Chloe. "Hot and fresh. I got it from the drive-through coffee place just down the hill. Consider it a peace offering."

She gave him a dark look of suspicion but took the drink from his hands. She held the thin, scalding-hot paper cup with ease. "Thank you. What's in it?"

"Strong flat white. No sugar. Real milk. Oh, and extra hot, just how you like it."

Her brows knitted together in confusion. Had she seriously expected him to have forgotten her coffee order? Theirs might have been a short, intense relationship but Jordan could remember just about everything that he and Chloe had done together. All the nights they had sat up late and talked. All the early morning coffee runs and then hiding the evidence from Marta's prying eyes.

Chloe moved closer and Jordan got his first real lungful of her perfume. The other day she'd been across the table from him, but now she was close. How was he going to survive the drive to Las Vegas if his senses were filled with her scent? Her perfume had lit the touchpaper for his cravings.

"Thank you, Jordan. That's very kind of you."

Jordan wanted nothing more than to close the car door and refuse to start their journey until she'd answered the thousand questions which filled his mind. He wanted to rip the Band-Aid off before they left Beverly Hills.

But a little voice inside his head cautioned him to take things slowly. That if he went down this road, they might never get out of LA.

The universe as always was listening. Jordan's cell buzzed and a message from Matthew popped up.

> Good luck today. Hope it all goes well. We need this. M.

His brother's message was a timely reminder. Confronting Chloe could well jeopardize this contract. With her wealth and fame, she mightn't need the Vegas gig, but he did. The company did.

"I am happy to bring you fresh coffee every day, Chloe. My job is to make you happy. Give you everything you need. I trust you will let me know if there comes a time when I don't measure up to expectations."

Measure up to her expectations, was he kidding? She'd come ready for battle, and Jordan had brought her favorite coffee. He'd even remembered how she loved her joe. Strong, and hot. And with real milk.

Chloe didn't miss the daily lectures she used to endure from Marta about the merits of oat and almond milk. She had no issue with any form of milk, figuring that everyone had their tastes as to how they liked their beverages. In the land of the free, people should be able to decide how they had their coffee.

That would make a terrible song lyric, but I reckon I could spin it into a jingle.

Only a matter of months ago she would have thought such an idea ludicrous, she was a multi award winning songwriter, and didn't need to write commercials. But Foster's betrayal had taught her that it paid to keep one's options open.

Jordan glanced over his shoulder at the SUV. "Was that bag all you are bringing on the road trip, or is everything else coming with your manager and the rest of your entourage on the *Chloe Jet?*"

Chloe stepped past Jordan and slipped her coffee cup into one of the cupholders on the passenger side of the SUV's cabin. "No, I have a couple more things."

She dashed back into the house and grabbed her statement Louis Vuitton rolling trunk. After pulling it outside, she went back for her aluminum trunk. This workhorse of a suitcase weighed fifteen pounds when it was empty, and usually only flew on the *Chloe Jet* as many of the commercial airlines refused to allow such oversized luggage.

"Here let me take that," said Jordan, as Chloe dragged the enormous silver suitcase over the threshold and onto the driveway. He tugged on it once, then grumbled. "What the devil have you got in here?"

"The devil wouldn't fit. He's still sleeping naked in my bed. The rest of the stuff are things I need," huffed Chloe.

That was a cheap shot, Chloe. Now he thinks I have someone else. Oh well.

It took the two of them to lift the suitcase into the back of the SUV. Jordan swore loudly as his thumb got caught between the suitcase and the car's floor board. Chloe wasn't going to apologize for having let go of the case a little too early.

"It's a good thing the tailgate opens up like a door, otherwise it might have been a struggle to get this inside," she said, offering him a smile.

The words "Shut up" followed her as she went back into the house. After grabbing her oversized bright red leather tote, Chloe set the security alarm system and locked the front door. A still grumbling Jordan slammed the tailgate closed.

Then silence fell.

She could almost hear the never ending list of questions that had to be rolling around in Jordan's head. Where were her people? What about her security team? And why the road trip?

Chloe pushed them all away. This was a moment for her to take stock. To acknowledge the changes that had happened in her life. And to calmly accept that there were more changes, and challenges, to come.

Removing the key from the lock, she stood staring at the door to her home. *I wonder when I will be back here again.* Placing a hand on the decorative glass side panel she made a silent vow. *This is my home. I will do whatever it takes to save this place ... for me.*

Wiping away an unbidden tear, she straightened her back and turned on her heel. Jordan was still standing alongside the car. A contemplative expression sat on his face. He knew she loved this house, she'd told him enough times. But Chloe couldn't find the strength to tell him the truth, that without the Las Vegas gig, she may have to sell her home.

Jordan was now a stranger to her, not someone in whom she could confide. Their relationship had crashed and burned, leaving no survivors.

He is here for the Vegas job, nothing more. Get through the next eight months and rebuild your life. And then forget you ever knew Jordan Royal.

As she approached the car, Jordan held out a black baseball cap. "You might want to put this on, along with your dark sunglasses. At least until we get out of the city." He pointed toward the windows of the SUV. Unlike the other vehicles in which Chloe normally travelled about LA, the Defender didn't have full black out on the glass. People would be able to see inside.

Chloe reached into her tote and with great flourish produced her own baseball cap. Hers was far superior to the one Jordan offered—it had its own sewn in blonde wig. Dropping the bag to her feet, she scooped up her hair and after tucking it under the wig, pulled the hat down low.

This isn't my first rodeo, buddy.

"Let's go."

CHAPTER FORTY

The LA mid-morning traffic moved at a stop, start pace, but they were actually making decent time. The only thing that annoyed Jordan was Chloe's choice of music.

After an hour and a half of what felt like hearing the same techno track being played on a continuous loop, Jordan hit the music symbol on the infotainment system. The techno beat disappeared and a '90s pop song filled the cabin.

Out of the corner of his eye, he caught a glimpse of Chloe's lilac painted fingernails as she reached out and punched the same button he had just hit. The deafening techno tune returned.

"If you don't like my taste in music, then at least have the manners to ask me to change it, don't just override my choices."

Jordan bit his bottom lip. They had barely made it out of the greater Los Angeles area, and with four more hours of driving ahead, he wasn't sure if his temper would hold. He had to let off at least a little steam.

"Alright. I hate this damn music. If you can call it music. And I would prefer that you played something else, something which won't have my brain exploding while I am behind the wheel of a fast-moving automobile. Was that clear enough for you?"

Chloe huffed. "I wouldn't say this traffic has us moving at any real speed, but that's because you were determined to take this route, rather than the I-10. You should have let me work the navigation system."

His teeth crushed once more into his bottom lip. At this rate, he was going to draw blood well before they reached Barstow. "I took the route which had the least amount of roadwork. When we left your house, the GPS said this was the fastest one."

She had changed, and not for the good. While he appreciated Chloe finally voicing her own opinion, Jordan was less than impressed that she seemed determined to ride his ass all the way to Nevada. Had Marta been giving her lessons? It sure felt like it.

"I want to stop for more coffee," she demanded.

"And I want you to turn that techno shit off," he snapped back.

He'd had years of experience in squabbling with Matthew to have him prize-fight fit for this sort of encounter. Jordan could go toe-to-toe, tit-for-tat for hours. If Chloe wanted another coffee, she was going to have to be the one to cave.

"Did you ever watch the TV series, Supernatural?" he asked.

"No, why?"

Pity. Because if you did, you would know the rules. Driver picks the music, shotgun shuts his cakehole.

"Nothing, just making conversation. Now would you like to turn the music down, or preferably off, so I can focus on finding a place to stop for coffee?"

Jordan would had loved to explain the Supernatural reference, but things were tense enough already. The last thing he needed was for Chloe to arrive in Vegas thoroughly pissed off and looking to have him bounced from the manager gig. He could just imagine having to handle the phone call from Bryce, his new boss.

His career was sitting on a bar stool at the last-chance saloon, and he was not going to stuff this up.

Chloe mercifully turned the music down, and Jordan began scanning the roadside for a place that sold coffee.

She'd gotten under his skin. Good. Payback was a bitch, and Chloe was going to keep leaning in hard. Last night she had spent some time online checking up on him. Trying to figure out why a Royal Resorts executive would have been tasked with the job of baby-sitting a pop singer. Except he wasn't an executive any more by the look of it. Jordan's name and photo were missing from the Royal Resorts website. She'd also uncovered some scathing press articles about the launch of the Laguna Beach resort.

Jordan coming out to Las Vegas for the launch made sense. He was part of the House of Royal family conglomerate, and the success of her residency would have an impact on the company's bottom line. But him willingly spending the next eight months in Vegas catering to her every whim didn't make a lick of sense.

Something has happened. Maybe he's fallen out with his father.

He was hiding something, but then again, she also had plenty of her own secrets. Things such as the real reason why her jet wouldn't be seen anytime soon in Las Vegas. Or the truth as to why Marta and Gabriela were no longer on the scene.

In time the questions would come, but first she had to get the Vegas residency announcement finalized. She'd feel a whole lot more comfortable about sharing things with Jordan once tickets had gone on sale. Once she was certain that no one could find a loophole to back out of the deal. If they discovered she was staring bankruptcy in the face, the Royal Resorts people might look to renegotiate the contract.

I can't have that.

Jordan changed lanes and the SUV slowed. "Does that place look ok to you?" he asked.

Chloe glanced in the direction of where Jordan was pointing. The store in question seemed to be a mom and pop operation on the side of the road. From here, it looked clean and respectable.

"As long as they serve a half-decent cup of coffee, I'm all good."

Jordan turned off the highway and onto the side access road. He pulled up in front of the store and killed the motor. "Did you want to come inside, or would you rather sit out here and wait?"

Chloe wanted this road trip to be just her and Jordan. And since no one knew, she was travelling to Las Vegas, and it was only a few hours in the car, she felt safe enough with him to take the risk.

Once they got to Vegas, it would be a different story. She would get Jordan to talk to the head of security at the hotel and decide what sort of protection they felt was necessary. Her contract with the resort included a full time security detail, but there was always a fine balance between being protected and feeling suffocated. Too many people had told Chloe what to do in the past, and she had paid the price for not listening to her own instincts.

"I'm sure I'll be safe in the store. Besides I have you for protection, I'm sure there's a clause somewhere in the contract that says you have to take one for the team if I am in danger."

Dang, I am on form this morning! Another coffee and I will be dangerous.

The wig and baseball cap were a great disguise, but they itched. As soon as they got out into the desert, Chloe planned to ditch them and be herself.

"Coffee. What else would you like, Chloe?"

The truth of why you are here, in a take-out bag, would be nice.

"Just the coffee. Though if they have anything that looks healthy and yum, I could go with that—or not. While you order the coffees, I'll just look around and see if anything else takes my fancy."

She got a small shake of Jordan's head in response to her vague answer. Without people constantly arranging her meals, and her mindlessly eating whatever was served up to her, Chloe was finding it hard to make her own decisions about food. Most of her recent menu choices had been heavily skewed toward pizza and tacos.

As soon as the announcement of the shows was done, she intended to get a trainer and get herself into concert shape. It wasn't just about looking good in her costumes, fitness gave her stamina. And stamina was what she needed for being able to perform on stage for several hours as well as hitting the high notes of her songs.

Live for today, tomorrow we start the workout diet.

They both got out of the SUV and headed for the store. He turned and met her gaze. "Are you really sure about this?" he asked, glancing around. "What if someone recognizes you?"

Chloe shrugged. "I'll risk it. And even if someone does recognize me, which I doubt they will, it might turn out to be good publicity. Get the millions of members of Chloe's Garden wondering why I was out on the road heading toward

Vegas. Social media rumors are gold if they get the fans talking about possible concert sales."

She wasn't afraid of the members of Chloe's Garden. They were her true fans. But like everything in the entertainment business, timing was critical. It would be better to manage the small breadcrumbs of rumors from the safety of her suite at the resort in Vegas, so the uncomfortable wig and baseball cap had to stay on.

Once inside the store, Jordan made his way over to the counter and ordered their coffees. Chloe wandered down one of the short aisles. It was a small place, not much bigger than the Snack Shop convenience store which was close to her house. They stocked the usual snacks, drinks, and random toiletries. All the stuff that people on the road would want.

Chloe absentmindedly picked up a box of tissues, and a stick of lip balm. Without people to anticipate her every need, she'd started running out of things. She'd recently had to learn how to handle online grocery orders.

A nearby display rack caught her attention. "Beef jerky!" she squealed with delight. Chips came next. With her arms ladened with goodies and snacks, an excited Chloe finally headed for the service desk. Jordan, who had a coffee in either hand, quickly stepped aside as Chloe leaned over and dropped her treasure haul onto the counter. "And these, please."

The cashier swiped her snacks through, and Jordan paid for them. With her paper bag filled with goodies in one hand and her piping hot cup of joe in the other, Chloe hip checked the door and marched outside.

He caught up with her at the car, opening the door just as she reached it. "Thank you, Jordan, you make a wonderful assistant," she said, climbing back inside. While he mumbled under his breath about being her personal manager *not bloody assistant*, Chloe spent a considered minute or two carefully arranging bags. She put her piping hot cup of coffee into the holder in the center console, humming to herself as she went about making sure everything was perfect.

Just before she reached for her seatbelt, she dragged the wig and cap off her head and tossed it over her shoulder. It landed on the passenger seat behind her. "Thank god for that, those wigs make my head sweat."

"Is there anything you would like before we set off again?" asked Jordan, climbing into the driver's side of the SUV. Chloe checked her snack collection—she had it all laid out on the dashboard tray in front of her. A veritable cornucopia of road trip foodie delights.

"So where do we start? Chips, jerky, gum, or candy?"

From out of nowhere Jordan magically produced a paper bag and handed it to her. "We start with these. Cinnamon rolls. They are pull-apart so if you are good to share one, we could save the second one for later."

Chloe took the bag and after poking her nose inside, gushed. "I'm sure these are very bad for you. Think of all the sugar. The calories. The carbs."

Jordan chuckled. "But the taste of enjoying your life to the fullest beats them all." His words took her back to that first morning in Paris. To the buttery goodness of the freshly baked croissants. He'd given her a brief glimpse of a life where treats were not forbidden. Where comfort and friendship came before trying to impress the world.

She'd wanted that world, thought that with Jordan she'd really had a chance of finally having it. But then she remembered how he'd failed her. How he'd walked away without looking back. He had never called. Not once.

"Jordan, when we get to Vegas, would you do something for me?"

"Of course, that's what I am here for, to cater to your every wish and desire."

The words rolled so easily off his tongue. But instead of filling her with a sense of reassurance, they only served to remind Chloe that his family were in the people pleasing business. He'd likely been spouting that sort of customer-service line from the day he'd uttered his first words.

But Jordan wasn't going to be able to find what she wished for in the in-house menu or have someone run out to a fancy store to buy it.

"When we get to Las Vegas, I want you to tell me the truth as to why you took on this management gig. I'm not buying the whole, 'it's good for business' routine. You are an executive at Royal Resorts, and I might not know a lot about how big companies work but I do know that they don't send their top people to do these sorts of jobs."

She ripped open the cinnamon roll and handed half of it to Jordan. He took it and gave a nod of thanks. For the next hour as Jordan drove, they sat munching their way through the snacks, neither one saying a word.

CHAPTER FORTY-ONE

"Can we please stop for a bathroom break?" Chloe had downed three coffees and a gallon of water already this morning. Her bladder was in grave danger of springing a leak. And all those sugary treats were playing merry havoc with her gut. She wasn't used to eating that much junk food in one sitting.

Jordan pointed to a rest stop a little way ahead. "Let's pull in there and you can go find relief."

Relief. It was sorely needed.

Chloe gripped onto the front rail of the SUV as Jordan turned off the highway and onto a dirt road. She could have sworn he made an effort to hit every bump and hole in the road. Her stomach was in knots and cramping badly by the time he stopped the car. He gave the brakes a little too hard a nudge and she glared at him.

Jordan didn't meet her gaze. He just sat staring straight ahead, before lazily pointing to a nearby sign which said *Women's Bathroom*. "You go on ahead and I will follow to make sure no super fans have tracked us from LA."

She muttered a few choice words in his direction, the last one being, "Asshole," and climbed out of the SUV. They were in the middle of nowhere and she wasn't going to bother with the hat and the wig. When her stomach gave a dangerous rumble, she knew she didn't have much time.

By the time she reached the washrooms, Chloe was sweating. Any moment now, and she feared the worst might happen. Her bowels threatened revenge.

No more junk food on this trip. I promise.

"What is wrong with me?" muttered Jordan, as he watched a clearly distressed Chloe make her way toward the ladies washrooms. He hadn't made any effort to avoid the bumps as he left the highway. And he'd been too heavy footed on the brakes. He was punishing her for no good reason. The silence in the SUV over the past hour had been just as much his fault as hers.

Las Vegas was still a number of hours away. When they got there, she wanted to talk. *No. She wants answers.* He'd barely survived the end of their relationship and the disaster at the resort, so the last thing Jordan wanted was to drag all that up again. To relive the pain that he'd spent the best part of seven months stuffing down deep.

His therapist had warned him not to suppress his emotions, rather he should form a healthier relationship with them. She'd cautioned him on the possible damage it could cause in the long run if he didn't embrace this way of thinking.

But he would choose short term sanity over the risk of future pain. Burying emotions was the only way he was going to get through this time with Chloe.

When her musical residency was over, and the board of

Royal Resorts finally cut him loose, then he would go back into therapy and dig it all up. Right now, his pain was resting under a headstone which read. *Here lies Jordan Royal's biggest mistakes—the ones he never learned from.*

After Chloe disappeared into the washrooms, Jordan sat watching the door for a few minutes. A mother and young daughter made their way in, and a middle aged woman came out. He glanced around the parking area. There were only a handful of cars. No paparazzi, or hordes of screaming Chloe fans were anywhere in sight.

"Better safe than sorry," he grumbled. He got out of the car and ambled over to the grassy area in front of the washrooms where there was a water drinking fountain and a couple of trash cans. A big metal map on an upright frame showed the local area and places of interest. Jordan moved past them and took up a spot with a direct line of sight to the entrance of the brick building where Chloe had gone.

Finally, she reappeared. The mother and daughter followed close behind. Jordan took two steps toward the group but catching Chloe's eye and the brief shake of her head, he halted in his tracks. She wasn't in any sort of danger.

The young girl, who Jordan guessed was around ten years old, was beaming from ear to ear. She kept smiling at Chloe and saying, "Oh my god. Mom. Oh my god."

His bratty pop star road-trip companion had met a fan.

Chloe made her way over to Jordan. She nodded at his phone, then handed her own to him. "Could you please take a photo of us on your cell, then take one on mine so I can share it to my Instagram?"

Jordan narrowed his eyes. "What?"

She turned and gave a finger wave to the girl and her mother, then came back to Jordan. "If you take one on my phone, then I can decide when it gets posted to social media, and I can tag Mandy and her mom. The other one, on your cell, well, that's for you. I wanted you to have something to remember this trip by."

"Oh."

"I figure a happy roadside snap would be better than remembering how you spent the whole trip to Vegas silently hating yourself for the shitty way you treated me." She leaned in close. "You know that bit where you walked out of my life and smashed my heart."

Jordan's phone slipped from his fingers. It landed on the stone edging near the water fountain with a horrible smack. He bent and picked it up. The screen was cracked all the way from the top left to the bottom right. It was broken, but still working. It was a small win, and after the past few months, Jordan would take any win.

I smashed her heart. Seriously? Was Zapp a figment of my imagination?

Fixing a smile firmly to his face, he righted himself. Chloe had already gone back to talk to Mandy and her mother, leaving Jordan with no other choice but to do as she had asked.

This is the gig, remember? Make the star of the Las Vegas show happy. Make Bryce, Dad, and the board of Royal Resorts happy.

The eyes of the young Chloe fan shone bright with delight. Even her mother looked more than a little starstruck. Jordan could just imagine their surprise at walking into the rest stop bathroom and finding a world-famous pop star at the basin washing her hands.

"Hi, are you Chloe's boyfriend?" gushed Mandy.

Her mother had the good grace to mouth. "Sorry."

Heat burned on his cheeks, kids certainly knew just how to skewer your pride. That question had Jordan drawing deep to find his best, award winning smile. "No, I'm just a friend of

Chloe's. We decided to go for a drive and ended up here. We will be heading back to LA now."

The last thing they needed was for word to slip out and for people to get in their cars and start looking for Chloe on the highway.

He took Chloe's phone from her, waiting patiently while she and her fans got themselves organized. For the next few minutes, Jordan took plenty of photos. There were pictures of Chloe and Mandy, Chloe and Mandy's mom, Chloe, Mandy, and Mandy's mom. And a dozen variations on poses, smiles, and kisses to the camera.

With his own phone, Jordan took a simple one of Chloe and Mandy hugging. Then when she wasn't looking, he snapped off one of Chloe as she stood saying her final goodbyes. Jordan got Mandy's address and gave a solemn promise that he would make sure to send her a signed copy of one of the photos. And a Chloe T-shirt.

Many 'I love you' and hugs later, Chloe finally said goodbye to Mandy and her mom. Jordan followed her back to the car, and after climbing in, gently placed his damaged phone into the center console. He pulled the SUV back onto the highway, feeling a touch guilty at having lied to Mandy about his and Chloe's destination.

"Thank you. That was nicely handled," said Chloe. She lay her hand on Jordan's arm for a brief moment. His body stiffened at her touch.

All his brave notions of not allowing Chloe another second of living rent free in his head and heart now revealed themselves to be nothing more than a thin layer of hope. Her touch had torn his resolve to pieces.

There was only one thing he could do to stay sane.

Get to Vegas, and then create as much space as possible between me and her.

As the tires of the SUV gripped the highway, he was certain that the universe was gently laughing at him, waiting for the moment when it could throw his life yet another curveball.

CHAPTER FORTY-TWO

Jordan decided he wasn't going to wait for that ball to hit him smack in the middle of his face. A little way past the town of Baker, California, he turned off the highway and onto a dirt road. He drove a good half mile before finally pulling the SUV over and turning off the engine.

Chloe hadn't spoken a word to him since their last stop and he couldn't stand the silence any longer. The tension was killing him. An isolated road in the middle of the desert seemed as good a place as any to have things out with her.

But Chloe was one step ahead of him.

As soon as the car came to a complete stop, she undid her seatbelt, and opened the door. She climbed out then slammed it behind her. Chloe was headed deep into the Mojavi Desert when Jordan finally caught up with her. He took a hold of her arm, and as she slowed her steps, he locked his elbow around hers. She was not going to get away.

"Let go of me," she snapped.

"No. Not until you explain that quip at the rest stop. What the hell do you mean I walked away? You were the one who took up with Zippo," he bit back.

Chloe came to a sudden halt, her boots scuffing up a small cloud of dust. She turned to face Jordan. "For the last time, his name is Zapp, and I didn't do anything with him. Foster had just signed Zapp, and his band and he wanted to create a fantasy for the fans. When he first suggested it, I said no, but then you abandoned me and went back to New York. I agreed to pretend Zapp, and I were a thing. Not because of the publicity but because I wanted to see if you really did give a damn about me. And your silence was all the proof I needed, that you didn't care."

What he'd seen on the red carpet at the All American Music Awards had been for show? It was just something to get a rise out of him. Chloe hadn't ever been with Zapp.

The truth was, his and Chloe's relationship had been crumbling long before the awards night. The album launch had really been its death knell.

I walked out of her home the night of the album launch. And I did go back to NYC. I made her believe I didn't care.

"Throw another man in my face all you like, Jordan, but you were the one who left my launch party. You were the one who decided I wasn't worthy of meeting your father. And you were the one who decided that the awards show didn't mean a damn thing, that I didn't matter. You went home and had a barbecue with your family instead."

He let go of her arm, taking a step back. It left them standing face to face under the bright California sun. If they were going to have it out, then he may as well get his side of the story told.

"You did matter, Chloe. More than you will ever know."

She rolled her eyes at his words and huffed. "Bullshit. I was a fling, a notch on your billionaire playboy bed post. If you had cared, you would have at least called the night of the awards."

There had been plenty of women in his life over the years,

some he had even fancied himself falling for on the odd occasion, but none of them came close to what he'd felt for her. Or the pain he'd endured when things had ended so badly between them.

"If I thought that what we had was just a fling, Chloe, I wouldn't be here. I would have told my father that I couldn't be bothered with you, and to get someone else to do this job."

I need to tell her the truth about why I left. About how she made me feel less.

"So why are you here, Jordan? I can't for the life of me figure out why an executive of Royal Resorts would be tasked with the job of babysitting a pop star."

Chloe didn't reveal that she'd discovered Jordan's profile was missing from the executive team page on the Royal Resorts website. And she wasn't going to mention the articles she had read about the Laguna Beach resort, and its initial failed opening. After the pain he'd caused her, she wasn't going to give him an easy way out.

Let him tell me the truth.

"Are you going to tell me that you are doing this job simply to stay on the right side of your daddy, to protect his company's investment in the deal? If that's the case then just have the balls to say so Jordan, and we can build from there. And when I mean build, I mean a twenty foot high wall between us with a small hole in it through which I can pass notes when I need things from you."

Her fingernails dug deep into the skin of her palms. She was not going to cry. She'd rather march out into the heat of the blistering desert, die, and let the vultures pluck out her eyeballs than do that in front of him. Jordan didn't deserve to see the fruits of his cruel hearted labor—to see her pain.

He closed his eyes and sighed. "No. It's not just about the money. But you're dragging all the reasons for our breakup from out of the past and turning them into fodder for an argument here and now. You keep trying to put all the blame on me. You still don't understand why I left. Or how small you made me feel. You are not the only one hurt here."

I'd hurt him. Made him feel small. What?

Chloe lowered her gaze to focus on the brown and white sand at Jordan's feet. She'd learned long ago not to look directly at the person who had come to deliver her bad news. Her memories of her parents were of not of their faces, but rather their shoes. Objects always held less pain than people.

"Tell me, Jordan. Why did you leave, and don't bother trying to sugar coat it, I would rather hear the truth. I can handle that much better than lies."

"Chloe, look at me."

She shook her head. No. That was not how things worked. Her heart and mind processed pain in a particular way. A way that offered protection. She kept her head down.

His boots shuffled forward, and Jordan's tall figure blocked out the sun. "Chloe. Please."

Damn. Why couldn't Jordan be like everyone else in her life? Just dump a world of pain and trouble on her head and then leave. At least then, she could get on with dealing with it. Alone. Like she'd always done.

Here in the middle of nowhere, he wasn't going to let her retreat into her usual safe place. He was going to make her look and listen.

Think of the house and how getting this Vegas gig will save it. Come on, Chloe.

She lifted her gaze and looked at him. "Alright. Talk to me, Jordan."

He gave her a soft, hopeful smile. "Things were tough for me in your world right from the outset. Your people made it very clear that I was considered a trespasser. An intruder. And unwelcome."

"I didn't do that. I never saw you as an outsider."

"No you didn't, but if I'm being honest, you did far worse. You refused to see how hard things were for me. You might have been dealing with your album, but I never once felt that you understood how big the resort project was, or how much I was struggling with it all." Jordan's hands balled into fists. "And on top of all that, was the constant feeling that you didn't want to fight for any of it. Not for us, and not for your freedom."

Chloe gasped. Words of denial were ready on her lips, but Jordan shook his head. He was going to make her listen, no matter how much she didn't want to hear what he had to say.

"You asked. Now I am telling," he said. "I saw how your entourage treat you. The horrible way Marta spoke to you on the phone that morning in Paris made me feel sick to my stomach. They control your life. Tell you what to do, what to say. Hell, even what to put in your mouth."

Chloe could just imagine Marta and Gabriela having a pink fit in the convenience store. Their voices had been protesting loudly in her head as she picked up the packet of candy. For the first time in her life, she had steadfastly ignored them.

"And when I tried to share anything with you other than what had been officially approved by your people, I was slapped down. I fought to break through to you, Chloe, but you let them make the decisions. From where I stood—and do stand—you've been manipulated and, dare I say, abused."

He was telling the truth about her former employees, that

for all intents and purposes she had been the victim of her own mean girls. She'd even paid them for the privilege of letting them bully her.

"As I recall, Jordan, you were simply just the other side of the same coin. On the one hand I had Marta and her team trying to enforce their opinions on me, while on the other I had you telling me to live my life while also constantly letting me down," she bit back.

Her heart was racing. She was dumping all this on him, and they hadn't even got the concert shows officially announced. Heck, she hadn't even made it to Vegas.

"You are right. I did let you down. But our breakup wasn't all one-sided." He moved away, now he was the one who looked like they were intending to walk into the desert.

Chloe threw up her hands in frustration. "Where are you going?!"

Jordan hurried back, and when he got to where Chloe stood in increasing confusion, he got right in her face. "Nowhere. I'm going nowhere until you hear the rest of it. I had to leave the album launch because of my work commitments. And I realize now that not bringing my father to meet you was a serious mistake on my part. It wasn't anything to do with you personally, it was about the resort launch. I was torn and angry with myself for getting on the plane and going back to New York, but I had no choice. Dad had called in a lot of favors to get me that gig, and I was worried that if he thought I was distracted by being with you, he might not think I was up to the task. He's never believed in me the way he believes in my brothers. And after we broke up, and I totally burned myself out at the resort, I proved to him that all his long-held reservations about me were right."

Jordan had failed. Now things made sense.

"Foster called me your deadbeat boyfriend, and a risk. And you agreed with him. I did my best to prove to you that

that wasn't the case, but you let Foster and your nest of vipers poison everything between us."

Marta had crowed about Jordan's departure for days. Banged on and on about how ungrateful he was. And how blind Chloe had been. But in his world, she wasn't the victim, she was villain of the piece.

"I get things were tense between us, and yes it was stupid of me to refuse your calls after the album launch, but I was angry and hurt, Jordan. The fake dating thing with Zapp was designed to make you stop sending me messages and flowers, and instead get your ass on a plane. All it got me was silence. I still can't believe you stopped calling."

Chloe held her hands together and brought them to her lips. The hot sun was beating down on her head, and this back and forth of unkind accusations was utterly exhausting. After their breakup, they'd each stayed in their respective hurt, neither daring to risk more pain by reaching out for the other.

Jordan shook his head. "I did call. On the night of the awards. I spoke to Marta, and she made it clear that I was out. That you didn't want to hear from me ever again. I saw you and Zapp kissing on the red carpet, and figured you were doing it to make sure I got the message that we were over and done."

He'd tried to call.

"Jordan, I didn't tell her to say that because none of it was true. And I swear I didn't know anything about your call. Marta must have deleted it from my phone." Chloe's shoulders sagged. It was just another in a long line of deceitful things she'd discovered about her former assistant. "Turns out Marta did a lot of things like that before I fired her."

Jordan's eyes grew wide. "You fired Marta? I gathered Foster was gone— but Marta, wow."

"Yep. She, Gabriela, all my employees are gone. And I have a whole new management team in place."

"So who are your new assistants, I expect I will be liaising with them?"

Chloe stepped away. If they kept up with this line of conversation, the subject of her money troubles would soon find a way to come to the surface. She wasn't ready for that conversation.

"I'm between support teams at present. Until I find new people, it's just you and me. And speaking of which, we had better get going." She couldn't do any more sharing today. Her heart was pounding hard in her chest as Chloe headed back toward the SUV.

A silent Jordan followed.

CHAPTER FORTY-THREE

When they got back in the SUV, Chloe put a podcast on. Jordan vaguely listened to it as he drove, but he suspected he took in as little of it as Chloe likely did. Today's revelations had left them both reeling. Misunderstandings. Lies. And both had been left in a world of pain.

He was still musing over every single word of his and Chloe's conversation as the sign for the Nevada state border came into view. While Chloe managed a tepid, "Yay," Jordan couldn't muster the energy.

"We should be at the Royal Resorts, Las Vegas hotel in about an hour. I checked with the team this morning, and they said everything is ready."

Their confrontation in the desert had left Jordan's head spinning. There'd been things he'd held to be the solid truth, which had now turned out to be false. People had lied.

What am I going to do about all this? That thing with Zapp was fake. Chloe never got my message. And she's gotten rid of all her entourage.

It would have been easy enough to pull the SUV back off the road and find somewhere to have another heart to heart with Chloe, but Jordan resisted the temptation. He sensed she had reached her emotional limit for the day.

Get to the hotel. Get Chloe settled. Call the office in New York, then go take a long hot shower.

It was a simple enough plan, and Jordan was determined to stick to it. Allowing his head to get further muddled over Chloe on day one of their eight month commitment would be the height of stupidity.

Today's revelations couldn't undo the damage. His behavior in the months following his and Chloe's breakup had cost Royal Resorts many millions of dollars. It had also cost him his father's trust. He couldn't put a price on that, nor on Bryce's willingness to give him one last chance.

He glanced over at Chloe. She was slumped against the passenger upright bar. Her dark sunglasses hid any real signs of emotion from his view. The upturned collar of her light jacket into which she had sunk meant her face was barely visible.

But if he didn't break the tension, it was going to be awkward as hell once they reached the hotel. "Have you been to Vegas before? I mean as a normal person," he asked.

Chloe shifted in her seat and sat upright. She rolled her shoulders back. "I forgot how stiff you can get on long car rides. I won't be rushing to do this again any time soon I can tell you." Picking up her soda, she took a long sip. "I don't know what it means to be just a normal person. I'm twenty nine years old and I've been famous since I was twenty. But in answer to your question, no I've never really been to Las Vegas. My trips here have always been ones where I fly in, do an awards or charity show, then fly out. Often on the same night."

Jordan saw an opening. "Would you like to do some touristy type things while you're here? I mean you probably won't be able to wander the Strip with a fanny pack and camera, but we could look to maybe slip you secretly into a show at the Sphere at the Venetian Resort. I hear the LED screen is amazing."

She let out a chuckle. "Heck, I'd be happy to go to a drive through for a greasy burger. That's the sort of thing I want. Oh, and the M&M store. My old team would never have allowed me to go inside one of those."

"So what happened? I mean with your entourage. Why did you let them all go? I thought they ran your life."

Of course Jordan wasn't going to let this go. He was like a dog with a bone. Marta had hated Jordan, and she was pretty certain that the feeling had been close to mutual. With his enemy now vanquished, Jordan would want to know the reasons why.

Chloe had practiced her response. Nancy had given her tips on what to say in public, or to the press about the recent changes in her management and private support team. And as much as Jordan might want to know all the sordid details, he was going to have to settle on getting the same bland explanation as everybody else.

"I just decided it was time to make some changes. And when you do that with any aspect of your life, it's inevitable that some people are not able to continue to share your journey."

It was a social media friendly, AI generated, group hug, publicist branded piece of utter bullshit, but apparently it was what people wanted to hear. They didn't want to know that you had real emotions or that relationships were hard and dirty, or that despite your best efforts people could still fail.

To the outside world she was Chloe. She was perfect. Untouchable. And she never made mistakes. Even her most avid fans in Chloe's Garden only got the rarest of glimpses of the real woman. Chloe was determined that it had to stay that way. If no one got in, then she couldn't get hurt.

She kept her gaze focused on the road ahead. Jordan wasn't stupid, he would want more than the *conscious uncoupling* public statement version of the truth.

"So how did your team take it? I mean was it a good parting? I'm only asking because we need to have a consistent narrative while you are performing at the resort," he asked.

You can keep pushing, but I'm not telling you.

"I have my own agent and lawyers to handle all that stuff, Jordan, it's not your concern. Rest assured that while I am working under contract with your family's company there won't be any negative publicity directly generated by me."

It was as close as she could get to telling him to mind his own business, without coming out and actually saying it. She didn't owe Jordan any more explanation than the one she had already given him. His job was to help her while she was in Vegas, hers was to put on a brilliant show for the fans. They should stick to their respective roles.

This gig was about shoring up her finances, making sure she kept her home. It was most definitely not about trying to make amends with her former lover.

That ship had sailed.

CHAPTER FORTY-FOUR

The bell of the private elevator dinged, announcing their arrival, but only Jordan and Chloe heard it. From the underground parking garage all the way to the twenty eighth floor, it had been just the two of them. The few staff who were in the know about the new resort resident had been instructed to keep well clear. Chloe's arrival was a closely guarded secret. Until the official concert series announcement, no one was to even mention her name. The sky villa was under the name of Jordan Royal.

Jordan was the first to step out of the elevator. "Welcome to your sky villa, Ms. Fisher. This is your Royal Resorts, Las Vegas, home away from home."

Chloe gave him an odd look. He hazarded a guess at what she was thinking. Why was he addressing her in such a formal manner?

Protection was the answer.

Before picking up her at her home this morning, he'd done his best to condition himself to not liking Chloe, to keeping his distance. Listening to "Bitter Babe" on repeat had been his latest attempt at exposure therapy.

In the past, facing his fears had worked but the road trip from LA had unfortunately undone a great deal of Jordan's best laid plans to protect his heart from further pain.

Discovering that she had been left as bruised and hurt from their breakup as he had, was something he hadn't anticipated. And while he was prepared to accept that was likely the truth, Jordan was now in a tight bind. Knowledge was one thing, what to do with it was quite another.

Get her settled, and then get the hell out of here.

"Let me show you around, and you can see what facilities are at your fingertips." Jordan ushered a still silent Chloe into the main living area. Floor to ceiling windows showcased the Vegas strip. The hotel across the road from the Royal Resorts Platinum Collection Las Vegas, didn't come up to the same height, so the view included the nearby mountains and desert. In preparation for Chloe's arrival, Jordan had spent a night in the sky villa, and he could attest to the magnificence of the evening sunset.

Chloe moved quietly about the space, taking it all in. She stopped and ran her fingers along the top of one of the luxuriously appointed deep-green couches which sat in the middle of the space, before moving toward the windows.

"So just to confirm the terms of the contract. This is your private space, it will be exclusively yours from today, until the end of your residency. You will have the access key and codes and can come and go as you please."

She nodded her understanding.

"If there is anything you would like altered before your rehearsals begin, such as the wall colors, drapes, or furnishings just let me know and I will have it changed. We want you to feel as comfortable as possible during your stay."

His words came out exactly as rehearsed; word for word how Bryce and the PR team had written them.

"No, it's all fine."

Why anyone in their right mind would want to change the warm cream and green design palette Jordan couldn't fathom, but then again, he hadn't much experience with people from the entertainment world. All he knew about them, and their reported demands were what he'd picked up from the gossip sites.

He barely remembered what the interior of Chloe's house looked like, recalling that there had always been too many people around for him to be able to sit and take it all in.

Being alone with Chloe brought back memories. Of the nights they had spent together. Of the hope he'd foolishly held for them to find a way to be together.

Jordan hurried over to a nearby coffee table and picked up an iPad. "This is your personal concierge for anything you want. It has the inhouse dining menu, as well as access to any VIP delivery service you might want, both here at the resort and in the greater city of Vegas. There are over four thousand restaurants in Vegas from which to choose."

Chloe set her oversized tote on the table. She looked ill at ease. Jordan's heart spoke its burning desire. *Take her in your arms. Hold her.*

"And what if I just want a toasted ham and cheese sandwich. Or even to cook something for myself. Can I order groceries?"

"Absolutely, but first let me show you the kitchen." He led her through a nearby doorway and into another part of the sky villa. This space contained amongst other things, a full chef's kitchen. "The refrigerator is already fully stocked with as many healthy things as I could remember you eating. All you have to do is either scan the products as you take them out of the fridge or use the keypad on the front to order something else. We can have anything you want brought up within the hour."

Jordan opened the French doors, proudly displaying the

delicious array of salads and bottles of freshly made protein smoothies. Chloe moved forward and examined the contents of the refrigerator. "Is there any chance of there being chocolate cake or a pie lurking in the back somewhere?"

Away from the iron fisted rule of her former entourage, it appeared that Chloe was now allowing herself some treats. It was nice to see her getting a little balance in her life.

"No, but that can be arranged. Just let me know what you want."

Chloe closed the fridge door with a tired sigh. "What I want is to have a shower and wash the day from my skin. Then I'll have a look at food." She turned, and lifting her head, met Jordan's gaze. "Will you be staying to eat with me?"

"Um, no. I have a few things I need to get sorted this evening." He held up his phone with its cracked screen. "I'll see you tomorrow."

Jordan held his breath. He was desperate to escape, to drive out into the desert and get some fresh air. He'd been living with Chloe's scent all day and had reached the end of his limit. But if she asked him to stay, if she commanded it, he would have no choice but to remain. To endure.

An unmistakable look of disappointment appeared briefly on her face. It lingered for a moment, and then it was gone. She'd ushered it away.

How am I going to survive the next eight months?

"Of course, I understand. You have your own life." He watched with growing anguish as Chloe reached out and took a hold of his hand. "Thank you, Jordan. Thank you for today. I'm glad that we managed to clear up a few misunderstandings. I hope it will make things easier for the both of us going forward."

Without thinking he bent his head. His gaze was fixed on Chloe's lips. On the soft, pink buds that he still tasted in his dreams. She needed kissing. There wasn't a single woman in the world who needed to be kissed more right now than Chloe.

Closer. Another inch or two and they would be lips to lips.

He could have wept with joy when his father's voice slipped into his mind and gently cautioned, *"Remember Laguna Beach. If you stuff this up, you will be gone"*. The board would ask for his immediate resignation. He would be out in the cold, relegated to running a bed and breakfast in some far flung corner of the world.

And yet closer still. A hair's breadth was all that stood between their lips brushing together. Just a taste. Nothing more.

Think of all the pain of the breakup, she wrote a revenge song. I am Bitter Babe.

Jordan snapped out of his kiss hungry daze. He took a quick step back. "Please take your time to get to know the sky villa. Don't hesitate to call me if you need anything." He moved quickly toward the door. "Good evening, Chloe."

Once downstairs, Jordan got back into his SUV. As soon as he was out of the resort, he turned the car toward the desert and hit the gas.

Chloe stood staring at the key pass which Jordan had pressed into her hand as he left the sky villa. She'd been certain he was going to kiss her. And if he had, she would have kissed him back.

At least one of them had an ounce of sanity in their head, and she knew for certain it wasn't her. The beautiful, romantic moment when he'd bent his head and his lips had drawn close had her hopes rising to a crescendo. *Yes. Yes. Oh, god yes.*

And then it had all crashed away.

"You're a silly little girl. He doesn't want you," she whispered.

If they had kissed, it would have been the height of stupidity. It would have put everything she was trying to protect at risk. She needed this gig, needed the money. If this deal went south, Jordan had family on which he could rely, whereas she had no one.

It was time to put her heart back on ice and start to think about how she was going to put together a kick ass concert experience for her fans.

CHAPTER FORTY-FIVE

Jordan kept his distance. Each morning, he would arrive bringing anything that Chloe had requested via the iPad the night before, along with a bunch of fresh flowers. He would stay and share a coffee with her before disappearing. Chloe wasn't entirely sure what Jordan was doing the rest of the time, so she filed it all under *Jordan's Other Stuff*.

And for the first couple of days, it was rather nice. She ordered print copies of some of the latest rom com books from the VIP ordering service, then lay on the couch snacking while she smashed her way through them. TikTok took up a shameful amount of her time, but she managed to half convince herself that it was all in the cause of fan engagement and research.

As soon as Jordan left each morning, she would slip back into the bedroom and fire up her battery operated little friend and get busy. Chloe hadn't masturbated this much since puberty had first hit. She'd thought she had got him out of her system with that revenge song, but her waning battery and near empty tube of lube proved otherwise.

By the middle of the third day, Chloe was about ready to

climb the walls. *Who knew you could reach the end of Tik Tok?* Lazing on the couch, she picked up her phone and dialed Jordan's number.

"Hi, Chloe. What can I do for you?"

Stop being so bloody solicitous and polite would be a good start.

She'd done a lot of thinking about him and what he'd said during their fight in the desert. There were many things left unsaid. There were deeper emotions that she wanted them to work through.

I know this is stupid, but I can't help myself.

"You said I could ask you for anything. So can you please come up to my suite, now?"

He was silent on the other end for a moment. "Actually, Chloe, I'm out of town. If it's okay, could I come and see you later today, maybe around six?"

Chloe sat bolt upright on the couch.

He's dumped me here in Vegas, and then gone home.

"Are you back in New York?" The notion of Jordan treating her like a delivery package hurt more than it should.

"No, I'm at a friend's house near Red Rock Canyon. It's about a forty minute drive into the desert from Vegas. If its urgent, I can come back to the resort."

The words were out of her mouth before she could stop herself. "What friend?"

Stupid. Stupid. Now you sound jealous.

"Just a family friend. I'm renting the house for the duration of your residency. It gives me a place to get away from the bright lights of Vegas and ... um ..."

Jordan was staying somewhere out in the desert alone.

"Could I maybe come and see you? I've been thinking about our conversation on the way over from LA and thought we should talk some more. If that's okay? I can call an uber or get someone to drive me. Do you have an address?"

A sigh drifted down the line. "Don't do that. I'll come and pick you up. I'm leaving now."

Damn. Another of his apparently not so well laid plans just went up in smoke. He'd chosen the desert house, well out of Vegas, as a place to go when Chloe wasn't in town, it was somewhere that he could continue to work on his mental health while also considering his future. He wasn't cut out to run hotels and resorts. Hours of therapy had seen him finally accept that being different from his high-achieving family members wasn't a failing, he just wasn't them. His passions lay elsewhere. Jordan was under no illusion that his career at Royal Resorts was all but over—much to his relief. The board and he were in agreement. This assignment was his swansong.

And now his sanctuary was about to be invaded by the one person he'd hoped would never set foot through the front door. He glanced at the open living space and gritted his teeth. This house was amazing. While the front was solid rock, the back which faced toward the desert and the mountains was a series of seamless glass panels. During the day, the view was a constantly changing palette of gray, gold, and red. The sand and rocks seeming to merge into one. The blue sky formed a frame for nature's art.

At night, the sky was filled with a billion stars.

If he knew Chloe as well as he once thought he had, she would take one look at this desert oasis and decide she didn't want to leave.

Resigned to his fate, Jordan snatched up his car keys.

The second Jordan stepped out of the elevator and into Chloe's sky villa, she leapt off the couch and came to greet him. "I'm sorry, that was selfish of me. You were taking time for yourself, and I just clicked my fingers and summoned you, like the ultimate diva. I promise it won't happen again."

He gave her a doubtful look. They both knew that was a lie. She might not be a diva, but she wasn't someone who was used to doing things for herself. Nor was she particularly good at being alone.

"Are you ready to go, or would you like to change?"

Chloe glanced at her sweats and dip-stained hoodie. The transition to couch potato had started not long after her people had all left, but over the past two days, she'd almost reached peak performance.

"I'm a bit of a home body mess right now. Give me a few minutes and I'll grab a clean T-shirt."

Jordan pointed at her dirty top, then to Chloe's bare feet. "Do you have anything warmer than those? The desert gets really cold at night. I thought we could go and look at the stars. The night sky over the desert at the house is beyond amazing. I'd love to show you, but you would need to be dressed in more than bare feet and a T-shirt."

She'd not put a lot of thought into her packing, rather she had just emptied a few drawers and tossed the contents into her suitcases. Bringing her heavy silver travel case had been more for effect than anything with any real purpose.

If I'm going to be in Vegas for a while, I will need clothes.

Chloe screwed up her nose. "I'm an idiot. I didn't bring any real warm clothes with me. Could we go somewhere and buy something? What stores offer private shopping?"

She couldn't just dash into a department store or wander the aisles of Target, but this was Vegas and there had to be somewhere that catered for the VIP shopper.

"We have arrangements with Neiman Marcus, Saks Fifth Avenue, and a couple of high-end boutiques."

They were all great sounding stores, but she doubted any of them would sell the sort of desert roaming gear she had in mind. "What about boots and jackets?"

Jordan pulled his phone from out of his back pocket and made a quick call. "Thank you, that would be perfect. We shall see you shortly."

He hung up. "That was the private client manager at Nordstrom. They will have a room ready for us in half an hour. I'll wait here for you to change and grab some things, then we can go."

CHAPTER FORTY-SIX

The private shopping area at Nordstrom was in a separate space next door to the main store. After parking in the underground garage, Jordan and Chloe took the lift to the third floor. There they were greeted by a small team of elegantly dressed VIP shopping assistants. Jordan introduced her simply as Chloe, and noted what they were looking to purchase.

The VIP team was well trained. They were efficient, respectful, and never once gushed over the fact that they were helping one of the biggest pop stars in the world to shop for jeans and boots.

Chloe was ushered into an enormous changing room, while Jordan sat sipping a barista-made coffee. The shoppers took her measurements, and then disappeared. They returned fifteen minutes later hauling three racks filled with clothes.

"Would you like us to assist you with trying on some of the garments, or would you rather we left you alone? Some clients prefer us to leave them to work in private," asked the head of the VIP team.

Chloe glanced at Jordan. It wasn't officially his job to help her buy clothes, but her heart told her she would be a fool to waste such an opportunity.

Take a chance. Reset things with him.

"Thank you. I'm happy to be left alone with my stylist."

As soon as the VIP team left, Jordan rose from his chair. He set the coffee cup on a table and ambled over. "Your stylist, hey? That's a heavy responsibility you have tasked me with, Ms. Fisher. I'm not sure if I'm at Stixxluv level."

Heat burned on her cheeks. If he only knew what it did to her when he teased her. Or the things she would let him do to her if he whispered the sort of deliciously filthy words he used to say whenever they made love.

Get your mind out of your panties. We are here for warm clothes, not sex.

"Few people are at Stixxluv level, but then again since he would never lower himself to actually coming to a department store to shop, you will have to take up the load."

Jordan reached over and plucked a puffer jacket off one of the racks. He handed it to Chloe. "I like this. The dark gray with the red trim is a great look, and it will keep you warm. How about I select a few things for you to try on. Things that my critical eye finds suitable."

Chloe nodded with a grin. A procession of sweaters, jeans, and various jackets soon followed. By the end of it, Chloe had sorted all the clothes into three racks. There was the definite *no* rack. The *maybe* rack. And the *yes* rack. Jordan had disappeared a minute or so ago leaving her alone.

She was feeling more calm than she had in quite some time. After all the drama of the past couple of months, Jordan's light hearted banter was a welcome balm. If only she could confide her troubles in him. Tell him the truth of all that had happened since their breakup.

Don't. I can't risk anyone knowing. There are only a few more days until the concerts are announced. I hope Marta doesn't go to the press before then.

There was a knock on the changing room door. "Come in."

Jordan reappeared carrying what Chloe hoped would be the last of the clothes. It was getting late, and she was getting hungry.

"The VIP team added these final pieces. I like the silver tank top, it reminds me of one of the outfits you wore at the Paris concert."

She took the tank top, swallowing down a lump of emotion at the thought of Jordan remembering such a minor detail. Men in her experience didn't tend to take notice of such things, but Jordan did.

"Speaking of concerts. I was going to ask if Stixxluv is coming to the launch announcement. Will he be arriving with Nancy on the *Chloe Jet*?"

All the joy she'd been happily embracing for the past hour deflated in Chloe's heart.

Rip the Band-Aid off, just tell him.

But she'd never been one for coping with a lot of pain all at once. Her childhood trauma had left her with poor skills to handle such hurt, and she could admit to still not having come fully to terms with Foster and Marta's deep betrayal.

Little bits. She would choose death by a thousand cuts.

"Stixxluv and I have parted ways on a professional level. He and I are still good friends, but we decided a few months ago that it was time for me to seek a new creative direction."

Jordan closed the door. "That sounds very much like something a PR team would write. If he was a casualty of the great cleanout, just say so."

"No, he and I parted before that, we just came to an amicable end. You can call him if you like, he will back me up." She held out her phone to Jordan, all the while praying he wouldn't take it.

"That's ok, you don't need to prove anything to me. But if he has gone, then who is your new stylist? I mean what are you planning on wearing to the announcement press conference? And when exactly is that going to be?"

I hadn't thought about clothes. What am I going to wear to the press conference?

She'd been so busy worrying about Jordan and how they were going to be around one another, that those details had entirely slipped her mind. Nancy would be coming out to Vegas to help, but only as her manager, not her assistant. It was Chloe's job to handle her entourage, or at least rebuilt it.

A strong hand took hold of Chloe's arm, steadying her. "Are you alright?" She blinked, then looked up and took in the expression of deep concern on Jordan's face.

"I ... I haven't done anything about the press conference, and no I hadn't settled on a date," she stammered.

She couldn't exactly tell him that many of the people she normally worked with in LA for her clothes and accessories were still owed money.

"Chloe. Look, I get that something is wrong, and you clearly don't want to share it, but can you at least tell me if you have anyone working for you at the moment? Give me somewhere to start."

She nodded. "I don't have any staff, and I don't have anything to wear to the press conference."

There would probably come a time, hopefully many months from now when they would have to talk about her problems. But Chloe was determined that it wouldn't be now. She was not going to spend the next eight months with Jordan giving her his pity smile.

I couldn't stand it.

He dumped the rest of the clothes onto the floor and

pulled out his cell. Jordan held Chloe's gaze while he made a call. "Hi, you. Yep. Good. And you?" There was some humming and nodding. "Listen I need a massive favor." Chloe couldn't make out what was being said on the other end of the line, but whoever Jordan was talking to spoke very fast.

"Her name? Um. Can you keep a secret?" More hurried words. "It's Chloe." More hurried words. "Yes, that Chloe." Chloe caught the high pitched squeal of delight as Jordan held the phone away from his ear.

"Who are you talking to?"

"My cousin Camille. She is a French fashion designer, currently working with Saks Fifth Avenue. I thought she might be able to help."

Chloe took the phone. "Hi, Camille. This is Chloe."

Snuffling and snorting came down the line. "Oh my god, I am such a fan. And ... oh my god. Whatever you need, you only have to ask. I am all yours."

The service mantra seemed to run in the Royal family.

"I need an outfit for a press conference being held in Vegas—let's say in four days' time. I know that's a tough ask, but if you have anything ..."

"Consider it done, Mon Chérie. Where are you now?"

She didn't want to tell Jordan's cousin exactly where she was right now, or her state of undress, which Chloe had just realized was a bra and boyleg panties. "I'm in Vegas staying at the Royal Resorts hotel in one of the sky villas. But no one knows I am here, it's top secret."

"I would love to work with you Chloe. We can do this, don't you worry. Could you please put Jordan back on?" Perplexed, Chloe handed Jordan his phone.

He did another round of humming and nodding. "Okay, see you tomorrow." And then he hung up. "Camille will be arriving in the morning. She'll bring her sewing equipment and materials with her and set up in your sky villa."

Wow, that was quick.

"How about we pay for the things you want to keep, and then let's take them back to the hotel. I'm thinking we will skip the desert house for tonight, which frees you up to talk to Cam. I'll give you her contact details, and the two of you can hopefully agree on a few things before she gets here in the morning. In the meantime I will let Bryce know that you have decided on a date for the press conference. How does that sound?"

It sounded like a sensible plan. Chloe was a little disappointed over the delay in their visit to the house, but super excited at the prospect of cousin Camille arriving in the morning. Once again Jordan had come through for her. "Thank you, that is amazing. You really do know how to make things happen."

Chloe reached out and took a hold of the sleeve of Jordan's light cotton sweater, drawing him to her. "Um. I mean it. Thank you for this, for bringing me here, and all you've done. I know I don't really deserve it."

A warm hand brushed over her cheek. "Everyone deserves to have friends."

"Am I your friend? I mean after throwing Zapp at you, and then that song. To be honest I expected that you would just hate me."

He lowered his head and their foreheads touched. "I was pretty pissed about Zapp, but it wouldn't have been a problem if Marta had let you know I called. And as for *Bitter Babe*, yeah, I'm nowhere near ready to begin to unpack that disaster." Jordan nodded. "You of all people must know that song rips me to shreds every time I hear it. You don't write a revenge song without intending to inflict maximum damage, and you did. Chloe, you cut me to the soul."

She'd poured her pain and anger into the lyrics, which had made the song so powerful. Millions of people had related to her heartbreak. It was too late for regrets, but she could try reaching out to him.

"Would sorry be a good place for me to start?"

Jordan breathed a soft. "Yeah, that would be nice."

Chloe had an even better place they could begin. Rising up on her toes, she slipped a hand around the back of Jordan's neck and as he lifted his head, she offered him her lips. Sensing his moment of hesitancy, she made the first move and kissed him. When she drew back, accepting that this was not what he wanted, Jordan clasped a firm hand to her ass and pulled her hard against him.

His lips came crashing down on hers in a fiery kiss that was dirty, messy, and full of the pain of longing. His tongue delved deep into her mouth, and she met him stroke for stroke.

"I'm sorry. I'm so sorry," she whispered.

"Shh, just kiss me."

Jordan wrapped her up in his embrace and kissed her once more. They were still a long way from finding one another, but *yes* this was a damn good place to start.

CHAPTER FORTY-SEVEN

Camille Royal stepped regally out of the elevator and into Chloe's private sky villa late the following morning. Jordan went to greet her, but his cousin gave him a queenly wave and advised, "Step back or be road kill."

Jordan rolled his eyes. Cam's English was near schoolbook perfect, but she still liked to pepper it with idioms she'd picked up from American television shows.

A team of resort bellmen and assistants pushing various luggage carts trailed in Camille's wake. She instructed them where to place things, before turning her attention back to Jordan. "What's the protocol on tipping in this situation?"

He'd anticipated her question. "We have an agreement with the resort to pay the team standard tips, and then monthly bonuses for the duration of our special guest's stay."

While their special guest remained out of sight in her bedroom, Jordan went and had a quick word with the head bellman, making sure that his team understood they would be receiving their tips at the end of their shift. They shook hands and the resort staff all filed back into the elevator, leaving the luggage carts behind.

His gaze roamed over the piles of boxes and cases. "Thank you for coming at such short notice and being so well prepared. Now, do I get a hug?"

A grinning Camile embraced him. "It's wonderful to see you. I know when I saw you on New Year's Eve, you weren't in a good place. How are things now?"

Her question took him by surprise. He hadn't considered how other members of the extended family would view his mental state. Now that he thought about it, Christmas and New Year's had all been a bit of a blur. He was finally coming out of his stress induced fog, and his mind was clearing.

"I'm a lot better. Once this new assignment gets bedded down, I will have some time for myself."

He wasn't making any promises to himself. The past year had taught Jordan not to make concrete plans. And for the first time he realized that wasn't such a bad thing. He'd learned to roll with the punches. But if the punches could stop coming for a few months, he would be most grateful.

Camille checked the room. "Is Chloe here? I know you think yourself a bit of a hunk, but I can't possibly use you as my mannequin for her gown."

Jordan headed for the master bedroom. He knocked on the door, and Chloe slowly opened it. He caught her shy smile and his chest tightened. They hadn't yet spoken about the kiss they'd shared last night. Instead, they had spent the rest of the evening making small talk and avoiding one another's gazes.

"Camille is here. If you are ready to start work with her."

As Chloe moved into the hallway, Jordan took a step back. His breath caught as she reached out and took his hand. "Thank you. I'm a bit embarrassed about all this, I mean having to ask your cousin to come and make me an outfit."

Jordan was acting on pure instinct when he wrapped his free arm around Chloe and drew her gently to him. "You don't ever need to feel embarrassed with me. I am here for you, Chloe." He dropped a kiss on the top of her long black hair, letting his face linger for a moment to take in Chloe's scent. His chest gave another squeeze.

I miss you. I wish we could have sorted all of this out long ago.

She let go of his hand and wrapped both arms around his waist. The silence they shared was enough for him to understand that last night's kiss hadn't been a mistake. No one was apologizing or suggesting it wouldn't ever happen again.

They both knew it would.

Camille Royal was the sort of woman every girl should have in her life. From the moment Chloe walked into the living room, and Camille took her hand, she was enveloped in a world of excited feminine energy.

"I brought the silks we discussed and a few other fabrics that I think might work. But let's get your measurements sorted first, and then we can decide how we wish to proceed. Seeing you up close gives me a better idea about colors, but again it's your decision."

Chloe wasn't used to dealing with someone who asked for her opinion rather than just telling her what she wanted. It was empowering, but it was also daunting.

Entertainment stylists were paid to deliver a package and until now she had gone along with whatever Stixxluv had chosen for her. With this new freedom of choice, came the expectation that she would have to pay attention and actually own her decisions.

Still holding Chloe's hand, Camille walked around the

living area. "So this is your sky villa—I mean it's where you are living? Sky villa, it's such a silly name, but it is what it is. A sky chateau would have been a better choice."

"Yes, until I finish the concert series, whenever I am in Las Vegas this is my home. It's got a lot of space. There are four bedrooms, and a full kitchen, along with a private gym. It's almost as big as my house in LA."

Camille softly hummed to herself, then approached Jordan. "Cousin, do you have your own sky villa here as well?"

Jordan shifted uneasily on his feet. Chloe sensed the question might be a loaded one. "Ah, yes. I have the one on the next level down. Why?"

"Excellent. I need your villa in which to work. In the meantime, you can move in here with Chloe."

As she let go of Chloe's hand, Camille transformed before her eyes. The friendly *BFF* disappeared and was replaced by a Boss Girl. She quickly took command.

Watching as Camille bossed Jordan around was a particular delight. At one point Chloe had to turn away while she held back a laugh. The warm banter of family had her rejoicing in its glow.

"But what if I don't want to move?" grumbled Jordan.

Camille snapped her fingers and like magic, Jordan stilled. "I didn't say no to you when you asked me to fly out here at short notice, did I? No. So you will do as you are told."

Wow. This Royal woman was feisty. Then again considering the sort of Royal male that Jordan was, she wasn't surprised.

A suitably chastened Jordan turned his gaze to Chloe. "Are you ok if I take one of the other bedrooms for a couple of days while Camille works on your gown? I could always get another room if it's a problem."

"Chloe is going to be representing Royal Resorts, so she

will need gowns, dresses, and gorgeous little suits. I will be here for some time," corrected Camille.

"Yes, Camille and I talked late into the night, and she has graciously agreed to make me a full Vegas wardrobe. I will be expected to dine with VIPs and make public appearances outside of my concerts, so ... yes, more clothes."

Chloe offered Jordan a gentle smile. "I would be more than happy for you to occupy one of my spare bedrooms. It does get a little lonely in here at times." He nodded his agreement.

"Speaking of VIPs, Jordan. When I called Bryce last night and told him I wanted an open budget for Chloe's wardrobe as well as use of one of the Royal Resorts jets, he not only said yes, but asked me to inform you that he is coming to Vegas. He wants you to arrange a private dinner for the four of us. Here in Chloe's sky villa. And that's tonight."

Jordan's *'fuck'* was whispered, but it was unmistakable. He got a slap on the arm from Camille for his troubles, then pushed toward the door. "Go and pack your things and bring them up here. Then you can help move my boxes and equipment down to your villa. Chloe shouldn't have to see how the magic is made. Maintenant, dépêchez-vous!"

As soon as he was gone, a softer, but still wicked version of Camille appeared. "I find that a little French drama goes a long way in this country. Americans don't quite know how to handle a fast talking European, and I've been known to use that to my advantage. Even with my cousins." Chloe was impressed. Camille Royal was a woman who got things done.

I could do with a few friends like her.

"You are evil. But I also think you are amazing. I hope one day that we might become friends."

Opening one of the black storage boxes she had brought with her, Camille pulled out a measuring tape. "While Jordan is downstairs sulking, we can get started on your measurements. And you don't have to hope for us to be friends, Chloe. If you are keeping Jordan in line, you can take that as a given."

CHAPTER FORTY-EIGHT

The second she laid eyes on Bryce Royal, Chloe could see the family resemblance. Bryce was a slightly taller, darker version of his younger brother. But unlike Jordan, his smile didn't do certain things to her lady parts, nor did shaking his hand make her heart go all a flutter. Only Jordan had that effect on her.

"Bryce Royal, CEO for Royal Resorts USA. It's both an honor and a pleasure to meet you, Ms. Fisher."

He had a firm, but pleasant hand shake. It was a nice change from the music industry heavyweight types who liked to crush a woman's hand just to prove to her that he could do high reps at the gym. "Please, call me, Chloe."

She ushered her guest into the living area of her sky villa. "Would you like a drink? Jordan brought up a bunch of different bottles of water with him. Or I could make you a coffee, I hear you are a bit of a caffeine fiend."

Bryce's eyebrows rose at that last remark, and Chloe's heart sank. So much for pretending she and Jordan barely knew one another.

"I mean, when he told me you were coming to Vegas, I asked your brother what sort of refreshments I should be offering."

Nice ass covering. Well done, Chloe.

"Thanks, but I'm good. I had a coffee not long ago. And to let you in on a little secret, my girlfriend is trying to get me to cut down to fifteen cups a day."

Whoa, that was a lot of coffee. Any wonder Bryce had a little bounce in his step, he was jet fueled. "I can see she might have her work cut out for her." Chloe laughed.

"If Vivian had her way, she would be here today. She's a huge fan. Instead, I had to play the boss card in order to get her on a plane to Chicago. But she will be coming to the first concert."

"Vivian works for Royal Resorts?"

"Yes, she is a recent hire in guest services. Her first project is doing an audit of our toiletries. At the moment our brand new apartment in NYC smells like the perfume section in Bloomingdales."

Did Bryce realize that he was smiling the whole time he spoke about his girlfriend? The pure joy in his voice was lovely.

I wish I had someone in my life who would talk that way when they mentioned me.

The elevator doors opened, and Jordan appeared. "Sorry, Bryce. I got caught up with moving some furniture for Cam. Our cousin is particular about where the rolls of fabric are stored." He motioned toward the kitchen. "Can I offer you a beverage?"

"Thanks, Chloe just offered me a coffee." The Royal brothers embraced in a warm hug which tugged at Chloe's heart. Families always made her envious.

"How is the wardrobe going?" asked Bryce.

"Camille and I worked through a few things last night and we've agreed on an outfit for the concert announcement. Jordan has graciously given up his suite so Camille can use it as her workroom while she creates a whole Vegas capsule wardrobe for me. As of this afternoon, Jordan's my new roommate."

"Housemate," offered Jordan.

"Aww, I but I like roomie better. And I am the talent."

Bryce laughed. "Roomie it is. Did Cam mention about us having dinner here tonight? I trust that is alright with you, Chloe."

She would swear on a stack of bibles that she could hear Jordan grinding his teeth from ten feet away. Poor thing. He'd been tossed out of his hotel suite. Made to move boxes, and now his older brother was treating him like the hired help.

Chloe caught Jordan's eye and he gave her a wink. "Dinner is all arranged. Tonight we are dining on the freshest sushi available in all of Las Vegas, accompanied by a crisp clean Pinot Gris. I hope that meets with your approval, Chloe?"

"But you ..." Chloe caught herself. She was about to mention that Jordan didn't drink, but again that would risk revealing the truth of their relationship.

"Yes, I was going to order us a sparkling wine, but I found a great French wine in the resort cellars," replied Jordan, easily covering her mistake.

Chloe didn't want to have to answer the question of where things stood between them. She wasn't entirely sure what to say. Until very recently Jordan had been her ex, and as best as she could manage, he'd been put firmly in the past.

In the days since their road trip from LA, things had definitely changed. There had been a thawing in the relationship. And that scorching kiss last night had put all manner of thoughts into her head.

It still doesn't change the fact that his family doesn't know about Jordan and my past. He's said he was sorry, but that's not enough.

If there was ever going to be a possible second chance for them, then Jordan was going to have to take the lead. She would not stay hidden in the shadows. He would have to be brave and let their love shine in the light. The only way she could see them having a future together was if they stood hand-in-hand and faced the world. As a couple.

She was still keeping secrets from him, and he was yet to explain what had really happened to him post their breakup.

And when we both discover the truth, will that future still exist?

"What time are we expecting the food?" asked Bryce. From the expression on his face he hadn't caught any of the undertone of the conversation. Chloe was counting on Jordan's brother having heard little else past the words food and wine.

"Sushi at seven. In the meantime, did you and I want to catch up on some Royal Resorts business?" suggested Jordan. "I'm ... I'm sure Chloe could do with a few minutes of peace and quiet. It's been a bit like Grand Central Station in here today."

It made her heart ache to hear Jordan stumble over his words. Bryce wasn't just Jordan's brother—he was his boss. The need for Jordan to make good over the failure in California had to be great.

"I'm going to go down and see Camille and settle on the final fabric for my announcement outfit, so yes let's all meet up here again just before seven. The sushi sounds fabulous, thank you, Jordan." She turned to Bryce. "Jordan has been a great help to me during my stay. He has a natural talent for anticipating and exceeding my every need."

That didn't sound the least bit staged or creepy.

"Then you are getting the true Royal Resorts service,

Chloe," replied Bryce. The awkward moment was saved when Bryce's phone pinged. As he glanced at it, Chloe mouthed *I'm sorry* to Jordan. He shrugged his shoulders, but she caught the hint of a tentative smile on his lips. His expression said it all. *Let's just get through this evening.*

CHAPTER FORTY-NINE

Thank god for Camille. The French connection was holding court, and everyone seemed happy to let her have the floor. From where he sat at Chloe's dining table, Jordan could sense she was relieved that for once someone else was handling the job of entertaining the crowd.

"And the models in New York this year. *Oh, mon Dieu!* I swear half of them didn't know how to walk a runway. I think the agency figured since I'm not a big name designer they would just send a dozen pretty girls they had on their books. I won't be using them again. I can't have the fashion critics laughing at me under their breaths. Not if I am going to try and book a venue at Paris Fashion week."

She might be complaining, but Camille was smiling the whole time she spoke. At one point, Jordan exchanged a knowing grin with Bryce. Their cousin was enjoying the freedom of being able to create and show her own designs. Her ready-to-wear collections were vastly different to the haute couture of her father's atelier workshop. Where Francois Royal measured everything down to the millimeter, Camille allowed her fabric to speak for itself.

Across the table from him, Chloe hung on Camille's every word. "And your father wouldn't let you work on your own creations at home in Paris? That's so sad."

The freedom to create her own pieces had come at a heavy price. Camille had struck out on her own and been banished from the family estate outside of Paris as punishment. If Francois had thought cutting his daughter off would bring her to heel, he'd badly misjudged how much Camille wanted to make her own way in the fashion world.

"My father said my work was not good enough. It didn't come up to his exacting standards. When he discovered I'd sold some of my collection to Saks Fifth Avenue, he exploded. *Je suis trahi!* I got on the next plane and came to New York."

"Yes, well Francois can be a little melodramatic," offered Bryce. "I don't think you selling a few dresses to an American department store actually amounts to betrayal. And as for your work not being good enough, believe me it is, my relationship is proof of that."

When Chloe's brows furrowed in confusion, Jordan stepped in. "Bryce's girlfriend, Vivian bought one of Camille's dresses, and that's how she caught Bryce's attention."

Camille picked up her glass of wine and saluted Bryce. "To my little blue rebel dress. Now I just need to create some other sexy designs to tempt the rest of the unattached Royal males. Bryce can't be the first and only one of my American cousins to have a girlfriend."

Jordan lowered his gaze to study the piece of masago sushi on his plate. The tiny pieces of fish roe suddenly held great interest.

"So both Jordan and Matthew have never had girlfriends?"

There was a sharp edge to Chloe's voice as she posed the question to the table. Jordan could just imagine what she was thinking. *What am I, chopped liver?*

He popped the sushi into his mouth, and lifting his head, made a point of giving Bryce his fullest attention. Out of the corner of his eye, he caught Chloe's death glare. She was going to make him pay for this at some point.

"Not as far as the rest of us know. I think they both like to play the field, but on the quiet. If you get my meaning," said Bryce.

Oh good. Keep digging that hole for me, bro.

Jordan slowly chewed his food, contemplating his response. He sensed things had reached a point in the conversation where he had a choice. He could simply laugh off Bryce's remark or take a stand. Send a message to Chloe.

"My private life has been just that for some time. After rehab, it made sense to keep a low profile." He looked straight at Chloe. "But I don't think that works any longer. I've learned that keeping things hidden can cause pain. The next time I find myself in a relationship, and it's with someone who wants us to go public, I will do as she asks. I will also introduce her to my family."

Chloe let out a gasp. She rose from the table, pushing back her chair. "Excuse me, I have to check for an email I was waiting on. I'll be back in a moment."

She hurried from the room, leaving an odd silence in her wake.

He was torn. Jordan desperately wanted to follow Chloe, but the fear of what Bryce would think held him back. If the CEO of Royal Resorts thought the company's investment in Chloe's residency might be put at risk by Jordan fooling around with the talent, he'd be forced to act.

And I might be on a plane out of Vegas, tonight.

"Bryce, do you think Vivian would like to come to my collection preview next month?" asked Camille.

Jordan could have kissed his cousin for so deftly stepping in and filling the void. "Where are you holding the viewing?"

He locked eyes with Bryce for a second, and slowly blinked. Of the two of them, Jordan was the better card player. Bryce had too many tells to be able to successfully keep a secret. Which meant, his worry over a possible connection between Chloe and his brother was written all over his face.

I'm going to have to tell him the truth.

If he didn't, if he continued lying, it would be game over. Bryce had to be able to trust him. To know that Jordan wasn't going to make a mess of things here in Las Vegas.

And Chloe has to know that she can trust me enough to give me another chance.

Chloe returned to the living room. She lingered at a distance from the table, wringing her hands. It was clear she didn't want to sit back down and resume the meal. His words had rattled her.

"Um, Camille, would it be alright if you and I went over some of the fabrics for my Vegas collection? I just want to be sure that we are on the same track. We can come back and eat some more of the sushi afterward."

"Of course, that's what I am here for. Excuse us, gentlemen," replied Camille. As she rose from the table, she picked up a couple of glasses and a full bottle of wine. "We won't be long, talk amongst yourselves. And don't eat all the good sushi."

As the women headed for the elevator, Jordan knew the time had come. He took a long drink of his water, then after setting the bottle on the table, he met Bryce's gaze. "About Chloe," he began.

Bryce nodded. "Yeah, about Chloe." He pushed his plate away and sat with his hands clasped gently together giving Jordan his undivided attention. It was his brother's listening pose, designed to give the other person in the conversation the opportunity to speak their piece without fear of interruption.

This is why he is CEO material, and I am not.

Jordan drew in a ragged breath. "I met Chloe in Berlin early last year. We became lovers. It was just before I took over the Laguna Beach project. At the time I didn't want Dad or the board thinking that I wasn't giving the resort my fullest attention. I made the decision not to tell anyone about us."

Bryce nodded. "I can see why you would do that. I would probably have done the same in your position. In fact I sort of did with Vivian. I kept her and my connection a secret, and it's something I came to regret."

Bryce and Vivian had been through their own dramas, but his brother's *never say die* attitude had seen him finally win the girl. Vivian was now Bryce's live-in girlfriend. And if the way Bryce talked about Vivian was any indication, an announcement of a bigger kind would be made before the year was out.

"I take it the two of you are no longer together? That's a pity, because from what I've seen tonight, I think you would make a good couple."

Jordan swallowed a lump of emotion. He hadn't been expecting to hear that from his brother. That Bryce would support him and Chloe.

"Why did you break up?"

"Chloe had a whole group of people around her who were determined to make things difficult—if not impossible—for us. In the end, when push came to shove, I thought she'd chosen them over of me. When we broke up, I was absolutely gutted."

Jordan raised his hands. "But you know me, king of second chances. I figured if I threw myself into the resort project, I could simply shut down my pain. Focus all my energies on trying to meet family expectations. And yeah, that was yet another thing I was wrong about."

There was more he had to tell Bryce, but it would have to wait. In confessing his and Chloe's secret relationship, he'd already risked more than enough.

His brother sighed. "We guys think we can ignore our feelings, but it never works. Things just fester and get worse. You have to live your life as you see fit, you can't keeping trying to be someone you are not."

"Yeah. At least pop stars get to write songs about their breakups. I mean ..."

The expression on Bryce's face went from one of quiet understanding to abject horror. "Oh no! The song Chloe had out last summer. The one about the guy she met in Berlin. Vivian plays it every morning without fail while she makes our coffee. Jordan, are you *Bitter Babe?*"

Jordan slowly nodded. "Yes, I am. I'm the selfish, heartbreaker she wrote about in *Bitter Babe* and all of it is true. I walked away when I should have stayed." He calmly held Bryce's gaze. "It's Chloe's greatest hit, and if winning her back means I have to stand to one side of the stage and listen to her revenge song every damn night for the rest of my life, I will do it."

His mind was made up, now he just had to convince the woman he loved that he'd never leave her again. Never fail her. In a lifetime of winning second chances, this was going to be Jordan's greatest challenge.

CHAPTER FIFTY

"Chloe! Chloe! Over here. Look to your right. Over here." Chloe stood in the center of the stage as a fireball of blazing camera lights went off all around her. At times Jordan worried she would disappear completely.

He had seen her perform in concert, but that had been at a distance. He'd been granted some perspective. But here on the stage at the brand new performing arena at Royal Resorts Las Vegas, there was no way of escaping the heat and light.

Bryce had warned him that the press were going to give heavy coverage to Chloe's exclusive *A Garden in the Desert* concert series, but Jordan hadn't been prepared for this level of insanity. The constant clicking of cameras and shouting of reporters bore deep into his brain.

And in the middle of it all, stood Chloe, calmly smiling, and waving to the cameras. Her gold strapless gown clung to her every curve. She looked like a goddess. A sexy, siren descended from heaven.

Camille's work was beyond stunning. Every drape of the silk fabric was perfection.

"The press frenzy is already lighting up social media." He

turned as Chloe's manager Nancy came to stand alongside him. "I expect you Royal Resorts people can't wait until the box office opens for ticket sales."

They were to the side of the stage. Only Chloe, Bryce, and Edward Royal had fronted the cameras. Edward had made the announcement about the new performance arena, then stepped back to let Bryce, the new CEO for North America, introduce Chloe.

"I'm just pleased Chloe is settling in and getting used to Vegas. She's been through a period of transition lately, and I think being able to focus on her music and the shows will be good for her."

Nancy fixed her gaze on him. "You seem to be getting along well with Chloe. I'm surprised she has shared any of her private life with you. I mean, considering that the two of you have only just met."

He caught the warning in Nancy's words. *Mess with my client and you will pay the consequences.*

"It seems that she is able to handle change well. We arranged Chloe's new stylist after she and her previous one decided to part ways." Jordan gestured toward Chloe. "You have to admit Chloe looks fantastic in that dress."

He'd been getting the evil eye from Nancy ever since she'd arrived from LA the previous night. All through the private dinner at Las Vegas's top Thai restaurant, Chloe's manager had grilled him on how things were going. She was protective of her client but not in the same controlling way that Foster or Marta had been. And despite Nancy's obvious wariness about him, Jordan respected her.

As Bryce moved off stage and made his way over to Nancy, Jordan stepped back. He and Bryce had agreed that in light of his previous connection to Chloe, it would be best if he stayed well clear of the stage and the cameras.

"Chloe's going to perform a song, then take some questions. After that, we will wrap things up. Nancy, is Chloe headed back to LA with you tonight?"

Nancy shook her head. "Apparently not. She says she wants to remain in Vegas and get the desert sand into her blood. I am content to go along with whatever makes Chloe happy."

Hallelujah! Finally a manager who listens to what Chloe wants.

"Are you alright with that arrangement" asked Bryce, turning his attention to Jordan. "You didn't have any other plans, did you?"

Jordan gave him his best smile. Even if he'd had plans, which he didn't, they would have gone out the window. He had one job to do, and that was to make Chloe happy.

"Unless it relates directly to Ms. Fisher, my schedule is entirely free for the foreseeable future."

Bryce raised an eyebrow but fortunately Nancy missed it.

She'd chosen to sing an acoustic version of one of her earlier hits. A song that had always resonated with her fans. The promotions team at Royal Resorts had wanted Chloe to sing her recent hit, but she'd held out. *Summer Flame* was her signature piece, a song that only true members of Chloe's Garden understood.

These were the people she wanted to have come to Vegas and enjoy her shows, not the tourists on an all-inclusive package deal. As far as she was concerned, those people would be better to spend their money on seeing the long running Legends in Concert show and playing the slots. Her original reluctance to play in Vegas still held.

Alone on the stage, microphone in hand, Chloe sang. Her

voice filled the auditorium. From out of the corner of her eye, she caught the looks of amazement on the faces of the press gathering. She was singing live and unaccompanied, something which many major artists refused to do. But there'd been no one playing along with her when she'd performed on the streets, no back up tracks. Just her voice. Her gift. When the song ended, a reverent hush filled the room —quickly broken by loud applause.

I still have it. And no one, and nothing, can take it away from me.
"Chloe, sing *Bitter Babe!*"

Grinning Chloe shook her head. "If you want to hear that song, you will have to buy a ticket and come see the show. Thank you, see you back here at the arena in a few months!"

She handed the microphone to a stagehand, then with a bow and a wave headed off the stage.

If Nancy and Bryce hadn't been standing near him, she would have gone straight to Jordan. Over the past few days they had barely seen one another. Jordan had been busy with preparations for the concert series announcement, while she and Camille had spent most days holed up putting the finishing touches to Chloe's Vegas capsule collection. Tomorrow, there would be more press engagements and some virtual appearances on morning TV shows.

But today, with the residency announcement now official, all Chloe wanted to do was to get out of town.

She and Nancy embraced. "Your voice is amazing, Chloe. And the fans will be ecstatic when they hear the news of the concerts."

"It will be good to get back on stage."

Bryce Royal, ever the gentleman, offered Chloe his hand. "So, what are your plans for the rest of today? Would you and Nancy like to come and dine with our executive team?"

Jordan's brother was a really nice man. So she gathered was his father, from the brief moment when she and Edward had been introduced just before she went on stage. But there was only one member of the Royal family Chloe was interested in spending time with, and that was the sexy, green-eyed man standing a foot or so back from the power gathering.

"I'm actually going to take the rest of the day off from people, if that's alright? I have a huge amount of promotion work coming up for the rest of this week." She turned to Jordan. "And Jordan said he would take me out into the desert to see the night sky. I was promised a billion stars, and I'm going to hold him to that promise."

CHAPTER FIFTY-ONE

"I think Nancy is suspicious of me," said Jordan, tossing an overnight bag into the back of the SUV. Chloe handed him her bag, and he carefully placed it alongside his, which for some silly reason made her smile.

Chloe had been waiting all week for this day. To get out of Vegas and finally, finally, see the desert house. "Do you have any real food at the house?"

He raised his eyebrows. "You've become a bit of a foodie, Ms. Fisher. And I'm pleased to see it. Yes, the refrigerator is fully stocked."

No more protein shakes ever.

She'd had a recent epiphany. The whole time Marta and her cohorts had controlled Chloe's diet, she'd never understood why she was always hungry, always craving junk food. Now she was out from under them, and able to make her own choices she was really enjoying food. Apart from the occasional snack attack, she was eating well. Good food.

She'd even managed to cook a curry one night from one of the prepared meal kits, silently watching as Jordan ate every bite. It had been a private moment of domestic bliss.

They were in the private VIP section of the resort parking garage, a secure area that allowed them to come and go from the hotel without using any public spaces. After leaving the arena, Chloe and Jordan had returned to her sky villa and changed into their casual clothes.

With Camille Royal flying home to New York City with Bryce and Edward later today, Jordan's suite was now vacant and ready for his return. Chloe didn't want her hot roomie to leave.

How do I ask him to stay?

The scorching kiss they had shared in the dressing room still hung silently between them. Neither seemed game to raise the subject. Hopefully this time away from everyone else would bring some clarity between them. Chloe wanted nothing more than for her and Jordan to finish the conversation they had started on the desert road on their way to Nevada.

"Are you ok if we cook something? I mean ... we could order in, but ... but," she stammered.

Her head was in a strange place. They were finally going to spend some time together, just the two of them, but Jordan's mood was guarded. She couldn't read him.

He opened the passenger side door of the SUV and motioned for Chloe to climb in. "Cooking would be nice. I tried doing a few stir fries when I was back in New York last year, and I think I got the hang of them. Well sort of ..."

Chloe moved toward the car. She stopped in front of Jordan, and as she raised her gaze to meet his. Her heart was racing. "Could we also talk? I mean have a real conversation?"

"Yes, but not in the middle of the parking garage." He bent and in one smooth motion dropped a kiss on her forehead, then stepped away. "Come on, let's get out of here."

A short time later, Jordan turned off Red Rock Canyon Road and took the SUV down a dirt track which from the main road appeared to head straight into the desert. A quarter mile down the track, a solid stone wall loomed into view. A smaller wall sat to the right of it, and Jordan drove toward it. It was only as they got close that Chloe realized the main wall was the front of a house, and the smaller one was in fact a garage.

Jordan slowed the SUV but instead of parking in the garage as she expected, he drove around back. He pulled up behind the garage and turned off the ignition. Chloe looked out, watching as the desert dust blew past the windows.

"Welcome to the desert house, Chloe. And in case you were wondering, the reason why I parked here was to hide the car from view. House of Royal security protocol is to have a vehicle always ready to leave a place."

She nodded. Sometimes it was easy to forget that Jordan came from money. That her experience of having security and bodyguards was something he had grown up with, had known all his life.

Chloe unclipped her seatbelt but stayed in the car. She was compelled to get something off her chest before they went into the house.

"They asked me to play *Bitter Babe* today, but as you no doubt heard I told them they would have to wait. I will of course eventually have to sing it in front of you, but before I do, I need you to know that I did write that song with pain in mind. It didn't start out that way. In the beginning it was a means to get my own anger and rage out of my system. Most of the lyrics were penned the night of the All American Music awards, after I thought, you hadn't bothered to call."

Jordan took a hold of Chloe's hand. "But I did call. Please tell me you believe me?"

"Yes, I believe you, Jordan. And I also believe that Marta deleted that call, just to make sure our break was permanent."

Shifting in her seat she turned, so she could face him

properly. "I went back to London and worked with Kevin Smith, he helped me to channel my pain. When the lyrics were done, I recorded it in one take. It's the purest song of my entire career. My biggest hit. And now every time I sing it, I will be reminded of how much I hurt you."

Jordan's thumb ran back and forth over Chloe's skin, sending shivers down her spine. "How about every time you sing it, you think of what we lost, and you use that to remember the power of forgiveness."

"Oh, Jordan."

CHAPTER FIFTY-TWO

Chloe barely had time to take in the front entrance of the house. Jordan turned off the alarm system, then reached for her. Bags and car keys fell to the floor as he wrapped her up in his arms. "Let's talk about things later, right now I just want you. Tell me that you want me."

"Yes. Oh yes, Jordan," she softly cried.

She rested her head against his shoulder as Jordan carried her into the master bedroom. He set her gently on her feet, then took a step back.

"We can take this like Paris, a slow, tender seduction. Or we can go crazy. My vote is we get crazy."

Chloe laughed. "Yeah, I think it's time Bitter Babe got naked and had his revenge."

Clothes and shoes were stripped away. Jordan broke several buttons on his shirt as he roughly ripped it off. An eager Chloe got her boots stuck in the hem of her jeans and fell to the floor. "Oof."

She didn't make it back to her feet. He pinned her to the carpet. His teeth nipping all the way down her neck, tearing at her bra. Chloe squealed. "Hang on let me get the clasp."

"Fuck the clasp," growled Jordan. He took hold of the flimsy lace confection and tore it from her body. Then he set to her jeans.

Chloe lay with her hand over her face doing her best not to laugh as Jordan manhandled her. He was rough, and she loved it. By the time there was only her panties left between her and being completely naked, his breath was coming hard. His chest heaved as he sucked in air. "Bitter Babe has a lot of revenge he needs to sexually inflict on your body."

Dropping her hand away, Chloe took in the magnificent sight of Jordan's hard erection. She licked her lips.

Oh god, I've missed this, missed him.

He crawled over her. Chloe let out a sob at the tears which shone in his green eyes. "Never again, Chloe. Promise me we will never let anyone ever come between us again. You and me. Tonight and forever."

She brushed a hand over his cheek, capturing one of his tears with the tip of her thumb. She kissed her thumb, symbolically taking Jordan's pain. "Forever." I love you, Jordan. I will always regret not saying it until now."

"I love you too."

He lifted her from the floor, and carefully lay her on the bed. She let her head fall back as Jordan slid her G-string down her legs. Her heart was racing in anticipation of his touch. When his tongue parted the folds of her sex, she grasped his hair and pulled hard.

"Jordan, please. Take it all, take everything you want. And when you don't think I can give any more, I want you to demand it from me. I am yours."

He pressed three fingers deep into her heat and began to stroke. "I'm going to make you offer me your soul, princess."

"Yes."

Chloe woke Jordan in the dead of night, her lips and tongue bringing him once more to a state of hardened arousal. In the hours since their arrival at the desert house, they'd come together three times, each time as magical as the last.

She prowled over him, like a lioness in heat, and he guessed where this was going. Chloe intended to ride his cock and bring him to submission. Her nimble fingers rolled a condom over his erection.

Gripping her hips, he flipped her over and onto her back. "Minx. Did you think to wake me and use me for your sexual pleasure?"

His cock parted her soft, wet folds and Jordan plunged deep into Chloe's sex. In the pale moonlight, he caught the wicked grin on her lips. This had been her plan all along, get him hard in the hope he wouldn't be able to resist fucking her this way.

"I think your pussy missed me." Jordan bent and kissed Chloe. "I know I've missed it, along with the rest of you."

Chloe sighed. "Show me how much you've missed me. I want no mercy. Hard. Deep. Please, Jordan."

She wrapped her legs around him, her finger nails digging into his back as he gave her all the punishment she could take. When she cried out with her orgasm, he let loose and pounded his way to his own release.

"My beautiful, amazing, Chloe. You are mine."

They still hadn't talked, but the time would soon come.

CHAPTER FIFTY-THREE

Colorado
  Two days later.
  Time to start repaying some debts.

Jordan caught sight of his brother the second he stepped out of the main building of Aspen-Pitkin County Airport. Matthew's jeep SUV was parked right out in front of the main door, and he was leaning against it chatting to one of the uniformed traffic team. Unlike most other airports, with their strict loading zone rules, the guy didn't seem in any hurry to move Matthew Royal on.

Catching sight of Jordan, Matthew gave a friendly wave. He shook hands with the airport traffic cop and made his way over.

"Morning." His gaze took in Jordan's tailored suit, and elegant woolen coat. He raised an eyebrow. "Way to fit in when you are in Aspen, bro."

Matthew was in jeans, a loose pale blue hoodie under a

thick winter coat and rocking a pair of Timberland boots. He fitted in, whereas Jordan was well and truly overdressed.

"Can I talk to you about the amazing investment returns that can be found in crypto currency?" said Jordan, slipping his sunglasses onto his face. He and Matthew both laughed.

"I thought you would have met me off the plane." Jordan had counted seven other private jets on the tarmac as the Royal Resorts jet came into land.

His brother shook his head. "Trying to be less billionaire and more of a local at the moment. Not that it seems to be helping me to make much headway. I might have to rethink my approach when it comes time to talk to the planning committee."

Jordan climbed into the front passenger seat of the SUV. It was a smaller vehicle than what he got around in on the West Coast, but its size made it nimble. As soon as they left the airport, Matthew was easily weaving in and out of the traffic. His snow tires gripped the icy roads.

"How did the big Chloe concert Las Vegas launch go? I saw the pics of her and Bryce on her Instagram feed, but I couldn't see you."

"It went brilliantly. The gold dress Chloe wore was from Camille's clever hands. You didn't see me, because I wasn't up on stage. Bryce is the CEO. My job is to keep our pop star happy over the next little while."

Matthew shot him a concerned glance. "And how are things between you and Chloe, I mean are you able to be in the same room and not feel awkward around her? Or is she giving you the solid diva treatment as punishment."

"Things between us are getting better, not perfect but I don't think any relationship can lay claim to that fiction. And no, Chloe's never been a diva. We are working through our issues, but to be honest I think we are both holding back on fully sharing. When I'm back in Vegas tonight, I'm going to talk to her about my stay in rehab."

He owed her that truth. Chloe had to know what a future with him might really look like, and what it could possibly entail. "And I need to explain about my breakdown last year."

Hopefully Chloe will then feel safe enough to tell him what had really happened with Foster and Marta. Whatever is was, she was keeping it from him, but he didn't want to press her. Something bad had to have happened for her to make such major changes in her life.

From what the Royal Resorts valet service had told him, Chloe's manager, Nancy, had arrived by a commercial flight when she flew into Vegas, leaving Jordan to wonder what had happened to the famous *Chloe Jet*.

"That's really great news about you and Chloe. I hope this is a second chance for the two of you." Matthew nervously tapped the steering wheel. "What about Mom and Dad, have you told either of them about your breakdown? Or Bryce."

Jordan shook his head. He could understand Matthew's worry. Keeping the news of Jordan's mental health problems from the rest of the family hadn't been easy. While he had a lifetime of keeping things secret from his parents, the more open and sharing Matthew had to have felt the heavy burden of lying to their parents. "Not yet. I need to get things with Chloe on more solid ground first. Telling the rest of the Royal family won't make any difference to what happened last year, but her knowing could impact how Chloe sees me."

And whether she wants me in her life.

Chloe's warm kisses were still on his lips when he boarded the jet to Colorado earlier that morning. And he would give anything to keep having his day's start the same way.

Today, Jordan was in Aspen to see his brother and talk about the stalled development of the Royal Resorts Aspen hotel.

On the outskirts of the town, Matthew slowed the SUV at a sharp corner and turned left. Soon the houses and hotels were left behind. The landscape became one of rocks and trees, with the snow covered mountains forming a stunning backdrop. Jordan hadn't previously been out to the site, and he was keen to see where Matthew was spending such a large amount of his time. And why he had made such little headway.

A mile or so further on, the trees cleared, and a huge rock faced resort loomed in front of them. "Wow. It looks like that big old lodge at Yosemite, the one we had Sunday lunch at all those years ago," observed Jordan.

"Yeah, the *Ahwahnee*. That's the exact same place I immediately thought of when I came here the first time. All that stone and timber." Matthew let out a sigh. "I just wish this resort was in half as good a condition as the one at Yosemite. If it was, it might be worth saving."

According to the executive reports Jordan had read, the Aspen resort was going to be demolished and a brand new steel and glass one built on the site.

That was of course if they could get the current owners to sell. Negotiations had been painfully slow, and from what Bryce had mentioned, difficult to the point where Royal Resorts were now having serious reservations about whether they should proceed at all.

Matthew stopped the SUV out the front of the main entrance. He reached over and from the rear seat passenger seat, retrieved two hardhats. Scowling, Jordan took the one he was offered.

"That bad?"

"Bits of drywall and the occasional lump of old ceiling have been known to drop on unsuspecting visitors. The owners only let me have a key and access if I agreed to sign a waiver and wear head protection," replied Matthew, with a resigned shrug.

They climbed out. Jordan followed his brother up the front steps and into the foyer of the resort. Bits and pieces of broken plaster and glass crunched under his feet. There were a number of broken windows, only some of which had been boarded up.

"How long has the place been empty?"

"About five years. They get the occasional idiot trespassers who come and inflict a spot of damage, but most of the problem comes from the weather. The snow and rain has gotten in under the roof in places."

The main foyer rose over two floors, and Jordan stood open mouthed as he took it all in. The grand staircase which swept up from the first floor had him thinking of the main staircase from the Titanic. This place had once been magnificent.

Why are we knocking it down, not renovating? This could be a fantastic hotel.

"It's a bit of a dive, but the land and the area around here is stunning," said Matthew, bending to pick up an empty vape that someone had obviously tossed away. He held it up. "Sooner or later one of these is going to burn this place down."

Jordan couldn't imagine that the sprinkler systems were still in working order. And if the resort did catch alight, it would be some time before anyone realized and probably far too late by the time the fire department arrived.

"Can I tell you something? I love this place. If it were up to me, I would save it. Bring it back to its old glory," suggested Jordan, his gaze lifting to the ornate but damaged plaster ceiling.

Matthew screwed up his face. "Unfortunately the costing estimates put that way out of any sort of sensible budget. I've had to come up with a whole new ultra-modern vision for this site."

He's changed. The old Matthew, the one who was all for saving and restoring, would have fought tooth and nail to keep this place.

Glass and steel frames would be an insult to the mountains.

"But all of it is still theoretical," said Matthew with a shrug. "I can't get the owners to sell. They are a nightmare."

"What does Bryce say about this place? I take it he's been out here."

As CEO, the final decision would be his, Bryce would be the one taking the project to the board for sign off.

"He still wants to buy it. Says once we get past the owners, any town planning regulations will be a piece of cake compared to what he had to deal with in Europe."

"Urgh," huffed Jordan. He had heard the same refrain from their older brother whenever Bryce mentioned his four years in Europe managing the House of Royal resort developments. "Every time he lifted a stone, there was a Roman ruin underneath. And if not, then there was an unexploded World War Two bomb."

This put the dealing with a crumbling roof and some broken windows firmly into perspective.

Jordan's phone buzzed. He would have ignored it, but the painful lessons of last year had taught him not to let calls go unanswered. Pulling his cell out of his pocket, he checked the screen.

Sheila.

Jordan never ignored his former assistant's calls. "Hi, Sheila. How's snowy New York City?"

"Hi, NYC is fine but freezing. I'm calling because Vegas has blown up."

His brows furrowed. "What's happened?" Matthew moved closer, and Jordan put the call on speaker. "I'm at the old resort in Aspen with Matthew. We're the only ones here, so you can talk freely."

"Hi, Matt. Long story short. That bitch Marta who used to work for Chloe has gone to the press. She's spilled the beans about Chloe being on the verge of bankruptcy. Did you know that the *Chloe Jet* has been repossessed?"

Jordan shook his head. "No, I did not. From my understanding the official line was that Chloe was looking to make some changes in her life."

The lie had never quite held water, but he'd decided to wait until Chloe felt ready to tell him the whole truth. Jordan scraped his hand over his face. So many things now made sense. If Chloe was indeed on the verge of going bust, then her need to hide out in Vegas was all a part of it.

Was it any wonder she didn't want to go back to LA?

"The main reason why Bryce has asked me to call you, is that no one can get a hold of Chloe. She's not answering her phone and she is not in her hotel suite. Oh, and according to the security team, your SUV is missing from the parking garage."

Bloody Marta. Determined to destroy Chloe at all costs.

He was standing in the middle of an abandoned hotel six-hundred miles from the woman he loved, and the shit had hit the proverbial fan. Chloe was nowhere to be found.

His stomach dropped as Matthew shoved his own phone under Jordan's nose. In big, bold letters across the front page of the LA Times were the words, "The Pauper Pop Princess: Secret insider tells all. 'Chloe's life is a lie.'"

"Are you still there? Jordan." Sheila's voice drifted down the line.

"Yeah. Matt just showed me this morning's LA Times, Chloe is the lead story. Listen I have to go. Can you let Bryce know I am handling this? We'll get a statement drafted. I will send it to him to review."

An annoyed huff echoed in his ear. "Sod the press, go find Chloe. Do what you should have done all those months ago. Pull your head out of your ass and go tell the woman you love how you really feel."

A loud click echoed in the empty lobby. Sheila had delivered the message, and her blunt ultimatum, and now she was gone.

Jordan met his brother's gaze. "I have to go."

"Yes, you do." Matthew lifted his phone to his ear. "Hi, Matthew Royal here. Could we please have the jet refueled and ready to leave asap? Jordan has to go back to Las Vegas earlier than expected. We should be on the tarmac in the next thirty minutes." He listened for a moment, nodded. "Thank you. See you soon." He hung up.

"Back to Vegas, Jordan, and make sure you find Chloe and protect her from the gutter-feeding press. After that, you might want to call the company lawyers and set them on this Marta person. She sounds like she is hell bent on revenge."

Jordan gave his brother a rare hug, then they both dashed for the door. He was down the front steps of the old resort and at the SUV before Matthew had got his keys out of his pocket. "Drive quickly, but don't go hitting any wildlife or skidding off the road and plowing into a snow bank."

"Get in, Jordan. Buckle up and shut up."

Barely forty minutes later, the Royal Resorts jet took off from Aspen-Pitkin County Airport. As soon as the plane leveled out, Jordan opened his iPad. He did a quick search for recent news on Chloe. If Marta had gone to the press, it would be on the gossip sites first. His heart sank as he took in the results.

"Oh no, it's everywhere."

Even the mainstream news media had picked up the story and run with it. Having been involved in the entertainment industry, Chloe's former PA must have known the right people in LA to talk to and where to sell her lies. The media had gone all in with the biggest show biz story of the year.

"Pop Princess Chloe and Her Life of Lies: *'She made me work for nothing for months, then fired me at Christmas. I feel so betrayed.'*— A tearful Marta."

He didn't bother to read the rest, knowing full well that Marta wouldn't be the sort of person to hold back. This was her one chance to destroy Chloe and she had taken it.

Jordan's calls to Chloe's number went straight to voicemail.

She wasn't at the resort. And she'd taken his SUV. There was only one place where Chloe would go to find sanctuary. Somewhere that only Jordan knew about.

Clever girl. You stay safe for me. I'm on my way.

He was going to find Chloe, then he was going to give her all the time and space she needed to share her secrets. And when she was done, he was going to finally do what he should have done all those months ago.

He was going to go into battle for the woman he loved.

CHAPTER FIFTY-FOUR

The first sign of trouble came in the early hours of the morning. After Jordan had left to go and see his brother in Colorado, Chloe had dragged herself out of bed and made a fresh brew of coffee. It had taken two strong cups to get her brain into gear. Jordan was a magnificent lover, but exhausting.

She was due to start costume fittings later this week, and there could be no hiding the marks and bruises that their vigorous love making was leaving on her body. "We might have to dial back on things until after the fittings." It was either that or ordering a truckload of flesh colored body stockings.

Phone in hand, seated at the island bench in the kitchen of her sky villa Chloe was mindlessly scrolling through TikTok when a text message popped up. It was from Stixxluv.

> Marta has sold story to press. Going live today. Thought you should know.

> What is she saying?

> You are bankrupt. Owe her tons of money. Jet seized. Lies.

> Thxs.

Chloe blinked back hot tears. *Fuck. What will the fans think? Will they hate me?*

The story was bound to break at some point, but she'd been hoping to have the opportunity to explain everything to Jordan. That had been in her plans for tonight. She cursed herself for having waited.

Thanks, Marta. Once again, you've pulled the rug out from under me.

It was just before seven thirty, and Jordan had left for Aspen an hour ago. His plane would be in the air by now. Not that her financial problems were anything he could do much about, but seeing a friendly face would have made things a little easier.

No. He's on Royal Resorts company business. I should leave him alone.

While she had been riding high in the music charts with *Bitter Babe*, the man she loved had been going through hell. He'd forgiven her, and she owed it to him not to let this business with Marta and her lies come between them.

Outside the window, the neon lights of the casinos were giving way to daylight. If the LA press had gotten hold of the story, she would be top of the early morning news. And once the LA press cohort got hold of the scandal, then Chloe Fisher would be prime morning news across the whole USA. She called her manager.

"Hi, Chloe. I was just about to call you, I didn't know if you were up yet. Apparently, there is a story about to break," said Nancy.

"Yeah, I just got a text from a friend. Marta my old

assistant has gone to the press. She's told them that I am broke and owe money all over town. Should we be issuing a press statement?"

Cunning Marta had obviously seen Chloe doing the press rounds over the past day promoting her Las Vegas residency and taken the opportunity to throw as much shade as possible.

"We will, but not until I've had a chance to talk to your lawyer and get an update from the accountants on who you still owe money to. I'm assuming since the Royal Resorts people have already paid your signing on fee that your finances are in better shape than they were at Christmas."

She could trust Nancy not to go shooting off first thing. Her words gave Chloe comfort. If people read that she'd had a blip with her money, especially around the time she was changing management, people wouldn't see that as much of a story. If they played it smart, Marta's story could be dead by midday. Disgruntled former employees of famous people were a dime a dozen.

"So we sit tight until Sandra and her people can give us the figures?"

There is no need to panic. No need to call Jordan.

"Yes, that's the first part of the plan. The other part is necessary, but definitely not nice. I want you to read the press articles when they hit the wire this morning. I will get my people watching and recording the TV shows, as no doubt will Sandra and the legal team. We—and I include you in that—Chloe, will have to know everything Marta has said, only then can we decide what course of action to take."

I can do that. I'll make notes in my journal.

"Oh, and one other thing. I know it might be tempting to call the press yourself, but I need you to lay low. I will let the Royal Resorts PR people know that we are waiting until we know everything that Marta has said. Then we will discuss our tactics."

Chloe had been around the business long enough to understand why. The last thing an artist ever wanted to do was to get involved in a tit-for-tat exchange with someone via the media. It never ended well. The fact that Nancy was going to include her in the discussions was a great relief. It was something Foster would never have done.

"I agree with our plans. Thanks, Nancy. I'm going to turn off my phone for the next few hours, and I'll call you later tonight."

"Good luck. And Chloe?"

"Yes?"

"Just remember, no matter what Marta has told the press, she can't hurt you anymore."

After ending the call, Chloe went and had a long shower. Under the hot water she gave herself a serious pep talk. It was the sort of conversation she hadn't had with herself in many years.

I can do this, I am Chloe. I have survived the streets, and betrayal. I am Chloe.

A short time later, dressed in fresh clothes, and carrying one of her oversized totes, Chloe headed downstairs and to the parking garage. Jordan's Land Rover Defender sat in its usual spot. After all these years of being told what to do by others, she was finally back to trusting her own instincts.

When the news broke this morning, she wanted to be as far away from the Royal Resorts hotel as possible. Her days of being a prisoner of her fame and hiding away in seclusion while the press circled her like hungry vultures were over.

Forty minutes later, Chloe turned the SUV off Red Rock Canyon Road and down the sandy track which led to the desert house. This house was far from town, and it was her secret refuge. A place of calm and safety, which Jordan had gifted to her.

Once inside the house, Chloe moved with care to close all the curtains, and check that the doors and windows were securely locked. She flicked on the TV and turned to *Good Morning America*, leaving the show to play quietly in the background while she fixed herself some breakfast. Jordan, bless that beautiful man, had made sure the refrigerator was well stocked.

With a plate of scrambled eggs on toast and a cup of orange juice in hand, Chloe took up a comfy spot on the couch and settled in to watch the start of the day's grubby events as they unfolded.

Marta did not disappoint.

CHAPTER FIFTY-FIVE

A hire car was waiting for Jordan when the Royal Resorts jet landed in Vegas midafternoon. He drove slowly out of the airport and onto the highway. Once he was out on the open road, he put his foot hard on the gas and brought the car up to the speed limit.

He'd given up on trying to reach Chloe, figuring she'd wisely gone to ground. Instead Jordan had spent the entire trip back from Colorado reading and watching every news item which concerned today's unfolding story about Chloe. By the time he stepped off the plane, he had a folder full of notes, and an endless hatred for Marta.

She'd done a real number on her old boss. Painted Chloe as a vindictive, narcissistic woman who didn't give a damn about anyone, including her fans. The first two accusations Chloe could easily brush off, but he knew that last part would hurt.

The twenty odd miles from the airport to the desert house felt like an eternity. Jordan let out a sigh of relief when the sign post for Red Rock Canyon came into view. His heart was thumping hard in his chest as he slowed the BMW and turned off the highway and onto the dirt road.

He took his time, glancing at his rearview mirror to make sure he hadn't been followed. His gaze checked the undergrowth left and right for any signs of paparazzi. Though considering how small the bushes were out here, he figured the only press who could successfully hide would have to be no bigger than garden gnomes.

Ok, no one is here. Good.

As he rounded the back of the garage, he whispered, "Thank you, lord."

His SUV was parked exactly where he hoped it would be, out of sight of the road. He locked the car and headed toward the house. He had to hope that Chloe was ready to trust him once more. Allow him to be the man he should have been for her in the first place. *I will never fail her again.*

From behind the living room curtains, Chloe watched as a dark blue BMW slowly approached the house. She glanced at the car keys which sat on the kitchen table. The idea of trying to make a run for it if the driver of the other car turned out to be a member of the press was only fleeting.

The desert house was secure. She had a phone. Worst case, she would have to call the security team from Royal Resorts to come and rescue her and hunker down until they arrived.

Her heart began to race as the car disappeared behind the garage. She moved toward the front door. Listening.

When the knock came, she jumped.

"Chloe," came a familiar voice.

Grabbing her phone, she turned it on and dialed Jordan's number.

"Is that you at the door?"

"Yeah, I figured it might be smarter to knock first."

"Good idea, I would hate to have to shoot you."

She punched the access code into the keypad and opened the door. Jordan crossed the threshold, and immediately shut the door behind him, securing it once more.

"It hadn't occurred to me that you might own a gun."

Chloe shook her head. "I don't."

He prowled toward her, his footsteps sending shivers down her spine. "How's your day been, nice and quiet?"

"Yeah. Not much happening. What about you?"

"Colorado was pleasant enough. I watched a lot of news and surfed the entertainment gossip sites on my way back, you know, just to kill the time. Slow news day."

Chloe blinked back tears. Her joking bravado was fading fast. "Yeah, you could say that."

Jordan held out his arms. Hot tears were falling as Chloe stepped into his embrace. He wrapped her up in his warmth and safety. "It's alright. I'm here for you now, sweetheart."

"Jordan. I'm sorry. I just didn't know how to tell you about the money. You tried to get me to listen to you about Marta and the others."

His hand rubbed up and down her back, and Chloe closed her eyes. "It's not your fault. They had you where they wanted, and you were alone. I'm the one who let you down. I should have stayed."

She clung to him like a limpet. "And then I wrote that song about you and made it all so much worse. Oh, Jordan."

"Yeah, you did. And it was shitty for a time. But *Bitter Babe* is now your biggest hit, and as much as I hate it, I'm going to have to get used to hearing it. That's of course if you want me to stick around."

Chloe drew back, gazing up at Jordan through the sheen of her tears. "Of course I want you to stick around. You know I love you."

"I love you too. I should have said that a long time ago. I love you and I will never fail you again."

CHAPTER FIFTY-SIX

If they were ever going to have a real chance at a future together, she was going to have to lay it all out for Jordan. Tell him everything. While he sat at one end of the couch, a bottle of fancy Japanese sparkling water in hand, Chloe took a seat at the other end, and began.

"Just before Christmas I got served a summons for an unpaid debt. When I got in touch with the debt collectors, I discovered I owed a lot of people a lot of money. After that, things unraveled pretty quickly, in fact so fast that I ended up running away from home."

Saying it now, it sounded all so vanilla and plain, but at the time her world had been crumbling around her.

He nodded. "I can see how you might have had to do that, as I recall Marta was always watching your every move. I used to hate it when she suddenly appeared from out of nowhere in your house."

"Turns out Marta and Gabriela were helping themselves to my money. Treating it as their own."

Jordan let out a foul curse under his breath.

"My accountant says all the evidence points to them

working in cahoots with Foster." Chloe took a sip of her bottle of water. "People throw the word gaslighting around as a bit of a joke, but I know that's what my life has been. I was so busy worrying about the music and touring, that I let other people take care of my finances. They dictated my entire life."

"And when you wanted to look at your finances, did they try to stop you?"

"They tried, yeah. That's when I realized just how deep they had sunk their claws into me."

She'd asked Jordan to keep his distance for this conversation, not wishing to have her need for his comfort cloud her thoughts. He'd accepted those wishes. It was refreshing to have someone in her life who respected her boundaries.

"But you got out from under them. You fired Foster and the others. You got new legal representation along with a kick ass manager. Dad said Nancy was a tough negotiator. As I recall you were all over the contract that you signed with Royal Resorts. That's fantastic. I'm really proud of you, Chloe."

She didn't feel proud of herself. Her money issues were on their way to being solved, but Marta had done some real damage with her accusations of Chloe being a liar. The members of Chloe's Garden would want answers.

"Did you hear the rest of what Marta said about me? That I'd made up my backstory, and I had lied to my fans."

"Yes. It was nasty, and personal." There was an edge of simmering outrage in his voice. "She may as well be wearing a printed T-shirt that reads 'bitch on the hunt for revenge'. I'm assuming you're going to set your legal people on her. If you want, I'm more than happy to sit with you when you do."

Chloe swept her fingers through her hair. The money was one thing, having her past dragged up for everyone to rake over and give their unwanted opinion of was the pits. She'd always known this day would come, but had hoped that when it did, she would be the one controlling the narrative.

While she valued Jordan's input, he didn't know the truth of her earlier years.

"Marta knows I can't sue her over any of the factual parts, because they are all true. Foster didn't sign me to his label after watching my YouTube video—he heard me busking on the street. I was singing outside the hotel he was staying at in Kansas City. I was twenty and I'd been homeless for four years."

Chloe got to her feet. She couldn't sit still while she told Jordan about the most painful day of her life. Of that bitter winter morning. "I was sixteen when I woke up alone in a motel in southern Nebraska. It was my birthday. My parents gift was to finally abandon me for the last time."

Until Marta's interview, few people outside her former team had known this painful truth. Now the whole world did. They knew that the Chloe Fisher origin fairytale was in fact an invention.

Chloe moved toward the window. She drew back the curtains and the late afternoon sun bathed the room in a muted light. "My parents are—since I'm assuming they're not dead—grifters. Con artists of the lowest kind. They are the sort of people who would see a man down on his luck and try to figure out what else they could steal from him. They abandoned me because I didn't want to live that life."

The irony of her ending up under the control of people like Foster and Marta wasn't lost on Chloe. But having a roof over her head and food in her belly had counted for a good deal over the past nine years.

Jordan rose slowly from the couch but kept his distance. "You were an incredibly brave young woman to have survived for all those years on your own. Chloe, you still are incredible."

She wasn't feeling incredible, Marta had done some real damage. She'd hit Chloe where she knew it would hurt her the most. "My fans think I'm a liar."

He held out a hand to her, but she refused to take it. "The only good thing Foster did when he signed me was to pay my parents off. They have an iron clad NDA, so won't be making any more money out my misery."

"The grifters were out-grifted."

"Hmm. I'm going to talk to Nancy and see what she thinks of me doing a full sit down interview with one of the major network shows. And maybe even a *Vanity Fair* piece. I want to set the record straight for my fans." The only way she would be able to rest was if she knew the Chloe's Garden heard the warts and all truth from her.

"And what about today, are you going to release a press statement?"

"No. Nancy and I talked this morning. We are going to wait. If I start responding to Marta's story, it will only give it more oxygen."

Jordan's phone rang, he glanced at the screen. "It's Bryce. I had better take this, he's been worried about you."

He answered the call and set the phone to speaker. "Hi, Bryce. I've just got back to Vegas, and I'm at the desert house with Chloe. You're on speaker."

"Chloe? Are you alright?"

"Yes, I am. Thanks, Bryce. Sorry for the radio silence, but it made sense for me to lie low. And I promise I will do everything I can to make sure this doesn't impact ticket sales for the concert series."

A rough laugh drifted down the line. "Impact sales? Chloe, there are no tickets left for the entire six months of your residency. Our booking website melted down within an hour of Marta's interview. Whatever damage she thought she might do, has had the opposite effect."

Jordan punched the air. "That's fantastic! The fans are with you, Chloe."

She'd thought she had run out of tears, but her wet cheeks told her otherwise. Chloe hugged her arms about herself, the fans hadn't believed Marta's story about having been treated poorly by her former boss. Chloe's Garden had seen through the lies and shown their support in huge numbers.

"I will leave the two of you in peace for the rest of today. I'm just glad you are alright, and that Jordan is with you. Let's talk later in the week when things have settled down. We might need to have a conversation about extending your residency."

Jordan grinned at his phone. "Just be ready for some hard negotiations from her management team." Bryce's laugh was still echoing down the line when Jordan ended the call and tucked his cell back into his jacket pocket.

Today was going to be a day for truths. After today, Chloe would know it all. Jordan was worried, but the thought of finally bringing all his secrets into the light was also liberating.

If she can be brave, then so can I.

"I love you, Chloe. I will support you no matter what you decide. And that includes what you want to do about us."

Her brows furrowed. "What do you mean about us? I thought we were kinda sorted on that. Or at least on our way."

Jordan drew in a deep breath. "I was in a really bad place after Marta told me you didn't want to hear from me again. And yes, I now know that was a lie, but at the time I didn't.

After I saw you and Zapp, I couldn't cope. I ended up booking myself back into rehab."

Chloe made a move toward him, but Jordan mirrored her earlier action and kept his distance. "I eventually went back to Laguna Beach and tried to keep going. I thought I could push through. Tough it out. Get the job done. Live up to my family's expectations. But I couldn't."

"What happened?"

He closed his eyes valiantly fighting back the tears. "Matthew sensed I was struggling. I flew home to New York with him for what was meant to be just a weekend, but on the morning, I was due to fly back to LA I found I couldn't get out of bed. My mind and body had finally collapsed."

Holing up in his apartment knowing full well that the rest of the world—including his father—had assumed he'd simply abandoned his commitments, had made his recovery even more of a trial.

"Matthew and Sheila knew what had happened, and they did their best to cover for me. I tried to work remotely, but it was a bust. After a few weeks I was able to muddle my way back into the New York office, but by then Bryce had been called home to the US to try and fix Laguna Beach."

The shame of his father giving him a dressing down and then sending him back to California had left deep scars. Over the past weeks, he'd finally accepted that they would never fully heal. Oddly, he was at peace with that notion. It had made him realize he wasn't cut out for the job and that walking away from Royal Resorts wouldn't in fact be the end of the world.

"Oh, god that's just awful, Jordan. I can't begin to imagine how hard that must have been for you. I'm so sorry."

Jordan nodded. "I'm not telling you these things to gain your pity, I'm doing it because you need to understand what sort of man I am. There will be times when I have to go and spend a week or two at a retreat to keep on top of my mental health. When we first met, I told you I was a high-risk recovering addict, and that still holds true."

"But you are clean?"

A valid question. "Yep, and I intend to stay that way, but it will take ongoing help. You should know that some parts of me are a little bit broken. The only thing that is one-hundred percent whole is that I love you and I will never stop fighting for us."

This time when she moved toward him, Jordan held out his hand. Their fingers threaded together. Tears shone in Chloe's eyes as she whispered. "Thank you for being honest with me. I love you, Jordan. Together we will make you whole. I love you, my *Bitter Babe*."

With this amazing woman, anything could be possible.

CHAPTER FIFTY-SEVEN

Las Vegas
Nine amazing and exhausting months later

"After one hundred and fifty shows, my extended Las Vegas residency has finally come to an end. I would like to thank all the amazing fans who have come to the Royal Resorts Platinum Collection resort to see the show. I can honestly say I have loved every single minute of every concert."

Jordan stood to one side of the stage watching as Chloe gave her farewell speech. She had played her final show in Vegas, and it was now time for them leave. The little black rings which had recently appeared under Chloe's eyes told him it was well past time.

"I'm also going to make a couple of other announcements today. I promised to be open and honest with my fans, and this is part of that dialogue."

After making a quick check of his tie and jacket, Jordan straightened his spine. They'd talked long about what Chloe was going to say, and he had offered his input, but in the end, he'd let her decide what she wanted to tell the public. And the members of Chloe's Garden.

Her recent *Vanity Fair* cover and interview had detailed much of Chloe's painful past. She'd been raw and honest with her fans.

"Firstly, I am going to take a long break from live performances. This past year has taught me that I need to work on more than just my music. I need to focus on Chloe, the woman. On the things which are important in my life, including this man. Jordan Royal."

Jordan was beaming as he moved into the light and came to stand alongside Chloe. It had taken some convincing on her part for him to step out of the shadows, but as he did, it felt right. This was where he should be, supporting his woman.

There is no more hiding our love from the world.

A thousand cameras clicked all at once. In reply to the calls of, "Jordan. Jordan. How did you meet Chloe?" Jordan simply smiled and waved. He had no intention of ever doing a press conference or one single interview. Their future branch of the Royal family only needed one star and Chloe shone brighter than anyone.

He'd been helping Chloe with the details of new contracts negotiated by Nancy and Sandra. In the spring there would be a new Chloe's Garden perfume and beauty range being launched. The products would be both affordable and make use of ethically sourced ingredients. Chloe was at pains to make sure that her fans knew she was taking care with the things she presented to them.

The high powered legal eagles at the House of Royal had got to work along with Sandra in dealing with Foster and Marta. Chloe's former personal assistant had seen reason and retracted her malicious lies. Foster had been determined to fight a dirty, protracted, and very public battle with his former client, but with a number of his other signed artists now calling foul on his business practices, Foster was having to deal with an ever growing pile of law suits. Even Zapp and Sibling Rivalry had fired him from their management.

Jordan was quietly confident that any day now Foster would be looking to make a substantial offer of settlement.

"Chloe, so what's next for you? Are you two planning on getting married here in Vegas? Can I get an invite?"

Jordan bent and placed a soft kiss on Chloe's lips. "I'll leave you to your press, see you in a minute." He moved back and off the stage. As he reached the bottom of the short set of steps a familiar tune filled the air.

Bitter Babe. He would forever feel a sense of pain whenever that song came on, but with it being Chloe's biggest hit, he was resigned to enduring it for many years to come.

His father was waiting for him. He offered Jordan a hug. "You did it. Well done on a fabulous job, I'm proud of you. And you won Chloe's heart at the same time." Edward pointed a finger in the air. "I wonder whatever happened to the guy from that song. Your mom showed me the lyrics the other day. He sounds like a complete ass. Bet he is kicking himself for ever letting Chloe go."

Today was a day for endings and new beginnings, he owed this much to his father. To finally tell him this one last truth.

"He did beat himself up over her, for a very long time. But the one thing I can say about *Bitter Babe* is that he's good at getting second chances. And this time he is never letting Chloe go. That's a promise. He's done with failing people." Jordan swallowed down tears. "I'm sorry, Dad. I was in no fit state to launch Laguna Beach and I should have said so. You gave me your trust and I failed you."

A few months earlier, Jordan and Chloe had flown to New York, and he'd officially introduced the woman he loved to his parents. During their visit, they'd spent some precious time with the Royal family and cleared the air over the events of the past year. From the reactions of Edward and Alice, they were both clearly devastated to hear the truth about Jordan's breakdown.

Edward shook his head. "No. I was the one who failed. I should have seen your pain, and that you were struggling, instead I just pushed you to keep going. If anyone is at fault here it's me. When you are back on the East Coast, I'd like you and me to carve out some time together. Let's sit down and have a real conversation about what you went through last year. There are lessons I need to learn. Then maybe we can talk about what you might want to do with your life, going forward."

"Thanks, dad. I think I have an idea about my future, but first I want to take Chloe away and just let her relax."

Chloe's revenge song ended, and she took some more questions from the press. No she wouldn't be writing a tell-all book, some things were best left in the past. The rumors of a Netflix reality series were also not true. But yes, she was working with an up and coming French fashion designer on a Chloe range of clothing, all based around the theme of Chloe's Garden.

"Thank you, that's all the time I have to answer questions. I have a dozen suitcases still left to pack, and a hot man waiting." When she flashed a grin in Jordan's direction, he laughed.

Chloe left the stage and headed toward him. Jordan met her half way. She slipped her hand in his. "I know we have a dinner planned with your family later this evening, but in the meantime could we go back upstairs to our suite? I want us to be alone for a while." He bent his head and she spoke softly in his ear. "And preferably naked."

Jordan placed a warm, tender kiss on Chloe's lips. "Absolutely, Ms. Fisher. You know I can never resist such a suite temptation."

EPILOGUE

The Royal family's private island
  The sunny Caribbean
  Christmas Eve. A jingle bells sunset.

The setting sun painted the horizon in a gold, pink, and orange hue. Above in the heavens, the first of the evening stars twinkled their welcome at her. Chloe's gaze lingered on them, then lowered to take in the gently rolling waves.

It was amazing how much her life had changed over the past year. This time a year ago, she had just left her accountant's office having been given the news that she was facing financial ruin.

And now I am digging my toes into the sand of a Caribbean island.

At the sound of footsteps she turned, smiling as she took in the sight of Jordan making his way down the nearby stone steps and onto the beach. The fading light shone on his white linen shirt and denim shorts. He looked like one of those men out of a health commercial. The after picture.

Jordan was soon to take up a newly created position within the House of Royal. Securing collaborations with artists across the global brands. He would have a team working on the day to day management of those contracts which would allow him the freedom to travel with Chloe and support her career and musical endeavors. It would also give Jordan the space to maintain his mental health and take time out when he felt it was needed.

"Hey, you," said Jordan, giving her a friendly wave.

"Hey yourself."

She greeted him with a long tempting kiss. *But not too tempting, his family is due to arrive any minute.* "Has the jet landed?"

"Yes, and they are now on board the boat. Which means Bryce and Vivian will be here within the hour."

Bryce and his fiancée were joining Jordan and Chloe on the island for the Christmas holidays. Matthew was still in Colorado but planning to make it in a day or two, weather permitting. The rest of the US based family members would be arriving in time for New Year's. Camille had gone home to Paris to spend the holiday season with her parents. According to Chloe's now *BFF* a ceasefire in the family row had been declared. How long it would last past Christmas Day , was yet to be determined.

"I'm looking forward to a family Christmas. It will be my first." Chloe's voice broke a little at the end. A real Christmas, with people who genuinely loved one another. She'd never dare imagine what that might look like, but she was about to experience it for real.

Jordan tucked his hand into his pockets and came to stand alongside her. "The sunsets here are amazing. Remind me to take some pictures for your Instagram feed. And mine."

Chloe laughed. "Your Instagram account is private, and

you only follow one person. I still can't believe your profile is @bitterbabenyc. You are a sucker for punishment."

"Yes well, @chloefisherofficial was already taken. And you only follow one person as well."

It was a silly, hopelessly romantic thing being the only followers of each other's accounts, but it still made Chloe's heart do a little dance every time she checked the app.

She gave a contented sigh and rested her head against Jordan's shoulder. "This is the happiest I have ever been in my life. I don't know if it is possible to be any happier."

"Oh," he murmured.

"What does that mean? Oh."

"It means I was hoping this would be your happiest moment." Jordan turned and took hold of both Chloe's hands. He sank down in front of her on one knee. "Chloe Fisher, I love you. You make every day the best. A man would have to be a fool not to want to spend the rest of his life with you."

She was lost for words. Was this really happening?

Yes. Yes. Yes.

"Chloe Fisher, will you make this *Bitter Babe* an honest man? I mean will you marry me?"

Tears filled her eyes, as she nodded. "Yes. Oh yes." Chloe bent and after taking Jordan's face in her hands, planted a long kiss full of promise on his lips. She whispered. "Hashtag Bitter Babe happily ever after."

She had finally found her forever man, and she would never let him go.

Do you want to read all the steamy, romantic things which

happen when former travel reviewer Vivian Holte finally gets the chance to go to Lake Como in Italy and write her last review? Was that a wicked billionaire following her?

For your free copy of **An Italian Villa Escape** join the VIP Suite at **Planet Billionaire.**

Planet Billionaire gives you VIP Suite exclusive updates on the happenings in the world of the Royal family, as well as beauty, fashion, a monthly tarot reading, and of course fabulous cocktail recipes.

Join the VIP Suite at Planet Billionaire

JOIN THE VIP SUITE AT PLANET BILLIONAIRE

When former travel reviewer, Vivian Holte travels to Italy to file her last review for her old magazine, a wicked billionaire can't reist the urge to secretly follow her...

For your free copy of **An Italian Villa Escape** scan the QR Code to join the VIP Suite at **Planet Billionaire.**

SOUNDTRACK

Set Fire to the Rain

Adele

Mr. Perfectly Fine

Taylor Swift

So What

Pink

Since U Been Gone

Kelly Clarkson

Shake It Out

Florence + The Machine

Tilted

Christine and the Queens

Waking up in Vegas

Katy Perrry

Royals

Lorde

ALSO BY JESSICA GREGORY

House of Royal

Royal Resorts

Room for Improvement

A Suite Temptation

The Last Resort (coming 2024)

An Italian Villa Escape

ACKNOWLEDGMENTS

A huge thank you to my editor Madeline Ash, your support and continued tough love helped to bring Jordan and Chloe to life.

To the design team at Qamber Designs & Media, especially Jennifer Silverwood. Creating the moodboards and images was a blast.

To my family. Thanks for your amazing support.

On with the next book!

ABOUT THE AUTHOR

Jessica Gregory writes sassy steamy rom com. She loves strong heroines and making her heroes grovel. She hopes to one day live on Planet Billionaire.

Jessica is the romantic comedy pen name for USA Today bestselling author, Sasha Cottman.

Visit
Jessica Gregory Books

Printed in Great Britain
by Amazon